DOWNFALL

DOWNFALL

Samuel E. Stone

Copyright © 2000 by Samuel E. Stone. TXu908-129

ISBN #:   Softcover   0-7388-2655-3

All rights reserved. No part of this book may be reproduced or transmitted in any form or by any means, electronic or mechanical, including photocopying, recording, or by any information storage and retrieval system, without permission in writing from the copyright owner.

This is a work of fiction. Names, characters, places and incidents either are the product of the author's imagination or are used fictitiously, and any resemblance to any actual persons, living or dead, events, or locales is entirely coincidental.

This book was printed in the United States of America.

To order additional copies of this book, contact:
Xlibris Corporation
1-888-7-XLIBRIS
www.Xlibris.com
Orders@Xlibris.com

CONTENTS

CHAPTER ONE
    OUR PERCEPTIONS AND EXPECTATIONS OFTEN CONTRADICT REALITY. 11

CHAPTER TWO
    IN ORDER TO RESPECT YOURSELF, SOMETIMES YOU HAVE TO FIGHT BACK. ... 40

CHAPTER THREE
    RETALIATION COMES IN ALL FORMS. 57

CHAPTER FOUR
    COURAGE IS HAVING THE STRENGTH TO DO WHAT YOU BELIEVE IS RIGHT. 90

CHAPTER FIVE
    JUSTIFICATIONS ARE SOMETIMES MERE WORDS, USED TO CAMOUFLAGE THE ACTUAL MOTIVE. 102

CHAPTER SIX
    A MICRO SECOND CAN INSTANTLY LAST ALL ETERNITY WHEN LIFE AND DEATH COLLIDE. 114

CHAPTER SEVEN
    INTIMIDATION TAKES ON MANY FORMS, DISGUISED IN A VARIETY OF DIFFERENT FACES. 127

CHAPTER EIGHT
    ONE'S OWN "DIGNITY" GIVES THE COURAGE TO CARRY ON
    WHEN THE WORLD SEEMS TO BE CRUMBLING AT YOUR FEET. 138
CHAPTER NINE
    SURVIVAL COMES IN MANY FORMS. IT CAN BE A DIFFICULT TASK, OR AS SIMPLE AS CHOOSING THE PROPER PATH. 152
CHAPTER TEN
    FEAR IS A STRONG MOTIVATOR OF COURAGE, FOR LIFE IS FRAGILE AND MUST BE PROTECTED. 168
CHAPTER ELEVEN
    THE COMPLEXITY OF LIFE IS MEASURED WITHIN THE MIND, NOT THE
    REALITY OF ITS EXISTENCE. 187
CHAPTER TWELVE
    ONE'S PEACE OF MIND INVOLVES MANY FACTORS. 206
CHAPTER THIRTEEN
    TRUTH A SIMPLE CONCEPT, YET DIFFICULT TO ACHIEVE, DISTORTED BY
    ONE's LACK OF COURAGE, OR JUST BY SELF- SERVING MOTIVATION. 221
CHAPTER FOURTEEN
    ENHANCING ONE'S CREDITABLITY HINGES ON UNDERSTANDING
    THAT ONE DOES NOT HAVE A HIDDEN AGENDA, AND ESTABLISHING

FIRM BELIEF, ONE'S STATEMENTS ARE TRUE AND ACCURATE. 256

CHAPTER FIFTEEN
A "LIE" EXPOSED CARRIED MORE IMPACT THAN THE TRUTH TOLD,
AND SERVES TO ENHANCE THE TRUE NATURE OF THE "BEAST." 270

CHAPTER SIXTEEN
JUSTICE IS ACHIEVED ONLY WHEN TRUTH TRIUMPHS OVER DECEIT,
AND MEASURES ARE TAKEN TO PREVENT ITS RECURRENCE. 287

*This book is dedicated
to my wife, Sherry
she gave me the strength
and the courage to carry on.
The downfall would not
have occurred without
her loving support.*

*Thank you,
my love.*

CHAPTER ONE

OUR PERCEPTIONS AND EXPECTATIONS OFTEN CONTRADICT REALITY.

It's hard to believe I'm sitting here in Federal court, but here I am in the Federal District Court House. I look around the room: the large columns, the marble floors, the boxes and boxes of paper work, more than 40,000 documents concerning my case alone. I'm the plaintiff in a case against my bosses; after 23 years as a cop here I am, taking them on in a court of law. I'm not alone in this battle; if I was, I probably wouldn't have made it this far. I guess I've always been an idealist who thought he was living the life of a realist; so as you probably guessed, it was a shock to my very being to actually discover that what I thought was true and correct was nothing more than a "sham."

I was living a good life. I liked being a cop, and enjoyed what I did for a living. I felt in my own way I was making a difference. Little did I realize that I was part of a system of power that had no accountability: power that did what it wanted, to whom it wanted, and when it wanted. Being a cop, you have an abundance of power, but all in all, you still have accountability. When you're the top administrators, it's another story. A story that I found out about the hard way, one that almost got me killed.

It all started in the spring of 1994; I was a patrol sergeant working the swing shift for Kingston County Sheriff office. Kingston County was a fast-growing suburb.

The military had expanded their operations in the county a few years back, bringing the area population up from 34,000 to some staggering 1/4 million people in less than ten years. It was a definite boomtown era.

The county government for years had been a "good ole boy" system. It was evolving with the changing times, and with the influx of people coming into the community. We noticed the population growth in the law enforcement field; the impact was overwhelming. Crime had risen beyond belief and we were understaffed. The deputies who used to investigate crime were now reduced to nothing more than report takers. A typical swing shift would start out with ten to twenty calls backed up, and end ten hours later with an equal amount of calls still pending. We would run from 12 to 14 deputies on a swing shift with an overlapping mid-shift coming in at eighteen hundred hours. As patrol sergeant, one of my jobs was to constantly shift priorities on calls, so the life threatening, or at-risk calls would be handled first. As we use to say in Kingston County, we have a response time to 911 calls ranging from 10 minutes to 10 days depending on the priority of the call, and the other calls pending. Well enough of that, let me get back to the story.

March 13, 1994: Swing shift line-up, the on-coming deputies had assembled to be given their area assignments and to be briefed on current events and information relating to criminal activities in their respective areas. Little did I know, as I began conducting line up, it was the beginning of the end of my career and would change my life forever. You know life is funny that way, sometimes the least little thing, something that might not even seem related to you can have such an impact that it changes your life. That is exactly what happened to me.

After a line-up, one of my deputies, Charles Atwater, came to me.

"Hey, Sarge, can I talk to you in private for a minute? It's important."

"No problem, closed the door." I responded.

Deputy Atwater and I were the only ones in the sergeant's office. All the deputies had just walked out and were getting ready to go on patrol to their assigned areas.

Deputy Atwater began. "You being my sergeant, I wanted to let you know what I'm about to do. Since I work for you, I figure it might affect you so I wanted to give you the heads up."

I nodded my head, and Atwater continued.

"Well Sarge, tomorrow I file my public disclosure papers to run for Sheriff in the November, 1994, election. I don't know how the Sheriff will react, so I wanted you to know in advance, just in case it causes career problems."

I replied, "Okay, well I appreciate the advance warning."

Deputy Atwater continued, saying he had given a lot of thought to running for sheriff. He and his wife had made the decision last year that he would run in the upcoming election.

The sheriff in Kingston County is an elected official. The elections are held in the fall every four years. The current Sheriff, Patrick Johnston, had a history of being vindictive and of crushing anyone that attempted to get in his way. I understood what Deputy Atwater's concerns were, when he advised me he wanted to give me the heads up on his intentions. I appreciated the advance warning and anticipated there would be problems.

In the past, other deputies had tried to run against Sheriff Johnston. They all found themselves without a job after the election. The battles were usually short lived, and when the dust cleared those deputies' reputations, along with their careers, had been destroyed. No one who had run against Sheriff Johnston had ever survived.

Deputy Atwater knew the risk he was taking. He remarked that he realized he had to win the election or his career was over. He then put me on the spot and asked me to support him in the upcoming election. I shook my head and looked up at him. I explained to him that I supported his right to run, but could not, and would not, support him in the election. I then explained to him that I had worked for Sheriff Johnston for more than 21 years, and even though I did not agree with all of his administrative practices, I owed him a certain amount of loyalty. I went on, advising Atwater that I also knew Sheriff Johnston to be a very vindictive person. I did not want any problems with the man, or with the remainder of my career. I was not political and did not wish to get involved with politics.

Deputy Atwater wouldn't give up; he then asked me if I would at least vote for him in the upcoming election. I told him that I felt how a person voted was an individual and confidential matter.

"That is why it's a secret ballot." I said.

I then wished him good luck and shook his hand.

At the time of this conversation, neither one of us had even a clue of the corruption taking place around us. Corruption surrounding Sheriff Johnston was controlled by him and by those he had put into power. The conversation between Atwater and myself seemed innocent enough, one you would expect you could have in a free country, like the good ole' U.S. of A. However, it was in fact the start of a series of events that would affect my life forever.

Atwater then walked out of the sergeant's office and went on patrol. I got busy doing the paper work of the day.

Part of my duties as a patrol sergeant was to approve all the incoming reports that came in. I was responsible for making certain that the reports were complete and accurate. If they were not complete, requiring additional investigation, I had to assign the report back to a patrol deputy for follow-up work.

Approving reports is a secondary function of a patrol sergeant. The primary function is that of listening to the police radio traffic, monitoring the computer's pending calls screen, overseeing all 911 calls, and operations of the shift.

Deputy Atwater did as he had stated. He filed his public disclosure statement stating his intent to run for sheriff in the November, 1994, election. It didn't take long for Sheriff Johnston to react. Approximately one week later, on March 21, 1994, he ordered an internal affairs investigation against Atwater. The normal procedure when an IA investigation is initiated, is to notify the officer's immediate supervisor, and to have the immediate supervisor do a preliminary investigation. This is an inquiry, to determine if a full IA investigation is warranted.

The charge filed against Deputy Atwater alleged improper conduct and inappropriate behavior while investigating a burglary to a church some three months earlier. I was never contacted nor advised of the investigation by my supervisors. I learned about the IA investigation from Sgt. Cantrell, who was assigned by Sheriff Johnston to handle the investigation.

Now, as I said. Kingston County is a county in transition, and the growth of the public services such as law enforcement has not caught up to the population expansion, nor to all the modern day procedures and built in safeguards. There is no IA division in the sheriffs' department as there are in larger departments. The sheriff himself appoints a supervisor to conduct an IA investigation when he feels one is warranted. There are 120 deputies in the department and each deputy is accountable to his or her shift sergeant.

I was rather upset to learn Sgt. Cantrell was assigned to handle the investigation against Deputy Atwater since I was Atwater's supervisor. I would have had the same concern for any of the deputies on my shift if it happened to them. Furthermore, I had known Sgt. Cantrell since his career started at Kingston County. He had a reputation of being a "yes" man, and a hatchet man for the administration. I decided to contact Chief Halsted and advised him that I was not pleased with Sgt. Cantrell being assigned to conduct an IA investigation against one of my deputies. Further, I asked Chief Halsted why I was not assigned to handle the investigation.

Chief Halsted advised me that Sheriff Johnston had made the decision to have Sgt. Cantrell conduct the investigation and that was the way it would be. I informed the chief that I wanted to go on record as opposing their not following procedure in regard to this case.

I later learned the IA investigation against Deputy Atwater was initiated by Sheriff Johnston's sister, after Atwater filed his public disclosure. Sheriff Johnston's sister apparently contacted a woman at her church where Deputy Atwater had handled a burglary investigation some three months earlier. She talked this woman into filing a complaint against Atwater. She then called Sheriff Johnston and informed him that this woman wanted to file a complaint against Atwater. Sheriff Johnston then arranged for Sgt. Cantrell to contact the woman from the church so an investigation could be initiated.

After talking to Chief Halsted, I also talked to Sgt. Cantrell. I informed him that I formally went on record opposing procedure not being followed, and the fact that he was handling the Atwater investigation. Sgt. Cantrell told me he did not know why he was assigned the investigation instead of me, since I was Atwater's immediate supervisor. Sgt. Cantrell then informed me he had only started the investigation yesterday, but had already determined that Deputy Atwater had behaved improperly and most likely would receive a written reprimand which would be placed in his file. He advised that the violation did not appear to be any more serious than a letter of a reprimand. I asked him if he had spoken to Deputy Atwater yet, and he responded he had not. Deputy Atwater was on vacation at this time and out of the area. Sgt. Cantrell advised he intended to contact him when he returned. I reminded him that department policy dictates notifying an officer of a pending IA investigation within 24 hours of starting the investigation. He responded he realized that, but it was no big deal; Atwater was only going to get a letter of a reprimand anyway. I walked away realizing it was a setup designed to put a blemish on Deputy Atwater's record prior to the election. I had seen it happen before when other deputies had announced that they were going to run against Sheriff Johnston. The sheriff would use the reprimand against Atwater in his campaign for re-election. It was not right but it was a reality. Sgt. Cantrell never did talk to Atwater, but the investigation concluded that Deputy Atwater acted improperly and he was given a written reprimand. Deputy Atwater never returned to work. He could see the handwriting on the wall. He requested a leave of absence to run for sheriff. It was denied.

He resigned to avoid giving Sheriff Johnston the opportunity to discredit or put additional blemishes on his record.

I went on with my normal duties as a patrol sergeant and tried to stay out of the election process. The department was basically split down the middle with 50% of the deputies supporting Atwater and 50% supporting Johnston. Most of the other mid-level supervisors and I tried to remain neutral and concentrate our efforts toward keeping the deputies focused on their mission and service to the community. For the most part, through the summer of 1994 it was business as usual. It was the calm before the storm, I was to discover: short lived and soon to pass.

In late August, the former Deputy Atwater approached Captain Hill asking him to be his undersheriff if was elected to the sheriff's position. Capt. Hill was rather reluctant, and had turned Atwater down when he had previously asked him. This time, however, Capt. Hill agreed to accept the position if Atwater won the election. The undersheriff is the second in command in the department. He basically runs the department for the sheriff. Capt. Hill has always been a fair, compassionate man who took pride in being a police officer and serving the public. He was constantly at odds with Sheriff Johnston and Undersheriff Dieter for their lack of fairness, and lack of consistency in dealing both with the officers and the public.

Capt. Hill realized accepting the position of undersheriff for Atwater, would cause problems with Johnston and his administration. He did not realize, however, how far reaching the effect would be, nor that it would bring an end to his career. Shortly after Capt. Hill made his decision concerning the undersheriff position; Atwater announced it at the sheriff's guild meeting. He wanted the guild to endorse him for sheriff. He felt, with Capt. Hill on his side he could win the sheriff's guild endorsement. This was a politically smart maneuver. Capt. Hill was probably the most liked and respected supervisor in the department. The end result was the division among the ranks grew even wider and more intense over the upcoming election.

The deputies became so divided that tempers flared and animosities grew. The other sergeants and I had a difficult, if not impossible task of attempting to keep the deputies focused on their mission. It was a known fact among the troops that Sheriff Johnston was vindictive by nature. Likewise, it was common knowledge that those who stood by Johnston would move up in the department. The combinations of these factors stimulated a lack of trust. There were deputies who would report to Johnston anyone considered to be helping Atwater. Johnston's supporters felt that anyone helping Atwater was disloyal. Paranoia continued to grow as the election approached.

I worked swing shift during July, August, and September, 1994, and was scheduled to start graveyard shift around October first. I requested annual leave for the last week in September and the first part of October. It was approved. I was scheduled to return to work October 10, 1994, on the graveyard shift. I was looking forward to taking leave, and then coming back to the graveyard shift.

I, in fact, remarked many times how: I was looking forward to going to a graveyard shift so I could stay out of the politics with the general election coming up in November.

My oldest daughter was getting married October first, in Oregon. My wife and I were focusing on the wedding. I was equally excited about getting a break from the turmoil at the sheriff's office.

My vacation and my daughter's wedding came and went. Both were extremely enjoyable.

October 10, 1994, I returned to Washington State, and was looking forward to starting a graveyard shift that night. I felt refreshed and ready to get back to work. In the afternoon, I stopped by the precinct office to get current on events, prior to going to work that night.

Capt. Hill contacted me. He advised that after the announcement came out that he was going to be Atwater's undersheriff he had received a call from Detective Wiggins, one of Sheriff Johnston's supporters. He told Capt. Hill that he was stupid for supporting Atwater and he had just flushed his career down the toilet.

Capt. Hill went on to tell me that the day after the announcement came out he was contacted by Chief Halsted. The chief was upset with him for agreeing to be Atwater's undersheriff. He told him that Sheriff Johnston was disappointed in him and reminded him the sheriff had ways of getting even. He went on to say the sheriff would get anyone who opposed him, and he had better be careful.

Halsted then remarked: "What you should have done was told Atwater to get fucked"

Halsted then got a serious look on his face and advised Capt. Hill that he should think about what he was doing.

Capt. Hill became more intense as he continued. He told me that yesterday he had been contacted by Undersheriff Deiter. Deiter also informed him that Sheriff Johnston was very upset and disappointed with him for agreeing to be Atwater's Undersheriff. Deiter then lectured Capt. Hill that he made a mistake, and the Sheriff would see that he paid for that mistake. He told him he should fix the mistake he made by telling Atwater that he reconsidered, and back out before it was too late. Capt. Hill said Deiter's demeanor was very intimidating toward him. I told the Captain I was sorry to hear all of this, then he said there was more. He went on to state that Undersheriff Deiter had told him that he and the sheriff had also learned you agreed to be Atwater's Chief of Detectives, if he wins the election.

"Me?" I asked.

Capt. Hill nodded his head, "Yes, you." He acknowledged.

He said, "according to the Undersheriff, they're both upset with you, as well."

I informed Capt. Hill I never agreed to be anything for Atwater or anyone else, for that matter. I have been trying to stay uninvolved and neutral in the election process.

Capt. Hill told me he understood my position but someone must have told Johnston and Deiter that I accepted the Chief of Detectives position. He said he did not mean to upset me, he only was trying to update me as to what has been occurring. Capt. Hill then informed me that Sheriff Johnston was in the precinct office this afternoon inquiring as to when I was due back from my vacation. He told me that he had advised the sheriff I would be in tonight to run the graveyard shift. The sheriff told him to tell me that the sheriff would be at the precinct office at the start of graveyard shift to talk to me. Capt. Hill then commented that Johnston also told him I had agreed to be Atwater's chief of detectives. I shook my head, and told the captain that I was not pleased with what was going on. I then checked my mailbox at the office as well as my office "in" box, and went home.

Later that evening, I returned in uniform to begin my first shift back on graveyard. As I came into the precinct office, I was greeted by Sgt. Newton who informed me Sheriff Johnston had been in the office half an hour ago looking for me. He stated the sheriff told him I had agreed to be Atwater's chief of detectives if he won the election. I told Sgt. Newton I haven't even talked to Atwater since he resigned six months ago. I further told him I never agreed to be anything for Atwater. Sgt. Newton responded that the sheriff told him he would be back later to talk to me. I said "fine." I looked forward to talking to the sheriff, and getting this matter straightened out.

My intention at that time was straightforward: I wanted to stay uninvolved in the election process and focus on my job. I enjoyed my job as a patrol sergeant, and was comfortable with it. I did not need or want a conflict with Johnston or his administration. I had personally witnessed the damage Johnston and his people had done to other deputies whom they focused on destroying. I have always been loyal to the missions and goals of the sheriffs' department. Johnston and his administration have always left me alone to do my job. The relationship I had allowed me the freedom to do my work. Johnston had always benefitted from the positive press he received from my successful operations. I wanted it to stay that way.

I began my line up and passed out shift assignments to the deputies working the graveyard shift. Sheriff Johnston arrived at the office during lineup. His demeanor appeared rather friendly and cordial. He sat down in the lineup room and listened while I finished conducting the line up. After completion of lineup, he made small talk with the deputies and me before they departed for their assigned areas. As the deputies started to depart, Johnston told me he needed to speak to me in private. He requested I go with him to the traffic division office which was vacant at that time. I asked for him to give me a few minutes to get the deputies all out on the road and so I could call Cen. Com. to brief them on some current events occurring that evening. He Said that would be fine. I took care of business at hand and then told the sheriff I was ready to speak to him. We then proceeded to the traffic office. Sheriff Johnston advised me to have a seat. As I walked over to a chair to sit down, he walked over and closed the door then immediately got right to the point. The small talk was over.

"You've been talking to the press and saying bad things about me, haven't you?" Johnston demanded in a loud and rather intimidating voice.

"I have not talked to the press or any news media; I haven't even been in the state for the last three weeks," I responded.

"Well," Johnston stated. "I got a call from some reporters and they advised me they had been talking to a deputy who implicated me in being involved in illegal narcotic activities."

He, went on to state that I was the county's expert in the narcotics field, having worked two tours of duty in deep cover and having supervised and set up other operations. He said the reporters knew things they shouldn't have known, so he concluded that I must have talked to them.

I once again assured the sheriff that I had not talked to anyone from the press. He looked physically shaken; his demeanor was full of anger and rage. As he spoke, his voice would rise and fall in a harsh tone. It was obvious to me that he was upset, irate, and close to being out of control.

I could see he did not believe what I was telling him. I also got the distinct impression that Sheriff Johnston had some skeletons in the closet relating to drug activities; Skeletons I did not know existed until that very moment.

The sheriff then demanded to know. "If you aren't the one who talked to the news media, who did?"

"I don't have a clue," I responded.

"Well," Johnston said once again as he appeared to be collecting his thoughts. "Are you aware of any illegal narcotic activities involving me?"

I shook my head no and advised "I am not aware of any illegal narcotic activities involving anyone in the sheriff's office. If I was aware of such activities, I would most certainly report it to the proper authorities and not to the press."

Sheriff Johnston, then raised his voice. His facial expression changed from anger to a serious look of concern. He asked:

"What is this I hear that you are going to be Atwater's chief of detectives if he is elected?"

I looked at the Sheriff; he was staring at me as if to analyze my reaction. I once again advised him I had been out of town on vacation for the past three weeks. I returned to learn of this rumor concerning me becoming Atwater's chief of Detectives.

I advised him I did not need this, stating "I am not political and I have been trying to stay out of the political process."

I demanded to know where this rumor came from, because it was not true.

Sheriff Johnston quickly responded, "Atwater is the one that started it by stating you are going to be his chief of detectives."

I remarked: "Well, Atwater never said anything to me; in fact, from what I heard today when I returned to the office, it is you sheriff and Undersheriff Deiter who are the ones spreading the rumor of me going to be Atwater's chief of detectives. I don't like it, I don't need this, I'm trying to stay out of politics," I repeated.

The sheriff's anger grew, as he raised his voice and once again claimed Atwater was the one saying it.

Realizing that I was aggravating the sheriff, I decided to drop it. I made my point. So I said,

"Well, I don't want the Chief of detective's job, I've been in charge of detectives before and your time is not your own. I like it here on patrol, I'm happy as a patrol sergeant and want to stay here."

Sheriff Johnston's tone switched. He began to lecture me. He said Atwater was not going to be elected Sheriff anyway, and he, Johnston, was going to win the election in November. He then went on, stating "all of those deputies who are supporting Atwater had better realize that they work for me and," he paused for a moment before continuing, "even if by some strange fluke, Atwater won the election, those deputies who supported Atwater, would have to work for me after the election for the three months before Atwater would take charge of the office." Sheriff Johnston stopped and swallowed hard.

Then he said, "A lot can happen in three months; careers can be destroyed and come to an abrupt end, for having made the wrong choices."

I took a deep breath, and tried to control my emotions. It was obvious to me I was being threatened—threatened by the top Law Enforcement officer in the County. My perception of this man had just changed. I wondered what he actually was capable of doing. I had always viewed Sheriff Johnston as a dedicated law enforcement officer; a poor manager, but a dedicated individual.

From past experience I had learned he had a temper, and would focus his attentions on those who opposed him. I had never been on the opposing end before; so I was seeing first hand the other side of the man a side I did not know. I knew Sheriff Johnston wasn't always fair and he would have his administration go after those who opposed him, but I thought he had a reason to do so. Throughout my career I had observed a lack of fairness and consistency within Johnston and his appointed administration toward those that worked for them.

I had written this off as poor leadership; after all no one is perfect. I had always been left alone to do my job, and I guess I developed an attitude that those whom Johnston had "come down on" (in the past) had done something to deserve it. I just gave Johnston the benefit of the doubt that he was justified in the decisions and the steps he took to discipline individuals within the department. Now, as this conversation progressed I came to realize I had been wrong, and it scared me.

Sheriff Johnston went on to say that there were individuals in the department such as Deputy Farrell who needed to do what they were told and keep their mouths shut. He said Deputy Farrell and others like him were a disruptive force to the mission and goals of the department. If they continued on the path they were on, they would all find themselves out of a job and losing their careers.

Deputy Farrell was one of the deputies vocally supporting Atwater for sheriff. He also was one of the few deputies that would stand up to the administration when they made some decisions which were unfair or lacked consistency. I viewed Deputy Farrell as an individual dedicated to trying to improve the working conditions within the department. He was one of the deputies involved in the union and guild affairs which, more times than not, put him at odds with Sheriff Johnston and his top administrators.

I told Sheriff Johnston it was he and those he appointed to run the department who have, in fact, created the demeanor of Deputy Farrell and those like him. I told him if his administrators would practice applying fair and consistent decisions and disciplinary measures, there wouldn't be people like Farrell causing problems. I realized as I was talking, I should have kept my mouth shut. Sheriff Johnston became enraged, furious that I would imply that they had done anything wrong. He began to yell at me, stating Deputy Farrell was a mental, and the department would be better off without him. Sheriff Johnston then kind of switched gears in mid stream, and demanded once again to know if I had talked to the news media. I again assured him I had not, and told him I resented the fact that he was questioning me again after we had already been through it and I had answered his questions.

I was upset now, and ready to just keep on speaking my piece; after all, he was the one who put me in this situation. I told him he needed to re-evaluate his administrative practices before the problems in the department became worse. I went on, telling him there was a real division in the department over the election and it was hurting the morale of the deputies and the effectiveness of the department. As a supervisor, I explained, I felt I had an obligation to point the problems out, in hope that measures would be taken to correct the problems. Sheriff Johnston wasn't even listening to me.

He raised his voice and stated: "I'm going to win the election, and after the election you will be working for me. All of you need to realize you will be working for me. You better get smart and do the right thing if you value your career. You know, Sarge, I always had a lot of respect for you; I know you'll do what is right in regards to this election. I'm glad we had this talk. I'm also glad to hear that you're not going to be Atwater's chief of detectives. Now you talk with the deputies, and help them to make the right decisions concerning the election, and their careers. I know they'll listen to you. Okay, good night Sarge, I'm going home now."

The sheriff then walked out of the room and departed. I stood there for a moment, bewildered. He had not heard a word that I said. I couldn't believe the man had just threatened me and my career. I was overwhelmed with feelings of disbelief, anger and fear.

Sergeant Newton walked into the office. He asked me how it went and if I was okay. He said he could hear the sheriff yelling at me. I gave him an overview of the conversation that took place. He told me to be careful, the sheriff was under a lot of strain over the election and he did not want to see me caught in the fallout.

After talking to Sgt. Newton I decided to write notes of the conversation between the sheriff and myself. It comes from the police training. You take notes to protect yourself. It's drilled into you, "documentation, documentation." It's for your safety and protection. I recorded detailed notes of everything Sheriff Johnston and I had talked about.

During the course of the shift, I talked to some of the other supervisors and deputies concerning my conversation with the sheriff. I don't really know why I talked about it. I guess I just had to. It bothered me, and it helped to talk about it.

The next morning when I got home from work, I woke my wife and told her what had occurred. We talked for a while about it. I could not sleep: I was all wound up about the entire situation. I think I probably would have been able to put it behind me and use the newly acquired insight I had gained concerning the Sheriff's demeanor to my advantage if it wasn't for the next series of events.

I tried to get in touch with Atwater over the next couple of days. When I finally reached him I asked if he told anyone I was going to be his chief of detectives. He said no, in fact the reality of the matter was he was not even considering me for the position. I remarked, "good," because I did not want the position. Atwater then asked me to publicly support him for sheriff. I once again refused.

October 18, 1994, was a beautiful, sunny day, crisp and clear. The events of the day would bring a significant impact to all those who were working at the sheriff's office. The sheriff's guild, which is like a union for the deputies, had a vote to determine whom they would endorse for sheriff in the election. The vote was open to all the deputies in the guild and the results of the vote would be printed in the local newspapers. The deputies who supported Atwater turned out in force, as did the deputies who supported Johnston. There was one distinct difference between the two groups. The deputies who supported Atwater all wore rubber gloves when they filled out their ballots. They feared Johnston would get a hold of the ballots and have them dusted for finger prints to determine which deputies voted against him. It was rather extreme and paranoid, but the fact of the matter was they were scared.

I did not wear gloves but I did vote. Who I voted for really wasn't important. The important thing was the impact of the vote. The result came in, Johnston with 46 votes and Atwater with 44 votes.

Thirteen deputies refused to vote, and four votes were thrown out because the ballots weren't done as instructed. No one really knows if the four votes that were thrown out were for Johnston or Atwater. No one, that is except those who counted the votes, and they weren't talking. At any rate, Sheriff Johnston got the endorsement, but neither side considered it a win.

Sheriff Johnston was furious. He was so upset over the nearly 50/50 split on the vote that he was over heard saying to many in the department that he would get those who voted against him, and they would pay. He would teach the deputies a lesson for not supporting him, he said. It wasn't even a real win for Johnston in the newspapers they reported the guild voted to endorse Johnston for sheriff in the election, but the article was focused on the department's division and the 50/50 split resulting in Johnston winning the endorsement by only two votes.

October 19, 1994, the day after the guild vote, proved to be a day that would forever impact my life. It was likewise a day Sheriff Johnston will remember for the rest of his life. An anonymous letter was delivered to all news media, all public officials, to all the school districts, and to other community leaders. The letter consisted of two pages of single spaced typing listing events and incidents of wrongdoing by Sheriff Johnston and his administration. It is my personal belief this letter was prompted by the guild vote and the frustration felt by some of the deputies.

To this day it is not known who authored the anonymous letter or who was involved in distributing it. When I arrived at work on October 19, 1994, for the graveyard shift the letter was the talk of the department, even though none of the deputies had actually seen the letter. Capt. Hill took me aside and told me about the letter. He said me Sheriff Johnston had contacted him earlier that day and questioned him concerning it (the letter). He said that one of the incidents listed in the letter stated that a certain captain had witnessed Sheriff Johnston breaking into a business, committing burglary. The sheriff read this to Capt. Hill, and then asked the captain if he ever witnessed him breaking into a business. Capt. Hill said he was caught completely off guard by the sheriff's questioning of him. He did not know what to say, so he answered the sheriff with a question.

"You wouldn't break into a business, or any building, would you, sheriff?"

The sheriff answered with, "Well no, certainly not, I would never do such a thing."

Capt. Hill then said Johnston changed the conversation to the anonymous letter in general and how upset he was over it. He told Capt. Hill he was going to get to the bottom of it, find out who was responsible and they would pay dearly. The captain then remarked that it had been a very intense day around the office.

Captain Hill was the only captain we had in the sheriff's office, so when the anonymous letter stated that a certain captain witnessed Johnston break into a building, it pointed the finger right at Captain Hill.

Capt. Hill got up from his desk and walked to the door. He looked out of the room to see if anyone was around. No one was about in the hallway. He then closed the door and motioned to me to come over to his desk. He sat down. He told me he did in a fact witness Sheriff Johnston break into a business. It was about 16 years ago, when Johnston was running for sheriff for the first time. He said, Johnston broke into a business, and then called the owner. He told the owner he was out patrolling and scared off some burglars who were attempting to burglarize his store. Hill went on to say Johnston then bragged to him that this was how he was gaining support and votes from the business community by making them think he was out protecting their businesses and scaring off criminals.

Capt. Hill also related to me that he was aware of two other incidents where Sheriff Johnston broke into businesses; one incident was witnessed by Deputy Houde and one witnessed by Officer White, a city police officer who was riding with Johnston one night.

He continued telling me about the incident where he witnessed Johnston break into a grocery store. Johnston, after breaking in, helped himself to a candy bar and a soda, then called the owner. He said the owner was very happy with Johnston for chasing off the suspects and protecting his business.

Capt. Hill then turned rather red and flustered as he related the story about the sheriff.

"The incident concerning Johnston breaking into stores in the anonymous letter is true. I just didn't know how to answer Johnston when he asked me about it."

Capt. Hill continued. "So I decided to answer him with a question to avoid a conflict. That's why I said, well, sheriff you wouldn't break into any business would you?"

Capt. Hill went on, stating the demeanor demonstrated by Johnston made him decide not to admit it and say, "yes I saw you break into a business."

He did not know what Johnston would have done if he had answered "yes." The fact of the matter was, he did not want to find out. Even 16 years ago Johnston was untouchable, and if he had turned him in it would have destroyed his career, not Johnston's. Capt. Hill lamented that he realized both then and now he was wrong for allowing Johnston to get away with his demeanor but did not really know what to do about it.

Capt. Hill paused for a moment. He began talking about the anonymous letter. He said Johnston had shown him the letter and it contained a lot of old things in it: things and incidents that were true, and had occurred a long time ago.

He remarked that whoever wrote the letter has been around for sometime and knows how corrupt Sheriff Johnston and his administrators are. The letter scared him and he feared things around the office were going from bad to worse, and that it had only just begun.

I was shocked and dismayed at what and Capt. Hill informed me. I was equally surprised and rather disappointed in the three officers, including Capt. Hill, for allowing Johnston to get away with breaking into businesses. In my 21 plus years as a police officer, I experienced police officers with poor people skills, and some that were heavy handed, but basically, they were all honest and upright people trying to do the best they could. I had pride in my profession, and pride in those I worked with. Pride, and a belief they would do the right thing. There were a couple of individuals over the years, whose behavior I had questioned but all and all, I thought we were the good guys.

Having been a police officer myself, 16 years ago when Johnston first ran for sheriff and knowing the political backing Johnston had, I guess I could understand why Capt. Hill and the others were afraid to do anything about Johnston.

I understood, but it wasn't right, and from the anonymous letter it sounded like the past was coming around again. Life is funny that way, we rarely get away with anything. It all has a way of catching up to us. I wondered what else was in the anonymous letter that caused Sheriff Johnston to be so upset and I wondered if all of it was true.

The rest of the week was basically routine. I never saw Sheriff Johnston, or anyone from the administration, for that matter. I heard talk about the anonymous letter—it was the topic of discussion for the week. However, none of the deputies I talked to had seen it.

October 25, 1994, I came into work to start a graveyard shift. I came in early as I normally did, so that I could get my paper work done and prepare for line up. I finished line up and got my deputies out on patrol. I had just settled down to read and approve reports when Lt. Booths walked into the room. Lt. Booths was in charge of "Pro Net" which was the undercover drug investigation unit for the county. He told me he needed to gas up his undercover vehicle and he had forgotten his gas key.

I told him, "No problem, you can use my gas key" and walked out to the gas pump with him. He gassed up his car and then returned my key to me. We stood in front of the precinct office talking. Chief Halsted drove up and parked his unmarked unit. He got out of his car and walked over to us. It was around 9:00 p.m. Chief Halsted was in uniform. It was not normal to see him out at night and even more unusual for him to be in uniform.

Halsted was the chief criminal deputy of the department. It was a position appointed by Sheriff Johnston. The chief criminal deputy was the third in command of the department, below the sheriff, and undersheriff.

Chief Halsted walked up, and said he was there to talk to me. He requested that when Lt. Booths and I were finished talking I would contact him in the sergeant's office. Halsted then went into the precinct building. Lt. Booths and I finished our conversation, which lasted only a couple of minutes, and I went into the office.

Chief Halsted was sitting in the sergeant's office. As I entered the room he stood up and told me to take a seat. He then walked over to the door and shut it. The chief and I were the only ones in the room.

Chief Halsted advised me he really did not want to be there talking to me, but he was ordered by Sheriff Johnston to do so. He then moved rather briskly over to where I was seated. He stood directly over me and got right into my face. He began almost yelling at me, in a very stern and strong voice.

He said in a demanding voice: "Did you write the anonymous letter?"

I was caught completely off guard and was totally surprised.

"No, I did not." I responded.

Halsted then asked: "Were you involved in the anonymous letter in any fashion?"

"No, I was not" I answered.

He continued his questioning asking me if I had seen or read the anonymous letter and I responded that I had not. Halsted then handed me the anonymous letter and told me to read it. I grabbed the letter from him and began to read. It was all in capital letters, single spaced, and contained a lot of spelling errors.

DEAR SIR:
I AM WRITINT THIS LETTER, BECAUSE THE PUBLIC SHOULD BE AWARE OF THE POWER BASE OF CORUPTION, FRAUD AND MISCONDUCT

CURRENTLY OPERATING IN KINGSTON COUNTY ADMINSTRATION UNDER THE DIRECTION OF PAT JOHNSTON. HERE IS A LIST OF SOME OF THE THINGS THAT HAVE OCCURRED.
- DESTRUCTION OF RECORDS AND PROPERTY EVIDENCE
- WAGES USED FOR OTHER THAN WHAT INTENDED FOR
- SHERIFF, UNDERSHERIFF AND CHIEF TAKE FAMILY VACATIONS AT TAX PAYERS EXPENSE
- SHERIFF AND UNDERSHERIFF HAVE ILLICIT AFFAIRS FINANACED BY PRIVATE SLUSH FUND SET UP WITH PUBLIC FUNDS
- LT. BOOTHS CONFESSED TO USING COCAINE, PRIOR TO SHERIFF PUTTING HIM INCHAREGE OF THE DRUG UNIT
- DET. WIGGINS LIED ON A SEARCH WARRANT IN A HOMICIDE CASE. SHERIFF COVERED IT UP. PUT HIM IN CHARGE OF GETTING SEARCH WARRANTS FOR SHERIFF OFFICE
- SHERIFF RECIEVES FEDERAL MONEY TO HIRE DEPUTIES BUT DOESN'T UNKOWN WHERE THE MONEY GOES
- SHERIFF CAUGHT TWICE BREAKING INTO BUSINESSES. BRAGGED THAT WAS HOW HE GETS VOTES BY TELLING OWNERS HE DISCOVERED THE BURGLARY AND CHASED THE SUSPECTS OFF.
- UNDERSHERIFF RECIEVES THOUSANDS OF DOLLARS FROM CONCERT PROMOTERS. THERE NOT ALLOWED TO HAVE CONCERTS UNLESS THEY PAY HIM OFF
- SHERIFF PAYED OFF A WOMEN IN GOT PREGEANT

- SHERIFF SECRETARY KEEPS A SECOND SET OF BOOKS CONTAINING MONEY BLED OFF AND PUT INTO A PRIVATE SLUSH FUND.
- PAST CHIEF OF DETECTIVES FORCE TO RETIRE BECASUE HE REFUSED TO COVER UP FOR SHERIFF.
- PROMOTION TEST ARE SOMETIMES FIXED TO INSURE YES MEN GET PROMOTED
- SHERIFF JOHNSTON WAS INVOLVED IN THE TRIPLE HOMICIDE AND THEN COVERED UP EVEDEINCE.
- NUMBEROUS QUESITIONABLE SUICIDES REALLL MURDER
- ONE DETECTIVE CAUGH STEALLING TWICE FROM HOMICIDE SCENES
- SHERIFF SISTER FILED COMPLAINT AGAINST ATWATER AFTER ATWATER ANNOUNCE HE WAS RUNNING FOR SHERIFF
- TOP APPOINTED PEOPLE IN SHERIFF OFFICE PUT THERE BECAUSE THEY WILL LIE AND COVER UP FOR SHERIFF
- LARGE QUANITIIES OF DRUGS HAVE DISAPPEARED FORM EVIDENCE ROOM THEN COVERED UP BY SHERIFF AND LT. BOOTHS
- SOME BUINESS PEOPLE ARE OFF LIMITS TOTHE DEPUTYS AND PROTECTED BY SHERIFF JOHNSTON
- SHERIFF JOHNSON IS INVOVLED IN DRUGS
- SHERIFF JOHNSTON AND UNDERSHERIFF DIETER RECEIVE KICK BACKS FROM DRUG DEALERS

THESE ARE ONLY SOME OF THE THINGS OCCURRING WHCIH I AM AWARE OF THERE ARE MANY MORE THING GOING ON. YOU PROPBALY WON'T PRINT THIS BECAUSE I LACK

> THE COURAGE TO SIGN THIS LETTER FEARING WHAT MIGHT HAPPEN TO MYSELF, MY FAMILY AND MY PRIMARY SOURCE OF INCOME . . . BUT IS'S ALL TRUE DO WHAT YOU CAN.

I finished reading the letter and handed it back to Halsted. "Well, what do you think?" Halsted asked.

"It's really heavy duty," I replied.

Chief Halsted then raised his voice and began to ask me a series of questions.

"Did you write the letter?"

"No, I did not."

"Were you involved in writing the anonymous letter?"

"No, I was not."

"Did you contribute any material or information to the writing of the letter?"

"No, I did not."

"Did you type the anonymous letter?"

"No, I did not."

"Did you assist in typing the letter?"

"No, I did not."

"Did you help in distributing the anonymous letter?"

"No, I did not."

"Did you meet with anyone concerning authoring the letter?"

"No, I did not."

"Do you know who wrote the anonymous letter?"

"No, I do not."

"Were you involved in the anonymous letter in any way, shape, or form?"

"No, I was not."

Chief Halsted advised me that he and others in Sheriff Johnston's administration were investigating the anonymous letter, and they had a deputy come forward informing them that I was involved in writing the letter.

I was getting very upset by Chief Halsted's line of questioning and was just about ready to jump back into his face.

I took a deep breath and said: "I wanted to know... no, I demand to know who said I was involved in this anonymous letter."

Chief Halted replied, "I can't tell you, all I can tell you is that we had a deputy come forward and say you were involved. He gave us a written statement stating you were involved."

I began to raise my voice, and said: "I have been a loyal employee for more than 21 years and I resent the fact that you come here and get into my face and accuse me of such a thing. I take it as a direct insult to my integrity. If you are going to tell me that someone said I am involved, you damn well better tell me who. I have a right to confront this individual and find out why he's saying such bull shit. I consider your actions, Chief, as a slap on the face and I do not deserve it."

Chief Halsted immediately began to justify his actions. He said; "We consider this anonymous letter to be a serious situation and we are going to investigate it until we know who was involved. There will be disciplinary action taken against any or all of the individuals involved in this letter."

He then asked me again, if I wrote the anonymous letter. I, again said, "No, I did not."

He went on to ask again if I typed the letter; however before he could finish the question, I interrupted. I told him that I had answered all of these questions twice already and I was finished answering his questions until he told me who said I was involved.

Halsted stopped dead in his tracks. Then he said: "Well... Well we're going to get them and they'll pay and if you are involved you'll pay."

I shook my head and asked Halsted if we were done. He said he was done for now, but they were still going to be investigating the matter, and they had a report from a deputy concerning the letter. I asked to see the report. Halsted told me he was not authorized to show me the report.

I informed Chief Halsted that I had a shift to supervise, and I had enough of this, and I was going to go back to work.

Halsted got a frown on his face; I could tell he was not pleased with my attitude.

"Well, very well then, go back to work but I may want to talk to you again. This matter is not closed and we will get to the bottom of it," he remarked.

"Whatever." I responded.

Halsted then got up, opened the door and walked out. He went directly out of the precinct office and got into his vehicle and departed.

I was very upset, to say the least. I walked out of the sergeant's office. Sgt. Newton confronted me and asked what Halsted was doing here. I started to answer him, and then stopped. I was too shaken to continue. I excused myself and walked outside to get some fresh air. Chief Halsted took pride in intimidating people. He didn't like the fact that I did not give him the satisfaction of being intimidated. He was angry with me. I was hurt and felt intimidated that he accused me of the anonymous letter. It did not show but I was shaking inside and needed to regain my composure. After about ten minutes I returned into the precinct office and contacted Sgt. Newton.

"Are you okay?" Sgt. Newton inquired.

"Yea, I guess that Halsted just gets to me." I replied.

I told Sgt. Newton what had transpired during my conversation with Halsted. Sgt. Newton advised me that the Sheriff, Undersheriff, and Chief have been having daily meetings with the detectives over the anonymous letter. He stated they were closed door meetings with a select group of detectives.

He knew something was going on, and they were upset over the letter. He did not, however, know exactly what was occurring. He told me that he thought the treatment I was receiving was inappropriate and he was sorry it was happening to me.

I called Capt. Hill at his residence and explained what had just occurred with my meeting with Halsted. He advised that he would check on the matter in the morning. I left the precinct office, after I hung up from Capt. Hill, and went out on patrol. I ended up having a roadside meeting with Corporal Dirk and Deputy Parkins. I told them about my conversation with Chief Halsted. Deputy Parkins informed me that he had heard just today, that the administration had information I was involved in the anonymous letter. He said Sheriff Johnston was going around the office telling everyone I was involved and they were going to handle the matter.

Corporal Dirk stated, the whole thing was a bunch of bull shit, and it appeared I was being targeted. He advised me that I had better get an attorney because once Johnston goes after someone, he does not stop until he destroys that person's career. He remarked that he has seen it happen too many times in the past. I needed to protect myself. Deputy Parkins agreed with Corporal Dirk, and added he would hire an attorney if it was happening to him.

I told both of them, I did not believe I needed an attorney at this time. I had always been loyal to the department and did a good job for Johnston. I thought Johnston would come around and realize my history with the department. They both cautioned me to be careful.

Later that night, I ran into Deputy Farrell; he had already heard about Chief Halsted's visit with me. He said he was sorry to hear I was being targeted by the administration. He went on to advise that he had not seen the anonymous letter yet but from what he was hearing, everything on it, all the wrong doing was true. He then added. "that is why Sheriff Johnston is so upset over the letter."

He told me to be careful. He believed Sheriff Johnston could be dangerous and was capable of just about anything. He went on to say that having all the allegations listed in the anonymous letter out in the open is causing Johnston to get desperate. "If he thinks you are involved in the anonymous letter, then he may fear that you know too much and you are a threat to him, and that is why he is targeting you." Farrell went on.

Deputy Farrell continued, stating he felt that Sheriff Johnston was nothing more than a criminal, and that he was involved in large scale criminal activities with some heavy hitters. He advised he had no proof, but if he ever got proof he would bring Johnston down. We talked for some time and when we were done, I was more bewildered and upset about my conversation with Halsted than I was earlier. I really did not know what to do or what exactly was going on.

In the morning, when I got off graveyard shift, I arrived at my residence and awoke my wife, Sherry. I told her about my night and about my meeting with Halsted. She was upset to hear what I was telling her and she remarked, "Well, now you know what the administration thinks of you."

Her statement hit home. It hit me extremely hard. I've always been a team player. I always considered the administration and all the deputies, including myself, to be on the same team. In my mind, I thought the sheriff and administration had respect for me and the accomplishments of my law enforcement career. Having been accused of writing the anonymous letter had even a greater impact on me than I had realized.

I stayed up all day. I could not sleep. I was too wound up. Normally, I would come home from a graveyard shift and go right to bed. Today, I didn't, I just couldn't sleep, my mind would not slow down. Later that morning, actually early in the afternoon, I received a call from Capt. Hill.

Capt. Hill told me he had called the detective's office and spoke with Det. Paris. He stated Det. Paris told him that Sheriff Johnston had a select group of detectives, including himself, working on determining who was responsible for the anonymous letter. Detective Paris went on to advise Capt. Hill that at one of the meetings where they had been discussing the anonymous letter, Detective Wiggins stated that he thought I could have written the letter. Detective Wiggin's reasoning behind thinking I was involved was because the letter listed wrong doing involving Lt. Booths and himself, Det. Wiggins. Wiggins made a comment at the meeting that I did not like him or Lt. Booths.

Detective Paris, advised Wiggins, was only speculating but Sheriff Johnston ordered Chief Halsted to contact me and interview me concerning the anonymous letter. Johnston's thinking on the matter was that he would shake me up and also lock me into a story, so if at a later date they could prove that I was involved it would give them grounds to fire me for lying.

Capt. Hill went on to say Detective Paris also told him Sheriff Johnston believed me to be an Atwater supporter in the up coming election. Sheriff Johnston was determined to destroy Atwater and anyone that supported Atwater. Paris then warned Capt. Hill to be careful, advising Johnston was also out to get him for agreeing to be Atwater's undersheriff. Paris then remarked the problems were just beginning and we should all be careful.

I got off the phone with Capt. Hill, and I really did not know what to do. I knew I was not going to take this lying down and that I was going to do something. I was equally disturbed to learn I was the only one being investigated for the anonymous letter and that Sheriff Johnston made a point of making sure all the deputies knew I was being investigated.

Over the next few days, I got very little sleep. I kept searching for solutions. I was searching for how to handle this situation. The realization hit me; it hit me like a brick—Sh—eriff Johnston has been stepping on deputies and destroying their careers over the last sixteen years that he has been Sheriff. I counted them. Seventeen deputies have either been fired or forced to resign over the time Johnston has been the sheriff. I was so into my own career, I never paid any attention. Every time a deputy got into trouble with Johnston, I just made the assumption that the deputy did something wrong. I never knew the situation completely. It didn't affect me, so I never worried about it. I was always busy working undercover or working on homicide cases. My career consumed my life. I actually never realized what was going on around me in relation to Sheriff Johnston. Now it was my turn to face off with Johnston and the reality hit home.

CHAPTER TWO

IN ORDER TO RESPECT YOURSELF, SOMETIMES YOU HAVE TO FIGHT BACK.

Around the 28th of October, 1994, I made up my mind as to what I was going to do, what I had to do. I decided to stand up and fight Johnston head on. I felt my problems were only just the beginning for all of us. I was not going to stand by and let Johnston destroy my career without a fight.

I called up the local newspapers. I wanted to go public and inform the citizens of the community what Sheriff Johnston was doing. My theory was if the public became aware of Johnston's actions; then Johnston would be held to a degree of accountability for his actions. I called up Mr. Henry Gains, editor of the Weekly Globe. I identified myself to him. I was immediately shocked and taken back by his response. After I introduced myself, his first comments were "Oh Hi, Sheriff Johnston called me and told me you might be calling me."

He went on to say that Sheriff Johnston had informed him that I was a disgruntled employee who had been passed over for promotion and I might be calling to say bad things about Johnston.

I was at a loss for words. I was not ready for this. I paused for a few seconds and then said;

"Oh, he did, did he? Well, I assure you, I am now and always have been a dedicated police officer. Further, I am not aware of ever being passed over for promotion."

I went on to say "The reason I am calling you is because I have never been political. I have never been involved in politics, but because of the actions of Sheriff Johnston and his administration I feel I am a victim of politics. I do not like it, and therefore, wish to go public at this time casting my support for Atwater for sheriff."

I told him the morale at the sheriffs' office was very low and that there is a definite need for change. I went on stating that Atwater is an honest, dedicated individual, who could bring about the changes needed in the department. I then told Mr. Gains about the incidents that had occurred to me concerning Sheriff Johnston's visit on October 10, 1994, and Chief Halsted's accusations of October 25, 1994. Mr. Gains listened rather intensely, interjecting a few questions here and there.

When we were done speaking, he informed me that he would publish an article concerning what I told him. He advised me, however, that first he would going to talk to Sheriff Johnston and get his side of the story. I told Mr. Gains that was fine with me, and I had no problem with him contacting Johnston.

Mr. Gains, informed me he had received calls from about 20 different deputies, all of whom wanted to remain anonymous. He said each of the deputies that called him told him negative things about the sheriff and about things that were occurring within the sheriff's office surrounding the up coming election. He remarked he was very interested in the problems and was pleased to finally have someone who was willing to go public and talk about the problems without remaining anonymous.

He made a comment to me which was very disturbing to me. He advised he wanted me to be aware that he has known Sheriff Johnston his entire life, and he has a lot of respect for the man. He has always supported Sheriff Johnston. He would try to be objective and not be prejudiced toward anyone in his article.

I made it clear to Mr. Gains, all I wanted was the truth exposed to the public. He thanked me for calling him and we hung up.

I called two other local newspaper editors. To my surprise, they both informed me they had already received calls from Sheriff Johnston.

Johnston had, likewise, advised each of them that I might be calling. He told them I was a disgruntled employee who had been passed over for promotion, and most likely, would be telling them negative things about him and his administration.

I was very careful not to interject any negative feelings or attitudes that I might have had concerning the entire ordeal. I tried to remain professional and stick to the facts involved. Once again, I advised them of my opinion, that I had always been non political. I advised them that I felt the actions of Sheriff Johnston made me a victim of politics, and I did not like it. I advised them the actions of Sheriff Johnston toward me were intimidating, and designed to influence my actions and vote in the up coming election. It was wrong, and a violation of my civil rights. I once again stated, I was "going public," supporting Atwater for Sheriff indicating, there was a need for positive changes in the sheriff's office.

Every one of us, I'm sure, knows the saying, "that for every action there is a reaction." The problem is, we never realize the impact the reaction will have upon us until after we put the action into motion.

November 2, 1994, the Weekly Globe head lines read;

"SHERIFF SERGEANT PUBLICLY SUPPORTS ATWATER FOR SHERIFF" Mr. Gains did an excellent job OF writing the article. He did not slant the article one way or the other. He stayed objective. He merely printed the facts that were related to him from Sheriff Johnston and me. That's not to say that I was happy with the article. Statements which were made by Johnston in the article were not true, and reflected poorly upon me.

Sheriff Johnston stated in the article that I was a disgruntled employee who had been passed over for promotion. He went on to say the only reason he came to talk to me on October 10, 1994, was because he received information from a local editor that I was involved in illegal narcotic activities in regards to the "Wild Willies" sting operation I had worked.

When I read this in the newspaper, I became furious, to say the least. I could not believe he would make up such a boldfaced lie. It was he who accused me of telling the press that he was involved in illegal narcotic activities.

The news article went on to quote Sheriff Johnston as saying he had never tried to influence my vote in the up coming election but I had bragged to him that I was going to be Atwater's chief of detectives if he was elected.

I guess I was naive, I thought to myself. I should have realized that Johnston would lie to the press. I should also have been aware that he would attempt to minimize the damages the article would cause him politically by attempting to discredit any statements I made to the media.

At any rate, I knew it was now my move and there was no turning back. Johnston would be more determined than ever to "get me," to fire me. They would invent a reason and I would be "history." I needed to do something to protect myself and to protect my career. I spent the evening talking to my wife and some of my closest friends. I was searching once again for a solution, or at least for the next step that I should take.

One of my friends suggested I should consult an attorney. He advised me that my civil rights had been violated and I probably had a good case to file litigation against the sheriff. He felt as I did, the next step the sheriff would take would be to suspend me and then cause me to be fired. He advised me that if I had legal action pending against the sheriff it might prevent him from firing me. He then told me about this guy he knew who was a retired police office and now a practicing attorney. He suggested I call him and that he might be able to assist me.

He said the attorney he knew was Randy Town, and he was familiar with these cases involving police officers. He told me Randy was an honest, dedicated individual, and he trusted him. He believed Randy probably could help me, and he gave me Randy's home number.

It was around 10:00 p.m., on November 2, 1994 when I first spoke with Mr. Randy Town. I called him at his residence. He was very receptive to my call. He seemed very concerned about my welfare.

I was impressed with him, after only talking briefly to him. I advised him time was of the essences. I needed to file my case against Sheriff Johnston before he has a chance to start action to fire me. Mr. Town listened to what I had to say, and then advised me to come into his office in the morning at 9:00 a.m., and he would go over my case in detail to determine whether or not I had a good case.

I had been keeping notes on everything that had been transpiring ever since Sheriff Johnston contacted me back on October 10, 1994.

I took all my notes with me, including some that I prepared, to present my case to the attorney. Mr. Town greeted me as I walked into the reception area of his office. He then escorted me back to his office.

He advised me from our brief conversation last night on the phone, it sounded like I had a good case but we needed to go over my case in detail before he could make a final determination. He explained to me that attorneys are not allowed to file a case that is frivolous. We spent the next couple of hours going over my notes. Mr. Town kept asking me a series of questions. He advised me that he believed I had a good retaliation and violation of my first amendment rights case if I wished to pursue it. He stated he would be more than happy to take the case, but before I decide I should understand and realize that once legal action was initiated, my career at the sheriffs' office could be in great jeopardy and there may be no turning back.

Mr. Town advised me of the procedure we would have to follow: first file a claim for damages with the county risk manager, then we have to wait for 90 days for them to respond. After the 90 days, whether they responded or not, we could file the lawsuit. He went on to say he would take the case on a contingency basis. He then explained to me how that worked. He explained, if we did not win our case, it would not cost me for his services except for any out of pocket expenses that occur. He advised that if we did win the case then he would get a percentage of the winnings. He told me that my "out-of-pocket" expenses could run between ten and twenty thousand dollars. At this point in time, I was not concerned about the cost, only about protecting my career and standing up to Johnston.

Mr. Town came across as a very sincere and honest individual who was more concerned about justice and my welfare than actively making money from me. He went on to say, if filing of the claim for damages serves the purpose of being a "wake up call" for Sheriff Johnston and I decided not to pursue it any further, he would understand. He said that if that happens there would be no charge for his services. I had explained to Mr. Town that I really was not out for money. I did not really want to sue the county. I just did not want to lose my job but feared I would be fired if I did not pursue legal action. I firmly believed that by initiating legal action I would hold Sheriff Johnston to some form of accountability.

I explained to Mr. Town I had already made my decision. I wanted him to file the claim for damages and I wanted them filed immediately, before Sheriff Johnston had time to take action against me, before he could fire me.

Mr. Town said "No problem, we can start on the paper work right now and I can have your claim for damages filed by tomorrow; let's get to work."

We made the amount of the claim for damages at two and one-half million dollars. It was a lot of money, but money was not the issue. The amount was set high in order to get the county's attention, attention to the fact that they had a serious problem with Sheriff Johnston, a problem which needed to be addressed and corrected.

Mr. Town advised me that he would call me tomorrow and let me know when the claim had actually been filed. He then told me that if anyone from the county or from the sheriffs' administration wants to talk to me concerning anything regarding the claim I should tell them to contact him and not talk to them about it.

I left his office with mixed emotions. Unable to predict the future, I could not help but wonder if I had made the right decision. Logic told me I did; yet the uncertainty filled me with apprehension as to what the future held in store. I decided to take the next week off. One of the ten most deadly errors that police officers make that causes serious injuries or death is "preoccupation." I was consumed with preoccupation over my future, consumed to the point that I realized I had problems focusing on anything except my current problems. I needed a break. I did not, at this point in time, need to be put into an emergency situation that required my full and undivided attention.

I went by the sheriff's office and contacted Capt. Hill. I submitted a request for ten days annual leave, which Capt. Hill approved on the spot. I felt relieved with the fact that I could take a break from the office and related pressures, while Mr. Town prepared my case.

November 4, 1994, at approximately 5:00 p.m., I received a call from Mr. Town advising my claim for damages had been filed with the county risk manager. I wondered what would happen next.

It wasn't long until I would find out. Around 9:00 p.m., on November 4, 1994, I received a hang up call, the kind of call where someone is just on the line breathing, but not saying anything. It was the first of more than one thousand, "hang up" calls my wife and I would receive over the next two years. The calls would come to our residence all hours of the day and night. Sometimes they would actually be threatening messages, but most of the times they were just breathing. We had an unlisted phone number. We rarely would give out the number, and then only selectively. Even after we changed the phone number, the calls continued. Over the next four or five days, nothing else really happened other than the hang up calls.

On November 8, 1994, around 5:00 p.m., I received a call from Capt. Hill. He told me that he and his wife were going to go down to the Republican Headquarters to hear the election returns come in. He stated they had an open house type of election party there and anyone could attend. He asked if my wife and I would like to go. I told him it sounded good, we had not been out of the house since the claim was filed. I advised him we would see him there. We needed to get out of the house. We had not been doing much of anything lately except worrying about our future.

We arrived at the Republican Headquarters around 8:00 p.m., and contacted Capt. Hill and his wife, Eileen. Atwater was trailing Johnston by about 900 votes in the early election results. There were not many precincts counted yet and the polls had just closed. Capt. Hill informed me that County Commissioner Heater was there at the campaign headquarters. He advised he was going to talk to Commissioner Heater concerning his fears of retaliation by Johnston against those that supported Atwater in the election. I walked over to Commissioner Heater with Capt. Hill. We got the commissioner aside, away from the crowds of people, and Capt. Hill explained his concerns to Commissioner Heater. He assured Capt. Hill and me that the county would not allow Sheriff Johnston to get away with any form of retaliation related to the election process. He went on to say that after the election was over things would get back to normal and our careers were safe. He then got a rather concerned look on his face and remarked if Sheriff Johnston does anything that we feel is inappropriate to contact him and he would correct the matter. We thanked him for his time, and walked back over to our wives. We both felt relieved knowing things were going to improve no matter who won the election. My wife, Sherry, and I only stayed at the Republican Headquarters for about another hour and then we went back home.

On November 9, 1994, the day after the general election, we learned that Sheriff Johnston won the election beating Atwater by a large margin. I had hoped with the election over, and the claim for damages filed, Sheriff Johnston would back off and things would improve. Once again, I was wrong. The weekly Globe came off the press with dual head lines. In bold print, it read:

"SHERIFF JOHNSTON DEFEATS ATWATER IN SHERIFF RACE"

and then directly across from it read:

"SHERIFF SERGEANT FILES TWO AND HALF MILLION DOLLAR LAWSUIT AGAINST SHERIFF JOHNSTON AND KINGSTON COUNTY"

I didn't even think about the news media picking up on the claim for damages. Looking back, I should have realized that the news media would be picking up on it and running with it. After all the papers these days are into sensationalism. My thoughts were more about survival, and so I hadn't even given the media a thought. That was a mistake on my part because with the article coming out in the local paper it violated the Sheriff's already damaged ego. It made him look bad in the eyes of the public and it gave him additional fuel to intensify his retaliation toward me. In fact, Sheriff Johnston and his administrators lost no time in retaliating against me.

Here it was the day after the election and the first order of business for Sheriff Johnston centered around Capt. Hill and me. Chief Halsted called me up at approximately 10:00 a.m., advising that he was sending two deputies out to my residence to pick up my patrol vehicle.

I told him that I did not understand why he would be having my patrol vehicle picked up. I advised him I was currently on approved annual leave and I was scheduled to return to duty on the following Monday. He advised me I needed to talk to Undersheriff Dieter concerning the matter so I called Undersheriff Deiter and inquired as to what was going on. He replied with: "You're suing the Sheriff and the county. You filed a claim for damages in the amount of two and half million dollars. We are not allowing you to return to work until you come in and sit down with the

Sheriff and me. We need to talk and you'll have to drop this lawsuit if you ever want to work here again."

I advised: "If you wish to discuss the claim for damages, you'll have to talk to my attorney. I have done nothing wrong, and I should be allowed to return to work."

Deiter responded with: "If you refuse to drop the lawsuit, then you are going to be suspended while we conduct an internal affair's investigation into your charges against the Sheriff and Chief Halsted."

Undersheriff Deiter continued: "We will be picking up your patrol vehicle today. I want you to call me tomorrow around 10:00 a.m. and I will advise you further as to what our intentions are after I have a chance to talk with the county's attorney."

A short time later, two deputies arrived at my residence and picked up my patrol vehicle. Later that same day, I learned of the second order of business for Sheriff Johnston, Undersheriff Deiter, and Chief Halsted. Capt. Hill was called into Chief Halsted's office. He was advised he no longer would be working day shift with weekends off. Capt. Hill had been working day shifts with weekends off for the last fifteen years, ever since he made captain. Halsted went on to advise Capt. Hill that starting tomorrow, Friday, Capt. Hill would be back in uniform, in a marked patrol car, working swing shift on the road. Likewise, Capt. Hill had not worked a swing shift or in a marked patrol car since he made captain.

Halsted then changed Capt. Hill's duties. He was basically stripped of all his administrative duties as a captain and reduced to a senior division sergeant position. His duties consisted of being the swing shift watch commander, a position that did not exist in the department up until this time. He was advised he was to oversee the sergeants and fill in where the sergeants needed him. He was basically reduced to a uniform officer working the streets. He did, however, retain his title as captain.

Captain Hill questioned Chief Halsted as to why this was happening to him at this time and without any prior warning. The chief responded with: "Because we just made the decision and that's the way it is."

Capt. Hill was devastated by the new assignment and wondered if it was retaliation for having supported Atwater in the election. Capt. Hill advised me of his concerns but admitted that at this point in time he did not know if it was retaliation or not. He did state that Sheriff Johnston himself told him that after the election, he would personally get anyone that supported Atwater and they would pay for not standing behind him.

Capt. Hill told me he believed the treatment I was receiving from the sheriffs' administration was nothing more than retaliation, and he warned me to be careful. I fully believe Capt. Hill realized the treatment he was receiving was also retaliation, but at this point in time he did not want to believe it.

On November 10, 1994, around 10:00 a.m., I called Undersheriff Deiter back at the sheriff's office as he had directed. I was advised that he was in a meeting and would return my call shortly. I grabbed the portable cordless phone and went outside to do some yard work. I took the phone with me so I would not miss the call.

A short time later the phone rang and I ran in the back door in order to listen to the answering machine to see who was calling. I heard Undersheriff Deiter's voice and clicked on the portable phone.

I said: "Hello," as I walked back into my bedroom. I sat on the floor where I had left a note pad and pen. I then took notes of the entire conversation as I talked to the undersheriff.

Undersheriff Deiter advised: "I have been talking with the county's attorney concerning your case and your claim for damages. There are some issues I need to discuss with you."

"Okay." I said.

Deiter continued: "The first issue is that I need you to come in and discuss your claim with the Sheriff and myself."

I responded: "If you wish to discuss my claim, you will need to contact my attorney. I will make myself available at whatever time is suitable for you and my attorney."

Deiter said: "That would be fine. The second issue, I wish to discuss with you is that the risk manager for the county will be conducting an independent investigation into your claim against the sheriff and the county. The risk manager is Barbara Becker. I have already spoken to her concerning your claim. I also spoke with Sheriff Johnston and Chief Halsted concerning your claim. I must tell you that their version of the incidents and what exactly occurred differs greatly from yours."

"We have decided that you will be suspended with pay while the investigation is being done. This is not punishment. It is just that, well, you said things about your supervisors that I do not believe are true and they need to be investigated."

I responded with: "When Barbara Becker has completed her investigation can I return to work?"

Deiter replied, in a rather strong and stern voice:

"No, and that brings me to the third issue. Now, after Barbara Becker finishes her investigation, the sheriff's office, I don't know this for sure yet, but I believe it's going to happen. The sheriff's office will conduct its own investigation. I mean to say, by that, well, what, I mean, is an internal affair's investigation into your claim. You will be suspended until that investigation is concluded as well, so you will not be allowed back to work for at least two months and it might be longer."

I was trying to take notes on everything Deiter was telling me and at the same time maintain my composure.

I advised Deiter: "Undersheriff, I do not understand why I am being suspended. The normal procedure when an internal affair's investigation is conducted is to suspend the person you suspect of wrong doing. I have done nothing wrong. Are you saying that I am being suspended and investigated because I filed a claim against the sheriff and the county?"

Deiter replied: "Well, no. We are going to investigate your claim. I've already talked to the sheriff and to the chief, as I told you, and their stories are different from yours. You made some serious accusations against your superiors that could be cause for your dismissal, so we are going to investigate them."

I responded with: "So you are investigating me for possible wrongdoing and not my claim as you previously told me?"

Deiter, at this point in time, began to get angry and very abrupt with me. He advised:

"No, we are investigating your claim and while that is occurring you are suspended. Do I make myself clear? You are not allowed to come to work, nor carry out any of the powers or duties of a police officer. At this point in time you are not a police officer . . . you . . . you are suspended. End of discussion. I will be contacting you sometime in the future to set up an interview with you. Do you understand?"

I answered: "I understand very well what you are saying. You can contact my attorney if you wish to contact me. Do you understand Mr. Deiter?"

Deiter replied "Very well then, that will be all."

And he hung up the phone.

Deiter had a way with words that always made him sound like he was in control. He would twist things around to his way of thinking. His demeanor was such that, he was right and you were wrong. It was obvious to me. I was the one being investigated and not my claim. It had gone beyond the point of backing down. I had passed the point of no return. I was not about to let it go; if I did, I would be more vulnerable than ever.

That very afternoon on November 10, 1994, there was a brass meeting at the sheriff's office. Now, a brass meeting is a monthly meeting which is conducted by the sheriff's administration with all the mid-level supervisors in attendance. It is designed to update the shift sergeants and corporals as to what is going on at the administration level as well as to pass out information and current assignments to the shift supervisors. It was announced at the brass meeting that until further notice, I was suspended with pay. Chief Halsted made the announcement advising that I probably would not be returning to duty this year, if I returned at all. He then explained to all the supervisors present that I was the focus of an internal affair's investigation where by they believed I had made false statements concerning the sheriff and him in the claim for damages that I had filed against them. He then told the supervisors present that he would keep them updated as to my status and the out come of the internal affairs' investigation.

Sheriff Johnston and his administration were implementing damage control for my actions. Once again, I should have realized it was coming, but I under estimated them. After all, I really never have been in this position of standing up and fighting back before and it was all new to me. Sheriff Johnston and his top aids were "pros" at it. They had "fine tuned" the art of justifying their actions. They had the power and control to discredit and destroy anyone who stood up to them or got into their way. The irony of it was that they would do it in the name of justice.

That afternoon about the time the brass meeting was going on, I made a discovery. I learned that my answering machine, the one connected to my phone, had recorded the entire conversation I had with Undersheriff Deiter. Apparently when I answered the phone on the wireless portable, it did not send a signal to the answering machine to disconnect the recorder. I normally have always answered the phone on the regular hard wired phone. We had just got the wireless portable, so I was unaware that when you answered the phone on it, it did not shut off the recorder.

I called up my attorney Mr. Town, and informed him of the answering machine recording my conversation with Undersheriff Deiter. He advised me that since the recording was not made intentionally, it was not an illegal recording. He further stated that I should remove the answering machine tape from the recorder and then turn it over to him. He then told me not to tell anyone that I had the tape. I had already informed him of the conversation that had taken place between Deiter and me. He advised that the undersheriff acted inappropriately in his demeanor and statements he had made during the conversation. Now, with this tape recording, there was evidence that existed that clearly demonstrated the Undersheriff's conduct.

The next day, I went to Mr. Town's office and turned over the tape recording. Mr. Town had his secretary transcribe the recording and then place the original tape recording and transcript in my case file.

On November 15, 1994, I received a letter from Undersheriff Deiter. The letter stated that it was a formal documentation of our conversation which took place on November 10, 1994. It stated that since I filed a claim against the sheriff and felt uncomfortable working under the current conditions, he was authorizing administrative leave with pay for me while the risk management conducted an investigation. The letter went on to say an internal affair's investigation into my charges against the sheriff and chief might also be conducted and I would be allowed to stay on administrative leave with pay during that process as well. The letter never once mentioned that I was suspended, nor did it mention the majority of the items that we talked about in our phone conversation.

I called up my attorney and advised him of the letter I had received from the undersheriff. It was decided upon by Mr. Town and I that I should respond to the letter. I wrote the undersheriff back, advising him that the letter he sent me was not an accurate documentation of our phone conversation of November 10, 1994.

On November 28, 1994, I received another letter from Undersheriff Deiter. This letter advised that the letter dated November 15, 1994, was an accurate account of our phone conversation of November 10, 1994. He advised in this letter he realized that I was emotionally upset over the entire incident and probably had trouble remembering what actually was said. He advised in the letter that I was probably just confused. He then restated in the letter that I was on administrative leave until the entire matter was resolved.

I took this letter, as I did the first letter, to my attorney. Mr. Town and I were now on a first name basis. I handed Randy the letter. He took it, read it, and just smiled.

He then winked at me, and made a comment that they just keep digging themselves a deeper hole. Randy had a way of just making me feel better. I do not know what it was, maybe just his demeanor and attitude. I would go to see him all depressed or all wound up, the next thing I knew, I just felt better and confident that things were going to work out.

With each day that passed, we kept getting increased numbers of "hang up" calls. I was beginning to wonder if I would ever be allowed to return to work. Capt. Hill would check on me every couple of days or so, as he did with some of the other deputies that supported Atwater and now they were having problems at the sheriffs' office. I believe the single most important factor, which kept me going, was the support of my fellow deputies, especially Capt. Hill.

Come the middle of December, December 12, 1994, to be exact,

I learned that the newly elected prosecuting attorney, Russ Roberts, went in and had a meeting with Sheriff Johnston and Undersheriff Deiter. He advised them that what they were doing to me by not allowing me to return to work was not only wrong but also illegal. He advised them that their conduct was criminal and it was obvious they were violating my civil rights. He then informed them that they needed to correct the problem, or else when he took office in January he might very possibly bring criminal charges against them.

The very next day, Capt. Hill delivered a letter to me, at my residence. The letter was from Undersheriff Deiter. It stated that I was being reinstated to active duty status effective immediately. It directed me to contact Capt. Hill and make arrangements to use my annual must leave prior to returning to duty. Basically, what the letter said was I could return to work after I used up the annual leave that I had on the books that were in excess of the amount allowed to be carried over to the new year. The "must leave" I had was more than enough to take me into the new year; this meant I would be off work until after the start of the year. I read the letter in front of Capt. Hill when he handed it to me. I asked him if he had read it; he had not. I handed him the letter when I was finished reading it. He read it and handed it back to me. He advised me he would do the paper work so that I could use up my must leave. We both thought it rather strange that the letter mentioned nothing about me being suspended or about an internal affair's investigation being conducted. In fact, there never was an internal affair's investigation on my claim for damages or on me. The subject of an internal affair's investigation was not mentioned again.

The patrol division of the sheriffs' department works rotating shift work. Each shift is ten hours long and they over lap. There are three shifts. Every three months the shifts rotate. The sergeants are responsible for drawing up the new shift schedules prior to the rotation. I advised Capt. Hill, when we discussed my annual leave, of the days off I wanted to take on the January, February, and March schedule. Days off, by past practice, are scheduled by seniority. I was a senior shift sergeant, so I would normally get the days off that I requested.

I felt good. I thought, just maybe the sheriff had come to realize the error of his ways, and that he too is accountable for his actions. I looked forward to going back to work. I believed things were possibly going to work out and be okay. I was once again wrong.

CHAPTER THREE

RETALIATION COMES IN ALL FORMS.

On December 21, 1994, the majority of the deputies who vocally supported Atwater in the November election began receiving anonymous letters. The letters were threatening in nature. The letters were all different, but designed to get to the individual deputies emotionally. There were about twenty deputies who originally started getting these letters. I was not one of the deputies receiving anonymous letters, at least not initially. Capt. Hill did not get any anonymous letters, either, when they first started appearing. Capt. Hill and I were, however, still getting hang up phone calls during all hours of the day and night.

Capt. Hill still had two young children living at home. After years of working day shift with weekends off, Capt. Hill was experiencing family problems over adjusting to working nights and weekends. The emotional stress over his current lack of stability in his position at the sheriffs' office created a hardship for both his wife and he. It took its toll.

Capt. Hill ran into Undersheriff Deiter at a local department store the morning of December 21, 1994. Capt. Hill was off duty while the undersheriff was supposed to be working.

He tried to explain to the undersheriff that he was having family problems and would like to go back to day shift, at least temporarily until he was able to get his family situation stabilized. Undersheriff Deiter looked Capt. Hill right in the eyes and advised him he would remain on swing shift for the rest of his career. Capt. Hill came to realize the undersheriff was taking great pleasure in seeing him squirm.

Deiter went on to advise Capt. Hill that if he decided to retire, the sheriff and he would not fight it but, rather, would support him and help insure that he get his retirement. Deiter then made a disturbing statement to Capt. Hill, a statement that gave all of us an understanding of the mental state of Johnston and Deiter. It was a statement that made us come to realize that it was not over yet.

Deiter stated, "If Atwater had won the election for sheriff, Johnston and I would be out on the streets without a job. It is only right that since Johnston won the election that those that supported Atwater should be worried about their future at the sheriffs' office."

Deiter continued remarking that, "The sheriff would fire all of them right now if he could get away with it."

"The sheriff has a way of getting what he wants done without it coming back on him. He will get rid of them, all of them in time and it will appear that they all deserve it when it happens. If I were you, I would reconsider retirement. I am only telling you this as a friend, after all, we have a lot of history here at the sheriff's office and I would hate to see you get fired and leave in disgrace."

Undersheriff Deiter then changed the focus of his conversation with Capt. Hill toward me. He told me Sheriff Johnston was going to figure out a way to take away my commission card so that I could no longer perform the duties of a law enforcement officer. Then, he would be able to get rid of me.

Deiter then remarked:

"Johnston has to be careful with the claim for damages filed against him, but it will not stop him from firing or getting rid of the sergeant. One way or another, he'll get rid of him." Capt. Hill just stood there listening to Undersheriff Deiter. He could not believe what he was hearing. He was in total disbelief. He was trying to digest the undersheriff's words. He had known this man for more than twenty-five years but until this very moment, he never really knew his true nature.

Capt. Hill called me later that day, and informed me of the

conversation he had with the undersheriff. He was very upset to say the least. He was a bowl of mixed emotions ranging from anger to despair. We talked for some time. Prior to the election Capt. Hill and I were, I guess what you would call professional friends. We had known each other for more than twenty years and considered each other working friends. We never saw each other outside of the work environment. Now, since the election, our relationship had evolved into giving each other mutual support. We were becoming much more than working friends. We were developing a trust and a bond that we could turn to each other in a time of need.

Capt. Hill further advised me that Chief Halsted took the new shift roster and changed my days off from weekends to mid week days. I was not pleased to hear about Halsted, but then I wasn't happy to hear about Deiter's conversation with the captain either. I came to realize that going back to work was not going to be easy. I was going to have to be very careful. I was going to be one of the main focus points of the administration's attention.

On December 26, 1994, I received a call from Deputy Farrell. He advised me that Capt. Hill's wife, Eileen, was in the hospital. She apparently suffered an emotional breakdown on Christmas day. The changes in her husband's working conditions and the threat of him losing his job created more pressure on her than she could handle. He then told me, he checked on her condition just before calling me and she is now stable, and Capt. Hill seems to be doing okay. Apparently Capt. Hill tried to reach me after taking Eileen to the hospital, but we had gone out of town over Christmas.

After my conversation with Deputy Farrell, I tried to reach Capt. Hill but was unable to do so. I was unable to reach him for the next three to four days. I finally got a hold of him.

He was not doing very well. He advised Eileen was home and had been improving quite well until the morning mail arrived. He informed me that this morning his wife received an anonymous letter. The letter stated it was no wonder that she was emotionally unstable, with a husband like Capt. Hill. The letter accused Capt. Hill of having affairs with women while he was at work. It made statements about Capt. Hill using and abusing her. The letter went on to state that Capt. Hill really liked working swing shift because it gave him time he could spend away from her. The letter was, by design, created to upset and stress Eileen, especially since everyone knew she was having a terrible time coping and was just released from the hospital.

Capt. Hill was really shocked and upset by the letter. He advised that he reported the letter to the Sheriff's office, and filed a report on it at the office. Undersheriff Deiter informed him the letter was not a crime, and there was nothing the sheriffs' office could do about it. Capt. Hill disagreed with the undersheriff and was angry at him for refusing to allow the office to investigate the letter. Capt. Hill told me other deputies who have received anonymous letters have reported it to the sheriff's office as well, and they have all been advised that the office would not investigate them. He felt it was wrong of the office not to investigate the letters. He also thought it strange, and wondered if their refusal to investigate had anything to do with their own involvement in the anonymous letters.

I was extremely unhappy myself with the entire situation. I thought it was nothing less than criminal for someone to send the letter to Eileen. Her condition made her very vulnerable. The letter was no more than an attempt to push her over the edge. The person that sent it had to be sick.

On December 27, 1994, in the morning hours, my patrol vehicle was returned to me. In the sheriff's office, each deputy was assigned a patrol car which he parked at his residence while on off duty status. Capt. Hill informed me that during the time of my suspension, my patrol car just sat in the parking lot at the precinct office and was not used. He went on to say that the night before my car was returned to me, Sheriff Johnston went by the precinct office and picked up my patrol car. He said the sheriff only used the car for a couple of hours and then returned it to the precinct office. Captain Hill thought it was rather strange and unusual that the sheriff would take my patrol car, especially since the sheriff had two patrol vehicles of his own, a marked patrol car, and an unmarked unit. Capt. Hill told me he observed Sheriff Johnston arrive at the precinct office after dark last night and take my patrol car. The captain lectured me, advising it might be a good idea for me to have my patrol unit checked out mechanically, just to be on the safe side. He was concerned with what the sheriff might be capable of doing and at this point in time he was just not sure.

The next day, I took my patrol vehicle by the south county road shed and had one of the mechanics there check the vehicle out. I thought Capt. Hill was just being paranoid, but decided to take the vehicle in to be checked anyway. I knew that Capt. Hill was trying to look out for my welfare and I appreciated it. I was totally surprised and dismayed when Wester, the mechanic, informed me that he found the bolts to the power steering hoses loose. The bolts were only hand tight, and according to the mechanic, in a short time the road vibration most likely would cause the hoses to start leaking power steering fluid. He then told me that it was good that I brought the vehicle in. If I was on a high speed run when the power steering unit started to leak it could cause me to lose control of the vehicle and crash. I asked him if he could tell if someone deliberately loosened the bolts holding the hoses on. He advised that there wasn't really anyway for him to tell. Then he remarked that my patrol unit was one of the new ones that came in last spring and that he personally checked all the bolts, fittings, and hoses before the vehicle was put out into the field and he knows for certain that those hoses were tight when he checked everything out. He went on to state it was unlikely that the bolts came loose on their own, however, it was possible. After Wester finished fixing my patrol unit, I returned home. There was no proof that anyone had actually tampered with the car, but it was highly suspicious. There really wasn't anything I could do about it. But now I really knew I had to be careful.

 I guess I was always considered a company man. Whatever the

assignment was, I would try to do my best at it. My career had been very successful at the sheriff's office up until these problems over the election. I believe a lot of the deputies thought I was one of Johnston's boys. "Pro" Johnston, I guess, you would say. Now, however, with the claims against Sheriff Johnston filed, many of the deputies looked upon me in a different light. They viewed me as an honest cop, standing up against injustice, and attempting to make a difference. The deputies' perception of me changed. It opened avenues of communication between the deputies and me that did not previously exist. I began to hear things about Johnston and his administration's activities that I never had a clue about. Deputies were opening up to me and relating stories concerning the administration's behavior and demeanor. Stories concerning criminal activities, as well as the administration's self-serving destruction of individuals to enhance their own power.

I began to receive documents and papers containing information on activities involving Sheriff Johnston, Undersheriff Deiter, Chief Halsted, and others in the department. The documents came to me anonymously. It started around the end of December of 1994, when my wife and I arrived home to discover an envelope lying between the screen door and the entry door to our home. I opened it. It stated that Sheriff Johnston was a criminal. He is involved in overseeing major drug transactions within the county. He receives payoff money from drug dealers for allowing them to operate. That was all it said. Not enough information to prove anything, just a statement to make you wonder.

This was only the start of things to come. A week later, I received an expense ledger of all Sheriff Johnston, Undersheriff Deiter and Chief Halsted's expenses for travel over the last two years. A note was attached, which read, "with a little research you will be able to determine that there was abuse of expenses taking place by the sheriffs' administration."

I turned the ledger as well as the previous note that I had received, over to my attorney, Randy. He informed me that people have been coming forward, giving him information on the sheriff's activities and he also was receiving documents and written notes anonymously. He then advised that he was to meet a woman this evening. She had contacted him concerning information she had about Sheriff Johnston. He said he would let me know what he learned from this woman.

I contacted Randy the next day to find out what this woman had to tell him. He informed me that she never showed up; so he still didn't have a clue as to what she had to say.

On January 2, 1995, I returned to duty as the swing shift supervisor. I was apprehensive but happy to be going back to work. On swing shift, you rarely see anyone from the administration. I was looking forward to getting back into police work, getting back to my normal routine. Capt. Hill was working swing shift as well, so we saw each other on a daily basis. Capt. Hill and I, as I have already said, had developed a relationship of trust where we gave each other moral support; so I was pleased that we would be working together.

The first week of work went by without any problems or incidents. On January 10, 1994, however I was contacted by Chief Halsted. He advised me that he had a special assignment for me to do. He stated that Sheriff Johnston told him that he wanted me to personally handle this assignment. The assignment consisted of doing a comprehensive study comparing the five days, eight hours shift to the four-day ten hour shifts with the emphasis on minimizing over time while enhancing training. I was to contact all the police agencies in the state that were comparable in size to our department and research how they were handling overtime and training. I was then to do a report on the facts that I developed, including an analysis on how our department could improve its current scheduling program.

I informed Chief Halsted there were two other sergeants in the department that were more familiar with scheduling and overtime. Both of them had worked on similar research in the past. I felt it would make more sense and avoid duplication of effort to have the assignment given to one of them. I further advised the chief that, as busy as swing shift was, I did not have the time to do the assignment. He told me once again that Sheriff Johnston wanted me to personally handle this assignment and there would be no discussion on the matter. He then advised I could work on the assignment when there were two supervisors on duty. He told me to let the other supervisor handle patrol, while I worked on the project. He went on to say as long as another supervisor was on duty and handling the calls, I did not need to listen to the police radio and would be free to call other agencies and do research. He then informed me that I was to have a written report on the Project finished and on his desk no later that February 1, 1995. I advised him I would handle the assignment and he would have the final report as requested.

This type of assignment was normally assigned to the administrative sergeant or a day shift sergeant. I found it rather peculiar that it would be given to me on swing shift. I did what I was told, however, and worked the assignment. I contacted Sgt. Didders and Corporal Timmons and advised them of the task I was assigned to do. They both said me they would cover patrol and the radio traffic while I worked on the project. I spent many hours over the next couple of nights calling other agencies and doing research.

One night in the middle of January, I was contacted by Deputy Farrell. He wanted to tell me about a meeting that Sheriff Johnston had with the "Dare Officers." These were deputies in the department that were assigned to work in the schools on drug education and prevention. Farrell advised that Sheriff Johnston was having this meeting with the Dare officers when out of the blue, the sheriff became very angry and went off saying how he was going to get the thirty plus deputies that supported Atwater in the general election and that those officers would pay for not supporting him. Johnston then remarked he has not forgotten, and the matter is not over yet. Farrell advised me that he thought I should know this, so I knew where Johnston's head was.

Later that same night, I was approached by Deputy Lori

Plankin, who was one of the Dare officers. She advised me of Sheriff Johnston's actions and statements made at the dare meeting, stating basically the same thing that Deputy Farrell had related. We talked for some time about the current situation and about our concerns.

The next day, I was contacted by Deputy Teri Willis, another Dare officer, who also advised me of Sheriff Johnston's statements and demeanor at the Dare meeting. It was quite obvious that she was upset and shaken up by the threatening remarks of Johnston.

Over the next couple of days, you could see the morale of the sheriff's deputies deteriorating. Deputies were still receiving anonymous letters that implied their future employment at the Sheriff's office was in jeopardy. Capt. Hill, himself, had received over a dozen letters since the first one his wife had gotten back in December. Many of the deputies were filing police reports on the letters, but nothing was being done.

Deputy Farrell contacted me. He advised me he was contacted by Chief Burger, the jail superintendent. Chief Burger pulled him aside and advised him to leave Sheriff Johnston alone. He stated that Sheriff Johnston is not capable of separating "Johnston the sheriff" from "Johnston the individual." Therefore, he takes everything personally. He went on lecturing Deputy Farrell that Johnston would destroy his career if he did not keep his mouth shut and just do his job. Chief Burger remarked he was just giving him friendly advice. Farrell said he took it as a direct threat toward him.

On January 26, 1995, there was another brass meeting. My wife's grandfather had passed away and the funeral was the same day. I was excused from attending the brass meeting so that I could go to the funeral. That evening at the precinct office during line up, Sgt. Didders briefed the deputies and me as to what took place at the brass meeting. Sgt. Newton and Corporal Davidson were also present at line up. Sgt. Didders advised all of us Sheriff Johnston was losing it and acting really scarey. He continued to state, Johnston is no longer the man that he once knew. Johnston's demeanor is that of a very angry, unstable individual who is bent on revenge. Sgt. Didders then warned all the deputies to be careful, especially if Sheriff Johnston showed up on one of their calls. He stated that Johnston is looking to fire a deputy and that Johnston made remarks at the brass meeting like: when his wife sees a deputy in uniform it makes her want to puke.

Sgt. Didders said "it was obvious that Johnston has not been able to get over the split in the department over the election last fall. Johnston has taken it personally that half the deputies voted for his opponent."

Sgt. Didders informed all of us that Johnston is considering taking away the four tens. This is a four-day work week with 10 hour shifts. He then planned to put the deputies back onto the five-day work week, with eight hour shifts. Didders stated that Johnston made a remark that he does not owe the deputies anything, and they needed to be taught a lesson.

Sgt. Newton spoke up. He reenforced the statements made by Sgt. Didders. He then stated he was going to advise the traffic division, which he supervised, to be careful around Sheriff Johnston. He continued by stating it was a dangerous situation and we all needed to practice extreme caution especially dealing with the sheriff.

Corporal Davidson was next to speak out. He advised that he believed that Sheriff Johnston was suffering from stress over the ordeals of the election and that he needed professional help. Sgt. Didders and Sgt. Newton both agreed with Cpl. Davidson. They both then stated that they intended to talk with Chief Halsted concerning the sheriff in hopes that something could be done before the problem becomes even greater.

The next day, Sgt. Didders and Sgt. Newton, did go into Chief Halsted's office and meet with him concerning Sheriff Johnston's mental state. Halsted advised them both that he realized Sheriff Johnston was having problems, but there was nothing he could do about it, and we all had to just weather it. He believed it would pass.

Sgt. Didders informed me of his conversation with Chief Halsted.

He said he did not agree with Halsted. He felt Johnston was sick and needed help. He feared Johnston could lose it anytime and become a danger to himself or others. He then remarked he had been told by many people in the community that Johnston has been bragging that he was going to fire all the deputies that voted against him in the last election.

Sgt. Didders, shook his head and said "I Just don't know what to do."

Later that evening, while I was out on patrol, I came upon Jerry Jackson. He owned a restaurant in the north end of the county for many years. He told me, he had read about my problems with Sheriff Johnston in the local newspaper. He advised that he was sorry to hear I was having problems. He then got a really concerned look on his face, and leaned over toward me and whispered to me to be careful. He went on to say that a few years ago, Sheriff Johnston came into his restaurant. He got into an altercation with one of his waitresses. Later that same day, he was contacted by Johnston who told him to fire the waitress. He got into an argument with the sheriff over the waitress and over whose decision it was to fire one of his employees. He said that he got in the sheriff's face and basically told the sheriff that no one, including the sheriff, was going to come into his business and tell him who to hire or fire. He recalled that Sheriff Johnston then stormed out of his restaurant, threatening him.

The sheriff was yelling at him "You should have done what I told you to do; now you will have to pay."

Jerry seemed to be overcome with emotion: he swallowed hard as if he was choked up. He had difficulty speaking as he continued. He went on, saying after the incident with Johnston he had experienced a run of bad luck and problems that eventually caused him to have to file for bankruptcy. He then told me how his restaurant was burglarized four times. Each time there was extensive vandalism to the establishment, which resulted in his insurance being canceled. This was followed by a fire which destroyed the restaurant. The fire was determined to be an arson fire done deliberately, but there never was any suspect developed or identified. He continued to relate other incidents of suspicious nature that caused him physical, mental and financial grief. He stopped, and remarked he was not saying that Sheriff Johnston was involved in his problems, he was just advising me to be careful. I got the impression he wanted to help me, and that there was something he was leading up to tell me, but he stopped short of actually telling me what was on his mind. He appeared afraid to say exactly what he knew about Sheriff Johnston, afraid maybe to compromise himself. He did however try to convey the serious nature of being at odds with Sheriff Johnston. I thanked him for his concern. We talked for a few more minutes, just casual small talk and then we each went our own way.

After Jerry left, I documented the things he told me in my notebook. I was still taking daily notes of everything that was occurring as well as everything I was hearing in relation to the sheriff and his administration. Ever since my conversation with Sheriff Johnston back in October of 1994, I've been taking notes. I believe it was my police training that caused me to keep notes. Cops call it "PTA." It stands for, "Protect Thy Ass," whenever a cop feels threatened he turns to documenting everything for his own protection.

Later that same evening, I received a call from Cen. Com. on the police radio. They requested I phone them at the 911 Center. I was close to the precinct office so I went to the office to call them. I walked into the office. Sgt. Didders was in the office reviewing reports. I picked up the phone and called Cen. Com. The dispatcher advised me that they had received a call from Sheriff Johnston. He advised them he had been monitoring the police radio traffic and was upset that no one had responded to a prowler call in the south end of the county. The sheriff wanted a deputy to respond to this call immediately. I thanked the dispatcher for the information and hung up the phone.

Sgt. Didders asked me what Cen. Com. wanted. I relayed the information about Sheriff Johnston's call and orders in regards to the prowler call. Sgt. Didders got a frown on his face and shook his head.

He advised me he would handle the situation and the sheriff. He remarked I was in enough trouble with the administration. Sgt. Didders then called a deputy off another call and sent him out on the prowler call. We were extremely busy that night, but we were always extremely busy. The supervisor's job was to monitor the calls and make sure they were handled by priority and in a timely fashion. Sgt. Didders and I always kepy the priorities handled properly and in a timely manner. It was uncommon, in fact, it just did not happen that the sheriff would interfere with the supervisor's overseeing the calls. We had to continually monitor the entire night's calls in order to maintain an understanding of the priorities. The "prowler call" the sheriff was complaining about was a chronic call. We had already sent deputies out to the call three times that evening. The situation was taken care of and it was not a high priority. The sheriff was not aware of the situation and should not have interfered.

It was just the beginning of the sheriff and Chief Halsted monitoring and interfering with the shifts that I supervised. This would continue until the end of my career. It became routine for them to scrutinize and find fault with some supervisory decision I would make on a regular basis. I concluded that while I was taking notes and documenting incidents and events, so were they. Police officers, especially supervisors, are called upon to make life and death decisions that affect people's lives each and every day. Decisions had to be made in a matter of seconds. It is a difficult task, to say the least, when you have the support of your administration. The pressure is intensified when your superiors are second guessing your decisions and analyzing your every action looking to catch you making an error of judgement. It becomes even more nerve racking when you make the right decision and the administration attempts to find fault with your actions. The Sheriff and Chief Halsted put forth a constant effort to micro manage my functions as a supervisor. This created undue pressure that I had to face head on in my daily function as a patrol supervisor.

On January 31, 1995, I completed the four ten's, verses the five eight's report concerning minimizing overtime and enhancing training, that Chief Halsted had assigned to me. I turned the report into Chief Halsted. He never said a word to me concerning the report as to whether it was satisfactory or not. He did, however, advise Capt. Hill that Undersheriff Deiter thought I did an outstanding job on the report. Capt. Hill advised me he believed that Sheriff Johnston intended to take the four ten-hour shifts away from the deputies and have them go back to working five days a week. He felt that the sheriff was setting me up, and they were going to use my report as their justification for going back to the five, eight-hour per day, work week. He advised it would get the patrol deputies to focus their anger over the shift change onto me rather than the sheriff.

On February 7, 1995, Chief Halsted called me into his office. He advised me the sheriff and undersheriff were concerned that I was slacking off on my duties and not listening to the police radio calls as I should. He advised they had aeen monitoring the radio traffic in January and there were many times I could not be reached on the radio. He went on to state it appeared the other supervisors, who were on duty with me, were handling the majority of the work. I took a deep breath, and did my best to remain calm. I then reminded him that he had assigned me the four ten's verses the five eight's investigation and told me to let the other supervisors handle the radio traffic and calls while I worked on the report. I told him I was off the radio while I did the research on the assignment. Halsted advised me he realized that I had that assignment to do but they still felt I was slacking off and not doing my job. He advised they had documentation of me missing radio calls. I could see what was happening, rather than blow up and giving them something to use against me, I swallowed my pride. I advised Chief Halsted that their concerns were noted and I would work on improving. The meeting was over and I departed from the chief's office.

On February 9, 1995, at approximately, 3:15 p.m., as I was just finishing conducting line up, Cen. Com. dispatched a call of two lost nine-year-old children in the woods up on Bear mountain. The lost children were a boy and a girl who had been missing for about six hours. I assigned a deputy to respond to the location of the parents at the base of the mountain and began calling out search and rescue. Chief Halsted came into the sergeant's office and advised me to call him later on that evening and brief him as to any progress that developed over the lost children. It was standard procedure to give the administration a progress report on lost children's calls. Sheriff Johnston viewed lost children's details as a photo opportunity session especially if the children were located without harm. He always made certain that he was at the command center soon after the victims were located so that he could talk to the news media and tell them what a great job his deputies and he did.

The children were lucky in this particular case. They were located by one of the search and rescue teams just prior to night fall setting in. I called Chief Halsted shortly after learning the kids were found, and updated him on the situation. After I finished telling him about the lost kids, he became very abrupt and rather rude on the phone. He wanted to know what meeting two of my deputies attended at the beginning of the shift today. He advised he was monitoring my shift's radio traffic and heard that these two deputies were at some kind of meeting. I told him that I did not know. I advised him that I was aware that they went to a meeting just prior to the shift starting and that the meeting ran into the shift. I had every intention of talking to them concerning the matter but it has been extremely busy on shift and I have not yet had a chance to talk to them.

Chief Halsted then inquired "Well, did you give them permission to attend this meeting that they went to?"

I replied, "No, I did not. I did not even know that they were going to a meeting until after the start of the shift and I discovered that they were still in attendance of some meeting down at the south office."

Halsted abruptly began shouting orders at me "I want you to talk to those deputies tonight and then write me up a detailed report as to what meeting they attended and by whose permission. I want that report on my desk in the morning, do you understand?"

"Yes Sir," I replied.

I again informed the chief I had every intention of talking to the deputies concerning the meeting prior to him bring it up, and he would have a report on his desk in the morning.

Later, during the course of the shift, I contacted both the deputies that were at the meeting in question. I learned the two deputies were guild representatives, and the meeting they attended was a guild/union meeting. They informed me they thought the meeting was going to end prior to the start of the shift and that is why they had not informed me of the meeting. By law, the office has to allow the guild representatives time off work to attend guild meetings. I informed them in the future to let me know prior to any meetings, so if the meetings run over into their respective shift, I could cover for them.

Prior to the end of the shift, I typed up a detailed report on my conversation with the two deputies. I thought about Chief Halsted's demeanor and actions toward me. The chief was not following the chain of command. If he was, he had told Capt. Hill about his concerns and then had the captain advise me to contact the deputies and write up a report on the matter. Capt. Hill was on duty, he should have been the one who directed me. I went and contacted Capt. Hill. I informed the captain of what Chief Halsted had order me to do and then I handed Capt. Hill a copy of the report that I had prepared for Chief Halsted. I requested Capt. Hill to witness me leaving a copy of the report on Chief Halsted's desk.

I left a copy of the report for the chief on his desk while Capt. Hill stood by as a witness that I turned the report in. I'm not sure why I requested Capt. Hill to witness my turning in the report. Just a gut instinct about Chief Halsted's demeanor that did not sit right with me, I guess.

The next day, around 3:30 p.m., I was in the sergeant's office working on approving reports; I had just finished roll call.

Chief Halsted stormed into the office. He jumped right into my face and began yelling in a harsh and stern voice.

"I gave you a direct order last night to leave a report on my desk concerning the deputies that attended some sort of meeting at the start of shift yesterday. Isn't that correct? Didn't I?"

"Yes sir, you did."

He began yelling again:

"Well why didn't you obey my order? Why didn't you leave the report as I directed you?"

"I left the report as you directed, sir." I replied.

Halsted was frowning as he stated:

"I didn't get it. If you left the report as you were ordered to, where is the report?"

"I don't know sir." I replied.

"You disobeyed a direct order, and I will not tolerate it." Halsted stated.

I responded with: "No, sir I left the report as you directed."

Just then, Capt. Hill walked into the room. He advised Chief Halsted that he could not help overhearing our conversation especially with the chief raising his voice as he did. He then informed the chief that I did turn in the report as directed and he had witnessed me turning in the report.

Chief Halsted seemed caught off guard and by surprise. He hesitated for a moment and then asked:

"Well, what happened to the report? I never got it. I do not have it. It was not on my desk."

Chief Halsted's demeanor had changed almost immediately. It was as if he was defending himself and trying to convince the captain and me that he had not received the report. Captain Hill informed the chief that he did not know what happened to the report, only that I had turned it in. I then spoke up and informed the chief that I had another copy of the report and I would get it for him. I went and got the copy and handed it to the chief. He thanked me, and remarked "very well" as he took the report and exited the sergeant's office. He appeared to be rather embarrassed. After the chief left,

Captain Hill smiled at me, and then made a remark that it was good forethought to have him witness my turning in of the report. The captain then joked that he had saved my ass again.

On the morning of February 13, 1995, I called my attorney. Randy informed me he also had been receiving a lot of documents concerning criminal activities involving Sheriff Johnston. He said the documents consisted of letters, memos, reports, and notes which he received anonymously. He stated that the documents contain a lot of information but no real facts or proof that Sheriff Johnston is corrupt. He then remarked the papers did imply that the Sheriff is involved in a lot of questionable behavior.

Randy then paused and told me that he might be on to something. He advised he received a call from a woman named Amy Tyler. He asked me if I knew her. I told him that I did not. He then told me that she informed him that she was Tom Johnston's girlfriend. Tom Johnston was Sheriff Johnston's nephew. She told Randy that she and Tom have been living together off and on for the last nine years and that they have three children together. She informed Randy that Tom is a drug dealer and he works drugs for his uncle, the sheriff. She went on telling a story of how Sheriff Johnston is behind many of the major drug dealers in the county. She advised that the sheriff receives payoffs from these drug dealers for supplying them with information on drug investigations and for, basically, protecting them. She then continued, relating that Tom is the go-between and handles all the communication between the sheriff and the major players.

Randy told me Amy was very nervous, and kept saying that if Tom or the sheriff found out what she was telling him that she would be killed. She refused to allow Randy to record her conversation with him. She, likewise, refused to give any written statements concerning the information she was telling him. She told Randy that if she was called into court to testify to any of this information, she would deny any knowledge of it.

Amy told Randy about a video recording she had of Sheriff Johnston, Tom, and some major drug dealers. She advised that on this video tape they are all talking about some major drug shipments coming into the county. She advised that they go into detail about distribution of the drugs and sharing of the profits. She remarked that it was obvious from the tape Sheriff Johnston is running the show. She advised that she kept the tape as an insurance policy; so if she and Tom ever had a falling out, she would have something to protect herself and her children. Randy asked Amy if he could get a copy of the tape or at least view the tape, but Amy refused.

Randy then cautioned me to be careful. He advised that from all the information which is surfacing he believed that Sheriff Johnston and his associates could be dangerous. We then talked for some time. Randy was concerned about me and how things were going at the sheriff's office. I advised him of the incident with Halsted involving the so called lost report. He warned me once again that Sheriff Johnston and his administration were going to fire me. It was only a matter of time until the administration trumped-up enough of a case that they felt would justify their actions and hold up in court. Randy inquired as to whether or not I was still keeping notes on everything that transpired at the sheriff's office. I told him that I was. He remarked that I should continue to keep notes on all of their actions, it could prove to save me in the end. I got off the phone, wondering where it would all end.

On February 22, 1995, Chief Halsted gave me another assignment. He had been giving more assignments than usual, especially since prior to this year, he never directly assigned anything for me to do. Capt. Hill normally issued all the tasks needing to be done. This new assignment was another one designed to keep me off of the radio and away from my regular duties. I was given the task of researching all the alarm systems in the local schools. There are more than three hundred schools in the county. I was then to submit a written report to the chief. Halsted informed me that Sheriff Johnston personally requested I be given this assignment. I informed the chief that I would take care of the task and I would have the report done and turned into him prior to the dead line he gave me of March 10, 1995.

The next night we had a shooting at a local tavern. It occurred just about five minutes prior to me going off shift. I responded, anyway, to assist Sgt. Cantrell who was just beginning his shift. The situation was handled properly and the suspect involved in the shooting was taken into custody. The following day, Sheriff Johnston contacted Sgt. Cantrell. He questioned Sgt. Cantrell concerning whether or not I showed up at the scene of the shooting and as to my response and actions at the scene.

Sgt. Cantrell advised me, he told the sheriff that I did arrive at the scene and I did a good job assisting him in handling the situation. Cantrell remarked he thought it odd that the sheriff would question him concerning the incident especially since I was senior to him. Cantrell actually knew beyond a doubt exactly what Sheriff Johnston was doing. He was one of the sheriff's boys and he was just playing the game. He would do anything the sheriff asked; in fact, I was rather surprised that they didn't come up with me doing something wrong or inappropriate.

On February 28, 1995, the deputies were all taken by surprise when an eight-year veteran deputy suddenly resigned. He was an Atwater supporter in the last election. He advised his fellow workers that he just could not take it anymore. He was constantly being scrutinized by the administration and had enough. Sheriff Johnston met with him one week prior to his resigning and informed him that his career was over and he had nothing to look forward to in the department. Johnston told him he was going nowhere in the sheriff's office, and he would never get promoted. This particular deputy always looked up to Sheriff Johnston and had considered him a mentor and a friend. He was devastated by the sheriff's demeanor toward him. He advised that he tried to talk to the sheriff, but the sheriff was not receptive to anything he had to say. He felt he had no recourse but to leave and seek employment elsewhere.

Like myself and others in the department, he was constantly under a microscope being micro managed daily. The administration was inventing things to use against him. The pressure was extreme and he came to the conclusion that it was no way to live. He decided to move on before his reputation was completely destroyed. Many of us could relate to his feelings and we have to do what is best for us to survive. A feeling of emptiness came over a lot of the deputies, who were realizing that in life just being right does not necessarily mean that you are going to win. The division in the department had grown even larger than it was during the election and the morale hit bottom. It was very low.

I was busy working on the school alarm's report that the chief had assigned me to do. It was an enormous task of contacting all the schools in the county. It was difficult at best trying to monitor the radio traffic and do the research. I was not taking any chances this time of being accused of slacking off and not hearing the police calls. It was especially difficult for someone like me. In 1980, I was involved in a vehicle accident while on duty in my patrol car. The accident almost killed me. It sent me to the hospital with severe head, neck and back injuries. The collision left me with more than 40% hearing loss in both ears and chronic back pain. I had to focus all my attention on the radio traffic in order to hear the police radio calls well enough to understand what was transpiring. It was quite hard for me to be talking to an individual and at the same time giving my attention to articulating the radio calls.

On March 1, 1995, around 9:00 p.m., Capt. Hill received a call from Chief Halsted. Halsted was upset once again, because I missed a radio call where one of my deputies was attempting to reach me. Capt. Hill advised the chief that I was busy making contact on the school alarm assignment. Capt. Hill further told the chief that he has been listening to the radio traffic and he must have missed the call himself because he did not hear it. That statement by Capt. Hill was a mistake on his part. The chief immediately became upset with Capt. Hill for missing the radio call. Chief Halsted advised Capt. Hill he has been monitoring the radio traffic and he would be documenting our lack of attentiveness. The chief stated any failure to perform our duties would not be tolerated. Later that evening, Capt. Hill informed me of his conversation with the chief.

Capt. Hill then told me of a conversation he had earlier that day. He said he was talking to Monica Santos, one of the records clerks for the sheriffs' office. Monica informed him that Sheriff Johnston and Undersheriff Deiter had been removing original reports from the record's division files. She was upset about it because she was one of the people who were responsible for maintaining the reports in records. She did not know what to do about the situation when the ones violating the rules were the administration. She remarked that she inadvertently caught them removing the files and they appeared angry at her for catching them. She admitted she was scared. She did not know exactly what documents they had removed.

After learning of the reports being removed, Capt. Hill checked the police computer files just on a gut instinct. He wanted to see if the reports that had been filed by deputies concerning the anonymous letters they had received were in the computer. Capt. Hill advised me that there should have been more than thirty anonymous letters or threats against deputies reports filed. He could not find even one report. None of the reports filed by the deputies were there. Capt. Hill then stated he went into the records division and checked the files for the hard copies of the reports and the reports physically just were not there. He could not understand why the sheriff, or anyone else for that matter, would have removed those reports from records.

The sheriff and undersheriff had both refused to allow the anonymous letters to be investigated, stating that no criminal laws had been broken, therefore nothing could be done about the letters. It went so far that Capt. Hill had one of the crime scene officers attempt to get finger prints off of one of the anonymous letters. Detective Tillery ran a finger print check on one of the anonymous letters. The process of checking for finger prints on paper is really a simple process. However, it takes a couple of days for the chemical reaction to work. Detective Tillery was in the process of running the test, when he was ordered to stop. The order came directly from Sheriff Johnston. The detective was then lectured concerning how busy the department was and how far behind they were on cases. Detective Tillery was then advised that if he valued his career, he should stick to handling only authorized investigation.

It seemed rather strange to say the least. You would think that the sheriff would want to have the letters investigated and the writer stopped. After all, the Sheriff, Undersheriff, Chief and half the detective's division were involved in attempting to learn who wrote the one anonymous letter the sheriff had received last year. It did not make sense that Sheriff Johnston did not want the letters investigated. It made even less sense that the letters disappeared from records. The only thing we could conclude from all of this was, possibly, the sheriff himself was involved in the anonymous letters being received by all the deputies that had supported Atwater.

Capt. Hill and I were standing in his office talking. The Captain walked over to the door and stuck his head out into the hallway. He looked around and then shut the door as he came back into his office. He then walked over to his desk and motioned for me to come over close to him. He began to speak in a low voice as if he feared that someone might hear what he was about to say. He informed me that he still has been receiving information from a variety of sources that Sheriff Johnston, Undersheriff Deiter, and Chief Halsted all are involved in illegal activities. Capt. Hill paused for a moment with a concerned look on his face. He informed me he did not know what to do about the information that he had received, and he did not know if any of it was true or not.

I informed Capt. Hill that I knew exactly where he was coming from. I had been receiving information on Sheriff Johnston and his administration as well, most of which had been coming to me anonymously.

Capt. Hill remarked that the majority of the information he

was receiving was coming to him anonymously as well. He was concerned as to why he was getting this information. He wondered if the deputies were supplying this information because they knew the administration was dirty. They were trying to assist us with our problems. Maybe, they thought with our problems, we could do something about it. He then paused, and made a statement. "Or is someone trying to set us up?"

Capt. Hill then remarked, that if even half the information that we were receiving concerning the administration was true, something should be done about it.

I suggest to Capt. Hill that he should contact my attorney, Randy Town. I advised him that I have been turning over all the information that I have received to Randy. He then told me he would contact Randy as well, and turn over the information that he had received. I told him I would go with him to Randy's office if he wanted. He told me he would like me to accompany him.

It was a couple of days before we were able to get in to see Randy. Randy had been really busy handling other court cases. We finally did meet with Randy on the morning of March 6, 1995. Randy advised us that ever since he took my case, bizarre things have been occurring to him. He stated he believed he has been followed while driving his vehicle and it has occurred on more than one occasion. He then advised that people keep contacting him and giving him information on illegal activities involving Sheriff Johnston and others in the sheriff's office.

Randy asked Capt. Hill and me, if we knew a girl by the name of Holly Hunt. Capt. Hill and I both replied that we did not know her. Randy told us that Holly Hunt is a woman about thirty years old, who resides in the north end of the county. He advised that she contacted him yesterday and then he met with her last night. She informed him that she believed Sheriff Johnston was involved in the triple homicide that occurred back in 1989, in the northern sector of the county. The triple homicide involved three young adults, two males and one female found shot to death in the woods. The murders were never solved.

Holly told Randy that she was a drug dealer and a drug user. She related how she used to purchase drugs from a city police officer by the name of Terry Doyle. She went on to tell Randy that the night before the triple homicide, Doyle showed up at her residence with a black brief case. The brief case was very distinctive, having a maroon stripe around the top of it. She stated that Doyle always kept his drugs in this brief case. She remarked that she and Doyle went way back, and he trusted her, and would tell her things. She stated that inside the brief case there was $250,000.00 in cash and four ounces of cocaine. She purchased one of the ounces of cocaine from Doyle. Doyle was bragging about all the money in the brief case stating the money had to be taken to Sheriff Johnston because it was his cut of the last drug shipment. Doyle was complaining that he did all the work, and Sheriff Johnston made all the money.

Holly advised Randy the very next day, actually only hours after she purchased the ounce of cocaine from Doyle, Ricky Dodge showed up at her residence. This was only a few hours before the triple homicide occurred in which Ricky Dodge was one of the victims. Ricky was carrying the very same brief case that Doyle had the night before. There were still three ounces of cocaine in it, but she was not sure if the money was there or not. Ricky pulled out the three ounces of cocaine and asked if she wanted to purchase one of them advising her to pick the one she wanted. She stated that she did purchase another ounce from Ricky. She said Ricky seemed very happy and high as if he had been partying all night.

The next afternoon, Holly stated she learned of the triple homicide and that Ricky was one of the victims. She was shocked and upset but really did not give it another thought until a couple of days later when Doyle showed up at her residence. Doyle was carrying the exact same brief case, the one he had before, and that Ricky had the night he was killed. Holly advised she believes that Ricky stole the brief case from Doyle, and was killed for doing so. She then remarked she learned later that Sheriff Johnston ordered the hit on Ricky, not just because he stole the brief case with their money and drugs, but because he knew too much and could not be trusted. She advised the other two victims were killed just because they were with Ricky. Ricky was the one that they were after.

Randy remarked to Capt. Hill and me that it was quite an interesting story that Holly had told him. I told Randy I had worked on the triple homicide case, and actually what Holly had related to him made sense and fit in with some of the things that we learned in the investigation. I remarked that the investigation revealed that Ricky did have a brief case that he supposedly stole from a drug dealer and it contained large amounts of drugs and a lot of cash. The three victims were killed over this brief case and that it was a contract killing. The brief case was never recovered. Furthermore, the brief case was supposed to be very distinctive, with some sort of colored stripe on it. I stopped and thought for a moment. I then informed Randy and Capt. Hill that the city cop named Jerry Doyle did come up in the investigation. We had received information he was involved in dealing drugs and possibly was involved in the homicide. The chief of detectives at the time was Chief Dave Logan. When Doyle's name came up, Logan advised us that Sheriff Johnston informed him that Doyle was clean and not to waste time investigating him. The sheriff remarked he knew Doyle personally, and the rumors concerning his involvement in drugs were not true.

Just then, Doug Botson walked into Randy's office. Doug was a retired crime scene detective from the sheriff's office. He was forced to retire in 1993, after having "a falling out" with Sheriff Johnston. Coincidentally, Doug's problems with Sheriff Johnston stemmed from another drug related homicide investigation.

Doug reported a coverup situation involving one of the detectives lying on a search warrant. The detective was a Detective Doug Wiggins, who was one of Johnston's "boys." Instead of anything happening to Wiggins when he got caught in the lie, the matter was covered up and swept under the table by

Johnston and his administration. Doug was then reassigned to the patrol division. Doug had not worked patrol in more than seventeen years and really was not physically able to work patrol due to a bad hip, so he ended up putting in for retirement and retiring.

I had spoken with Doug Botson around the time of the election in 1994, and had advised him then about my problems with Sheriff Johnston and that I had filed a claim against Johnston and the county. He mentioned at that time, he too was considering filing a claim against Sheriff Johnston stating that what happened to him was not right. Apparently, the reason that he came into Randy's office was to retain Randy to handle his case and start action against Sheriff Johnston on his behalf.

We all trusted Doug, so we updated him on the information that we had been receiving concerning Sheriff Johnston and his administration involving illegal activities. Doug had additional information concerning the triple homicide which tied into what we already were aware of. Likewise Doug had other information concerning illegal activities involving members of the sheriff's office.

The matter was of a serious nature and we all concluded that something needed to be done. I made a comment that I felt it was not appropriate for us to investigate our superiors; so what should or could we do?

Randy came up with the idea of a group of us getting together and contacting the Federal Bureau of Investigation, the FBI. He suggested that we request a grand jury probe into the allegations of misconduct committed by Sheriff Johnston and his conspirators. We all thought that would be a wise way to handle the situation, and that would be the approach we would take. Randy advised us to gather up all the documents and notes we had that contained information or evidence and he would put the material together to submit to the FBI. Randy then advised he would contact the appropriate people in the FBI and arrange the meeting. He would then let us know when the meeting would take place.

Randy stated that he intended to talk to Holly Hunt again and see if he could get more information from her. He believed she knew more than she was telling. She was afraid of Sheriff Johnston and reluctant to tell everything that she knew. Randy remarked that he was not sure what motivated Holly to come forward, nor why she told him what she did, other than just-maybe, she was having trouble with her conscience bothering her, over the triple homicide.

It was decided that Capt. Hill and I would discreetly talk to deputies that we felt could be trusted and see if any of them were interested in going with us to the FBI, or if any of them had any documents or evidence they wanted to submit to the FBI.

We all talked about the anonymous letters the deputies had been receiving and decided to collect all the letters and submit them to the FBI for investigation as well. The FBI is responsible for handling not only federal crimes but also crimes involving misconduct of police officers, so we felt they were the appropriate agency with the proper authority to investigate these matters.

March 7, 1995, proved to be a difficult day, to say the least. First, I was contacted by Deputy Scott Gibson. He was one of the K-9 handlers and was in charge of the county's drug dog. He took me aside and advised me that last week, he was ordered to take the drug dog and check my locker for drugs. I was rather taken back by what he told me. I asked him who gave him such an order, to which he replied that he was given the order by Corporal Timmons. He stated that Corporal Timmons gave him the order, but Timmons told him that Chief Halsted was the one who requested it be done.

Deputy Gibson went on to state he told Corporal Timmons he would obey the order, but only under protest. He then had the drug dog check my locker at the precinct office. The dog did so with negative results. The dog gave no response or reactions that there ever were any drugs in or about my locker. Gibson advised me, he felt bad about having to do the check and he wanted me to be aware of it. I thanked him for his concern, and for informing me of the fact that it occurred. I then told him not to worry about it, that he was just doing his job.

The main concern I had from my conversation with Gibson,

was that this could be the prelude to someone planting drugs in my locker, and setting me up for a fall. I decided at that time to remove everything from my locker. It would be difficult to plant drugs in an empty locker. That night, at the end of shift, I proceeded to take everything out of my locker. I filled the trunk of my patrol car with all the stuff I had in the locker. I took most of it to my residence and stored it there. I kept only that which I would need while I was working with me, and those items, I kept in the trunk of my patrol unit. My wife was not a "happy camper," to say the least when I brought home boxes of files, and all the stuff I had accumulated. She helped me find a place to store everything that was easily accessible but out of the way.

Shortly after my conversation with Gibson, Chief Halsted came into the sergeant's office. I was on the phone with Cen. Com., the 911 Center. Chief Halsted began to yell that I just missed another radio call. I put my hand over the mouth piece of the phone and advised the chief that I heard the radio traffic, and would take care of the radio call, as soon as, I was off the phone. Halsted paused for a moment, and then just stood there staring at me, waiting for me to get off the phone. I finished getting the information from Cen. Com. concerning a police call and hung up the phone. The chief began to speak to me just as I put the receiver down on the phone. I looked up at him. Halsted advised me that he needed me to submit a written report to him, justifying my use of the K-9 units last night on a felony in progress call that I handled. He advised me that Sheriff Johnston was monitoring the police radio last night, and he did nor believe I had proper justification for my use of the K-9 units. I looked up at Halsted. I stared right into his eyes. I could not help but notice that he was taking great pleasure in screwing with me. I advised the chief I would do the report tonight and that he would have it on his desk in the morning. Halsted advised me to see that I did, he then turned and walked out of the sergeant's office.

The next day, Chief Halsted advised Capt. Hill he received my report on the K-9 call out. He then told the captain that I did a good job, and it appears that all the actions taken were justified. Halsted then smirked, and made a comment to Captain Hill, that "I guess we'll just drop the matter; "we won't be able to fuck him on this one."

Capt. Hill advised me it was as if the chief wanted him to know that they were out to get me. Capt. Hill thought it odd that the chief would confide in him, when they were out to get him as well.

Capt. Hill then changed the subject and informed me that he received another anonymous letter last night. This one accused him of being a wife beater and threatening that he would be taking a fall. It stated that he was going to be arrested and taken to jail on domestic violence charges. Capt. Hill looked up at me, shook his head, and commented that he has never touched his wife and he was not a wife abuser or beater. He remarked that he and his wife have had some heated arguments. Capt. Hill continued, that between him working shift work, the pressure at the office over just trying to survive, and these anonymous letters, it is all taking a toll on his marriage. He became all choked up, and remarked he hoped that his wife and he could survive the ordeal. The sensitivity in Capt. Hill was always intense, he was really a nice guy and I hated to see him suffering.

Since our last meeting with Randy, Capt. Hill and I had been contacting deputies, the deputies, we felt, who would not say anything to Johnston or his Administration. We had been advising them of the pending meeting with the FBI. Almost immediately we began to receive more anonymous documents and information concerning inappropriate behavior involving Johnston, Deiter, Halsted, and some of the deputies that used to do their dirty work for them. Some of the deputies we contacted began preparing their own packets of information to submit to the FBI. To our surprise, the knowledge of a meeting being set up with the FBI never got back to Sheriff Johnston or anyone in the administration. It did, however, get back to Johnston that some of the deputies were investigating him. This was not accurate information. In fact, I do not believe any of the deputies were investigating him. Johnston, however, believed that they were. The sheriff became very irate over his belief that the deputies were investigating him and intensified his scrutinizing of certain deputies he thought were involved, which included me.

One deputy in particular, Deputy Farrell, was removed from my shift and assigned to Sgt. Cantrell's Day Shift. Farrell's areas of patrol duties were also change from the central area which was his normal beat to the south end district. Farrell was called into the office by Chief Halsted and advised that he had a poor attitude, and was setting a bad example for the younger deputies. He was told that he was being transferred so they could keep an eye on him and monitor his demeanor. Dep. Farrell was also called into the detectives office. He was interviewed by Det. Paris as to whether or not he was involved in investigating the activities of Sheriff Johnston. Dep. Farrell had a reputation of being honest and straight forward. He would always call a spade a spade, and never worry about diplomacy. He denied that he had been investigating Sheriff Johnston or anyone else in the department, for that matter. He did make it quite clear, however that he felt there was a need for Johnston, and others in the department to be investigated. He basically told Det. Paris that he refused to conform to Johnston's lack of standards and selective enforcement. He would not allow himself to be intimidated by their conduct. He filled Det. Paris's ears, and actually, would have been better off if he kept his mouth shut and didn't say so much, but that was just his nature.

Within the next couple of days, after Dep. Farrell's interview with Det. Paris, the sheriff initiated an internal affair's investigation against Dep. Farrell. Dep. Farrell was basically, tried and convicted by the IA investigation which was conducted by Sheriff Johnston's "good ole' boys" system. Johnston appointed people he trusted to do what he wanted to handle the investigation. Dep. Farrell was found guilty and received a written reprimand for unacceptable conduct and behavior concerning statements he made about Sheriff Johnston. Dep. Farrell thought the entire IA investigation was nothing more than bull shit. He was not pleased, but decided to be less vocal and just to do his job. He realized that you did not have to do anything wrong to get in trouble at the sheriffs' office. He really did not want to lose his job.

During this same time frame, another deputy, Deputy Ed Taylor, found himself the subject of an IA investigation. He was an Atwater supporter during the last election and in fact was Atwater's campaign manager. He too, was found guilty of conduct unbecoming a police office, and received a written reprimand. Likewise, two other deputies who were Atwater supporters also had IA investigations conducted against them and received written reprimands.

It was the belief that the written reprimands were the first steps in establishing a matter of progressive discipline so that they could justify eventually firing the deputies. It also appeared to be obvious Sheriff Johnston was proceeding to carry out his threats of getting rid of all the deputies that supported Atwater.

On March 28, 1995, Chief Halsted called me into his office. He advised me that he was assigning me the task of conducting an IA investigation into the conduct of two officers that have been accused of using excessive force while taking a suspect into custody. Halsted then continued to inform me that the administration has already decided that the two deputies acted properly, but they needed to give the appearance that the incident was being investigated. I informed the chief that I refused to become involved in any type of cover up and I resented the fact that he would make such a request of me. He became extremely aggravated. He began to yell at me, stating there was no cover up and that I misunderstood him. He was ordering me to interview the two deputies concerning the incident and that was all there was to it. He advised me the detectives would handle the rest of the investigation. He then demanded to know if I was refusing to obey a direct order. I advised him that I was not refusing to obey a direct order, and I would handle the interviews. Halsted tpld me to have my report on his desk in the morning.

I felt I pushed the issue as far as I dared. I did not have a problem with interviewing the two deputies. What I did have a problem with was the Chief's statement that they had already predetermined the outcome of the investigation, an investigation that had yet to be conducted. The administration constantly operated on verbal orders and demands. They refused to put anything in writing. It was their built in protection system. If they got caught doing something inappropriate, they would deny their involvement. Having nothing in writing it was always your word against theirs and you would not be able to prove that you were in the right. I felt I had no choice but to interview the two deputies and objectively report what they told me.

I contacted the two deputies involved later that evening, one at a time. I conducted the interviews and then typed up my report. I then contacted Capt. Hill and gave him a copy of the report and had him witness me leaving the report on Chief Halsted's desk. I was not taking any chances that the chief might once again accuse me of not turning in the report.

I told Capt. Hill about my conversation with the chief and his attempt to get me involved in the cover up. Capt. Hill advised that he was not surprised and he thought I handled the situation appropriately.

Capt. Hill and I spent some time going over some of the material that was going to be submitted to the FBI. The majority of the material Randy already had. We wanted to do a cover sheet and a list of the crimes and violations that Sheriff Johnston and his followers were reported to be involved in. We thought by submitting a list of violations at the front of the material, it would give us a guide to use when the information was explained to the FBI.

CHAPTER FOUR

COURAGE IS HAVING THE STRENGTH TO DO WHAT YOU BELIEVE IS RIGHT.

On March 30, 1994, eleven deputies, including Capt. Hill, and I went with Randy Town to the FBI central headquarters. There was a lot more deputies who wanted to go, but feared for their careers. They did not want to risk retaliation by Johnston and his administration. I believe it was that fear that caused us to receive anonymous documents concerning illegal activities of the administration. The deputies knew things were not right and wanted justice served without directly putting themselves at risk. Randy was pleased there were eleven deputies that had the courage to stand up and take the risk.

The FBI offices were located on the 27th floor of a high rise building. There was a major bank on the main floor of the building. The offices were secured with a reception area separating the receptionist from the public by a glass divider. As soon as we walked in, Randy told the receptionist who we were, and we were immediately taken in the security door. All twelve of us walked into the office together, they were expecting us. We were directed back to a large conference room and told to be seated, and that the director would be in to see us shortly.

We met with Mary Jo Robinson, the Regional Director, and with Jason Bolton, the Agent in Charge of the White Collar/Organized Crime Unit. They introduced themselves, and then asked us to be seated. Randy then identified himself as an attorney, and our spokesman for the presentation.

Randy made the presentation to the FBI. He began by introducing the deputies that were present. He then advised he thought it best to start off by reading the cover sheet and list of violations that had been prepared by the deputies present, stating it would give them an overview of exactly why we were all there. Randy then began to read from the cover sheet.

"We are dedicated, veteran police officers, who have devoted our lives to protect and serve the public and the community of Kingston County. We have chosen and feel it is our responsibility and duty to come forward to pursue an investigation against Sheriff Pat Johnston and his top administrators for misconduct, violation of public trust, and violation of civil rights. Further, it is our belief, as the facts will demonstrate, that Sheriff Johnston has been involved in cover-ups ranging from homicide investigations to other incidents in and about the county of Kingston. We respectfully request a grand jury investigation into this matter in order to restore the law and order to the degree the citizens justly deserve and have a right to expect of their public officials."

Randy then read the list of the violations that we believed Sheriff Johnston and his administrators have committed. He read:

The violations we believe have been committed consisted of:

#1. Malfeasance in office
#2. Civil rights violations
#3. Misconduct in public office
#4. Conspiracy to obstruct justice
#5. Retaliatory action/denied access
#6. Violation of Americans with Disabilities Act
#7. Perjury under oath
#8. Harassment/intimidation
#9. Public misconduct
#10. Discrimination
#11. Misappropriation of public funds

#12. Negligence in the line of duty
#13. Participating in bribes, blackmail, and extortion for Political gain
#14. Granting and receiving "special favors"

Randy paused for a moment and looked around the room.

It was obvious that he had gotten the FBI agents' attention. They looked intent, waiting for Randy to continue. Randy went on:

"The following are incidents of wrong doing involving Sheriff Pat Johnston and his top administrators. This is not a complete list and other information can be obtained by contacting the witnesses listed in the documentation submitted."

Randy then began to read from the list of 66 allegations of wrong doing that was prepared for the FBI.

#1. Sheriff Johnston receives kickback money from the major drug Dealers.
#2. Chief Halsted has ties with organized crime.
#3. Sheriff Johnston was involved in ordering the contract Killings in regards to the triple homicide which occurred in 1989.
#4. Sheriff Johnston was involved in a cover-up in regards to the Cummingham's drug related homicide.
#5. Undersheriff Deiter receives kickbacks from the concert Promoters for allowing rock concerts to be performed in county.
#6. Sheriff and his administrators have been involved in removal and destruction of reports form the records division.
#7. Drugs have continually disappeared from the property room, at the direction of the sheriff.
#8. Sheriff Johnston has been caught on more than one occasion breaking into business and then bragging that

he scared the suspects off in order to promote support in upcoming elections.

#9. Sheriff Johnston and Undersheriff Deiter maintain a double set of books in order to cover up for misappropriation of funds.

#10. Johnston lied under an oath; reference civil service appeals case, in regards to promotions.

#11. Johnston has in the past shut down undercover drug operations because they were getting too close to getting major dealers that he was protecting.

#12. Johnston orders predetermined Internal Affairs investigations in order to get rid of deputies that do not go along with his programs.

#13. Sheriff and undersheriff are involved in blackmail of certain individuals that they have things on. They gain money and favors from these individuals

Randy continued to read from the list of 66 allegations of misconduct. The list went on and on, describing other incidents involving drug related homicides that Sheriff Johnston and his administration were either involved in setting up or covering up.

There were also events involving extortion, racketeering, and profiteering. The list named individuals who were victims as well as suspects in many cases. In others, where the information was not available, it only gave the issues that raised suspicion that wrongful acts have taken place. He had the undivided attention of the FBI agents. After he finished reading from the list, he once again advised the agents that the concerns were real and that we respectfully request a grand jury investigation into these events of misconduct.

Randy remarked that,

"As you can see, we are, dealing with well organized and dangerous individuals who will stop at nothing to get what they want. Sheriff Johnston and those that work for him must be stopped. It would not be appropriate for the deputies here today to investigate their own superiors; that is why we are here to turn over the evidence we have gathered and request that your agency handle the investigation."

Randy handed Agent Jason Bolton two black binders both about three inches thick. He advised these books contained evidence and documentation of the actions and conduct of Sheriff Johnston, Undersheriff Deiter and Chief Halsted. He further stated there were others within the sheriff's department that are "dirty" and need to be investigated as well.

The meeting with the FBI lasted for about three hours, during which time Agent Bolton asked us questions concerning the 66 allegations and the sheriffs' administration. He took notes on just about everything. He informed us of the procedure that the FBI followed. He advised that their procedure consisted of first, opening a preliminary investigation, whereby they would look into the material presented and make a determination as to whether there was enough evidence to warrant a grand jury investigation. If they found that there was enough evidence, then they would request a grand jury inquiry.

Randy then advised the FBI agents that the deputies in Kingston County, in general, were afraid of Sheriff Johnston and might not cooperate with their investigation. He then remarked the majority of the deputies are good, honest individuals and will tell the truth under an oath in front of a grand jury. Agent Bolton advised he understood Randy's concerns and they would open a preliminary investigation immediately and would be in touch with us.

It was our belief that Sheriff Johnston had no knowledge that any of us contacted the FBI. We did, however, have a feeling he was aware that something was in the wind. Over the next two months, two of the deputies that had gone to the FBI had their residences broken into. Their computers, including their floppy disk files were stolen, along with notes that they had on Sheriff Johnston and others in the department. The only other items taken in the burglaries were guns.

About ten of us, including Randy, Capt. Hill, and me also

began to notice that we were being followed by strange vehicles.

At first, we all thought it was just our imagination and it was not happening, that maybe we were just paranoid. We observed not only vehicles following us, but then these same vehicles and others began to stake out our homes from a distance. We would observe them parked down the street, or in some cases on another street with an overview of the deputy's residence. It was not until we began to talk to each other and compare notes that we realized that the same vehicles were following and watching each of us at different times.

During this same period of time we inadvertently discovered that illegal phone taps had been placed on our phone lines. They were cheap, inexpensive type of trap that anyone could purchase at any number of local electronic shops. We never could learn who was responsible, or should I say, obtain proof of who was involved, but we all believed that it was Sheriff Johnston. It was apparent to all of us involved, that someone wanted desperately to learn what exactly we were up to. The ironic part of it all was the fact that none of us were actually trying to hide anything that we were doing. We just were not broadcasting the fact that we had gone to the FBI.

In the middle of April 1995, Randy filed my civil lawsuit in federal court. The lawsuit was filed against Sheriff Johnston, Undersheriff Deiter, Chief Halsted, and Kingston County for violation of my civil rights and retaliation. The sheriff being an elected official required that we also name Kingston County as a defendant in the lawsuit. Around this same period of time, Randy also filed claim for damages with the county on behalf of Capt. Hill and retired Detective Botson. Both claims were against Sheriff Johnston and his administration for violation of civil rights, and retaliation. It goes without saying that Sheriff Johnston was extremely upset over the lawsuits and claims being filed.

At about this same time frame, mid April of 1995, I was contacted by Sergeant Newton. He was extremely upset. He advised me the state was conducting an audit of the sheriff's office. The state audit, I learned at a later date, was done at a request from the FBI. Sgt. Newton informed me that he was ordered by Sheriff Johnston and Undersheriff Deiter to conduct an inventory of all the accountable items within the sheriff's office that were involved in the state audit. They advised him to sign off certain items even though he could not physically account for those items. He advised that he refused to sign off on any item he was not able to account for. Newton then remarked the administration was not pleased with him for refusing to sign everything off without accountability, but he was not going to lie and get himself in trouble for anyone.

Sgt. Newton changed the subject and advised me that the current state attorney general is considering running for governor. She supposedly has promised Johnston the position of head of the state patrol, if she gets elected governor, in return for him handling her campaign. Sheriff Johnston has agreed to be her campaign manager. Sgt. Newton remarked for me to be careful, advising that Sheriff Johnston and the attorney general are tight.

Sgt. Newton was aware of the FBI investigation. He was concerned if the FBI got the state attorney general's office involved in the investigation that Johnston might find out about it.

Sgt. Newton began to relate his concerns to me, in regards to the major rock concerts that perform at the fair grounds off and on all summer long. He said the promoters have to hire Undersheriff Deiter as their security consultant for the concerts. If they do not hire him, he refuses to sign them off, and without the undersheriff's signature they cannot get the county to issue the concert permit. Sgt. Newton advised he did not know whether or not what undersheriff was doing was illegal, but he, himself, did not want to be involved in anything illegal. Sgt. Newton had the job of setting up the actual security for the rock concerts and worked directly under Deiter's supervision. Sgt. Newton was aware that the FBI was looking into the circumstances surrounding Undersheriff Deiter and the rock concerts. In fact, he was the one that requested that it be brought to the FBI's attention. Now he was having second thoughts and concerns that the FBI might think he did something wrong. It worried him. He was equally concerned that the records on the concert security work including the financial records could disappear. He went to his locker and began to remove all the concert records. He advised me that if the FBI wants the concert records, he was going to make certain that he had them and that they would be available for the FBI.

Sgt. Newton remarked he knew how documents seemed to have a way of disappearing around the sheriffs' office, especially if the documents related to the administration and were the topic of some sort of investigation. He advised me he was going to make copies of all the concert papers and have them ready to give to the FBI when they requested them. He further advised he was going to take all the documents to Capt. Hill and give him one copy of the documents to hold onto for safe keeping.

Since November of 1994, all the mail and correspondence that I received at the sheriff's office as well as the mail other deputies who supported Atwater in the election received came to us opened. Some of us had been constantly complaining to Capt. Hill about the mail being opened. Come the middle of May 1995, Capt. Hill decided to do something about the mail tampering. He decided enough is enough. He contacted Jenny Perkins, the chief civil deputy, concerning the mail situation. They had words, in which she finally advised him that it was departmental procedure for them to open all correspondence that came directly to the sheriff's department. Capt. Hill informed her that the practices of opening the deputies mail was illegal and it should stop immediately.

The very next day, Capt. Hill was called into Undersheriff Deiter's office. Deiter jumped into Capt. Hill's face. He began to yell at him. Deiter told him it was legal and it was office policy to open all the mail and that practice would continue. Capt. Hill was then verbally reprimanded for not being a team player and told if he continued to make trouble around the office, he would find himself losing his captain bars. Capt. Hill, you could say, was in the same boat as I was. He was always getting in trouble and being held to a higher degree of accountability. Capt. Hill was well aware that it had never been an office policy to open all correspondence. He was also aware that all the deputies' mail was not being opened, only the mail of those who had supported Atwater. He realized Deiter was just attempting to justify their actions without admitting that they were doing anything inappropriate. Capt. Hill was satisfied he made his point and that was really all he intended to do. He also put them on notice that they were violating the law and the time would come at a later date to pursue it further.

Around the end of May, 1995, Randy requested Capt. Hill, Doug Botson, and I deliver some papers to Special Agent Bolton at the FBI office. Randy handed me a packet containing additional evidence and documents relating to the investigation. He wanted the three of us to go in hopes that we would get an opportunity to talk to Agent Bolton and learn how the investigation was going. We arrived at the FBI office around 10:00 a.m. that morning. Jason Bolton greeted us at the security door and escorted us back into his office. His office was located on the top floor of one of the high rise buildings in the downtown section of the city. He had a panoramic view of the city and Bay from his coroner's office. Jason advised the three of us that the FBI had initiated the investigation against Sheriff Johnston, but that the case was moving at a slow pace and his agents have been rather busy with other priorities.

We related to Agent Bolton that we had concerns about leaks in his office informing Johnston of the investigation which would cause the sheriff to cover his tracks and hurt the investigation. We advised that our concern for leaks centered around the fact that Sheriff Johnston, himself, was an FBI academy graduate. Bolton assured us they were taking every precaution to prevent any leaks from occurring. We then informed him about Johnston's connections with the state's attorney general. Agent Bolton paused, it was rather obvious that he was not aware of Johnston's relationship with the attorney general. He then made a comment that Johnston's relationship with the attorney general did not sit well with him, but there was nothing they could do about it. He advised we have to realize that when you're investigating a person who is as well connected as Sheriff Johnston, it is only a matter of time until confidentiality is breached, and he knows what's going on. Bolton then commented that he would not be surprised if Johnston already knew about the FBI probe. He continued to state it really did not matter, anyway, because once they concluded their preliminary investigation, they would be contacting and interviewing Johnston and his administration, so they will learn of the investigation, anyway.

He gave us an update on the investigation. He advised that he and his agents met with the U.S. Attorney and the State Attorney General and went over the violations the sheriff and his administrators are suspected of being involved in. They discussed the entire case at great length and divided up the task that needed to be performed in the investigation. He stated the State Attorney General ordered the state audit to be conducted on the sheriff's office and that his agents are investigating the charges of misconduct and law violations. He went on to say we had to realize that when dealing with upper level corruption, unless you have a witness directly involved in the corruption who is willing to give statements concerning the participant's involvement these types of cases are very hard to prove.

Agent Bolton shocked the three of us with his next statement. He advised us that we have to realize Sheriff Johnston is a very powerful man politically, and the FBI cannot afford to walk into the sheriff's office and make accusations against the sheriff without having strong probable cause against the man. We need a case so strong that we have it on a silver platter prior to coming down on the sheriff; we do not want to end up with egg on our faces. The FBI is, sad to say, a politically supported agency. The democrats are in power and Sheriff Johnston is a democrat. If we make the wrong move in this case, it could have severe repercussions on the FBI.

Agent Bolton paused and looked at each of us. I think he could see the shocked reaction on each of our faces. He advised he personally believed that Sheriff Johnston is corrupt and he will see that the FBI does everything it can to build a case against the man. Johnston is a powerful and dangerous person and he needs to be stopped. In the mean time, Bolton advised us to continue with our civil cases against Johnston. He remarked, that more times than not, the way to succeed in destroying political corruption is through the civil courts. He advised from his review of the material, there is a clear case of civil rights violations which in and of itself is illegal but which is handled through the civil courts.

I turned over the packet of material that Randy had given to me to give to Jason. He advised he would review the new material and add it to the case file. He remarked the State Attorney General's office most likely will be investigating the state law violations and the FBI will be investigating the federal law violations. Agent Bolton advised he would keep in touch with Randy and keep him updated as to how the case is progressing. He told us the investigation would take at least another three months to complete. He wished us luck and we departed.

The three of us left Agent Bolton's office with mixed emotions. We wondered if the FBI would make a case against Sheriff Johnston. We wondered if they really wanted to make a case. It was obvious to us that Agent Bolton was concerned about Sheriff Johnston's political ties and power. It was equally obvious that he viewed Sheriff Johnston as a corrupt and dangerous person. The trip back to our county was one more of silence than talking. I think each of us felt that even though Agent Bolton thought Johnston was guilty; the FBI was not going to be able to make a case against him.

It was too late to turn back now; we had involved the FBI and now we would have to live with the outcome, no matter what it came to be. The future scared us. We felt as if we were standing alone. We had each other, and for that we were thankful, yet we each still felt alone. I guess it was because we felt insecure in our thoughts, our thoughts of what we were doing, what we should be doing, or not doing. Uncertainty seems to work as a catalysis to enhance one's own insecurities.

June and July of 1995 passed and it began to feel like part of the routine for Capt. Hill and me, to have to justify everything that we did. We were surviving at the sheriff's office, but it was a challenge just to make it through the day. Each day as we put on our uniforms and went to work, it felt like we were playing "Russian roulette." I lost more than twenty pounds. I was eating antacids like they were candy. Capt. Hill had to change his blood pressure medicine three times and still was not able to get his blood pressure under control. Our wives felt helpless, they wanted to do something to help relieve our pain, but they felt as is there was nothing they could do. They were wrong, however, because it was from their love and support that we gained the strength to endure. There were other deputies who had supported Atwater in the 1994 election, who were not as fortunate as Capt. Hill and myself. Many of them were receiving disciplinary actions in one form or another. The Administration continued in their effort of creating a paper trail to justify terminating them and destroying their careers.

There was not a word mentioned or heard concerning the FBI investigation over these last two months. We did not know how it was going, or even if it was still being investigated. Randy kept saying that he had to call Agent Bolton, and get a status report on the investigation. He found himself rather busy at work and the days seemed to roll by without him finding out or taking the time to call. We were not pushing him, the FBI was going to do what they would do and it was out of our control. Handling our own responsibilities and just surviving was our main focus of concern.

CHAPTER FIVE

JUSTIFICATIONS ARE SOMETIMES MERE WORDS, USED TO CAMOUFLAGE THE ACTUAL MOTIVE.

On August 1, 1995, I was called in to give a deposition on my pending lawsuit against Sheriff Johnston. It would be the first of five depositions I would be required to give in my case alone. The deposition lasted all day. The deposition process is basically a discovery process, whereby the other side is allowed to ask you questions to determine exactly what evidence you have against them that could come out in court.

Present at the deposition was Sheriff Johnston, Undersheriff Deiter, Chief Halsted, the county's attorney Ms Pitts, the county's risk manager Barbara Becker, my attorney Randy Town, and of course, myself. Without going into a lot of detail about what occurred, I can summarize by saying that I was asked questions concerning the administration's behavior and demeanor toward me. I answered each question asked without hesitation calling "a spade a spade."

My answers seemed to work like a catalyst to intensify Sheriff Johnston's anger toward me. In fact, I believe this first deposition was actually the single factor that brought the reality of the lawsuit home to the sheriff.

I believe that part of Sheriff Johnston's strategy was to pressure me into dropping the lawsuit by having himself, Deiter and Halsted all present at this deposition while their attorney drilled me with questions. They wanted me to feel intimidated to the point that I would back down. All three of them glared at me with piercing stares during the entire line of questioning. Ironically, the more intimidated I felt, the stronger my convictions became to stand tall and have the truth prevail. It's funny how the human mind and body function; it's as though when you increase the pressure you are under it works to fine tune your senses. My mind was acute and my body actually felt relaxed. It was not because I was in fact relaxed; I think it was more because I was concentrating so intensely on each and every question being asked.

During the deposition process, the administration learned for the first time that I had been taking notes on everything that had been occurring since my confrontation with the sheriff back on October 10, 1994. They were not happy to discover that I had notebooks full of documentation of incidents and events.

I asked Randy how he thought I did after the deposition was over. He told me that he thought I did just fine. He said I had given them a lot of things to think about. He said he felt good about it and he thought we had a strong case against them. He then remarked that they were attempting to get me to back down in there. Now that I stood up to them, the battle lines have been drawn. He felt my future with the sheriff's office was not secure, and could end at any time. He advised their only defense was to discredit me. They wanted to make me look like some sort of paranoid nut case. Randy warned me to be careful and to cover my rear, remarking that it is really only starting. We had a long battle ahead of us and it was all up hill.

I had walked out of the deposition feeling good about myself and about the way I handled the questions, not to mention my own emotions. After talking to Randy, that good feeling turned out to be short lived. I was once again faced with uncertainty, which is probably the one feeling that disturbs me the most. I appreciated Randy's comments. I needed the input to maintain my objectivity.

Randy's perception was accurate. The very next day, Johnston, Deiter, and Halsted attempted to discredit me with the deputies. They used the fact that I had been keeping notes on incidents and events to inform the deputies that I had been spying on them. Each of them went around the department telling the deputies that I was writing down everything negative that any of them said concerning the department and the administration. They instilled a feeling of paranoia among the deputies which was enhanced by the fact that many of the deputies had been saying negative things about the administration. In some of the deputies, they likewise instilled a resentment and lack of trust in me. The deputies feared not knowing whether what they might say to me could end up being documented.

I never made it a secret that I was taking notes nor did I broadcast it. Many of the deputies were well aware prior to this first deposition, that I was in fact taking notes, and keeping a log or journal, however, there also were many that were not aware. Some of the deputies, especially those that were Johnston supporters, tried to make an issue out of me keeping notes.

The administration's attempt to discredit me and create a hostile work environment for me among the deputies failed. Too many of the deputies knew me; we had a history, a history built on experience and trust. It prevailed. Likewise, the deputies possessed an acute understanding of the administrations demeanor which helped to enhance my support.

Another attempt was made by Sheriff Johnston and his administration designed to turn the deputies against me. This second attempt was more personal in nature. They contacted all the deputies that I had to list as potential witnesses in my case against them. They informed each and every one of those deputies that they knew they were witnesses for me, and then put them on the spot, demanding to know what exactly each of them was going to testify to. The administration did not wait to go through proper channels and take the deputies depositions, instead they called them one at a time into the office and questioned them.

The deputies all felt intimidated by the administration. They felt that if they testified for me their jobs would be in jeopardy. Once again, however it back fired on the administration. The majority of the deputies were angry, but not at me rather at the administration. They were upset and resented the fact that the administration tried to intimidate them. All but a handful of the deputies stood firm. There were a few that did become angry at me for causing them to be put in the position of being at odds with the administration but then I guess that was to be expected.

I talked to Randy concerning the actions of Sheriff Johnston and the others toward attempting to destroy my character and reputation among my coworkers. I felt strongly that it was a deliberate attempt to weaken my case by discrediting me and intimidating my witnesses. Randy agreed with me, but advised at this point in time there was nothing that we could do concerning Johnston's actions. He stated it was not right, but it was a fact of life. Johnston, being the chief executive, had the capability to get away with a lot of unethical conduct. It's to be expected that he will try. After all, if it was not for his demeanor and lack of ethics, we would not have a lawsuit pending against him to begin with. I had to agree with Randy. I cannot expect that Johnston will play by any set of rules, he sort of makes up his own rules as he goes.

A week after I gave my first deposition, the county hired a management consultant to conduct an independent investigation into my lawsuit. The investigation was conducted by a Howard Higgins. He was paid twenty thousand dollars to conduct the investigation, which only took two weeks to conclude. His investigation became known as the "Higgins Report."

Higgins contacted witnesses on both sides and questioned them concerning all the details and evidence involved in the case. I was interviewed by Mr. Higgins with my attorney present to represent me. I was impressed by Mr. Higgins's professional and friendly demeanor. He seemed to remain totally objective throughout the investigation. We were advised that we would not be allowed to learn the outcome of the investigation nor have access to the report itself. It was considered part of the county's case in representing Sheriff Johnston and was to serve to evaluate Johnston's defense. Therefore, it was considered privilged and confidential. It was not part of discovery. The report was also to determine if the county wanted to settle the case or take it all the way to court.

Although we never saw the "Higgins report," we did learn at a later date that the report recommended to the county that they settle the case out of court. The report stated Sheriff Johnston violated my civil rights, and the county would most likely lose the case if they proceeded to go to court.

We also learned that after the "Higgins Report" came out, Sheriff Johnston went over to the County commissioner's office and had a meeting with the commissioners. Johnston pleaded his case, promising the commissioners that if they stood behind him and gave him unlimited resources to fight my lawsuit that he guaranteed them he would run me into the ground and destroy my case against him. Probably the most significant factor in persuading the commissioners to back Johnston was when Johnston informed them that if they settled my case, there would be a lot of other deputies filing lawsuits against him and the county.

Johnston convinced the commissioners to support him and allow him to take my case to court. The commissioners wanted to save money and avoid additional lawsuits, so they chose to ignore the "Higgins report" and give Sheriff Johnston whatever resources he needed to destroy me and my lawsuit.

The commissioners were made up of a "good ole boy system." They all got to their positions by receiving and granting favors. Sheriff Johnston was considered one of the boys." The commissioners felt if they backed Johnston, he would end up owing them. Johnston was considered to have a lot of political power and it was self serving for the commissioners to have Johnston owing them.

The commissioners, however, advised Sheriff Johnston, that if

I won my case against him, they would not stand behind him on any of the future cases that should develop. Johnston agreed to the commissioner's terms.

The commissioners' decision would have an adverse effect on Capt. Hill and myself. Sheriff Johnston was now even more desperate than before. He had to win the case against me or he would lose the commissioners' support. He was prepared to stop at nothing to destroy my case. Shortly after his meeting with the commissioners, he called Undersheriff Deiter and Chief Halsted into his office. He wanted a meeting without the county's attorneys present. He wanted only those he trusted to assist him in developing a plan of attack. He would stop at nothing to get what he wanted.

Sheriff Johnston then hired a high-priced attorney to represent Deiter, Halsted and himself. He now had an unlimited budget for his defense, at the tax payers expense and with the blessing of the county commissioners. He hired one David Custington, attorney at law. Mr Custington had a reputation of successfully making cases go away.

He was an expert in distorting the facts and effectively minimizing the testimonial evidence of the opposing witnesses.

Mr. Custington also had never lost a case. He like Sheriff Johnston, would stop at nothing to win. In fact, he had represented Sheriff Johnston in the past on other issues. He was known for also handling litigation involving employees. He possessed a skill to effectively intimidate witnesses while staying within the so-called letter of the law.

Although my attorney never said it, it was rather obvious to me he was intimidated by Mr. Custington's reputation. Randy was a local attorney, and not really experienced going up against the skilled hard hitters. Randy was about to face the challenge of his career as an attorney. The opposing side had money, power, and experience in their corner, while we, on the other hand, had only the truth on our side to see us through. It was most definitely a case of the "little guy" against the establishment. Since I was a small child I have always heard "you can't fight city hall." I guess I never really gave any thought to the significance of that statement until now.

My wife and I, regardless of the odds against us, still believed in our hearts that the truth would triumph in the end.

Sherry's only comment to Randy after Sheriff Johnston hired Mr. Custington was that when Randy won our case he would be famous.

We constantly spoke in the positive. We had to, it was the nourishment that allowed us to survive.

Early in September of 1995, Sergeant Newton contacted me in the sergeant's office. He had a serious frown on his face and it was quite obvious that he was upset. He informed me he had just learned that the administration was taking away our four, ten hour shifts and putting all the deputies back onto the five days, eight hours per day work week. He advised the change would take place at shift change in October. He went on to state the reason that Sheriff Johnston was making all the deputies go back to the five-day work week, was to get even with the deputies. Sgt. Newton paused for a second and then continued, stating that Sheriff Johnston is obsessed with power and that power has completely corrupted him. He has turned the entire department against him and he does not even care. Newton said he just came from a meeting with Chief Halsted over the shift change.

Sgt. Newton was very upset, you could hear it in his voice and see it in his demeanor. He told me the sheriff's administration had no logical reason to go back to the five-day work week. He and Chief Halsted discussed the topic in length until he finally blew up at the chief. He said he had to apologize to Halsted.

Newton continued advising that Chief Halsted had told him Sheriff Johnston was having all the deputies go back to the five-day work week to punish them. He was blaming his decision on those deputies that filed grievances and lawsuits against him. Johnston hoped that by punishing all the deputies, it would turn the majority of them against those deputies that were standing up to him, and trying to fight him in the courts. Sgt. Newton shook his head and remarked that he felt Sheriff Johnston's career was over and it was only a matter of time until all of his deeds were going to catch up to him.

The next day, the sheriff deputies' guild had a meeting. The deputies were upset about having to go back to the five-day work week. One of the deputies called for a vote of "no confidence" in Sheriff Johnston. This motion stirred a rather heated argument among the deputies. There was a lot of verbal support for taking a vote; however, the deputies were afraid of Johnston and did not really want to do anything that might further cause him to come down upon them. It was decided to table the motion for thirty days to observe whether the situation between the deputies and the administration might improve. It was, basically, just wishful thinking on the part of the deputies.

The deputies' guild over the last six months had conducted a survey rating the department on its functions from the administration on down to patrol. The majority of the deputies felt it would be more productive and in their best interest to submit the results of the survey to Sheriff Johnston and his administration than it would be for a vote of no confidence. The result of the survey in regards to the administration was not favorable. The survey rated the administration on issues such as leadership, guidance, and practicing fairness and consistency in governing the deputies. The results of the survey rated the administration either "poor", or "needs improvement", in basically all areas involving their practices in handling personnel matters.

The deputies' guild members hoped that the administration would view the survey as a wake up call and want to attempt to improve themselves in regards to Personnel relations. They were wrong. Sheriff Johnston and Undersheriff Deiter viewed the survey as a slap on their faces. Their attitude was, "how dare the deputies judge us, we will teach them." Things went from bad to worse.

Even though things got worse around the department, there were no signs of improvements. The issue of a vote of "no confidence" in

Sheriff Johnston was never mentioned again. The deputies were all fearful and scared for their own job security and did not want to make matters worse.

Two days after the guild meeting in September, every deputy in the department, including myself, received an anonymous letter. The letter came out pleading for unity and support for "our brothers, who have been wronged by the sheriff and his administration." The letter was basically a support letter for Capt. Hill, me, and the other deputies that Sheriff Johnston had been targeting. I don't know who wrote the letter, but I am certain Johnston suspected Capt. Hill or myself of being involved in it. The same day that I received that letter, I also received another anonymous letter. This second letter, I viewed as a direct threat or, I don't know, maybe an indirect threat against myself. It read, "the wrong of the wrong doers will be the very ropes that capture and bind Solomon."

Now, I read this letter, and thought to myself "anyone who uses quotes from the Bible to threaten someone has got to be one sick puppy." It upset me, in fact, I dare to say it pissed me off, but then too, I would not be totally honest if I didn't admit it scared me at the same time.

I took the letter to the precinct office. I had received it at my personal box at the post office. Sgt. Cantrell was in the precinct office. I advised him I wished to file a report of harassment by mail and showed him the letter. Sgt. Cantrell read the letter and then filed a report on the letter for me. After he was done, he gave me a copy of the report for my own records.

Two days later, about one third of the department received another anonymous letter. I was included in that one third. The letter was titled "Irony." This letter was sent only to those deputies that were known to oppose Sheriff Johnston. The essence of the letter said that you had better support your administration or else. The letter implied if you didn't support the administration the sheriff's office would not be a safe environment in which to work. It basically stated support or leave before it's too late or else you will regret that you didn't. The "Irony" letter was viewed as a threat among the deputies.

I hung up copies of the "Solomon" quote and the "Irony" letters on the bulletin board at the precinct office. I felt that all the deputies should see and come to realize exactly what was going on in the department. A couple of days later, I noticed that someone had signed Sheriff Johnston's name in bold print to the bottom of both the letters. The two items hung on the bulletin board for about a week before someone removed them.

About a week later, another letter titled "Lord Grant" was found hanging on the bulletin board at all the precinct offices. It was more of a poem than a letter. I did not notice the poem until Deputy Baker pointed it out to me. He came up to me appearing physically shaken. He advised me he was sitting at one of the computer stations typing up his reports, when Sheriff Johnston entered the room. Johnston read the poem out loud to Deputy Baker.

The poem read:

> "Lord grant me the serenity
> To accept the things I cannot change
> The courage to change the things I can
> And the wisdom to hide the bodies of
> Those I had to
> KILL
> Because they PISSED ME OFF. . . ."

Sheriff Johnston turned to Deputy Baker and remarked,

"This is a dangerous place to work. A person could get killed here." Johnston smiled at Deputy Baker and walked out of the room. Baker stated it was really strange and the sheriff's comment gave him a knot in his stomach. He felt as if the sheriff had just threatened him. Deputy Baker was active in the deputies' guild, and had vocally opposed Sheriff Johnston and the administration in the past on guild issues. Baker took the reading of the poem by Johnston personally.

Deputy Baker and I talked for some time. I attempted to reassure him and calm him down. After our discussion, I removed the poem from the bulletin board. I felt that it was inappropriate for it to be hanging there. I decided to keep it with my notes as to what has been transpiring around the office.

On September 20, 1995, when I arrived at the precinct office to start my shift, I was met by Sergeant Newton. He appeared upset once again. Newton grabbed me by the arm as he motioned me into the traffic office and closed the door. He informed me he had to go to the Sheriff and Police Chief's quarterly meeting today with Sheriff Johnston. The sheriff brought him to the meeting to put on a demonstration of "the total station." This was a laser measuring system designed for reconstruction of accident scenes. It was used to develop diagrams and sketches for crime scene evidence. Sgt. Newton said after the demonstration, there was a luncheon. He stated at the onset of the meeting that Sheriff Johnston was friendly and appeared to be in a good mood. After the luncheon there was a social event and all present spend time visiting and talking. He went on to say an FBI agent cornered the sheriff and took him aside.

Johnston concluded his conversation with this FBI agent and then went over to where Sgt. Newton was standing and confronted him.

Sgt. Newton remarked the sheriff was furious. He advised him that the FBI agent just informed him that eleven deputies went to the FBI headquarters and requested a grand jury investigation of him and to incidents of wrong doing.

Johnston appeared flustered as he remarked: "I could end up going to prison."

Sheriff Johnston became so enraged that he was unable to even speak. He grabbed Sgt. Newton and took him out into the parking lot. The sheriff then told Sgt. Newton that he knew that Capt. Hill and I were behind the FBI investigation. He stated he was also aware that some of Sgt. Newton's people were also involved.

Sheriff Johnston then began to yell and make threats. He screamed. He would get every one of them; those deputies that went to the FBI would pay and they would pay dearly. The sheriff then questioned Sgt. Newton as to his knowledge of the FBI investigation, and who exactly went to the FBI. Sgt. Newton "side stepped" the issues, as to whether he had knowledge about the FBI investigation, and responded instead with he did not know exactly who all went to the FBI.

Sgt. Newton advised the sheriff just kept repeating himself, saying,

"They'll pay, they'll pay, I will teach them for trying to get me into trouble; I could go to prison, they'll pay."

According to Sgt. Newton, Sheriff Johnston's demeanor made him feel very uncomfortable. The sheriff was acting very weird and irrate. He was full of anger and hate. He had a strange look on his face, one that he had never seen before.

Sgt. Newton warned me to be careful, advising that Johnston was a very vindictive person and he definitely was out to get me.

I thanked Sgt. Newton for his concern. I then walked out of the traffic office and went into the sergeant's office to conduct line up. I knew how Sheriff Johnston felt about me. It did not make any difference, I was going to continue to do what I felt I had to do.

Capt. Hill contacted me later that evening, saying that Chief Halsted was once again upset with me. This time it was over some overtime that I approved for one of my deputies. I remarked to Capt. Hill that it never ends, and to inform the chief that his complaint was noted. I updated Capt. Hill as to what Sgt. Newton had told me concerning the sheriff and the FBI investigation.

CHAPTER SIX

A MICRO SECOND CAN INSTANTLY LAST ALL ETERNITY WHEN LIFE AND DEATH COLLIDE.

The day after Sheriff Johnston learned of the FBI investigation things began to get even more serious and I began to wonder if I was going to survive. I was working a swing shift and was out in my patrol car driving around the county. It was just turning dark, kind of twilight, as I drove through a business district. All the stores and businesses were closed with the exception of some restaurants. I observed a vehicle, a mid-size, dark colored car behind me. I got the impression that it was following me. It had been behind me for some time and seemed to take the same turns that I did. It was too dark outside to get a good look at the license plate. I could not make it out. I decided to make a series of turns to determine for sure if the vehicle was actually following me, or if it was just a coincidence. Just when I concluded that the vehicle was in fact, following me, it turned off. I felt relieved and that maybe it was just my imagination making me paranoid. I got about another mile down the road, when the police radio broadcast a prowler call. The location of the call was about a half mile back down the road that I had just traveled. I advised Cen. Com. that I was in the area of the prowler call and would be responding to the scene.

The call was dispatched that there were two subjects in a dark sedan in the alley between a large retail computer outlet and a jewelry store located at 41277—Greenwich Blvd. We had been experiencing burglaries to local businesses as of late; so I anticipated that it could be a burglary call. As I arrived at the scene, I turned off my headlights and drove into the entrance to the alley. I observed a vehicle parked approximately sixty feet down the alley. I turned on my spotlight and shone it on the vehicle. I instantly recognized the vehicle as the same one that had been following me, just prior to the call being dispatched. I had just hit the vehicle with my spot light when within a split second shots rang out. Sheer panic overwhelmed my entire body, as bright flashes of light lit up the alley. Time instantly slowed down beyond belief. The windshield in my patrol vehicle was hit by one of the bullets. It shattered upon impact. As the adrenalin in my body rose, I watched in amazement as small fragments of glass from the windshield appeared to just flutter ever so slowly about the vehicle. The small pieces of the windshield glistened like sunlight reflecting through crystal as the light from the muzzle lit the darkness. It was as if these fragments were almost suspended in the air. All of my senses seemed acutely aware as I ducked to the floor of the patrol car seeking to avoid the gun fire and flying glass. I could actually feel the impact of each of the bullets hitting the patrol vehicle. There even seemed to be a delay from the moment the flash of light appeared until the bullet made impact. The really uncanny part of the entire episode is the fact that I never once, after the first round was fired, heard the sound of the guns actually firing.

I grabbed the police radio as I dropped to the floor of the car and called Cen. Com. yelling into the mike

"Shots fired, Shots fired, Officer under gun fire, request back up"

I just dropped the microphone and opened the passenger door. I rolled out onto the pavement and away from the vehicle, laying prone on the ground next to a bunch of garbage cans that were lined up by the side of the building. There was no thinking process involved in my actions. Everything was just instinctive reaction. I lay there on the ground with my service revolver in my hands looking for the location of the shooter. As instantly as it had started, it was over. I believe the entire incident really only lasted a few brief seconds but it seemed like eternity. I just lay there. I did not hear a sound. The shots had stopped but I was not sure if the suspects had fled the scene or if they were just lying in wait. I could see the outline of the suspect's vehicle standing in the darkness in front of me. It had not moved. I kept scanning the area, looking for movement. There was none. I was afraid to move myself, fearing that I might draw more gunfire. I don't know exactly how long I just lay there; it seemed like a very long time. Finally, two patrol units arrived as backup. They lit up the alley with their spotlights. A search of the area determined that the suspect had in fact fled the scene on foot.

Twelve shots in all had been fired into my patrol car. Four rounds hit the grill, three rounds impacted the driver's side column post, and the rest hit the windshield. It was quite obvious that the suspects made a deliberate attempt to kill me. The locations of the bullets implied that they were not fired just to scare but rather to kill.

I was covered with blood. My injuries were minor having been caused by the flying glass fragments. In the excitement of the moment, I did not realize that I was injured. In fact,

I didn't even notice until one of the "back up" deputies pointed out to me that I was bleeding.

The vehicle which the suspects left at the scene turned out to be a stolen car. It was stolen earlier that evening from another county and at the time we recovered it, had not yet even been reported as stolen. I had no description of the suspects. I believed from the shots fired that there were two suspects but I never saw anyone. The deputies that arrived as backup searched the area for possible suspects, however they located no one.

Capt. Hill responded to the scene. He was concerned about my welfare. I assured him that I was okay; a little shaken up, aut basically all right. He called Chief Halsted on a cellular phone to advise him of the shooting. It was standard procedure that when an officer was involved in a shooting related incident, you notified your supervisor, who in turn would advise up the chain of command. Capt. Hill got off the phone with the chief and walked over to my location. He was shaking his head. The captain advised that the chief told him to have the deputies handle the crime scene and initial reports. He would not be sending out detectives to the scene. The detectives would review the patrol's investigation tomorrow and handle any follow up that they deemed necessary.

We could not believe the chief was not following procedure by not having the detectives' respond to the scene and conduct the initial investigation. Capt. Hill got the impression from talking to the chief that Halsted was minimizing the incident.

If the detectives did respond, it would be harder to down play the incident. The patrol handling the investigation gave the impression that it was just a routine occurrence. We had a lot of good patrol officers, however, the most of them lacked the experience and expertise to properly process a crime scene. The patrol officers also, did not have the time available to them that it takes to adequately do a crime scene investigation.

Capt. Hill had Cen. Com. trace the 911 call that came into the dispatch center advising them of the prowler call that led to the shooting incident. The call was made from the public telephone booth located on the edge of the alley where the incident took place. All of the events leading up to the shooting; from the vehicle following me, to the call being made anonymously, to the shooting itself; raised the suspicion that it was a planned attack. Capt. Hill and I both agreed that it appeared that I was targeted. It was planned and a deliberate attempt on my life. There was no sign of any attempt at a forced entry to any of the businesses in the alley. There actually was no evidence that would lead us to believe that the incident was anything but a set up and planned to lure me into the alley. Capt. Hill had one of the deputies at the scene attempt to lift finger prints from the pay phone used to call Cen. Com. There were not any prints found on the phone. It appeared the phone itself had been wiped clean. Usually we have little success in obtaining prints from a pay phone because there are just too many prints, one on top of another, making it impossible to get a clean print. This was not the case. The fact that there were no prints at all raised our suspicions even more and made it look like a professional job.

Later that night, after I cleared the scene, I went back to the precinct office and wrote up a detailed report of the incident. I included the facts relating to the suspect vehicle following me for sometime just prior to the call coming in. I wrote the report objectively but did imply that it was probably a planned attempt on my life.

Things just didn't add up right. I thought about my conversation with Sgt. Newton, concerning Sheriff Johnston's demeanor the day before. Sheriff Johnston was blaming Capt. Hill and me for the FBI investigation. I couldn't help but wonder if the sheriff was behind this shooting incident. It was all just speculation. There was nothing substantial, no real evidence to prove that I was actually set up as the target. My gut instinct told me that Sheriff Johnston was involved. I believed that Chief Halsted's refusal to send detectives to investigate the crime scene was a strong indicator that he too was involved.

My suspicion of their involvement was enhanced by the actions of the administration over the next couple of days. No official investigation was ever conducted, nor were the detectives ever involved in any investigation into the shooting.

I was never contacted or interviewed, which would have been standard procedure. The only thing that was ever mentioned was a brief statement by the sheriff. He advised the deputies in a written memo that the department concluded that the shooting incident was a random act of violence and encouraged the deputies to practice extreme caution when responding to calls, especially when responding to remote or isolated locations.

Capt. Hill and I were upset with the way the office down played an act of attempted murder. There was nothing we could do about it, so we tried to just get on with our lives and not worry about it. I thanked God that the bullets all missed me and that I survived. I wondered what would happen next. I realized that if the sheriff was involved, it was not over.

Just about three weeks later, on October 13, 1995, I responded to a 911 call in the remote countryside of the western region of the county. The call was a man acting violently, who physically assaulted two men and a woman. Cen. Com. did not have any other details of the incident. I was not going to have a repeat of the detail that occurred in the alley and be caught at the scene alone. I broke some of my deputies away from non-priority calls and advised them to respond to the scene with me. Three deputies and I arrived at the location of the call just as the darkness of night was setting in. I made contact with the two male victims, while the deputies with me checked the surrounding area for the suspect. I was standing with one of the victims in the front yard of the residence, next to some vehicles that were parked in the driveway. Another deputy was talking to the other male victim. They were just off to my right between the vehicles in the driveway and the house. The female victim was still in the residence.

One male victim advised me that he, his wife and brother were all just sitting down for dinner, when the suspect came storming in the front door to their house and assaulted them. He said the suspect was carrying a rifle and beat them with the butt of the gun. He started to tell me they did not know who the suspect was when out of nowhere, a loud explosion suddenly rang out. It was a rifle shot. The projectile made a thud as it created a gaping hole in the rear quarter panel of the vehicle parked next to where we were standing. The muzzle blast from the weapon lit the darkness with a blinding light. The blast from that first shot was so loud that it sounded like someone had just touched off a case of dynamite. Again, it seemed like the second and third shot carried no sound, whatsoever, other than the thud of the metal as they hit the car parked by where we were scrambling for cover.

I grabbed the victim standing next to me and pulled him down behind one of the vehicles in the driveway. The deputies at the scene all spread out as they searched for cover and concealment. It was rather easy to determine that the suspect was moving; changing his location as he fired the weapon at us. We could see the muzzle blast moving across the darkness. I motioned to the deputies at the scene, directing them to different locations so that we could set up a perimeter of containment. We did not know exactly where the suspect was, but had his position pinned down to the south side of the residence, somewhere between the back yard and the adjoining woods. We did not want to give him the opportunity to circle around behind us.

I called Cen. Com. on the police radio and advised dispatch that we were pinned down by a suspect with a gun and shots had been fired. I requested emergency traffic, and that they notify command. Everything and I mean everything was once again slowed down beyond belief. Adrenalin had overcome all of us. It's a strange and rather unreal feeling; instead of being overwhelmed with excitement and fear, you experience a sense of calming. It is as if you have all the time in the world to articulate your every action. Your mind is captured by the moment and over come with concentration of survival.

I tried to talk to the suspect, yelling out continuously, trying to get a response. I was attempting to accomplish two things. One, was to pinpoint his location by hearing his voice and the other was to try and talk him down and to get him to surrender his weapon. Actually there was another reason behind yelling at him it's hard for a person to think about what he is going to do next, when he is constantly being distracted by someone trying to talk to him.

Finally, the suspect yelled out:

"I'm going to kill all of you fuckin deputies!"

He did not say much and he did not repeat himself, but it was enough for us to be able to pinpoint his approximate location. We moved in on him. We moved slowly, trying to maintain some sort of cover to protect ourselves. We did not want him to become aware that we were closing in on him. We did not want him to feel pressured to react and do something impulsive or stupid and get himself or one of us killed. Our intentions were mainly to tighten up the perimeter so that we could safely keep him contained while we negotiated his surrender.

I kept trying to talk to him. I was trying to build a relationship, a bond established by the fear and anxiety of the moment. I needed him to trust me in order to get him to even consider surrendering. I needed him to realize the danger involved in our current situation; the danger to his well being and the safety he would have if he trusted me. I kept telling him that the situation was still "fixable," no one has been hurt seriously and we could minimize his problems if he would surrender his weapon. The suspect would not respond. I was at a disadvantage by not even knowing his name. I decided to tell him my name, still working on establishing a bond. I told him my first name, and did get a response, but not the one I was looking for. I no sooner said my first name, and he fired another shot in my direction.

I yelled out:

"Come on man, if you don't like my name, you can just say so, you don't have to kill me."

I still did not receive a verbal response. I continued for some time to try to communicate with the suspect, however with negative results. I just could not get through to him.

Then suddenly out of the darkness he yelled:

"You're DEAD."

At that very second, one of the deputies sensing he was real close to the suspect, shined his flashlight in the direction of the suspect's voice. The light lit the suspect up. He had moved from the location where we had determined him to be. He had crawled over to within ten feet of another deputy. The suspect was in a kneeling position with a raised rifle which was point directly at the deputy that was closest to him, the deputy with the flashlight. The deputy froze staring down the barrel of the suspect's gun. At that very moment, realizing the threat to that particular deputy's life, another deputy fired his shotgun directly at the suspect.

The shotgun blast was so powerful that when it made impact with the suspect's chest, it literally raised his entire body off the ground and threw him through the air upwards and backwards approximately five to ten feet. The suspect had left us no other choice but to react to neutralize the threat. The deputies rushed the suspect location. The impact of the shotgun round was tremendous, killing the suspect instantly. The deputies contacted the suspect, checked for any signs of life. There weren't any. They then rolled him over and handcuffed him, per departmental procedure, and secured his weapon.

I walked up to the deputy who did the actual shooting. He was in shock. He was just standing there, holding his shotgun and staring at the suspect lying dead on the ground. I looked at him and took the shotgun from his hands. I told him that it would be all right. I gave the shotgun to another deputy to secure.

He looked at me. He had tears in his eyes. He responded:

"I had to Sarge. I had no choice. He, he was going to kill Deputy Gibson."

I nodded my head, and I told him, he was right. He did the right thing and had saved lives tonight. It was going to be all right.

I called Cen. Com. on the police radio and advised them to clear emergency traffic and to notify command that we had an officer involved in a shooting with one suspect down. I requested that the Captain, and crime scene, and detectives respond to my location.

I directed the deputies at the scene to secure the area until the detectives arrived, while I took the officer involved in the shooting aside, away from the body and scene. I took him back to my patrol car and stayed with him until the other units arrived. He was shaken up to say the least, and I was concerned that he might go into shock. He was traumatized by the ordeal. There was nothing I could really do for him except to comfort him and keep reassuring him that he did the right thing. I told him that it was a justified shooting, and I would stand behind him.

Within the hour after we had the scene secured, Undersheriff Deiter, Chief Halsted, Sgt. Paris and the detectives that would be involved in the investigation arrived at our location. I updated them as to the situation. Sgt. Paris and the detectives took charge of the scene. The deputies and I, who were involved in the incident, were all ordered to clear the scene and report to the south office to be interviewed.

I arranged for another officer to drive the vehicle belonging to the officer that did the shooting. I did not feel he should be driving at this time, so I had him ride with me down to the office. We all arrived at the south office about the same time. None of us talked. We were all silent. We went into the computer room and each sat down at a station and began to do our reports on the incident. We were all filled with mixed emotions. We were happy we were alive, but it affected all of us that someone had to die, especially at our hands.

We each typed up our version of what we observed and of exactly what happen. The reports were reviewed later and found to be very consistent. One at a time, a detective would come into the computer room and take one of us to the detective's office to be interviewed. Undersheriff Deiter and Chief Halsted both came to the south office and supervised the interview process. After we all finished our reports and all my deputies had been interviewed, we were all ordered to go home. I was not interviewed. I went to Chief Halsted and inquired as to why the detectives did not interview me, since I was the officer on the scene supervising and handling the incident. He advised me that it was not necessary, the review team had all the information that they needed. He then told me to go home and that if they needed to talk to me, that they would contact me at a later date.

I thought it strange that they were not interested in my version of the incident. The adrenalin built up in my body from the threat of the incident was wearing off. I was getting tired and was at the point that I did not care whether they wanted to interview me or not. I was ready to go home and get some sleep. It was around noon and I had come into work at 1:00 p.m., yesterday, so it had been an extremely long shift.

I walked out the back door of the office into the parking lot. I was met there by Deputy Gibson. He advised me that he needed to talk to me for a second. I went over to where he was standing by his patrol car. He advised that he got the impression from the interview the detectives conducted with him, that the administration was going to rule the shooting justified. He paused and looked right at me.

"But", he said, "they are focusing their investigation on you and whether you acted properly in supervising and handling the situation. They wanted to know if you followed procedures, if you maintained control of the situation. They were investigating you rather than the shooting, Sarge."

Just then some of the other deputies involved in the shooting incident came over to where Deputy Gibson and I were standing. We all talked. Each of the deputies was under the opinion that the Administration was out to get me. They all stated that their interviews were about how I conducted myself and if I acted properly. They advised the line of questioning was slanted in such a fashion that they were fishing to get something improper that they could use against me. They all agreed the detectives and administration were not investigating the officer involved in the shooting or the suspect. In actuality, it was I that was being investigated.

Each one of them, in their own way, tried to reassure me they told the administration that they felt I followed procedure and acted properly during the incident. They knew the type of pressure I was under from the administration and did not want to give them anything they could use against me. And, I too, believe, I handled the matter properly. The deputies were just telling the truth, but that took courage, especially when you're dealing with people like Deiter and Halsted, who sometimes get angry and take it as a personal attack against them, just for being honest.

I was rather disturbed with the fact that the administration was trying to nail me to the wall for doing my job. Then again, I guess I should have expected it. We all departed from the south office and went home. We all were exhausted, but none of us were able to sleep. When your life is put in jeopardy, and then someone dies, you can't just let it go. It stays with you for a long time.

When I arrived at home that morning, I told my wife, Sherry, of the incident. She was a great comfort to me. I could tell she was frighted, but did not express her concerns. She appeared more interested in making sure that I was handling the situation. I don't know what I would have done without her.

I found myself laying in bed with thoughts of the shooting running through my mind. I analyze the events of the incident over and over again. I was questioning my own behavior. Did I act properly? Was there something I could have done differently to have prevented the fatal outcome? Was my supervision of the situation the best it could have been? The questions raced through my mind. Did I have control of the situation or did the events of the incident control every one of us at the scene? I don't know that I will ever know the right answers or if there are any answers. I do believe that I did the best job I knew how and I guess that is all any of us can do.

I did not have a problem with the administration investigating my actions in supervising the shooting incident. I did, however, have a problem with investigating my actions as the primary focus of their investigation. I believed they needed to look into the entire incident, and first, determine if the officer involved in the actual shooting was justified. Then secondary to that, review my actions as a supervisor to determine if I acted properly. Both of theses issues needed to be addressed, but in the proper order with the correct priority.

I do believe that Undersheriff Deiter and Chief Halsted, viewed the shooting incident as an opportunity to find something they could use against me. I guess it was their motive more than the actual focus that disturbed me the most, about the interviews. Like everything else that had been happening, I would get over it and survive. A few days after the shooting the official ruling came out. They found the shooting was justified and non preventable. There was never a word mentioned about whether I supervised the incident correctly or not. The mere fact that nothing was mentioned made me believe the administration must have concluded that I handled the situation correctly. Otherwise, they would have made an issue out of it.

After the official ruling came out that the shooting was justified, the incident was over and done, except for those of us that were there at the scene that night. Those of us that were involved would never forget. It would never really be over. It would stay with us the rest of our lives. It was sad. We won because we survived. We won because our actions were justified. The reality was there were no winners that night, just scars and mixed emotions that would last a life time. Police work has its rewards but it also has its own consequences. In a split second, any given situation can turn on you and affect you forever.

CHAPTER SEVEN

INTIMIDATION TAKES ON MANY FORMS, DISGUISED IN A VARIETY OF DIFFERENT FACES.

The rest of the month of October 1995, was basically business as usual. By that I mean things had not changed since the election. Chief Halsted did not miss a chance to ride me.

Nor to come down on me, for anything he could find. Sheriff Johnston continued to monitor the police radio calls during the shifts I worked and they were still giving me more special assignments than normal. The atmosphere I was subjected to at work was micro management to the highest degree.

I was still under the misconception that as long as I did nothing wrong, the administration would not be able to touch me.

I had an unrealistic opinion that Sheriff Johnston and his people had to play by the same rules I did. I guess that I gave them credit for having some degree of moral ethics.

On October 30, 1995, I turned in another report as requested by Chief Halsted. It concerned a fire commissioner's meeting the chief had ordered me to attend. I gave Capt. Hill a copy of the report, so that he could witness that I turned the report in. It had become standard procedure for me to give the captain a copy of the reports in order to protect myself. The next day, October 31, 1995, once again Chief Halsted accused me of failing to obey orders by not turning in the report as directed.

Chief Halsted became furious when he learned once again Capt. Hill had witnessed me turning in the report and Capt. Hill had a copy of the report in question. He advised me, in a rather loud and stern voice, that he did not care how many witnesses I had or how many copies of the report I made. He stated that if he did not get his copy when he required it to be turned in, then I did not turn it in. He remarked that I was responsible and if he did not have it, then I disobeyed a direct order.

I could not believe Chief Halsted demeanor and I had had enough. I advised the chief that with all due respect, he should be careful of accusing someone without having all the facts to back himself up or it might just come back and bite him.

I continued to tell him that I was getting tired of the bull shit. I was tired of justifying my every action. Chief Halsted just stood there and looked at me. He then turned and left the room without saying another word. He never mentioned the report to me again. I learned later, from Capt. Hill, that Chief Halsted conveniently found his copy of the report.

We all finally learned the identity of the suspect that was fatally wounded in the stand off a couple of weeks ago. He was a Samuel T. Irving, a 34-year-old, single male with a history of assaults, burglaries and drug related charges. It was believed he went to the victim's residence to collect on a drug debt and things got out of hand and that is when 911 was called. The autopsy revealed that Irving was under the influence of cocaine at the time of his death. The victims that Irving assaulted were not admitting that they were involved in drugs or that they even knew him. They kept claiming that the attack on them by Irving was random, and they did not know why it occurred.

The entire circumstance surrounding the shooting incident was strange at best and left a lot of unanswered questions. No one could explain how Irving got out to the victim's residence in the first place. Their home was located way out in a remote area of the county, and it would not be practical to believe that someone walked there. The fact that Irving stayed around to confront the police after they arrived at the scene was even more bizarre. It made no sense whatsoever. He had every opportunity to just disappear into the night, but he had chosen to confront the officers. These questions, and others, haunted our minds. We did not have the answers and most likely never would. We just had to assume, for our own peace of mind, that the drugs he was on caused him to attack rather than flee. The drugs are what most likely caused his death. It gave us a rationalization that helped to justify the actions taken and the end result.

Sgt. Newton came into the sergeant's office around November 1, 1995, needing to talk to me. He was upset over the treatment Deputy Teri Willis was receiving from the administration. Deputy Willis was a ten-year veteran of the department. She also was the first female deputy ever hired by the department. Newton advised me that Deputy Willis received a written reprimand over an incident she was involved in, and that she did not deserve to be written up. He claimed the administration was coming down on her because she was an Atwater supporter in the last election, and also because she was outspoken about Sheriff Johnston eliminating the "Dare Program."

An interesting part of the Sheriff eliminating the "Dare Program" was the rumor he did so because his children were at the age that they would be taught "Dare" in school, and he did not want his children learning about drugs. He feared if they learned too much that they might come to realize he was involved in drugs. I'm getting away from the point here concerning my conversation with Sgt. Newton. Let me continue:

Sgt. Newton went on to say he did not know where it was all going to end. I heard him make this statement time and time again concerning the actions of the administration. He was frustrated and fed up. He advised that about half of the deputies who were known supporters of Atwater in 1994, had now received disciplinary action against them in one form or another. He paused for a moment and just looked at me. Newton then sighed, and remarked,

"You realize, don't you? Almost everyone who went to the FBI last spring has now been disciplined by the administration."

Sgt. Newton was concerned and fearful that Sheriff Johnston was going to destroy all of our careers and there was nothing any of us could do about it. Newton then quizzed me as to how the FBI investigation against the sheriff was going. I told him that I did not know. I knew the FBI was still conducting their investigation, but that was about all that I knew. I had been told when the FBI becomes involved in political corruption cases, it can take years before they complete their investigation. Apparently, there are no statues of limitations involved in political corruption cases, so they take their time.

Sgt. Newton remarked he hoped the FBI would do their job and they would do it well. He hoped criminal indictments would be issued against those that broke the law, so that the department could grow beyond the current situations and problems that exist. It was obvious Sgt. Newton was aware of inappropriate and illegal behavior on the part of the administration. He wanted to see it corrected. His demeanor demonstrated he was concerned and scared that he could possibly get caught in the fall out of the FBI investigation. I had always looked upon Sgt. Newton as an honest, hardworking cop, and a good person. His demeanor, however, raised concerns in me as to how deeply involved he was in the criminal activities of the sheriff, and his administration.

On November 11, 1995, Chief Halsted walked into the sergeant's office and asked me if I was aware that Deputy Teri Willis had filed an E.E.O.C. complaint against the sheriff's office. The E.E.O.C. is the Equal Opportunity Commission. They handle complaints like discrimination. Halsted advised that Deputy Willis is accusing Sheriff Johnston, Undersheriff Deiter and himself of sexual harassment and discrimination toward her.

I informed Chief Halsted that I was not aware that Deputy Willis had filed a complaint. The chief then handed me a document. It read, "Statement of Affidavit." The document was typed and completely filled out in my name. It stated, I was not aware of any misconduct involving Deputy Willis committed by Sheriff Johnston, Undersheriff Deiter, or Chief Halsted. The chief then directed me to sign the affidavit and return it to him. He advised he would be up in his office. He then walked out of the sergeant's office. I read the document again and shook my head. I knew things about the administration's misconduct toward Deputy Willis, as well as inappropriate behavior toward others in the department, including myself. It was unbelievable. The mere fact Halsted even asked me to sign this statement I guess you could say pissed me off. The manner in which they abused their employees and then expected us to cover for them and protect them really pissed me off. It was not going to happen. I was not about to sign the statement they prepared for me. I was equally upset that they would have the nerve to write a statement that was supposedly coming from me, and then order me to sign it. The very least they could have done was to come to me and request I write up anything I might be aware of, instead of giving me a statement that I was not aware of any violations. What they wrote was a lie. They could intimidate me all they wanted by ordering me to sign it, but I was not about to do that.

I walked into Chief Halsted's office and advised the chief that I read over the affidavit that was prepared for me to sign, and I could not sign it. It contained untrue statements and I was not about to sign a false statement, even under direct orders. Chief Halsted became irrate and very upset. His face became flustered and he glared into my eyes. He had a stern look on his face, a look that could kill. His voice became very deep and abrupt as he once again ordered me to sign the paper. He advised me that I had no choice, he needed the affidavit signed today so he could return it to the prosecutor's office. I advised the chief that with all due respect, I refuse to sign a lie and the affidavit contained untrue statements. Before the chief could say another word, I continued advising him that his request was illegal. I would not tolerate it. He should reconsider before he finds himself having additional legal action taken against him.

Halsted did not know what to say. He was the one normally doing the yelling and shouting the threats. He was not usually on the receiving end. After a long pause, he paced back and forth behind his desk. He looked back toward me with his face drawn. He advised me to contact Deputy Prosecutor Peters, and to advise her I was refusing to sign the affidavit. He also directed me to inform her exactly what statement I would sign, advising they needed the statements done today.

I later learned that Chief Halsted and Deputy Prosecutor Peters were both involved in writing the statement the chief tried to get me to sign. In fact, they wrote the affidavits for all the supervisors in the sheriff's office to sign. Each one of them contained the statement that they were not aware of any misconduct taken by the administration against Deputy Willis. All of the supervisors, including all the sergeants and corporals signed the affidavit as written. The only exceptions were that of Captain Hill and me. It was a known fact among all the supervisors that Deputy Willis was treated differently, and discriminated against, yet only the two of us refused to sign their lies.

I contacted Deputy Prosecutor Peters as directed. I advised her the statement the chief attempted to get me to sign was not accurate and contained untrue statements. I told her that I refused to sign it. She requested to know exactly what part of the affidavit was inaccurate and what exactly the statement had to say in order to get me to sign it. I then advised her of two separate incidents in which chief Halsted and Sheriff Johnston acted inappropriately toward Deputy Willis. Peters listened to what I had to say. She did not say a word or make any comments. When I was done, she advised that she would prepare my statement and fax it to the precinct office for me to sign. She told me it would take her about forty minutes to prepare the document. She requested that when the fax arrived I should sign it and fax it back to her. About an hour later her fax arrived.

The statement I gave her over the phone was not contained in the affidavit she prepared. The conduct of Sheriff Johnston and

Chief Halsted toward Deputy Willis was down played and the facts distorted. The statement still contained untrue statements which gave the appearance that the Administration had done nothing wrong. I called Deputy Prosecutor Peters once again. I informed her that I would not sign the affidavit that she prepared the second time. I explained to her it still was not accurate.

During the course of the afternoon, I went back and forth with Peters. She faxed me four additional statements for me to sign. They were sent one at a time. Each time they were incorrect and I refused to sign them. Each time key issues of the truth were omitted. Finally on the sixth attempt, the affidavit contained the basic truth, but still down played the inappropriate behavior. I signed the document because it did basically contain the truth.

Capt. Hill went through a similar situation with Deputy Prosecutor Peters. He too, eventually signed an affidavit that had enough of the truth in it, he could live with it. Neither one of the affidavits we signed was written the way that we would have written them, if allowed to have written them ourselves. We were both dismayed and in a state of shock over coming to the realization that the prosecutor's office was involved in covering up the truth. We were equally dissatisfied and rather disappointed that all of the other supervisors would sign a form just to protect the administration, when they knew what they were signing contained false statements.

It undermined our own sense of worth as part of the law enforcement community. It just cut against the grain as to what being a cop is all about. After all, cops are supposed to be honest. Their power comes from the people in the community, and is based on trust. Trust that the power will not be abused. Trust that they will do the right thing, no matter what the consequences. The other sergeants and corporals were individuals, whom Capt. Hill and I trusted with our lives. These were individuals we were depending on to tell the truth when called upon in our own cases. Yet, these supervisors lacked the courage to be honest even when it involved a fellow officer.

Capt. Hill and I understood from that point on that when it came to the other supervisors, we most likely would be standing alone. We had each other, but other than ourselves, there was no one. The other supervisors feared for their own jobs. We understood their fear. Their fear, however, was no excuse. It did not justify their behavior. There is no excuse that justifies a lie. You can sometimes rationalize a reason to lie, but you can never really justify it.

Later, that same night, Capt. Hill and I learned about a meeting Sheriff Johnston had attended at the Mental Health Residential Center. Johnston was said to be bragging to a group of doctors. He told them that those deputies that opposed him in last year's election, as well as those deputies who went to the FBI would pay. He was not done with them yet; he was, in fact, only just beginning to come down on them. Their careers would be over when he was finished teaching those deputies a lesson.

One of the doctors in attendance at the meeting was a family friend of Capt. Hill. He called Capt. Hill that night after the meeting concluded, to warn him to be careful. The doctor further advised Capt. Hill that Sheriff Johnston was a powerful man and in his professional opinion a mentally unstable person. He continued by remarking the combination of power and instability Sheriff Johnston possessed can make for a very dangerous person. The doctor made it clear to Capt. Hill he did not want to become involved professionally or in anyway whatsoever. He was only relating the information to Capt. Hill as a friend. He was concerned about Capt. Hill's welfare. The good doctor then told Capt. Hill that he, himself, was fearful of Sheriff Johnston and did not want to have any problems with the man. He told Capt. Hill that this conversation he was having with him, actually never took place and then hung up the phone. The words the doctor told Capt. Hill, just reaffirmed our own thoughts and belief concerning Sheriff Johnston.

Two days after the E.E.O.C. affidavit incidents concerning Deputy Willis, Chief Halsted came into the sergeant's office and handed me back an overtime slip. The overtime slip was one that I had submitted some two weeks' prior and had been approved. Chief Halsted advised me the overtime slip had been approved in error and I was now being denied the overtime pay request. I tried to discuss the overtime slip with the chief. He was very abrupt, stating there was to be no discussion about it. The overtime was denied and that was the end of it. Chief Halsted had not spoken to me since the E.E.O.C. affidavit incident. As he was walking out of the office, he made a comment, kind of half under his breath but loud enough that I would hear it. He stated, "if you can't help us, then you'll get nothing." It was quite apparent to me that denying the overtime slip was just one of his little ways of getting back at me for refusing to sign the E.E.O.C. statement. I shook my head. Halsted's demeanor disgusted me. I pulled out my notebook and documented the conversation and Halsted's comments. I still continued to keep detailed notes on everything since my conversation with Sheriff Johnston back in October of 1994. In fact, I was just finishing up my third full notebook of notes.

Come the end of November of 1995, "Discovery" was due to be turned in, reference my lawsuit against Sheriff Johnston and his administration. I received a call from Randy, advising me discovery was due. He informed me that discovery was where we had to turn over a copy of all physical and testimonial evidence we intended to use in the trial. He advised it included all papers and documents concerning Sheriff Johnston and others that we may want to use in the court case. This evidence had to be submitted to the courts, and also to Sheriff Johnston's attorney, Mr. Custington.

Randy went on to say that anything we do not supply to the courts and to the other side in discovery, we would not be allowed to bring up in the trial. Randy advised he was going to turn in all my notes, the tape recording of Undersheriff Deiter, and all the documents that were turned over to the FBI. He advised he felt it was safer to turn in everything than to omit something, and then learn later that it was an important piece of evidence in our case and we would not be allowed to use it. I agreed with him.

All of the documents were submitted to the Federal Court where the trial would take place. A copy was also given to Sheriff Johnston's attorney, Mr. Custington.

Randy spoke with the FBI agent in charge, Jason Bolton, prior to submitting the documents in discovery. Mr. Bolton advised him, the FBI investigation was out in the open and no longer a secret, so he had no problem with the documents being surrendered to the courts, or to Johnston for that matter. Agent Bolton advised Randy he was convinced that Sheriff Johnston was a dirty cop, but he had concerns as to whether his agency would be able to make a case against Johnston. He remarked that Sheriff Johnston has covered his tracks extremely well, and people are afraid to give statements against Johnston. Agent Bolton then remarked the only way to bring Sheriff Johnston down, might be through the civil court process. He wished Randy luck in handling my case and advised the FBI would be continuing their investigation against Sheriff Johnston.

Randy advised me to be careful. He stated that once he turns in all of our evidence, things could get extremely hot for me around the sheriff's office. He remarked:

"You just do not know how Sheriff Johnston will react when he sees all the evidence."

Randy told me to tell Capt. Hill that all the evidence was being turned over, so he could be prepared and extra cautious. I advised him I would inform the captain.

All the evidence was submitted in discovery. To my disbelief, and rather pleasant surprise, nothing happened to me or anyone else at work. In fact, it appeared that Chief Halsted had backed off. He in fact, even acknowledged my presence with a "Hello" from time to time. I thought, maybe, seeing all my notes, and all the evidence we had against the administration, they came to realize that they needed to leave me alone. Just let me do my job. I had high hopes. The evidence would play a positive role in the survival of my career. The next two weeks went by and everything seemed to be going well at work.

It was the first time since I returned to work in January that I was not under the gun and micro managed on a daily basis.

While everything appeared to be going well at work, there were other events happening that raised my concerns. Within days of submitting the evidence in discovery, my wife and I noticed strange vehicles parked on the side of the roadway near our residence. Our neighbors also noticed. They called us to advise that it appeared there were people watching our home. I got some license plate numbers from the vehicles that seemed to have us under surveillance. All the license plates I ran in the computer came back "no record found." We observed a blue mini van, a green four door sedan, and a white Jeep pick-up truck. Each of these vehicles seemed to appear at different times. They all would stop on the side of the roadway just up the street from my residence and in a location they could perform surveillance.

I began to notice these three vehicles, as well as a couple of other cars that I really was not able to identify. They seemed to follow me whenever I drove anywhere. It appeared I was under surveillance both at home and at work. I learned Capt. Hill and part of a group of deputies who were to be witnesses for me in the trial, also were being followed.

Captain Hill and I concluded that the evidence submitted in discovery had Sheriff Johnston running scared. We believed he ordered the surveillance. He was concerned that we knew too much and wanted to keep track of everyone we made contact with. It was speculation on our part, but it was the only logical reason we could come up with. After all, the surveillance didn't start until after the evidence was submitted. There had to be a connection.

CHAPTER EIGHT

ONE'S OWN "DIGNITY" GIVES THE COURAGE TO CARRY ON WHEN THE WORLD SEEMS TO BE CRUMBLING AT YOUR FEET.

Suddenly, without any advance warning, I was taken completely by surprise, on December 13, 1995. My career as a law enforcement officer, my chosen profession that I had dedicated my life to, came to an abrupt end. It began when I arrived at the precinct office that day. Chief Halsted contacted me. He advised that after I conducted line up and got my deputies out on the road, he needed me to contact him in his office. I told him I would. He then advised me to bring Corporal Brown, who was my corporal, with me when I came to his office.

I really did not give it much thought. The chief was always calling the supervisors into his office for one thing or another. It was just sort of routine. Halsted's demeanor on this particular day was out of the ordinary. He was acting overly friendly. He had somewhat of a smile on his face and his voice did not have that stern harshness in it as it had over the last year. I still did not see the warning signs. I thought he was just in a good mood for one reason or another.

I went into the sergeant's office and prepared the assignments for my shift. The deputies came in and assembled. I conducted line up, passing out shift and area assignments, never realizing it was the last line up I would ever conduct. After getting my deputies out on the road to their respective areas, I contacted Corporal Brown and advised him the chief wanted to see us in his office. Corporal Brown and I then walked down to the chief's office.

The door to the chief's office was open, we walked into the office and found the chief sitting at his desk. He once again appeared friendly, in fact, overly friendly. He even seemed rather happy and excited. It struck me as odd, something just wasn't right about the situation. Chief Halsted got up from his desk and greeted us with a kind of a smirk of a smile on his face. He advised us to have a seat and motioned over to where two chairs had been positioned in front of his desk. Normally there were not chairs sitting in that location. It was as if the chairs were set up just for our meeting. Halsted then walked over and closed the door, as Corporal Brown and I went over and sat down. The chief then returned to his desk and sat down. He put his elbows on the desk and folded his hands together. He then seemed to take a deep breath and stare right at me. There was what felt like a long pause and the room filled with a piercing silence. I was not feeling comfortable about this so called meeting. I was only now just starting to realize that something was up, and it was not in my best interest.

Chief Halsted reached across his desk and picked up an envelope and handed it to me. He had a glitter in his eyes, and it appeared that he was trying to restrain himself from smiling. I was beginning to get uncomfortably nervous, but I still did not have a clue as to what was about to transpire. I took the envelope from him. His voice rang out in a loud and abrupt echo.

"Open it now and read it."

I looked at the chief. He was staring at me. There was no emotion on his face. Just a sternest that sent a chill down my spine. I opened the letter, my hands were beginning to tremble as I read the bold print that caught my eyes.

"YOU ARE HEREBY SUSPENDED PENDING AN INTERNAL AFFAIR'S INVESTIGATION INTO YOUR BEHAVIOR AND MISCONDUCT."

It took every ounce of my self control to maintain my composure. I was taken aback, caught completely off guard. Totally surprised. I could feel my face flushing as my insides began to tremor. My hands felt like they were shaking. I took a deep breath, while attempting to maintain control.

Chief Halsted's demeanor had suddenly changed turning cold. He had a chilling tone in his voice as he yelled:

"Well, read the letter. Read it now."

I looked back down at the letter and began to read. It read.

"You are at this time relieved of duty, pending an internal affair's investigation for dismissal. The charges against you are as follows:

#1. Possession of unauthorized documents.
#2. Illegal tape recording of Undersheriff Deiter
#3. Failure to report sexual harassment, reference Deputy Willis case.

You will surrender your "Police Commission" card, keys to the office, your patrol vehicle, service revolver, and all items that belong to the sheriff's department at this time. You are no longer a law enforcement officer and will not conduct yourself as a "Law Enforcement Officer" from this point on."

I finished reading the letter. I was shaking inside but tried not to let it show. I looked up at the chief. Chief Halsted was staring at me. He remarked:

"Well, you read the letter. Give me your commission card and keys to the office."

I guess that I did not respond fast enough to his demands. I was taken back by it all. I just stared back at him.

Chief Halsted began to yell, this time getting in my face,

"Well," he said. "Don't you have a commission card?"

The chief getting into my face and yelling must have jolted me back to reality. I asked him, "What, what did you say?"

Chief Halsted, yelled even louder. "Don't you have a commission card?"

I said, "Yes I have a commission card."

Chief Halsted demanded that I turn over my commission card to him. I reached into my wallet and pulled out my commission card and handed it to him.

"Now the keys to the office. Give me your keys. I need your keys now."

Chief Halsted's demeanor was becoming very excitable. It was as if he was getting off on bring me down and stripping me of my police powers.

I took my keys out of my pocket and removed the office keys from the key ring and handed them to him. He smiled, as he sat back in his chair and stared at me. It seemed as if we just sat there staring at each other for a rather long period of time, but it was probably only seconds. Chief Halsted then opened his mouth and began to speak in a demanding tone.

"I'll take your service revolver and badge. Give them to me now."

It was obvious to me that he was getting great pleasure at my expense throughout this entire ordeal. I was barely keeping it together, fighting my emotions. I was not about to give him the satisfaction that he was tearing me down. Halsted was taking his sweet time, dragging out the process and enjoying every second of my agony. I wasn't about to lose my temper and kick the living shit out of him, even though I really wanted to reach across his desk and sweep the floor with that sick smile of his.

The stares back and forth between the two of us were deadly, to say the least. The reality of the moment was being screamed back and forth between us with our eyes in the midst of the silence. I guess my adrenalin kicked in, and everything slowed to a point of articulation. I began to get my confidence up and take control of my emotions. I was no longer nervous or intimidated by Halsted's actions.

I handed the chief my service revolver and police badge.

Chief Halsted then advised:

"You are no longer a law enforcement officer. You have no police powers and furthermore, you are not welcome around the sheriff's office or any of the substations. You are to have no contact with any of the deputies nor with the employee of the Cen. Com. office. You are not to call the sheriff's office or Cen. Com. for any reason. Do you understand what I am telling you?"

I looked at him and remarked:

"I do not see a restraining order attached to this letter of suspension. I believe you are out of line and violating my civil rights. I will not tolerate such behavior."

Chief Halsted jumped up from his seat. His demeanor changed and he began to stutter. He was not prepared for my response. He acted defensively as if he felt he lost control of the situation. He responded with:

"You, you heard me, you do what, what I tell you to do. You're not welcome here. We, we don't want to see your face. You stay away and leave us alone. That's it. We're done. Corporal Brown will escort you around the office so that you can pick up your personal items and, and then, He'll, he'll give you a ride home."

"We're done, get out of my office. I want you to leave. Leave now, we're done, get out."

I walked out of the chief's office with kind of a smile on my face. Not that I was not upset and devastated by the letter and the action of the administration, but rather because even with the ball in the chief's court, I got the best of him. I did not allow him to get to me. All of his attempts at destroying me failed. In the end he was the one that lost control and he came to realize that he could not destroy my spirit. It was not over yet and he knew it. I think when I walked out of his office he was the one that actually felt intimidated, and he realized that they had made a vast mistake in their dealing with me. He knew I was not going to tolerate it, and was not going down without a fight. I also believe that he was acutely aware that their actions were wrong and that they were violating my rights. He knew it was going to come back around on them because I was not going to let go.

Corporal Brown escorted me around the office while I picked up my personal belongings, he was very quiet and never said a word. It was obvious that he was upset over what was happening. He then gave me a ride to my residence. It would be the last time I would ever ride in a police car. Just prior to arriving at my residence, I asked him to pull over to the side of the road. He pulled over onto the shoulder of the roadway and stopped the car. I asked him if he had read the letter that the chief had given to me. He advised me that he had not. I handed him the letter. He read it and then handed it back to me. He looked genuinely sad. He remarked that he was sorry that this was happening to me. He did not know what to say. I advised him that I had done nothing wrong, and this entire situation including my suspension was not right. He shook his head, and once again stated he was sorry this was happening to me. I told him that I understood his feelings. We then proceeded to my residence.

As we drove up my driveway, my wife was out in the driveway. There were eight or nine young children standing in the driveway singing Christmas carols to her. The neighborhood children had gotten together and gone around the neighborhood singing carols. They just happened to be at my house when I arrived escorted home. Sherry looked up at me. She had a concerned and curious look on her face. She was wondering what I was doing home and why I had been driven home instead of driving my own patrol car. I got out of Corporal Brown's vehicle. He wished me luck. Then backed his patrol car down the driveway and departed.

I was unable to talk to my wife. The children were singing Christmas carols to her. I stood next to my wife and listened to the children singing. I tried to listen intently and with pleasure to the children singing. My mind wasn't into it. I tried not to let it show. Sherry and I kept making eye contact. I could read the concern on her face. It was obvious she wasn't listening to the Christmas carols either. We both just stood trying to be polite, and acting like we were enjoying the children's singing. They were very good and in other circumstances we would have really enjoyed listening to them.

It seemed like the singing lasted forever. The kids finally finished their last song, we thanked them, praised them and they departed.

Sherry and I went into the house, and I told her what had happened. She was very supportive and I believe even more upset and angry at the Sheriff and his administration than I was. After we talked for a while, I called my attorney. Randy was in his office and I was able to reach him right away. I briefed him as to what had transpired. He seemed very concerned. He reminded me that when I first saw him and filed the claim for damages that he told me then that Sheriff Johnston would do everything in his power to destroy my career.

He remarked that frankly, he was surprised I had lasted as long as I did at the sheriff's office. He advised me that he would defend me in the internal affair's investigation. He knew that the charges were all bogus and trumped up to discredit me.

Randy reminded me that I had to realize the internal affairs investigation was an in-house investigation. Sheriff Johnston appoints whomever he wants to conduct the investigation and then the final determination of my guilt or innocense is made by Sheriff Johnston and Undersheriff Deiter.

He advised that he was certain they had already found me guilty or Johnston would not have ordered the internal investigation in the first place.

Randy advised that the reality is that they are setting me up to fire me. I made an appointment to see Randy at his office in the morning.

That night was one of the longest nights of my entire life. I could not sleep. My mind just would not shut down. I felt helpless. I kept analyzing my situation, attempting to determine what I should do or what I should not do. I kept searching for some sort of solution, a solution that would save my job. I not only loved my job, I needed it to survive and pay my bills. I was at a complete loss. I knew the fact was that I was going to be fired. I tossed and turned all night long going over and over everything without coming up with anything solid or positive that would give me some sort of relief. Morning finally arrived. I was exhausted but happy the night was over.

I arrived at Randy's office around 9:00 a.m. Randy greeted me with a cup of coffee as I walked in. It tasted good. I needed the coffee, not to mention his positive, cheerful demeanor. We sat in his office and began to go over the charges cited against me in the internal affair's investigation. Randy advised me that he had already been on the phone with Ms. Pitts from the prosecutor's office. She not only represents the sheriff's office on civil cases, but also represents them as an advisor in disciplinary and civil service matters. He told her he was representing me in the internal affair's investigation. She then gave him some insight into the charges against me. As we went over the charges, Randy briefed me as to where they were coming from. We took each charge against me, one at a time. Randy began. The first charge is:

#1. Possession of unauthorized documents:

"This charge stems from the documents and variety of papers that you turned over in "Discovery," in your lawsuit against Sheriff Johnston and his administration. It includes all the evidence that was turned over to the FBI as well. Sheriff Johnston contends that it was illegal and violates departmental policy for you to have possessed these documents. He further is accusing you of resorting to illegal means to have obtained some of these documents. They are implying that the only way you could have gotten these documents would have been to break into their respective offices and steal them."

I interrupted Randy:

"Well, that's bull shit, I never broke into anyone's office and all the documents and papers that I received, I turned over to you. And as far as discovery goes, you turned in all the stuff that you felt could be evidence in the case and a lot of it you collected from people. I didn't, and I never possessed a lot of those documents."

"It's okay, It's okay," Randy responded.

"Let me continue. There's no sense to get all worked up about it. I was getting to that. It is all bull shit. They do not have a case against you for possessing unauthorized documents. Even if you were in possession of anything that could be labeled unauthorized it would fall under an exception called "evidence," but the fact remains, that you were not. Any documents that you received anonymously, you immediately turned over to me as evidence. The majority of the documents they are referring to under this charge were directly turned over to me, and not you. I maintained the documents as evidence in your case, not you."

"Now lets go on."

Randy stated, as he began to read the second charge against me.

#2. Illegal tape recording:

"This charge is in reference to your answering machine inadvertently recording the conversation between you and Undersheriff Deiter."

Randy went on to say that the administration did not have a case against me for this charge. Then he proceeded to explain why. He advised, that first of all, the recording was not made intentionally. Secondly, I had no knowledge the conversation was being recorded at the time of the recording. And thirdly, as soon as I discovered that the conversation had been recorded, I notified him.

Randy stopped for a moment and paused. He then advised that Sheriff Johnston intended to hold an in-house internal affair's investigation against me on the first and third charges listed. The second charge, the illegal tape recording, Johnston plans on sending to another county, to have a prosecutor criminally charge me. He advised I have nothing to worry about concerning the illegal tape recording, no prosecutor will ever charge me. They can't, in order to charge a person with a crime by state law, you have to show intent. There was no intent to break any laws and therefore there is no violation of the law.

Randy continued:

"You did not know the answering machine did not shut off. The recording was done without your knowledge and as soon as you discovered that the conversation had been recorded, you notified me. I instructed you to turn the tape recording over to me. It was possible evidence. It would have been illegal to destroy it.

They have no case against you. This charge would not hold up in any court. The prosecutor that will be handling this charge will realize this, and you will never be charged."

"Now lets go on to the third charge,"
Randy remarked.

> #3. Failure to report sexual Harassment reference to Deputy Willis Randy shook his head, and a smile grew across his face.

"This charge is the most unbelievable of them all. I just can't believe they would be so stupid as to try and charge you in regards to Deputy Willis, when they in fact tried continuously to intimidate you into signing a false affidavit."

Randy stated "we have copies of all six of the affidavits that they tried to get you to sign. Each one of them shows that they tried to cover up the truth, but you refused to be part of their lies. We also have Capt. Hill, who will testify that they tried to get him to lie on an affidavit as well. The captain will also testify that you made certain that he was aware of Deputy Willis's complaints. They have no case against you. We can stick this one right down their throats and they'll regret that they ever mentioned it."

Randy stopped talking, and sat back in his chair. He put his hands up to the back of his head, folding his fingers together. He paused and a serious look grew on is face. Silence filled the room as I waited in anticipation of his next words.

"The reality of the situation," he stated, and then he stopped.

I was on the edge of my seat waiting to hear what he had to say. My life, my career, was on the line and I was depending on

Randy to protect my future. He finally, after a moment, continued, repeating himself.

"The reality of the situation, is that Sheriff Johnston was going to appoint the internal affair's investigation to one of his "yes" men to investigate. They will give the appearance that it is being conducted in a fair and impartial manner. The fact of the matter is that there will not be a fair investigation. They will determine you are in fact, guilty, and then they will fire you. The entire matter, from the letter you were given stating that you are currently suspended while they investigated you for termination, implies their intent."

I was taken back. I knew what Randy was saying, was true. I thought the same thing myself. It's different, though, thinking something, and the reality of actually hearing the spoken words.

Randy then advised:

"On the positive note, when that happens, we will take the matter to court to appeal their ruling and we will win in court.

There is not a judge in the land that will not be able to see through their bull shit. However, on the down side of the situation; you will be out of a job. You will have no income for anywhere from six months to a year, until we can get your case in front of a Judge."

Randy could read the look on my face. I was devastated. He knew that I needed my income to survive. He could see the despair in my eyes. I just sat there. The entire situation had gotten completely out of control. I did not know what to do or where any of this was going. I originally filed the claim for damages in an attempt to protect my job. The entire situation just escalated beyond belief. Now, not only was I in danger of losing my career, but I also was facing the possibility of criminal charges being filed against me.

Randy stated:

"I got an idea. Do you have any physical injuries that would be considered disabling in nature? If you do, you should apply for disability retirement. If you apply for disability retirement, you are automatically given six months disability leave while the state board investigates your claim for retirement. Once the state puts you on disability leave status you fall under state control. Sheriff Johnston would not be able to fire you. He could not do anything to you during the six months leave status. After the six months are over, if your retirement is approved, Johnston still would not be able to touch you. However, if the state board did not grant your retirement after the six months, then you would go back under Sheriff Johnston's control."

Randy paused again for a moment and then continued.

"I realize you do not want your career to end, but frankly I do not believe you have a choice. It is out of your hands. You now have to think about protecting some sort of income for yourself, and I think retirement would be the way to go, provided you have a legitimate disability that would entitle you to retirement."

Randy shook his head, a frown grew across his face as he stared right into my eyes. He remarked, with concern in his voice:

"You need to realize your career is over; even it you beat these charges against you, it will only be a matter of time until other charges are trumped up against you. Sheriff Johnston will eventually get rid of you. He and his administration will, one way or another, destroy your reputation and fire you. The reality of the matter is there is nothing that you can do about it. If you continue to work for Johnston you will lose."

Randy didn't cut me any slack. He called a spade a spade. I did not like hearing what he had to say, but I appreciated his concern and straight forwardness. I really didn't have to think about what he was saying. He was right. I knew it in my heart and soul.

I advised Randy that a few years back, a drunk driver hit my patrol car while I was sitting in the vehicle writing up an accident investigation. The vehicle made impact with my patrol car at sixty plus miles per hour while I was parked on the side of the roadway. It destroyed my patrol vehicle and sent me to the hospital. I was out of work for nine months recovering from head, neck and back injuries. The accident left me with 41% hearing loss in both ears and chronic back problems.

Randy remarked:

"Well, that's great . . . "

I looked at him with a rather disapproving look upon my face. Randy said.

"Well, what I mean to say is, that is your disability. You can apply for a duty related disability. I'll draw up the paper work and we can apply immediately before Sheriff Johnston has an opportunity to proceed with firing you."

Randy explained to me the procedure for applying for disability. He advised, first, you apply for disability before the local state board. They review your request at a hearing. If they feel you have a valid claim, they automatically put you on six months disability leave. During the six months disability leave, they will send you to their state doctors to evaluate your medical condition and claim. At the end of the six months, the local board will have another hearing to determine if you are in fact disabled. The determining factor the board will look at is if you can perform your current position with average efficiency. If the board decides you cannot perform your duties with average efficiency, then they will grant you permanent disability. On disability retirement, you will receive 50% of your base pay every month for life.

Randy remarked and repeated himself:

"The best part of it is that as soon as the local board approves your disability leave, you will fall under state control. The sheriff will not be able to fire you."

Randy advised:

"Sheriff Johnston will most likely continue with the internal affair's investigation against you while you're on disability leave, so if you're not successful in getting the state to grant you disability retirement at the end of the six months, then he will be able to fire you."

I had mixed feelings. I did not want my career to end, but realized that I really had no choice. The only possibility I had to prevent a total loss of income was to go for the disability.

I told Randy my feelings, and then I told him I would go for the disability.

Randy advised he would prepare the paper work and we could present it to the retirement board at their next scheduled meeting. He looked up the next meeting and advised me that the next local retirement board meeting was scheduled for December 21, 1995.

Randy and I spent the rest of the morning going over my case. We spent time working to prepare my civil case for trial, and also working to set up a file for the disability board hearing.

Randy kept me busy, giving me research work to do on the case. It was good for me. It helped to keep my mind off of my problems and focus on something positive. Around two in the afternoon, we broke for lunch. Randy insisted on paying, and took me to a fancy restaurant located in the downtown section of town. At lunch we talked about a variety of subjects. He took my mind off the sheriff's office and my problems. I needed the relief. The day went by rather quickly. I arrived at my residence later that night with a new outlook and a positive focus that things were going to work out. There still were a lot of uncertainties, but I was confident. I had a positive attitude, and no longer was just feeling sorry for myself.

CHAPTER NINE

SURVIVAL COMES IN MANY FORMS. IT CAN BE A DIFFICULT TASK, OR AS SIMPLE AS CHOOSING THE PROPER PATH.

On December 21, 1995, Randy and I went to the disability board hearing. Randy presented my disability case to the board and I was granted six months disability leave. I still have mixed feelings over applying for disability, but felt genuinely relieved that I was guaranteed an income for the next six months.

I would be able to financially survive as I pursued my fight of injustice, masterminded by Sheriff Johnston.

Randy and I were unaware that while we were attending the disability board meeting, Sheriff Johnston was busy striking out again. This time the focus of his attention was Capt. Hill.

Capt. Hill was called into Chief Halsted's office. He was given a letter of suspension, relieved of duty and advised that he was the subject of an internal affair's investigation for termination.

Capt. Hill was charge with:

"#1. Possession of unauthorized documents.
#2. Failure to report sexual harassment, reference to Deputy Willis
#3. Misconduct and inappropriate behavior in regards to failing to report incidents to the Sheriff."

Capt. Hill was required to turn in his police badge, service revolver, and other police equipment. Then, like myself, he was escorted around the office while he retrieved his personal belongings and then transported to his residence.

Later that day, I was contacted by Capt. Hill. He was devastated. He advised me that he now realized exactly how I felt and what exactly I was going through, especially since it happened to him. I put him in touch with my attorney, advising him that I trusted Randy and felt he would be able to assist him with his problems. We both agreed the entire situation was wrong and we needed to stand together and fight. We had no other choice at this point in time. We did not want to face it, let alone believe it, but the reality was that Capt. Hill's career as well as my own, was over.

Right after the first of the new year, Randy called me up on the phone. He had some interesting and rather disturbing information that he had learned. He did not want to discuss it over the phone, so we arranged to meet at a local restaurant. I met with Randy about an hour later. We sat down and had some coffee. He looked tired, rather worn out, like he had been overworking himself. We engaged in small talk for a brief period and then he focused on the information he had learned.

"You remember that guy that one of your deputies shot and killed a few months back?" Randy asked "A Samuel T. Irving, was his name."

"Yes, I remember him" I remarked.

Randy continued "Well I received information today that he was also one of the two people that took shots at you in the alley. It's really too much of a coincidence, don't you think? I mean this guy Irving shoots at you two different times, and in two different locations, in a very short time frame."

I nodded my head,

"Yes, that is very interesting. Tell me more; who was the other guy? What else have you learned? Continue, tell me more."

Randy advised me that there was more. He began to tell me about the person that had contacted him, earlier today. He stated that:

"This guy told me that Sam Irving was a drug dealer, and that Irving worked for Sheriff Johnston's nephew Tom, selling drugs. Apparently Johnston arranged through Tom to hire Irving and this other guy, to have you killed. They were to be paid two kilos of cocaine after they completed the job and you were dead.

It was no accident that you were being followed, nor that the prowler call came out. They made the call to Cen. Com. to lure you into the alley to eliminate you."

Randy continued, stating that "The disturbance call you responded to, where Irving was killed, was a set up to kill you as well."

Randy then told me to just think about it, advising that no one could figure out how Irving got to the location or for that matter, why he stuck around after the cops arrived.

Randy advised:

"According to this informant that came forward, there was a second subject with Irving. This second guy was parked on a parallel road located a couple of hundred yards through the woods from the scene of the shooting. This guy was waiting in the get away car for Irving to return. Irving did not leave because he wanted the cops to show up and knew you were the supervisor on duty and would respond. He lay in wait in the darkness for you and your officers to arrive so he could shoot you. The first shots fired were intended to kill you."

Randy paused, then he remarked.

"It makes sense. It explains why Irving stuck around, and did not flee the scene when you and your deputies arrived. Irving most likely felt he could shoot you, and then escape in the darkness through the woods to where the other guy with the car was waiting for him. His plan got spoiled when he missed you, and then you had the deputies set up containment, eliminating his escape route."

I shook my head in amazement and disbelief. The realization hit me, Sheriff Johnston was extremely dangerous; more so than I ever imagined. I could feel my body shaking from the inside out. Randy went on "I think, this guy that came to me, well, I think he was the second guy in the alley, and most likely the guy that was waiting in the get away car the night Irving was killed. He never said it, but I got that impression. He told me he was Irving's roommate, but he would not give me his name. He advised me that if Johnston found out he was talking to me, he would be dead. He then remarked that he was getting out of town: if he did not get out soon, he would be a dead man."

Randy told me that this guy refused to put anything he knew in writing and also refused to allow the conversation to be tape recorded. He explained to Randy the only reason he came forward was because he guessed his conscience was bothering him and he wanted to warn us that Johnston was serious about killing anyone who got in his way.

He advised Randy to be careful and to warn me of the serious nature of the situation.

Randy then stopped and looked at me. "You know what this means, what it implies don't you?"

Randy asked.

He caught me off guard, and I really did not know what he was talking about.

I replied,

"No, what do you mean?"

Randy stated,

"Well, it means everything we've learned about Sheriff Johnston being involved in setting up the triple homicide on Trinity Island to his involvement in drugs is probably true. It means that he is a very dangerous person and that our lives, especially yours, is in danger."

I asked Randy if we would be able to use this information he just learned against Sheriff Johnston. He hesitated for a moment and advised that we probably would not, at least the way it stood now. He advised that he was going to get in contact with Jason Bolton at the FBI office and advise him of the new information. The FBI might be able to identify the subject that contacted him, and possibly they can develop a case against Sheriff Johnston from the information.

Randy said "We'll just have to wait and see. In the mean time, be careful and practice extreme caution. Remember, we are playing for keeps and our lives are at risk."

Randy and I spent another hour or so at the restaurant just talking. The entire situation seemed unbelievable, like something out of a movie. It just did not seem real. I had trouble coming to the realization that Sheriff Johnston was actually trying to have me killed. It was hard to accept, but it made sense: up until this time the incident in the alley, as well as the shooting incident that resulted in Irving's death, had made no sense to me. Now it was all coming together. I needed to talk about it and Randy gave me as much time as I needed. I think he had to talk about it, as well. Neither one of us had ever been in a position like this before. It scared us. It helped both of us to talk it out. I began wearing my bullet proof vest from that point on. I would wear it whenever I went out in public, even if I just ran to the grocery store to pick up some items.

The rest of the month of January, of 1996, was a busy one.

I spent the majority of my time at Randy's office going over my case file, and working on the witness list for the civil trial.

The date of the trial was set for October 1, 1996, in Federal court. Randy was extremely busy working on my case, setting up depositions. He also filed two additional lawsuits in federal court against Sheriff Johnston and his administration. One was on behalf of Capt. Hill and the other was on behalf of retired Det. Doug Botson. Retired Det. Botson had problems with Sheriff Johnston, approximately two years prior to Capt. Hill's and my problems with the sheriff. Botson was forced out of the department by Johnston, and had taken an early retirement. After the media made it publicly known that Capt. Hill and I had filed litigation against

Sheriff Johnston, Botson came forward and decided to pursue legal action against the sheriff as well. Needless to say, I felt reassured about the situation, knowing I was not standing alone.

Capt. Hill, Doug Botson, and I each lent moral support to each other. The three of us were, I guess you would say, working friends or working associates. We all got along well but really were never involved in each other's lives. Our only association with each other was at work. Now, through this ordeal where we all shared similar experiences and treatment from Sheriff Johnston and his administration, we came to rely on each other for encouragement and support. I suppose in looking back, one of the most important things that evolved from all this was the lasting friendship and trusting bond that developed between us.

A couple of days later, Randy advised me that the county had scheduled a mediation hearing. The hearing was set to be heard in front of a mediation judge on January 21, 1996. The procedure was in all Federal court cases. Prior to going to trial you were mandated to have a mediation session. This was designed as an attempt to settle the case out of court, in order to save legal expenses. Randy advised it was to our advantage to go to mediation prior to taking depositions. He told me that when we deposed our witnesses, it would be very costly and the expense would come out of my pocket. If we could settle the case now, we could avoid the cost. Randy also felt it was a good sign that the county requested mediation on behalf of Sheriff Johnston, Undersheriff Deiter and Chief Halsted. There was a possibility that just maybe after receiving all of our evidence in discovery, they have come to realize their liability and want to settle the matter, rather than take it to court. Apparently, either side could request mediation at anytime during the pretrial process. The side requesting the mediation has to pick up the cost of the hearing, so it also saved us money because the county requested the mediation.

On January 21, 1996, at 09:00 a.m., my wife, Randy, and I arrived at the conference room at the county court house for the mediation hearing. Present at the hearing was the presiding Judge,

{Judge Framton}, Sheriff Johnston, Undersheriff Deiter, Chief Halsted, their attorneys, David Custington and Leila Pitts. Also, present were two individuals from the county's risk pool. Neither my wife, Sherry, nor I knew what to expect. We had never been to a mediation hearing before and we were nervous, to say the least. We were both full of apprehension. We felt a little shaky. We complained to each other how we both felt warm, but cold and clammy at the same time. Our stomachs were full of butterflies and tied in knots. We both tried to give an outward appearance of being calm and in control. It was extremely difficult at best.

Sheriff Johnston's attorney, Mr. Custington, gave the opening statement to the judge as the proceedings began. It became obvious from his first few sentences that this case was not going to be settled out of court. Mr. Custington began by stating that this was not a mediation hearing to reach a settlement in this case, but rather a hearing to resolve this case and to have it dismissed. He then advised the judge and all those present that what he was offering, on behalf of his clients, was that if the sergeant and his wife would drop this lawsuit, then Sheriff Johnston would allow the good sergeant to retire.

Mr. Custington paused for a moment and then continued, repeating himself.

"Sheriff Johnston will allow the sergeant to retire and will drop the internal affair's investigation against him if he drops the lawsuit. If the sergeant refuses to drop the lawsuit, then Sheriff Johnston will fight the sergeant's retirement, pursue criminal charges against the sergeant for the illegal tape recording of Undersheriff Deiter, and will also proceed with the in house investigation, the internal affair's investigation to bring about "just cause" to fire the sergeant."

I could not believe the words coming from Mr. Custington's mouth. I was under the impression that "blackmail" was a crime; that "blackmail" was illegal. Yet, as I sat there in this court of law, what I was hearing Mr. Custington state was nothing more than "blackmail." It totally infuriated me. I felt Mr. Custington's statements were both inappropriate and illegal, and I was not going to be intimidated by such improper actions. After all, as far as I was concerned, I was the victim here, and I had done nothing wrong. His statements were not acceptable.

Mr. Custington ended his opening statement by stating:

"The sergeant can drop the lawsuit and walk out of here today knowing he will be granted his retirement, or he can lose everything; the choice is his."

Randy looked over at me. I could see from his eyes that he was as shocked as I was at Mr. Custington's remarks. He was equally upset and not pleased with their tactics. He then got up and gave his opening statement. He advised the presiding judge that this case dealt with an issue of violation of protected speech and the rights of an individual to support the candidate of his own choosing. This is a case of intimidation and retaliation by Sheriff Johnston and his administration against his client. Randy continued highlighting facts and the issues involved which occurred over the last sixteen months. He covered everything that had occurred since October 10, 1994, when Sheriff Johnston had first accused me of going to the media and of going to be Atwater's chief of detectives, on up to the present date. I was impressed with Randy's presentation and demeanor. The Judge had a detailed overview of the problems that I had encountered by the time Randy concluded.

After both sides gave their opening presentation, Judge Framton separated both parties and place us in separate rooms. The judge then kept alternating back and forth between the rooms, listening to each side's demands and attempting to bring about some sort of compromise to settle the case.

I advised the judge that I had never experienced the mediation process before and I was taken back by Mr. Custington's opening statement. I explained to him that in my mind, what Mr. Custington was attempting to do was nothing more than "blackmail" and I did not understand why he as the judge would allow such behavior. Judge Framton explained to me that basically, anything short of physical contact was allowed in a mediation hearing. I shook my head, dismayed that a court proceeding of any type would allow such illegal acts to take place. The mediation process lasted all day. At the end of the day, nothing was settled, nothing was resolved. In fact, the only positive thing that I believe came from it was the fact that the sheriff and his administration came to the realization that I was not going to back down. I was going to see the lawsuit through to the end, no matter what the consequences might be.

The following day, and over the next serval months, I would spend hours upon hours with Randy getting everything in order preparing our case for trial.

First, I met with Randy at his office to go over the witness list for trial. We had over one hundred names on our side, listed as witnesses. The list had to be cut down to approximately twenty-five people. It was explained to me that the list had to be scaled down in order to be able to present our entire case in a three to four weeks of trial. Randy told me that our case would be stronger if we only called our best witnesses and avoided a lot of duplication of testimony. We spent the entire day going over the witnesses, deciding which ones to call and which ones to eliminate. It was a tedious process.

Secondly, we had more than 40,000 documents that we had to get entered as evidence in the case. The documents all had to be organized so that they could be presented in a timely and non-confusing manner. We also needed to pull out those documents that would not be relative to my case. Randy was a gifted speaker, and a sharp attorney when it came to strategy. However, his organizational skills were poor at best, especially when it came to paperwork. All the documents that Randy received, including all the papers and evidence that I turned over to him, were thrown into boxes. There were a total of eight boxes. Each aox was two feet wide by three feet long and approximately one foot tall. They were all full of papers and documents in no particular order. We had to get them organized by time, dates, who they involved, and by importance.

Another thing that we were busy doing was determining whom we were going to call in for depositions, and devising the questions we wanted to ask in the deposition process. Taking depositions was the next step before trial. Depositions are investigative tools each side uses to see exactly what testimonial evidence the other side will have available to them for use in court. The way it worked was that Johnston's attorney, Mr. Custington, would take depositions from the witnesses that we intended to call in the trial. Then Randy would depose Johnston's witnesses.

The trick to depositions is, basically, asking the right questions. If you do not ask the right questions, then you just waste time and money. You have to make certain you cover anything and everything that could be asked of that witness when he or she is called upon to testify in court. Depositions are probably the most expensive part of the lawsuit. It cost approximately $40.00 per hour for the court reporter, and then an additional $3.00 per page for the typed deposition. The average deposition would run between 200 and 300 pages. The cost rises dramatically with each person that you depose.

Randy and I had to decide exactly whom we were going to depose. Then we had to articulate questions to be asked of those we were deposing. It was a tedious process. We kept going over the questions again and again, attempting to insure that we were not leaving out anything of importance. I had been involved in criminal cases throughout my career, but never a civil or constitutional law case; so the entire process was an education for me.

We had until June of 1996, approximately six months to complete the depositions that we wanted to get done. This was a lot of time in one respect, but very little in another. We had to have everything turned in by then. Anything not turned in, most likely would not be allowed in the trial. The process is called "discovery." Discovery is, I guess, letting the Judge and the other side involved in the trial know basically everything and every piece of evidence, both oral testimony and physical evidence, that you intend to submit or attempt to use in the trial. It's designed to allow the other side time to prepare a defense for any evidence that may come up in court. It is not like on T.V., where one side comes up with a surprise witness. In fact, I would dare to say that there actually are very little surprises by the time you get down to the trial. Both sides are acutely aware of the other side's case long before the jury is ever impaneled in the court room. The only real surprises come when you are able to trip up a witness on the stand and turn his testimony around. I did not like the entire process, but had little to say about it. I felt that discovery just gave Sheriff Johnston and his administration time to make excuses and come up with justification for their actions.

Sheriff Johnston and Undersheriff Deiter did not waste anytime following through with Mr. Custington's threats towards me, which he made at the mediation hearing. The first of February of 1996, they scheduled me to be interviewed in regards to the internal affairs investigation they had initiated against me. Randy advised me that since I was on disability leave status, Sheriff Johnston did not have control over me and I did not have to respond to their request to be interviewed. Randy recommended that I cooperate, however, and allow the interview to take place stating, if I cooperated with them and for some reason was unable to be granted my permanent disability retirement, I would have grounds to fight any negative decision they reached in the internal affairs investigation. He further advised me that if I refused to cooperate with the administration, I would not have a case to fight their decision. There is a departmental policy in the sheriff's office that states if you refuse to cooperate with an internal affair's investigation, your refusal is grounds for termination.

I advised Randy that I had no problem with being interviewed and would go along with the internal affairs process, remarking that I had nothing to hide. I knew if the internal affair's investigation was done fairly and honestly, I would be cleared of any and all charges. I also was quite aware that it was a biased investigation and the sheriff had already determined my guilt. Randy just enhanced my feelings by informing me that the internal affair's investigation was just a formality; Sheriff Johnston makes the final decision on guilt or innocence, and he has already decided my fate but had to give the appearance that his actions were justified. He advised that it does not matter, however, we needed to document the fact that I cooperated fully and have nothing to hide, so if necessary we can appeal their decision at a later date.

On February 10, 1996, Randy and I arrived at the county's personnel conference room for my scheduled internal affairs interview. Chief of Detectives, Jim Weatherbee, conducted the interview. My wife, Sherry, came along to give me moral support.

She realized how traumatic the ordeal was for me. She wanted to be by my side to ease the pain.

I found it ironical that Weatherbee was conducting the interview. He was one of Sheriff Johnston's "puppets." He would say or do anything that Johnston wanted without question. He was also one of the detectives that I had trained when he was a "rookie," and first made detectives. Randy and I went into the interview room and sat down. The interview was tape recorded, with my permission. Not that I really had a choice. If I refused to allow them to tape record the interview, they would have declined to continue. They would have advised that I refused to cooperate with the investigation. They would have really liked that, since it would have given them grounds for my termination for failing to cooperate. I had no problem with them recording the interview process; in fact, I wanted it recorded because I did not trust them, and did not want to give them the opportunity to twist my words. I viewed the tape recording of the interview as a positive thing for my own protection.

The interview started out with Detective Weatherbee advising me of my rights. I had advised people of their rights many times over the years that I had been a cop, but I, myself, had never had my rights advised to me. It suddenly gave me a realistic insight of the psychological impact it has on a person when you advise them of their rights. Throughout my career, I never really understood the effect of it, having never been on the receiving end before.

I took a deep breath, and tried to remain in control. It was an emotional experience for me. After twenty-two years as a dedicated police officer, I was sitting there being the accused. The impact of the situation made me physically sick. I focused on my belief that the truth would be the driving force and we would win in the end. I was not afraid of the interview nor of the line of questioning, but I was not exactly comfortable being there. I kept wondering if the truth would make any difference.

Chief Weatherbee began by questioning me concerning the documents that went to the FBI. I advised him that I did not know exactly what all the documents were that went to the FBI. He wanted me to identify each and every document. I told him I could not do that because I did not know each and every document that went to the FBI. He was very persistent. He showed me a specific document, such as Sheriff Johnston's expense ledger. He asked me if I ever possessed that particular document for each document that he showed me. I answered each question as accurately as I could. The majority of the papers that Chief Weatherbee showed me, I never had in my possession. I had however seen many of those same documents in the packet that went to the FBI.

Weatherbee then questioned me as to whether or not I ever broke into Sheriff Johnston's or Undersheriff Deiter's offices and stole papers. I advised him that I never broke into anyone's office, nor have I ever been involved in criminal activity.

I tried to explain to Chief Weatherbee that after my problems started with Sheriff Johnston, I began receiving documents anonymously and every document that I received I turned over to my attorney. He really did not want to hear anything that I had to say. He was focused on the questions he had prepared. The questions were all typed out and seemed to follow a sequence. He was very careful not to stray from the order that the questions appeared to be in his folder. It made me wonder who prepared the questions for Weatherbee.

He continued to ask me detailed questions concerning specific documents. The process lasted for hours. Finally, Weatherbee was done with the questions concerning the documents and we were given a break. Randy advised me, during the break, that I was doing fine. He thought that things were going well and I was doing a good job. He informed me that he got the impression that the entire process was nothing more than a fishing trip whereby they were attempting to learn if the FBI had more information than the administration was aware of. He remarked that they do not have anything on me, nothing substantial that they could use to fire me. I was upset and disturbed over the fact that here I was the victim in this entire ordeal and yet I was the one that was being treated like a criminal. I pointed this fact out to Randy, and he reminded me that ever since I initiated the complaint against Sheriff Johnston, I have been treated as the suspect. I agreed with him and said that was my point. He explained to me that their only defense was to try and make me out to be the bad guy. They had no real defense for their actions and they knew it.

The interview started back up again with Weatherbee reminding me that I had been advised of my rights and that the interview was being taped recorded.

I thought to myself, "Like I had to be reminded."

I guess I was developing a bit of an attitude over being put through the whole thing. Chief Weatherbee then questioned me concerning the answering machine recording of my conversation with Undersheriff Deiter which had occurred back in October of 1994. I was accused of knowingly making the tape recording. I advised that I was not aware that the conversation was being recorded until sometime afterwards when I discovered the recording on my answering machine. I was asked why, when I discovered the recording, I did not notify the Undersheriff that I had the recording. I stated that I did not say anything on the advice of my attorney.

During the course of the interview, Weatherbee kept referring to the recording as the "illegal recording of Undersheriff Deiter."

He continuously attempted to get me to acknowledge that it was an illegal recording. I refused to acknowledge that it was an illegal recording. I kept repeating that it was an inadvertent recording picked up on my answering machine without my knowledge.

Chief Weatherbee asked other questions of me concerning the recording, and finally informed me that a prosecutor would make the final determination as to whether or not I would be charged criminally with making an illegal recording.

The last segment of the internal affair's interview consisted of Chief Weatherbee questioning me concerning Deputy Teri Willis's sexual harassment complaint. Weatherbee started his line of questioning by asking me,

"You did not report the sexual harassment complaint reported to you by Deputy Willis, did you?"

I answered the questioned, telling him,

"My supervisors were made aware of the complaint."

I stated that I made certain Capt. Hill was made aware of the complaint and he had informed me that Chief Halsted also had been told of Deputy Willis's complaint.

All of the pre written questions Chief Weatherbee had, were worded in such a way as to try to trick me into incriminating myself and admitting that I did something wrong. It was obvious from the line of questioning that the focus of the investigation was not to determine the truth of the matter but rather to gain evidence that they could use against me.

The day, and the questioning, finally came to an end. It was over and we departed. Randy shook his head as we walked down the steps from the personnel building.

He remarked:

"The day was nothing more than a waste of time, a fishing trip, whereby they were trying to trap you into saying something that they could use against you. Just bull shit."

Randy looked at me, and continued:

"You know that dimwit Weatherbee didn't prepare those questions. You know Custington prepared the questions don't you?

This was nothing more than a set up, an attempt to trap you. You didn't let them do that; you did a good job."

Randy then repeated that I did well, and that they had nothing. He then reached over and put his hand on my shoulder and advised: "But they are going to find you guilty and fire you anyway."

I looked over at him but did not say a word. I did not have to. Randy knew exactly how I felt about this entire situation.

I was at least relieved that the internal affair's interviews were over. I did not want to have to go through that again. It was not fun.

CHAPTER TEN

FEAR IS A STRONG MOTIVATOR OF COURAGE, FOR LIFE IS FRAGILE AND MUST BE PROTECTED.

About a week later, I received a call from Randy. It was around 8:00 p.m., on a Wednesday night. He was rather excited. He told me that he just got off the phone with Holly Hunt. She called him, requesting to meet with him. She wanted to see him right away. Randy said she sounded scared and very nervous. She told Randy she was now willing to come forward and tell him everything she knew about Sheriff Johnston, including his involvement in drugs and crimes of violence.

It had been approximately one year since the first time Holly Hunt had come forward with information about the triple homicide on Trinity Island. She had refused to become directly involved or give Randy any written or recorded statement at that time. Now she was telling Randy she had proof that Sheriff Johnston was involved. She needed to see him in person, and did not want to go over any of the details on the phone. Randy made arrangements to meet with her at a roadside rest area. It was an out of the way little rest stop, just to the north of town. She told Randy she had some documents and photos that he could use as evidence against the sheriff. She was afraid to meet Randy in a public place, saying she thought she was being watched. She did not want it to get back to Sheriff Johnston that she was talking to Randy. Arrangements were made for Randy to meet with Holly around 9:00 p.m.

    I asked Randy if he wanted me to go with him. He advised that Holly sounded like she was on the up and up, but you never knew. He remarked, it could be a set up and he would not mind having company if I wanted to go with him. I told him to swing by and pick me up. Randy arrived at my residence about ten minutes later and we headed out to the rest area.

We arrived at the rest area just before 9:00 p.m. It was a dark and rather isolated place. There was absolutely no one around. Randy and I looked at each other. We each knew exactly what the other was thinking; this was the perfect place for a set up. Randy backed his pick-up truck into a corner of the parking lot, allowing us to view the ingress and egress of the entire parking area. We were both feeling a little apprehensive as we sat there in the darkness waiting for Holly's arrival.

    Randy began to tell me that when he talked to Holly on the phone, she told him that she feared for her life and needed protection. She wanted out of the drug scene before it was too late. She told him that last year when she spoke with him, she did not tell him everything, and recently she was at the wrong place at the wrong time. She overheard a conversation that she should not have heard. Her voice was breaking on the phone and she sounded shaken. She related that, as of late, she has noticed vehicles following her and she believed her phone was bugged. Holly insisted that Randy supply her with protection if she came forward with the information she had.

    Randy told me he planned to talk with Holly to determine if she was just blowing smoke or if she actually had good information. He remarked how you can never tell with drug users whether what they have is real or just their own paranoia setting in. The fact is, many times drug users read more into a situation than actually exists. You just have to evaluate the information and determine for yourself whether or nor it appears legitimate. There is a term that law enforcement and drug dealers alike use to describe drug users who go off the edge of reality and fall into their own paranoia. It's called "Tweekin," and those that "Tweek" are referred to as "Tweekers." Until we actually talked with Holly and evaluated the information she had, there was no way of determining its value. Both Randy and I were anxious for Holly to arrive and hear exactly what she had to say.

Randy advised me that his plan was to find out what Holly knew and get it down on a tape recorder. Then, if he thought it was good information, he planned to hide Holly somewhere for the night, until he could get in contact with Jason Bolton at the FBI office in the morning.

He was hopeful. The information and evidence that Holly said she had, were good. It would be a break in our case against Sheriff Johnston; not that it had anything directly to do with our case other than the fact that anything that showed the true demeanor of the sheriff helped our case.

Nine p.m. came and went. Holly never showed. Nine thirty p.m., Randy tried calling Holly at her residence. There was no answer. Ten p.m., still no show. Randy kept trying to reach her on his cell phone. There was no answer. By ten thirty p.m., we were getting impatient. We decided to run by Holly's residence to check on her. Randy feared something was wrong. Holly was very insistent to see him right away. It did not make sense to us for her not to show. Randy did not believe that in her current state of mind, she would have just backed out.

As we were pulling out of the rest area, Randy stopped the vehicle and slapped his hands down onto the steering wheel. He had just remembered that he only had Holly's phone number: she had moved. He did not know the location of her new residence.

It was decided that we would return to our homes and wait for Holly to contact Randy. In the meantime, Randy would continue to attempt to reach Holly by phone. We assumed Holly most likely had gotten "cold feet" and changed her mind about giving Randy the information she had on Sheriff Johnston. We were both disappointed she hadn't come when Randy dropped me off at my residence. There was nothing we could do about it and we joked that at least it was not a set up and we were still alive.

The next day, around mid morning, I received a call from Randy. I could tell by the tone of his voice that he was excited and extremely upset.

"You're not going to believe this."

"What's that?" I inquired.

The phone went quiet. There was a long pause.

"What is it Randy?"

Randy responded:

"I just learned that Holly Hunt was killed last night. She died when her car went over an embankment then rolled and caught fire. It was a one car accident and she was the only one involved."

He paused again and then continued. "Apparently while she was driving to meet with us last night, is when the accident occurred. The vehicle was totally destroyed by fire, and dental records will have to be checked to determine for sure if the body found at the scene is actually Holly. The vehicle registration indicates that it was her car and I'm rather certain it was she in the car."

Randy then remarked:

"And here's the kicker. You won't believe this. It's just too coincidental. Sheriff Johnston was supposedly out driving about last night in his patrol car. He is the one that came across the scene of the accident and called it in. Can you believe that? It's unreal. Oh Wow, what have we got ourselves in the middle of here? You know, when I talked to Holly on the phone last night, she said that she was in fear of her life. Her demeanor was, I mean she was scared. This is too much to be merely coincidental. She was murdered. It had to be murder." Randy just kept rambling on. He was in shock over the news of Holly's death. It was also obvious that he was feeling somewhat guilty that he was not able to protect her.

Randy added "I'm just sick. I feel responsible. Maybe, I should have driven directly to Holly's house and picked her up. Maybe I should have gotten the FBI involved as soon as she called. I just don't know. All I know is she called me up wanting me to protect her. She feared her life was in danger and it really was. I should have done something. I let her down and now she is dead."

I told Randy he was beating himself up over Holly's death and it was not his fault. He did not kill her and he had no way of knowing that her life was in actual and immediate danger. There was nothing he could have done. I also reminded him that Holly did not want him to go to her residence and she picked the location for the meeting.

I was, also, in a bit of shock over hearing of Holly's death. I was even further taken aback by the fact that Sheriff Johnston was supposedly the officer that found the accident scene. It all seemed highly suspicious, to say the least. I was under the same opinion as Randy that Sheriff Johnston was directly involved in Holly's death.

Randy advised me that he would be contacting Jason at the FBI, and updating him as to the information that Holly had told him and the fact she died while en route to meet with us last night. We arranged to meet later on that day to talk. We were both taken aback over Holly's death and the implications involved.

We later learned another interesting fact concerning the accident. It was that Sheriff Johnston called out certain off duty deputies from their residences to assist him in investigating the accident. He did not use the deputies that were on duty working patrol, which would seem to be the logical thing to do. The accident was determined, by Sheriff Johnston, to be a one car over the embankment accident caused by the driver losing control of the vehicle.

An autopsy performed at a later date determined the body was in fact that of Holly Hunt. She had died of a skull fracture caused by a blunt object. It was believed that she possibly hit her head in the accident, which resulted in her death. At least that was the official ruling. We were not buying it: life is never simple, and there are always more questions than answers.

The fact remains, we will never know for sure, nor be able to prove, if Holly was a victim of homicide or just a freak accident. Further, we most likely will never know for certain what proof and evidence Holly had against Sheriff Johnston, or if she even had anything at all. In our own minds, there were no doubts. Holly was murdered and Sheriff Johnston "just happening upon the accident scene" enhanced our feelings he was responsible.

Holly's death served as yet another reminder to all us of the serious nature of the situation we were involved in. Those of us who went to the FBI were convinced Sheriff Johnston would stop at nothing to protect himself and the empire of power he controlled. Over the next couple of days, we noticed that there seemed to be an increase in the amount of times that we were being followed. We also became acutely aware that vehicles were staking out our residences. Surveillance of all the deputies involved seemed to be increased. Capt. Hill, Deputy Farrell, Deputy Tooney, Deputy Willis, and others involved, all observed vehicles following them and staking out their respective houses.

Deputy Willis informed us that one of her neighbors observed a white sedan parked up the hill from her home. It appeared that the subject in the vehicle was pointing what looked like a radar traffic gun at Deputy Willis's residence. It was determined from the neighbor's description that the item being pointed at Willis's residence was more than likely a parabolical microphone. A parabolical microphone is a listening device used to intercept conversations, or what is referred to as an "eavesdropping device."

The same white sedan was observed hanging around all of our houses from time to time over the next couple of weeks. It would show up at different times and always seemed to park in different locations. Interestingly enough, all of the deputies who had their residence staked out, or were followed, were deputies who had gone to the FBI. We concluded that Sheriff Johnston was attempting to determine exactly what we knew and how much evidence we had against him.

Randy advised the FBI of the surveillance that was happening to us. The agent in charge, Jason Bolton, assured Randy that it was not the FBI that was watching us. He also advised Randy that the FBI was still investigating Sheriff Johnston, and they had brought in the D.E.A., Drug Enforcement Administration, to assist them. What exactly they were doing with the investigation, we did not know.

We just did not know for sure who was involved in the surveillance. The FBI really would not tell us even if they were in fact, staking us out. We concluded that Sheriff Johnston was behind the surveillance.

All of us involved became acutely aware of our surroundings.

You might say we were becoming paranoid but I don't believe that would be accurate. Paranoia is based on an illusion and an over active imagination. What we were experiencing was based on the reality of the moment. It was the reality of life and death. We could not afford to be too careful or cautious.

We all began to practice our own security measures. We were very careful of what we talked about on the phone. We never talked about anything important without background music to drown out anyone that might be attempting to eavesdrop with a parabolical microphone. We looked for any vehicles that appeared to be following us and got a license number and basic description of any and all vehicles. We would then compare notes on the cars we thought could have been following us. We wanted to determine if the same vehicle was seen at more than one of our residences. Whenever we needed to meet and talk about something of importance, we always picked a secure location. We would never meet in the same location twice. Security became a part of our daily lives.

The rest of the month of February, as well as March and April of 1996, the days were spent calling in witnesses for the Federal court case against Sheriff Johnston. Depositions were scheduled by both sides. It was a busy three months preparing questions unique to each person being deposed and then taking that person's deposition.

I was called upon by Mr. Custington to be deposed. Mr. Custington's questioning of me under oath through the deposition process lasted five days. Each one of the days consisted of long drawn out hours of question after question.

The deposition process, by design, is where by the opposing attorney asks the witness a series of prepared questions in order to lock the witness into their story, while at the same time attempting to trip the witness up so that they can discredit their testimony. I personally do not like the deposition process and feel that it is in fact an unjust practice and abuse of our justice system. Attorneys claim that the deposition process is an investigative tool and part of the discovery process to get to the truth and the issues involved in the case. Observing Sheriff Johnston's attorney in action, I found the process as a legal means to harass and intimidate the witnesses that were scheduled to testify for me against Sheriff Johnston.

Mr. Custington was an expert in designing questions that would obscure the truth. He would ask a single question, then change the wording just slightly. He would then ask the question again. He would do this over and over again, each time clouding the issue at hand and attempting to destroy the creditablity of the statement made by the witness.

In my own deposition, when Mr. Custington would be questioning me, I would answer each question asked truthfully and decisively. Mr. Custington would then move to have my answer stricken as "non-responsive to the question." I got the distinct impression that it did not matter whether my answer was responsive to the question, the only thing that mattered was whether Mr. Custington liked the answer that I gave.

The days spent in the deposition process were extremely exhausting, both mentally and physically. I went into the process of giving my own deposition with the realization that every question asked of me was a trick question by design. I developed a technique to protect myself while answering the questions asked of me. What I would do was listen to the question asked, then repeat the question silently in my mind analyzing each and every word involved in the question, itself. If there was a word that I did not understand or that had multiple meanings, I would ask Mr. Custington to explain what exactly he meant by the word. Then and only then, after I was satisfied that I understood the question, would I give my answer. I would answer the question as accurately and as briefly as possible making sure to only answer the question that was asked. The more information that you give in your answer, the more "fuel" you give. The more "fuel" you give, the greater the risk that your words will be twisted and used against you.

Mr. Custington continually became very frustrated and sometimes angry, with my articulating his every word. There was nothing, however, that he could do about it. I had the right to understand the question that was asked of me. Once he asked a question he was obligated to explain any segments of the wording that I requested.

I was not extremely pleased with having to give five full days of depositions. Once again just as it had been through this entire ordeal, I was the victim who felt he was being treated more like a suspect than a victim. It did not sit well with me.

All of my witnesses, or I should say a majority of them, were deputies that worked for the sheriff's office. Mr. Custington, being Sheriff Johnston's attorney, had access to all the deputies at their work place. Each deputy that I listed as a witness was ordered in to talk to Mr. Custington prior to giving their individual deposition. The deputies were not given a choice as to whether they wanted to talk to Mr. Custington or not. The interviews were scheduled and they were informed as to what time they were supposed to go for their respective interview. The interviews were designed to intimidate the deputies to the point of believing that their own careers would be in jeopardy if they testified against Sheriff Johnston. Randy and I learned at a later date from one of the sergeants that Mr. Custington told each deputy how to answer the questions asked of that deputy. Mr. Custington even, in some cases, told the deputies exactly what to say in their answers to certain individual questions. Many of the deputies who were fearing retaliation, went along with Mr Custington's advice to them on how to answer questions. They basically, compromised their own morals and values to protect their careers.

There was, however, a group of deputies that refused to be intimidated. These deputies answered each and every question asked of them honestly and non-restrictively. They did not hold anything back and basically told it like it really was. I will always be grateful, and thank God for the courage of those deputies that stood tall and told the truth; without them all would have been lost.

In the interviews that Mr Custington conducted with the deputies, he advised each of them that I was the enemy of the Sheriff's office. He told them, I had "spied" on each and every one of them by taking notes on every conversation I had with them. He also informed them that I kept notes on their actions and interactions within the sheriff's office. He did everything in his power to alienate the deputies against me. Then he would appeal to their sense of loyalty to the sheriff's department and their pride as a law enforcement officer, in an attempt to convince them to testify in the manner he desired. Mr. Custington was successful in some cases in persuading the deputies either out of intimidation or a warped sense of loyalty. I dare say, however, all the deputies, even those that Mr. Custington got to, knew in their hearts and minds exactly what was going on.

I found the deposition process very traumatic and emotionally trying. Each time a deputy denied the truth of an issue or said something to discredit me it hurt. I could not help but to take it personally. I realized now, after all is said and done, that it wasn't about me. Rather, it was about that individual deputy trying to survive as a deputy working for Sheriff Johnston and his administration. I understand why some of the deputies lied and denied the truth. I even understand why some of them made statements to put me down and discredit me. I understand but will never condone their actions, nor do I agree with what they did. I lost all respect for them as individuals and more importantly as law enforcement officers who took an oath to up hold the truth.

Sheriff Johnston developed his power and control over a long period of time. His power grew due directly to the deputies being passive and afraid to speak up when they felt that something was unethical or just wrong. I now know, in order to hold people in authority accountable, you have to speak up and become involved, otherwise you have no one to blame but yourself when that power is abused.

The morning of February 27, 1996, my attorney, Randy took the first of two depositions he would take of Sheriff Johnston. Present in the room for the deposition process was the court reporter, Sheriff Johnston's two attorneys, Mrs. Pitts and Mr. Custington, Randy, and myself.

Sheriff Johnson's deposition lasted about three hours. Randy asked the sheriff questions concerning the October 10, 1994, meeting he had with me. Questions about the anonymous letter of October 19, 1994, that he received. Questions about things the sheriff had told the news media. I took notes on the entire deposition. After the deposition concluded, I found it interesting to discover that Sheriff Johnston answered 104 questions by stating "I don't recall." Just as interesting was the fact that, out of the questions he did recall, we were able to determine that he lied 79 times.

Undersheriff Deiter's deposition was taken on April 9, 1996. He admitted in his deposition that he had a conversation with Capt. Hill in which he mentioned that if Sheriff Johnston did not get reelected he would have lost his job. He told Capt. Hill after the election, and after the sheriff won, that those that supported Atwater now needed to worry about their jobs. Deiter attempted to defend the statement by remarking that Sheriff Johnston could not fire anyone without "just cause." Deiter also answered questions in which he admitted that he was the one who told Capt. Hill that I was going to be Atwater's chief of detectives. He advised he made that up as a joke when he told it to him, and that was what started the rumor that I was going to be Atwater's chief of detectives. Deiter could not remember if he had told that rumor to Sheriff Johnston or not. It infuriated me. This rumor that was destroying my career was nothing more than an irresponsible joke. I could not believe it. I felt sick, as if I had been kicked. My career was sabotaged at the expense of this man's sick humor.

Undersheriff Deiter was then questioned by Randy concerning the conversation that he had with me that got recorded on the answering machine. Deiter admitted that the onset of the conversation began by him talking to the answering machine. He advised that I came on the line and he began talking to me. He just assumed the answering machine shut off, but never gave it a thought. He tried to minimize the damages of the things he actually said. Knowing that it was on tape, he could not deny them so he tried to explain his statements away.

Deiter related that back in 1994, Sheriff Johnston and he made the decision to conduct an internal affair's investigation against me. They also made the decision to suspend me pending the outcome of the investigation. He stated that they made the decision because I made demeaning statements against my supervisors. He further stated the decision was made to suspend me after I filed my claim for damages with the county risk manager, in which I accused the Sheriff and him of misconduct. Randy, asked Undersheriff Deiter who made the decision to conduct an internal affair's investigation and to suspend Capt. Hill and the Sergeant in December of 1995. Deiter said that Sheriff Johnston and he met with Mrs. Pitts and Mr. Custington. They discussed the situation concerning Capt. Hill and myself and what their options would be.

He stated,

"I guess the Sheriff made the decision to suspend them and conduct an internal affair's investigation for termination against them."

Undersheriff Deiter's deposition lasted about four hours. He contradicted statements made by Sheriff Johnston in his deposition—not on key issues, but on items that were still of significance. Deiter admitted, in his deposition, Sheriff Johnston told the news media that I was a disgruntled employee. Johnston on the other hand, in his deposition, denied that he told the press that I was a disgruntled employee. There were a lot of other issues that they contradicted themselves on, as well. Randy said afterwards he was pleased with how the depositions were going so far.

He remarked,

"With each lie we catch Sheriff Johnston and his administration making, it enhances our case against them that much more."

On April 17, 1996, Chief Halsted was called into Randy's office and his deposition was taken. More lies and contractions were told and established between statements made by Sheriff Johnston, Undersheriff Deiter, and Chief Halsted.

In Chief Halsted's deposition, he was questioned concerning his treatment and demeanor toward me during the year of 1995.

He attempted to justify his actions concerning some of the incidents and others he denied ever took place. In many cases he would simply advise that he was just following orders given to him by Sheriff Johnston or Undersheriff Deiter. He basically tried to minimize his involvement.

Randy changed the line of questioning away from me and asked Chief Halsted if he was involved in organized crime. The question took Halsted by surprise. His demeanor changed from bold and rather self-confident, to meek and nervous.

Halsted answered Randy's question with "No, absolutely not."

"Do you have friends that are involved in organized crime?"

"No absolutely not. "Halsted repeated himself. You could see the change in Halsted's demeanor. He looked like a young boy who just got caught with his hand in the cookie jar, and then was trying to deny his involvement. He appeared scared and uncomfortable with Randy's line of questioning, afraid as to where Randy might be leading.

"Do you know Jack Meeker?" Randy inquired.

Chief Halsted paused, as his face turned a bright red.

"Yes."

"Are you and Jack Meeker close friends?" Randy asked.

"No, not really, we just know each other." Halsted remarked.

"Isn't it true that you and Jack Meeker have been friends ever since childhood? Isn't it also true, that whenever Jack comes to town you entertain him and take him out on your yacht?"

Randy began hitting him with one question after another before he had time to react or even answer. It shook Halsted up even more and he began to stutter.

"Well, I mean, you know, we have kind of been friends since grade school. We grew up across the street from each other and used to play together, but we are, well, you know not really close. I, I, don't, I mean not really, I don't entertain him when he comes to town, but yes, I guess, I might have taken him out on my boat once or twice over the years."

Chief Halsted paused, he had figured out where Randy was going with the line of questioning, and he did not like it. His emotions were written all over his face as he began to glare at Randy.

Randy continued with his line of questioning.

"Isn't it also true that you on many occasions went to Texas to visit Jack Meeker and stayed at his residence there?"

Halsted reluctantly answered. "I might have stayed at Jack's place once or twice. I, well I really don't remember. I mean, I did not go there just to see Jack. It would have been like I was passing through and just stopped by, while going some place else, after all, we were childhood friends. Not really friends now, but childhood friends."

Halsted was recovering from Randy's line of questioning and attempting to minimize and rationalize his actions, something that he actually wasn't very good at doing.

"What does Jack Meeker do in Texas?" Randy inquired.

"He's a businessman. He runs small businesses."

Halsted answered.

"What kind of businesses?" Randy came back with.

"Well there, there, Jack runs topless clubs in Texas, Okay?

But, I want you to know he is an honest person and does not go around breaking the law."

"Is Jack Meeker connected to organized crime?" Randy asked.

"No, absolutely not." Halsted answered.

"He is connected to organized crime isn't he?" Randy asked again.

"I don't know that, I don't know that to be true, no." Halsted remarked.

"Isn't it true that the Federal Organized Crime unit, in the past, has investigated Jack Meeker?" Randy inquired.

"I don't know that either." Halsted answered.

"Isn't it also true that the Federal Organized Crime Unit investigated and questioned you concerning your connections with Jack Meeker?"

"Well, I, Well yes, they did." Halsted remarked.

You could tell that these were the questions that he had hoped Randy would never get to and he was upset that Randy was bringing this stuff up.

"So, are you aware that Jack Meeker is connected to organized crime?" Randy asked again.

"No, I don't know that for sure" Halsted reluctantly stated.

"Are you involved in organized crime?" Randy repeated.

"No, I am not."

It was obvious that Chief Halsted was very uncomfortable and at a loss for answers with Randy's line of questioning. Randy dropped the subject of Jack Meeker, and did not ask Halsted any further questions. Randy liked to use the deposition process to determine the demeanor of potential witnesses, as to what buttons to push to bring that person up or down. Knowing the right nerve to hit was a useful tool when it came to court.

There were a lot of other depositions taken and many more lies told as we proceeded with the deposition process. Sergeant Newton, Sergeant Didders and Corporal Davidson all denied that they were "concerned" about Sheriff Johnston's demeanor. They denied advising the deputies that Sheriff Johnston had "lost it, was scarey and dangerous." The interesting part of their depositions was the fact that as each one of them denied making any statements concerning Sheriff Johnston, they actually admitted that they heard the other two supervisors making such statements. I believe it was out of fear of reprisals that they laid the blame on each other, rather than admit to the truth.

Of the three supervisors, Sgt. Newton was the biggest disappointment to me. He had witnessed first hand Sheriff Johnston's actions and inappropriate behavior many times. He was the one that kept remarking something needed to be done to correct the actions and misconduct of the administration. He came to me after my problems had started and advised me that he would stand up and support me. He actually came to me and told me that he knew what was going on; he knew it was wrong, and that I was the victim. He promised. He would be there for me. Now, he was not. They had gotten to him. (The administration had gotten to all three of them.) All I wanted was for them to stand up and tell the truth. It doesn't sound like that big of deal to me to just tell the truth. Then, I guess the truth is sometimes a difficult task which opens the door to serious consequences. Consequences that some people do not have the courage to face. The irony of it is in the long run the lie holds far more devastating consequences.

Another one of the deputies we deposed was Detective Wiggins. A few years back, Detective Wiggins lied on a search warrant involved in a homicide case. He got caught lying on the search warrant by another detective who turned him in. Sheriff Johnston had the incident covered up in order to protect Detective Wiggins. He was one of the sheriff's boys. Knowing the history and of Wiggins's loyalty to the sheriff we did not anticipate getting anything of value from his deposition. We were extremely surprised and rather pleased when Detective Wiggins actually admitted under oath during his deposition, he lied on the search warrant a few years back. We were equally excited when Detective Wiggins admitted he was aware that Sheriff Johnston protected him and had the incident covered up. We couldn't believe he was telling the truth. We expected him to lie.

Randy, however, pointed out that Wiggins was probably afraid to lie. He most likely was afraid we could prove the truth and he did not want to get caught in another lie. None of us, could understand why Sheriff Johnston had hired Wiggins some twelve years ago. He had a rather shady past and supposedly had been involved in criminal activities, which resulted in his arrest. The charges were later dropped and he was never convicted.

On April 23, 1996, Randy deposed Sheriff Johnston for the second time. It was approximately two months after his first deposition. Randy waited to depose the sheriff the second time until after he deposed everyone on the administration and all the deputies that Mr. Custington intended to call as witnesses for trial. Randy wanted to gain knowledge from the other witnesses to articulate questions for Sheriff Johnston in the second deposition. His plan was to catch the sheriff in more lies.

During the second deposition, Johnston was questioned concerning the investigation that he had initiated against Atwater shortly after Atwater disclosed that he was running for sheriff against Johnston in the 1994 election. Johnston admitted in his deposition that he talked to his sister concerning Atwater running against him. He then advised that his sister had a friend of hers file the complaint against Atwater. He defended his actions by stating that Atwater acted inappropriately and he was justified in ordering an internal affair's investigation into Atwater's conduct. He further advised he was justified in punishing Atwater for his conduct.

Randy asked Sheriff Johnston a series of questions concerning his involvement in criminal activities. The questions that Randy asked were directly related to the allegations that were submitted to the FBI. The sheriff's demeanor changed. He lacked confidence, his voice was breaking, and he appeared shaken. It was obvious he was not comfortable with Randy's line of questioning. Johnston denied any involvement in organized crime. He, likewise, denied involvement in any cover ups in reference to any homicides that occurred in the county.

All in all, Sheriff Johnston was prepared for the depositions and questions asked of him. His answers were all short and defensive. It was as if he had answered the very same questions before.

Randy changed the subject, and asked the sheriff about his nephew, Tom Johnston. Sheriff Johnston became very nervous. He denied that he had a nephew named Tom and then requested a recess so that he could talk to his attorney.

After a short break, Randy once again began questioning the sheriff. This time, Sheriff Johnston admitted that he did have a nephew named Tom. Randy then questioned him concerning Tom's criminal history and his involvement in drugs. Johnston informed Randy that his nephew, Tom, has had some problems with the law. The "Tom," that is involved in drugs was not his nephew. He stated there is another Tom Johnston, and that is the subject that has a history of drug related activities. Johnston advised he does not know that Tom Johnston.

Randy asked the sheriff about his nephew's girlfriend of nine years, an Amy Tyler. Johnston denied he knew her or that he ever met her. The subject was then changed, and Randy questioned the sheriff about his involvement in drugs. Sheriff Johnston denied he had any involvement, whatsoever, in drugs or anyone related to drugs other than in his official capacity as a law enforcement officer. You could tell, however, that Randy had struck a nerve. Sheriff Johnston was no longer in control of his demeanor, nor prepared to respond to Randy's questions. He was visibly shaken, appeared upset, and kept drinking a lot of water from the pitcher on the table.

Randy did not want to get too involved in the questions he asked. The purpose of the questioning was to get a feel for the person's reaction and to lock them into their lies. Randy did not want to give them too much information, so that they could be better prepared when the case went to trial. He then switched his line of questions to incidents and conversations involving Undersheriff Deiter and Chief Halsted. Randy covered statements that they had made in their depositions. Sheriff Johnston's answers continuously contradicted statements made by the other two individuals.

Mr. Custington kept objecting to the questions asked by Randy. One of the last questions Randy asked the sheriff was concerning the deputies that went to the FBI requesting an investigation be initiated against Sheriff Johnston.

Randy asked "How many of those deputies that went to the FBI requesting an investigation against you have now, themselves, become the subject of an internal affair's investigation within the sheriffs' office under your direction and request?"

Sheriff Johnston replied "I don't know."

"Isn't it true that all the deputies who went to the FBI have now, at your direction, been the subject of an internal affair's investigations?"

Sheriff Johnston replied "Well, I guess that's correct."

Mr. Custington objected to Randy's questioning.

"Did you, Sheriff Johnston, order those internal affair's investigations to be initiated against those deputies that went to the FBI?" Randy asked.

"Well, yes I did."

Mr. Custington once again objected to Randy's line of questioning.

Randy advised that he had nothing further and the deposition ended. Randy felt relieved that we had locked Sheriff Johnston into a lot of answers. Answers that would serve to be helpful to our case when we went to trial.

The deposition process was interesting, to say the least. We had deputies whom we thought we could rely on let us down, and we had others that surprised us with their honesty. When the depositions were done they totaled approximately forty. Randy had deposed eighteen individuals that were listed as witnesses for Sheriff Johnston's case. Mr. Custington deposed twenty-two witnesses that were listed to testify on my behalf.

The case was coming together and the trial date was getting closer. There was still a lot of work to be done before we would be prepared to take Sheriff Johnston on in the court room.

CHAPTER ELEVEN

THE COMPLEXITY OF LIFE IS MEASURED WITHIN THE MIND, NOT THE REALITY OF ITS EXISTENCE.

Come June of 1996, every one of us who went to the FBI had concluded that we were being followed and were under surveillance. It was not constant. It seemed to be sporadic, but it was not our imagination. Two of the deputies who had gone with us to the FBI, had their residences burglarized. Papers and notes that they had containing information against Sheriff Johnston and others in his administration were stolen while nothing else in their respective residences appeared to have been touched.

I believe my residence would have been broken into if it were not for my security system. In the late 1980's I worked undercover and was involved in investigating and bringing down members of organized crime. Fearing reprisals, I had a video monitoring alarm system installed in my home. The system consisted of eight video monitors and an infrared motion surveillance system. The video monitor received images that are transmitted to a remote site. No one could set a foot on my property, without their photo being captured and preserved on video. I believed this device most likely deterred anyone from breaking into my residence. I never kept any documents or evidence at my residence anyway, so it would have been a waste of time and energy for anyone trying to break in.

Also, in June of 1996, the prosecutor's office came back with a ruling concerning Sheriff Johnston's attempt to have me charged with illegal tape recording of Undersheriff Deiter. Johnston and Deiter both had been pressuring the prosecutor's office to have me charged. The prosecutor declined prosecution citing no violations of the law occurred. The ruling cleared me of any wrong doing and stated there would be no further action on the matter by the prosecutor's office. I was relieved and very pleased with the decision. Even though I knew I had done nothing illegal or wrong, I still had been worried and concerned over the possibility of being charged with a crime. My joy was, however, short lived.

Approximately one week later, I received a letter from Undersheriff Deiter. The letter advised that the sheriff's department had concluded their internal affair's investigation against me. They had determined I violated departmental policy in regards to unlawful possession of documents. The letter further stated that even though no criminal charges would be pressed against me in reference to the answering machine recording of Undersheriff Deiter, I was found guilty of violation of departmental policy in regards to unlawful recording. The letter then stated that, thirdly, I was found guilty of failure to report a sexual harassment complaint in regards to the Willis case.

The letter went on, stating if any of the charges, I was found guilty of were sustained, they would constitute grounds for termination. It then stated, that since I had applied for disability retirement, and currently was on disability leave, no action would be taken against me at this time. The letter advised that if I failed to get my disability retirement, disciplinary action would commence, which could result in my termination from employment.

After reading the letter, or I should say after reading the letter over and over, I contacted my attorney. Randy advised me he received a copy of the internal affair's determination letter as well. He commented he was happy with the letter. I was taken back by his comment, advising him that I, myself, was not pleased with the letter. I informed him I found the letter offensive and very upsetting.

Randy went on to explain to me that now that Sheriff Johnston and his administration found me guilty of the charges they trumped up against me, it demonstrates their retaliation toward me. He went on to say, the letter also was a form of blackmail, "retire or get fired." Randy then commented that Johnston and Deiter just shot themselves in the foot with this letter. A jury, without a doubt, will be able to see that this letter, in fact the entire internal affair's investigation, was nothing more than retaliation on their part.

I understood what Randy was saying. It made sense. It still however, pissed me off and upset me beyond belief. I had said, all along, since December 13, 1995, when I was suspended, that the internal affair's investigation was nothing more than a "sham." Sheriff Johnston had decided prior to initiating the investigation that he was going to find me guilty on all charges. He would then use that as grounds to fire me. The problem was, I guess, that saying it, knowing it, differs greatly from the reality of actually holding the physical piece of paper stating in black and white that you are guilty. I had thought I was prepared for it emotionally, but I was not. It took its toll both physically and mentally.

I got off the phone with Randy. I no sooner put down the receiver than the phone rang. It was Capt. Hill. He had just received a determination letter on his internal affair's investigation. It read exactly the same as the letter I had received. In fact, the only thing it appeared they changed were a few words and the name on the top. He, like myself, was devastated. I knew exactly how he felt. We talked and vented on each other. We both were full of emotion and anxiety.

I am sure Sheriff Johnston and Undersheriff Deiter wrote the letters in an attempt to tear us down by destroying our careers, and our stability in the process. They did not realize, however, that by sending the letters to both of us at the same time, it would have a catalectic effect of enhancing the bond between us. Sharing the same emotions creates a situation whereby there becomes no doubt of what the other is thinking or feeling. The bond between Capt. Hill and me grew to new bounds as we talked. We in turn drew strength and courage from each other. By the time we finished our phone conversations, we had gone from negative to positive thoughts. We actually felt good. We were determined more than ever to succeed. We agreed with Randy, we were going to use the internal affair's determination letter to our advantage, to expose Sheriff Johnston and Undersheriff Deiter for what they actually were. Randy was right and the letters were good news. They were evidence, physical evidence.

Capt. Hill had also applied for disability retirement. His current status was like my own, that of being on disability leave. Johnston could not touch either of us until after the disability board made its final determination on our retirements. If we were granted the retirements, we were in the clear. If the retirements were denied, we would be fired. The situation, without a doubt, added to the frustration and pressure we were experiencing.

After the depositions were completed, I kept getting feed back from the deputies who were to be called as my witnesses. They advised that the administration was applying pressure to them. Deputy Willis was fired. Deputy Tooney was suspended. Deputy Farrell and Deputy Talgon both received written reprimands. In fact, every one of the deputies who went to the FBI, received disciplinary action against them in one form or another. The morale at the sheriff's office was at a low. Each blow delivered by the administration seemed to bring us all closer and served to enhance our determination and desire to succeed. My lawsuit against the sheriff was not about money. Nor were the other lawsuits that would follow. They were, in fact, concerning the principal of standing up for what you believe in. They were attempts to correct the injustice and restore accountability. Corruption and abuse of authority hurt us all.

A few days later, Randy received a call from Amy Tyler. He had not heard from her in almost a year. She was in the county jail. She had been arrested and wanted to see him. Randy dropped what he was doing and ran over to the county jail. He arrived at the jail and walked up to the booking counter. He requested to speak to Amy

Tyler, advising that he was her attorney. The Deputy Jailer working the counter told Randy it would be about thirty minutes before he would be able to see his client. Randy objected to the wait, advising that attorneys have the right to see their clients without undue delay. The jail supervisor, Chief Burger, came out and spoke with Randy. He said the reason for the delay, was that they were in the middle of doing a shakedown for drugs in the female section of the jail. He advised no one is allowed to visit the inmates during the drug shake down, not even attorneys. He told Randy it should not be long until the shake down is completed. He continued to make small talk with Randy. Chief Burger was always friendly and a likeable person. Randy was aware, however, that Burger was one of Johnston's boys and totally loyal to Johnston.

Randy was finally allowed to talk to Amy. He was escorted to one of the private interviewing rooms. Amy was already sitting down in the room. She was crying hysterically.

Randy tried to comfort her and find out what was going on. She advised him that she and her boyfriend, Tom Johnston, broke up. She stated it was over between them and that Sheriff Johnston was helping his nephew, Tom, destroy her life and take her three children away from her.

She told Randy that last night she left Tom. She took their three children and was attempting to get out of the county. She did not make it. Prior to reaching the county line, Sheriff Johnston pulled her over in his police car. Her children were taken away and she was arrested. She advised she was charged with domestic violence. Tom accused her of the beating on him. She continued to cry and Randy kept attempting to calm her down.

Amy paused; with a blank stare on her face she looked directly at Randy. She began to cry again. She advised Randy that they just did a drug search in the women's section of the jail and found drugs in her cell. She swore up and down to Randy the drugs they found were not hers, that she was being set up. She feared she would never see her children again. Randy asked her what kind of drug did they find? She replied cocaine. Amy was shaking. She could not speak.

Randy told her to take her time. He advised her that he would help her and everything would be all right. Amy regained control and began to speak. Randy could tell by the tone of her voice that she was scared to death. She once again advised Randy that she did not have any drugs on her when she was arrested and she was being set up by the sheriff. He told her that he believed her and he was there to help her. She seemed to calm down somewhat and changed the subject.

Amy advised Randy that she really did have a video tape of Sheriff Johnston dealing with some major drug dealers. She said the tape would show Johnston is a dirty cop. She advised that in the tape, Johnston is negotiating for his cut of the drug profits. Johnston is arguing percentages of profit with some major players. She then stated that on the video there is also some talk about having someone eliminated. Johnston talks about teaching them a lesson.

Amy paused, she began to shake, and her voice cracked as she spoke. She continued telling Randy that she wanted him to have the video tape, but that she needed protection and wanted her children returned to her. Randy advised her he would help her, and he would get her protection. He told her the first thing he needed was to get his hands on the video tape. He told her that the safest place for her right now was in jail, while he made arrangements for a safe house for her. He said he would take care of the details. He went on, stating that tomorrow she would be arraigned on the charges against her and he would be there at the arraignment. At that time, he would get her out, and everything would be set up, including a place for her to stay. Amy seemed to calm down and was pleased with what Randy was telling her.

Randy inquired as to how he could get his hands on the video tape. He told her that the sooner he had the tape, and had it protected, the better it would be for her. He told her he needed the tape before he could contact the FBI and arrange for a safe house for her.

Amy replied: "If Johnston knew I had this video tape, I would be dead."

She stated that she really was not certain Johnston didn't already know of the tape's existence. Amy then told Randy that she could arrange for him to get the video tape.

She told Randy to contact her girlfriend, Wendy White. She gave Randy Wendy's phone number and address. She advised Wendy does not have the tape, but that she could take him to Ralph Monroe's residence. Ralph was keeping the tape for her. Amy remarked neither Wendy nor Ralph knows what is on the tape. They just knew that it is important to her and that she referred to the video tape as her insurance policy. She advised the tape is locked inside a green canvas bank bag. She told Randy to just rip the bag open to get to the tape, she did not have access to get the key while she was in jail.

Amy then wrote out two notes for Randy. One letter was to Wendy White, requesting she take Randy to Ralph Monroe's residence. The other letter was to Ralph, directing him to turn the green bank bag containing the video over to Randy. She gave Randy the notes warning him to be careful: remarking that both Tom, and Sheriff Johnston are dangerous and if they found out what he was doing, they would kill him. Randy told her he understood her concern and he would take precautions to make sure everything went right. He assured her that everything would work out and be okay. He told her he would get the tape, and then set everything up for her release in the morning. He then cautioned her not to mention anything to anyone about their conversation. When Randy departed from the jail, Amy's demeanor had changed. She was still scared, but seemed encouraged that things would work out.

Randy also felt that things were coming together and would be all right.

Randy left the jail and immediately tried to get in touch with Wendy. There was no answer on her phone. He decided to drive by her residence in the hopes that she might be home or arriving home shortly. There was no one at home. Randy spent the next three hours calling Wendy every fifteen minutes, to no avail. Finally, he reached her. He explained who he was, and that he was Amy's attorney. He advised her that he needed to talk to her in person. He told her he did not want to discuss what he had to say to her over the phone. Wendy was rather reluctant to meet with him. She finally agreed to meet him at a local coffee shop. She told Randy that she had to get a baby sitter, and it would be about an hour before she could meet with him. Randy agreed to meet with her in an hour at the coffee shop.

Randy was excited. He was finally getting the proof that Sheriff Johnston was dirty. He wanted to get the video and review the contents. He needed to insure what Amy had told him was actually on the tape. He already decided if the evidence was on the video, the first thing he was going to do was to make copies of the tape. He wanted to make sure he had enough copies that the video couldn't get stolen, lost, or destroyed. While he waited the hour for Wendy, he went by one of the department stores and purchased a dozen blank video tapes. His intentions were to get the tape, make copies, and then secure the original and some copies in different locations. Randy kept a watchful eye of his surroundings. He had been followed in the past. He did not want to have anyone trailing him when he went to meet Wendy. He went by his office and picked up his pistol. It was a "Smith and Wesson" nine millimeter automatic. He wanted to be prepared for whatever might happen. He was not taking any chances.

Randy arrived at the coffee shop about ten minutes early. He sat down and ordered a cup of coffee. His old instincts from when he was a cop came back to him. He sat down positioning himself so that his back was to the wall, and he had a clear view of the door and anyone that entered. As the time passed, it seemed to go by extremely slowly. He waited for Wendy's arrival. He kept checking his watch. He was full of anticipation, and the realization that until he had the tape in his hands, he was no closer to having the proof that he needed. He checked his watch again. Wendy was late, fifteen minutes late. He began to worry. Another half hour went by, no Wendy. Randy was beginning to wonder if she was going to show. He decided to give her another fifteen minutes and then try calling her again. He had to get that tape and he needed to get it that night. The time continued to creep on by as he grew impatient. Wendy had not yet arrived. Randy decided to call her. He went over to the public phone located in the hallway by the rest rooms. He began searching his pockets for Wendy's phone number. Panic started to set in when he could not find the phone number. He continued to search frantically. Just then he looked up and observed a woman in her early thirties walk into the restaurant. She looked like she was searching for someone. Randy walked over to her. He asked her if she was Wendy, and she nodded her head affirmatively, and replied that she was. She inquired if he was Randy. He told her that he was, and escorted her back to the table where he was sitting. Randy handed Wendy the note that Amy had hand written for him to give to her. Wendy read the note and then looked up at Randy. She asked if Amy was okay. Randy advised her that Amy was fine and that he was going to take care of her. She seemed relieved to hear that Amy was all right. Randy could tell that Wendy was a good friend and concerned about Amy's welfare. Wendy agreed to take Randy over to Ralph Monroe's residence. She advised him that Ralph's place was about a half hour drive from the restaurant. They spent little time in the restaurant beyond the introduction stage, then departed.

Ralph lived out in a sparsely populated area of the county. Upon arriving at his residence, Randy immediately got a gut feeling that something just wasn't right. His heart sank, and his palms began to sweat as he observed the front door to the one story rambler house standing open. It was not that warm a night, that a person would have purposely left the door standing open. Randy pulled up to where an old car was parked in front of the house. He advised Wendy to wait in the truck while he checked the place out. He got out and approached the residence. It was an old home which appeared to have been neglected over the years and was showing its age.

Randy walked up to the doorway of the residence. He cautiously looked inside. He observed the figure of a body laying on the living room floor. His heart began to race as his eyes focused on the stillness of the body. Just then, Wendy came up behind him and gently touched his shoulder asking him if everything was okay. Randy jumped. She scared the daylights out of him, and he harshly replied:

"No," as he pointed to the body lying on the floor in front of them.

The two of them walked into the residence and approached the body. Wendy recognized it to be Ralph. His skull was crushed. Laying next to him was a crow bar dripping with blood. Wendy remarked that it was Ralph and then began screaming hysterically.

Randy himself got caught up in the excitement of the moment and began to yell.

"Oh my God, Oh my God."

They backed out of the house. Randy was quick to regain his composure as he came to realize that Wendy had lost it, and was in shock over seeing Ralph laying on the floor in a pool of his own blood.

Randy tried to calm Wendy down, while at the same time coming to the realization that the suspect that did this to Ralph might still be in the area. His eyes scanned the area surrounding the residence and the driveway. Wendy was shaking and crying. Randy held her in his arms as his eyes scanned the surroundings. Ralph's residence was isolated. The driveway leading to the residence was long and winding. The location was back in the woods away from everyone. It was a dangerous place for them to be if the suspect had not yet departed.

Randy reached down to the small of his back and pulled out his pistol that he was carrying. He just stood there for a moment with one arm around Wendy and the other hand holding his gun.

He was at a loss as to what he should do. He knew he needed to stay with Wendy. She was in no condition to be left alone. He wanted to go back into the residence and search for the green bank bag containing video tape. Yet as the thoughts raced through his mind, he realized that he should not go back into the residence. If he disturbed anything in the house, he could be charged with destroying evidence, or even implicated in Ralph's murder.

He kept scanning the area, concerned that the suspect might still be in the vicinity. There appeared to be no one around except Wendy and himself.

Randy put his gun back into the small of his back and grabbed Wendy with both hands. He began to shake her yelling all the while.

"Listen, listen to me."

He kept attempting to get her to respond and get her back into control of her senses.

She finally calmed to the point where by he got her attention. He kept reassuring her. It was going to be all right. He kept telling her that the person that killed Ralph was long gone and they were safe even though he was not certain of that himself. She was still traumatized by the sight of Ralph laying dead on the floor, but no longer hysterical.

Randy wanted desperately to go back in the house and search for the tape, but decided that the prudent thing to do was to just call the police. He took Wendy over to the driver's side of his truck and opened the door. He reached in and grabbed his cell phone and called 911. He advised Cen. Com. of the murder and of the location. He then hung up the phone and turned to Wendy.

Realizing that the sheriff's office would be the police department that would response to the scene' he had to brief Wendy as to what to say and not to say before they arrived. He did not want Sheriff Johnston to know about the video tape or that they were out there attempting to retrieve the tape.

Randy advised Wendy that they could not tell the police why they were at Ralph's residence. She did not understand and did not want to get in to trouble with the police. She had a puzzled look on her face as Randy repeated himself. We cannot tell the police why we were here. Randy continued, trying to explain to Wendy that if Sheriff Johnston finds out about the video tape their lives could be in danger. Then it hit him. Randy became white as a ghost as he thought to himself that it was just possible that his conversation with Amy at the county jail was monitored. Someone could have been eavesdropping on their conversation. They might have overheard Amy telling him about the video tape. Ralph could have been murdered over the tape. The thoughts ran through Randy's mind. He attempted to refocus his attentions onto Wendy.

Wendy was just standing there, with a dazed look on her face. Randy asked her if she understood what he was trying to tell her. She nodded her head advising him that she did not trust the cops anyway and she would not tell them anything. To re-enforce what he was saying Randy told Wendy that some of the cops that work for Sheriff Johnston could have been involved in Ralph's death. He stated that he just did not know, and he did not know whom he could trust. He asked her again if she understood. Tears were still rolling down her face as she nodded her head that she understood what he was saying to her.

Randy stood by his truck, holding Wendy in his arms. Her head rested gently on his chest. He was still at a loss. He just stared at the open door to the residence. He felt helpless. He was so close to retrieving the video tape, and now he might never get it. It could be lost forever. It may not even be at the residence any longer, and if it was, Sheriff Johnston and his deputies would most likely find it when they conducted their homicide investigation.

They just stood there, waiting for the police to arrive as Randy fought the emotions within his mind. He kept wrestling with logic over his desire to search for the video tape. In the end, his common sense won out and he gave up on the notion of searching for the tape, realizing that their survival was his most important consideration.

Approximately fifteen minutes passed before deputies began to arrive on the scene. They were followed by detectives from the sheriffs' office and then the coroner. The first deputies to arrive secured the scene and briefly questioned Wendy and Randy. One of the deputies stood by Randy and Wendy until the detectives took charge. Detective Sergeant Paris arrived at the scene and took charge. Randy knew him to be one of Sheriff Johnston's boys and did not trust him.

About an hour went by Wendy and Randy were still standing by a patrol car that they had been escorted to by one of the deputies. The deputy who was basically assigned the task of watching them, was still standing with them. Finally, Randy asked the deputy if they were free to leave, advising he had other business to attend to. The deputy told him he would check with Sergeant Paris and let him know. A short time later, Sergeant Paris walked over to where they were standing. He advised them that, at this point in time, they were not free to leave. They were considered suspect's in Ralph's homicide and were going to be detained for questioning.

They were both then separated, and placed into the rear seats of different patrol vehicles. As they were escorted away from each another, Randy made eye contact with Wendy. He could see from her eyes that she trusted him and was not going to say anything to the cops. Randy asked Sergeant Paris if all this was necessary, and if he could just drive his truck down to the Sheriff's office to answer questions. Sergeant Paris advised him that he could not and that his truck would have to be impounded at this point in time, and he would be transported by the deputies. They were both then transported to the sheriff's office.

They arrived at the sheriff's office approximately forty-five minutes later. Wendy and Randy were both placed in separate interview rooms. Another hour passed before Sergeant Paris and another detective came in to interview Randy. They were both detained the entire night and asked question after question concerning Ralph, the murder, and what they were doing at Ralph's residence. Randy kept insisting that he was not at liberty to tell them anything, claiming attorney/client privilege. The detectives were not pleased with Randy's response. They kept threatening to have him charged with homicide and/or obstructing their investigation. Randy stood firm with his response. Wendy likewise refused to answer any questions for the detectives and kept insisting that she did not do anything wrong and that they just discovered Ralph's murder. She really did not know Randy, but she felt that she could trust him. She also knew that Amy trusted Randy. Otherwise, Amy would not have arranged the meeting between herself and Randy. She trusted Amy and she knew that the situation was serious. She was scared and felt that only Randy could help her. After all, she did not even really understand what was going on just that Ralph was dead and her life might also be in danger. And she knew she could not trust the cops, especially the ones that worked for Sheriff Johnston. She had experienced situations in the past with some of the deputies that led her to the belief they were not the ones to be trusted.

She also kept requesting to talk with Randy, advising that he was her attorney. Her requests were not honored.

The detectives, under the direction of Sergeant Paris, refused to let up on them. They were questioned for hours upon hours. Finally, Sergeant Paris advised both Wendy and Randy that they were free to leave at this time, but they were not allowed to leave the county. He advised them both that they were still considered suspects in the murder investigation and they would be contacting them again later.

Randy inquired as to where his pick-up truck was, and if he could have it returned to him. Sergeant Paris advised Randy that his truck was parked in the back lot of the sheriff's office and he could take his truck at this time. He then handed Randy the keys to the truck. It was a little after nine a.m., when the two of them were finally released. They had been detained the entire night. They walked out to Randy's truck. Randy observed that everything in his truck had been gone through. He questioned the motive behind the search; wondering if it really was related to the homicide investigation or to seeing exactly what information Randy, himself, had on Sheriff Johnston. Either way, it did not matter, Randy did not have anything in his truck that would be of interest to them.

Randy gave Wendy a ride home to her residence. They spoke barely a word during the trip. The two of them were both exhausted from the ordeal they had been through. They arrived at Wendy's residence: as the truck stopped in front of her house, their eyes made contact. Randy could see the fear and confusion she was experiencing in her eyes. She in turn could see Randy's concern for her welfare. Nothing was said for a few moments. Randy advised her to be careful and to get some rest. He told her that he would keep in touch, and for her to call him if anything suspicious happens, or if she is contacted again by the sheriff's office. Wendy was scared for her own welfare. Randy tried to reassure her that she was going to be okay. He told her that he would not allow anything to happen to her. He then told her that she was not a threat to anyone. She did not have the video tape or any information that would make her a threat, to anyone. All of a sudden a thought ran through her mind as she asked Randy what was on the video tape that made it so important anyway. Randy told her that she was better off not knowing. He then told her it was incriminating evidence against Sheriff Johnston, and that was all she needed to know. She became silent and the conversation ended. Randy walked her up to her residence and went inside with her. He checked the place out to make sure no one was there or had been there. Her home looked fine and undisturbed. Randy once again told her to call him if she had any problems whatsoever. He then departed.

Randy decided to run by his office before he went home. He had to cancel some of his appointments for the day, and then intended to go home and get some sleep. After arriving at his office, he called Jason Bolton at the FBI office. Jason listened intently as Randy detailed the events that had occurred over the last twenty four hours. Jason seemed very receptive and responded that he would have his agents look into everything. He advised Randy that it created a unique situation since the sheriff's office was investigating Ralph's homicide. He stated that, the fact of the matter, was, the FBI could not actually become involved in the homicide investigation without notifying the Sheriff. It was a matter of policies and procedures. He advised they would focus their investigation on the video tape and incidents related to and surrounding the tape.

He stated.

"We will have to "back door" the homicide investigation, if you know what I mean?"

Randy knew exactly what Jason was telling him. He was satisfied and pleased with Jason's response. Randy really did not want the FBI to contact the sheriff's office directly. He feared that if they did it, would just make Sheriff Johnston cover up his involvement even deeper.

Randy got off the phone with Jason. He was exhausted, however, the adrenalin built up in his body over the events of the night had not as of yet worn off. He sat there at his desk pondering everything that had occurred. A cold sweat broke out over his entire body as he recalled his conversation with Amy that occurred yesterday in the jail interview room. They must have monitored our conversation he thought once again.

How else would anyone know about Wendy and Ralph? It was just too much of a coincidence that it could not be ignored. He did not know for sure if the video tape and Ralph's death were connected, but felt strongly that they were related.

If Sheriff Johnston had his conversation with Amy monitored, then Sheriff Johnston would have known about the video tape, and also that he was about to retrieve it from Ralph. It took him so long to get a hold of Wendy that Sheriff Johnston would have had time to go, or tosend someone to Ralph's residence before he could have gotten there. The thoughts kept going through Randy's mind. It all made sense. Then suddenly Randy's thoughts turned to Amy.

Randy found himself facing a dilemma. He was concerned for Amy's welfare. He was afraid to go to the sheriff's office to check on her fearing that any contact he might have with her could jeopardize her safety. Yet he needed to know she was all right, and he had promised her that he would be there at her arraignment. He decided he had no choice; besides, if their conversation was monitored, she was already in jeopardy. He left for the court house.

Randy arrived at the court house just as arraignments were beginning. The procedure followed by the jail staff was to bring the prisoners down to the court room just prior to there being arraigned. The prisoners to be arraigned were all sitting in the back row of the court room. Randy glanced at the prisoners that were sitting there, looking for Amy. She was not there. Randy scanned the entire court room for Amy; however, she was no where to be found. He approached one of the Deputy Jailers and took him aside. He inquired as to where Amy was. The Deputy Jailer advised that he did not know. He did not bring her down for arraignment. He advised Randy to check with the jail to find out her status.

Randy left the court room and proceeded over to the county jail. He contacted the desk sergeant in the women's section of the jail. Randy inquired as to Amy's status. The jail sergeant scanned the computer for information about Amy. He then advised Randy that according to the computer, Amy posted bail last night and was released. Randy was rather taken back and shocked to hear that Amy had been released. He asked the sergeant who posted Amy's bail. The sergeant checked the computer once again and remarked that he did not know, it was not listed on the computer. He advised that it was kind of strange, because normally that information is listed on the computer. Randy thanked the jail sergeant, then departed. He was rather baffled. The last thing Randy expected was that Amy would be gone. He knew he had to find her.

He did not have a clue as to where to even begin to look for Amy. He decided to go by Wendy's residence and check on her. She, being Amy's best friend, might know where she would be or might have had contact with her. Randy drove directly over to Wendy's residence. He knocked on the door. There was no answer. He waited a few moments and knocked again.

A voice came from inside, inquiring as to who was there. It was Wendy's voice. Randy told her that it was he. The door swung open. She was crying. It appeared she had not gotten any rest since Randy had dropped her off earlier that morning. She looked puzzled as to why Randy was there, but invited him into her home. She directed him to the living room, advising that she would be right back. She returned within a minute or two, wanting to know to why he was there. Randy asked her if she had been in contact with Amy since he dropped her off this morning. She told him that she had not. Randy informed her that Amy had bailed out of jail late last night, and now he did not know where to find her. Wendy appeared shocked to hear that Amy bailed out of jail. She remarked that, as far as she knew Amy did not have any money for bail. Wendy advised Randy that Amy would contact her before anyone else, if everything was all right, but she had not heard from Amy. Wendy then made eye contact with Randy. She told him that she was scared, and began to cry. Randy extended his arms out to her and she came willingly into his arms. They hugged each other. It was a hug of concern and protection.

Wendy agreed to help Randy locate Amy. She went into her bedroom and got dressed. She returned to where Randy was sitting in the livingroom, stating that she was ready to go. They spent the day searching for Amy. There was no sign of Amy at her residence. It did not even appear that she had been there. Wendy had a key to Amy's place, so they went inside to look around. There were still two days of messages on the answering machine. All of Amy's belongings were also about the residence which tended to imply that she had not taken off. Wendy then took Randy by some of the mutual friends of hers and Amy's. No one had seen her or had any idea as to where she might be.

Wendy had the idea to contact a friend of theirs that got along with Tom, but actually didn't like Tom. She had the woman contact Tom at his parent's place and see if Amy's children were still there. The children were still there. They had not seen their mother in two days. Tom told this woman that he did not know that Amy had gotten out of jail. He did not have any ideas as to where Amy would have gone after getting out. This woman advised that when she inquired about Amy, Tom acted really nervous like he knew something about Amy, but he wasn't telling. She advised that she just didn't believe Tom.

It was after nine p.m. that night when Randy returned Wendy to her residence. They were no closer to locating Amy than they were when they started. Randy dropped Wendy off and then drove on home to his residence.

Around ten thirty p.m., Randy called me on the phone. He sounded extremely exhausted and rather frustrated. He spent the next hour or so filling me in on all the details of what had transpired. It was unreal, it was more or less like something out of the movies, not what actually happens in real life. I listened intently to his every word. I had no answers, just questions. Randy finally finished by telling me that he was going to try and get some sleep. He informed me that in the morning he would call Jason at the FBI's office again and update him to the fact that it appears that Amy is missing.

Things were becoming more bizarre and serious all the time. I hung up the phone. I feared for the welfare and safety of all of us. In the beginning, back in October of 1994, I perceived Sheriff Johnston and his administration as poor managers but not criminals. Now my perception had changed. The events since then had convinced me that they were dangerous and capable of just about anything. It was an unsettling feeling. I realized that my up and coming court case threatened to expose their true nature to the public. It enhanced my belief that the sheriff would stop at nothing to prevent this exposure. The sheriff, in his current state of desperation, was capable of just about anything. There was no doubt in my mind that Ralph's murder was linked to his involvement in the video tape. Further, I had little doubt that Amy being missing was directly connected to Sheriff Johnston. Randy likewise had little doubt about the sheriff being responsible, but yet, we still lacked the proof.

CHAPTER TWELVE

ONE'S PEACE OF MIND INVOLVES MANY FACTORS.

The month of July 1996, seemed to linger on, passing extremely slowly. I was experiencing a lot of concerns, and mental anticipation, all surrounding my retirement hearing which was scheduled for the 26th of the month. I was pleased when the day of the hearing finally arrived. Randy kept telling me my 41% hearing loss and the fact that we had documentation it occurred in the line of duty meant there would be no problem with the retirement board approving my disability. He had been continually reassured me over the past six months, while I was out on disability leave. It helped, however, the fact that my financial security for the rest of my life hinged on the disability board decision weighted heavily on me.

My stomach was full of butterflies, and my palms were sweating as I rode with Randy to the disability board meeting. I anticipated Sheriff Johnston and Undersheriff Deiter would be at the meeting in an attempt to circumvent the board from granting my disability retirement. I was, however, wrong. They were not at the meeting. In fact, no one from the sheriff's office was present at the meeting. The review of my medical condition for disability retirement was over almost as soon as it began. The board had previously reviewed one of my medical documents, and the police reports which clearly showed my hearing loss occurred in the line of duty.

The meeting consisted of my attorney giving a brief statement of the facts surrounding justification of my request for disability retirement, and then making a formal request that the disability board grant my retirement. Randy was also there to argue the facts and points of law, if there was any opposition raised against granting my retirement. To my surprise, there was no argument raised against my disability retirement, not by Sheriff Johnston, or anyone from the sheriff's office, nor from the prosecutor's office. In fact, after Randy gave his statement of facts, the disability board unanimously granted my "duty related disability retirement."

It was as if a tremendous burden had been lifted off my shoulders. I had won. No matter what the out come of the up and coming civil trial would be. I had won. I now had financial security for the rest of my life. I would receive 50% of my base pay for the rest of my life. That would amount to approximately $2000.00 per month, with an annual cost of living raise every year, starting after the first year. I had always been the sole supporter of my family. If I had lost my request for disability, Sheriff Johnston would have regained control over me and I would have been fired. If that occurred, I would not have been able to pay the bills. We could have lost everything we had worked our entire lives to achieve. It was probably the most predominate concern that plagued my mind during this entire ordeal. It was what I considered a major victory, especially since at the mediation hearing Sheriff Johnston and his attorneys tried to blackmail me into dropping the lawsuit by holding my retirement over my head.

Physically, emotionally, and mentally, I felt good, the best I had felt for a long time. After the disability board meeting ended, I ran to find a phone and call my wife, Sherry. I wanted to advise her of the good news. Little words were spoken between us on the phone. I told her that my disability retirement had been approved; we both cried, thanked God, and expressed our love for each other. Sherry was my support and the driving force, giving me the strength and courage to carry on. I would not have been able to survive without her.

Randy and I left the court house. He could tell I was over whelmed with excitement. He congratulated me on my retirement.

He added "We now have to get down to business, and finish getting prepared for the civil trial October 1, 1996, will be here before we know it."

He informed me that he had kept the day open on his calendar, so after the disability hearing, we could go back to his office and work on the civil trial. We then proceeded to Randy's office.

Looking back on my victory, of getting my disability retirement—it was, I guess you could say, a "bitter sweet victory." I wasn't really ready to retire. I loved my job and had every intention of working in my career for another ten years. I was forced into the position of having to pursue my retirement or be fired. When the excitement of the moment wore off, and the reality set in, I actually experienced a loss. My career was over, gone. I really had no idea as to what I would be doing next with my life after the court case was over.

Randy and I spent the entire rest of the day working on my case. We covered key issues we wanted to present in court. We also, set up the order we wanted to call witnesses involved in the case to testify. From that day forward, until the actual trial, many hours were spent daily working on preparation for court.

After my retirement was approved, my wife and I began receiving more hang up phone calls. More than we were usually experiencing. We also began to receive threatening phone calls over the next few days. Randy also began receiving hang up, and threatening phone calls as well. We made attempts at trying to get the phone company to trace the calls. We even had the phone company put taps on our lines. We had little success. It was determined that the calls were being made from a cellular phone. Cell phones unfortunately can't be traced like a conventional hard wired phone.

We also came to the conclusion that our phone was once again being "tapped," that is to say, that someone was listening in on our line. We would be having a conversation with another party when, all of a sudden, a fax machine noise would come on the line, drowning out our conversation. This occurred on more than one occasion, and it only happened when the topic of the conversation focused on Sheriff Johnston.

We notified the telephone company, who confirmed our suspicions concerning our line being "bugged." The person from the phone company, however, informed us that our phone line, was what they called a hard line. The line ran approximately four miles to a switching station. The problem was anyone who knew what they were doing could "splice," into the line anywhere over the four-mile run. It would be next to impossible to locate the exact location of the splice.

We had little success in trying to prove who was making the calls. Randy changed his phone number. I could not, or should I say, I would not. I have had the same phone number for almost thirty years. My phone number was unlisted. I did not want to risk losing contact with friends and family members from my past, the ones we may have lost contact with over the years. The old phone number is the only connection we have to them in the event that they try to reach you. In any event, I refused to give up the old number.

Changing his phone number really didn't help Randy. It only lasted about two days that he did not receive any anonymous phone calls. He made the mistake of giving his new number to the prosecuting attorney that was representing Sheriff Johnston. It wasn't even twenty-four hours after he gave out his new telephone number that the calls started back up again.

It seemed like the closer the trial date got, the more intense was the surveillance of Randy, the deputies that were to testify, and myself. One of my neighbors alerted me to a vehicle, a white sedan. It was continuously seen parked down the road from my residence. My neighbor described the driver as a white male in his late thirties or early forties. This same vehicle my wife and I observed following us on many different occasions as we would run errands around the county. Randy and some of the other deputies observed this same vehicle and others following them as well.

One of the deputies, Frank Tooney, hired a private investigator to do counter-surveillance on the vehicles that were following him. He did this after his residence was broken into and his notes and diary involving Sheriff Johnston were stolen.

He and his wife were traumatized over the burglary and felt violated. He also experienced great concern over the fact that one of his weapons, a 9-millimeter semiautomatic pistol, was also stolen in the burglary. He was afraid that the pistol might be used in a violent crime, and he could end up being framed for the crime. He was equally concerned that the weapon might end up being used against one of us.

The detective that he hired traced one of the subjects following us back to Mr. Custington, Sheriff Johnston's attorney. Apparently this subject was an ex-cop who had worked for one of the major cities. This particular subject left the police department after he had an internal affair's investigation focus on his involvement in drug transactions. He was never convicted or charged with a crime. Since resigning from the police department, he worked off and on as a private investigator for Mr. Custington. During the counter surveillance, the investigator Deputy Tooney hired witnessed meetings taking place between this subject and Mr. Custington.

Randy confronted Mr. Custington on more than one occasion concerning all of us being followed. Mr. Custington denied any knowledge or involvement in the surveillance. He also denied he was having any of us investigated. We came to the conclusion that Mr. Custington was less than an honest person. Mr. Custington and Sheriff Johnston had a long history that went back more than twenty years. Johnston would use Mr. Custington to get him out of trouble whenever the need arose. Custington had a reputation of being hard hitting and underhanded. He would manipulate the law to his advantage and destroy his opponent's witnesses through intimidation techniques. His reputation was not of winning a case in court, but one of tearing the heart and soul out of a case before it ever reached court. We believe that all the surveillance and harassing phone calls were all just part of his scheme to keep the pressure on everyone involved in our side of the case, in hopes of preventing the case from ever getting to court.

Around the middle of August 1996, Randy received a call from Jason Bolton, agent in charge of the FBI investigation against Sheriff Johnston. He told Randy that they had not been able to locate Amy Tyler. They had contacted friends and family including relatives in West Virginia. No one has seen or talked to her since just prior to her getting arrested two months ago.

It was as if she has fallen off the face of the earth. He went on to advise Randy that he had agents contact Amy's sister in West Virginia, and the sister was aware of the video tape involving Sheriff Johnston and major drug dealers. The sister had viewed the tape, and was able to verify its existence. FBI agents showed the sister pictures of Sheriff Johnston, and she identified him as one of the people in the video negotiating drug transactions and percentages. She told the agents that Amy was always referring to the video tape as her "insurance policy." The sister did not know Sheriff Johnston personally, and never actually had met him. She, further, told the agent the video was filmed inside a large room that was full of growing marijuana plants. In the video the man that was pointed out to her, to be Sheriff Johnston, was discussing his cut of the marijuana and cocaine distribution for their west coast operation. He was insisting on an increase of his percentages, justifying the increase by stating that he made sure the competition was being eliminated.

Jason advised Randy that Amy's sister didn't remember all of the conversation on the video. She did, however, say the subject Amy referred to as the sheriff appeared to be really scarey. He made some sort of comment or threat that they could not operate without him and they should remember what happened to the kids on the island. Jason commented that he feared Amy was most likely a victim of foul play. He had little hope of finding her alive. He advised Randy they were bringing in D.E.A., the Drug Enforcement Agency, to assist them on the investigation. He then remarked their investigation was far from being over.

Late in August of 1996, summary judgement was held in regards to my civil trial. It is a process whereby the judge reviews all of the evidence that was submitted in discovery and makes a determination as to whether or not to proceed with the trial. The judge also, at this time, decides what evidence he will allow to be used in the court proceedings. Each side had to submit written arguments to the judge as to why a certain piece of evidence should not be allowed to be introduced in court. It is an attempt by the attorneys on both sides to eliminate evidence the other side is attempting to use against their case in court. The arguments usually center around a certain piece of evidence or testimony that could prejudice the jury prior to all the facts being presented in the case.

The judge assigned to my civil trial was The Honorable J. D. Swanlund. He was what was called a Magistrate Judge. He had presided on the bench as a judge for more than twenty years. He was sharp, always attentive and very articulate. He was a fair man, and a no nonsense type of judge. His initial ruling in my case was that there was sufficient evidence to warrant the case to go to trial. The case was a civil rights suit for violation of my constitutional rights to wit: freedom of speech, for supporting Atwater, talking to the news media, and going to the FBI. It also covered retaliation against me for my participation in the above acts.

Sheriff Johnston, Undersheriff Deiter, and Chief Halsted, through their attorney, Mr. Custington, had all filed counter claims against me. They were in fact, suing me for suing them. The counter claims were all reviewed by Judge Swanlund, as well. He threw out every one of their counter claims. Citing, they were "groundless." The nice part of this, as Randy explained it to me, was that the judge did not just throw the counter claims out and dismiss them, but rather he ruled on them and found them to be "groundless." According to Randy, by ruling on the counter claims Sheriff

Johnston and the others would not be able to file them again or ever bring them up in another court. It was the same as if they lost in court.

The second part of Judge Swanlund's ruling was what is referred to as "Motions in Liminee." These are the issues and items that are not allowed to be brought up in court by either side. Any mention of any item on the "Motions in Liminee" list could be grounds for immediate dismissal of the case as a mistrial. Randy explained it to me, that the judge wants the jury to be able to try the case based on the testimony, evidence, and merits of the case. Therefore, each attorney submitted the items and topics they desired to have included in "Motions in Liminee" to the presiding judge. The judge then rules on each item and composes the list containing those items that do not directly relate to the case, or that could damage, or prejudice the jury. It is referred to as the list of "forbidden topics."

The "Motions in Liminee" list came out and was distributed to both sides. Randy had informed me just how important the list was to our case. He advised that the judge could rule that we can proceed to trial and restrict so much of our evidence through "Motions in Liminee" that we are left without a case to even try. We read the list, and then we read it again. Randy looked over at me and touched my shoulder. He advised me that we were all right, we lost a few items that we wanted to get into court but then we gained some as well.

He remarked,

"In looking at this list, Sheriff Johnston's side lost some too, and lost some critical issues that they wanted to try to use against you, that will help us."

Randy appeared pleased with the judge's ruling.

I gave a sigh of relief. I did not want to have come this far and then not be able to proceed to court. I wanted the truth to come out. Court was where I felt the truth would become known and I would be able to clear my name from the charges against me.

Equally important, I had hopes the trial would expose Sheriff Johnston's true agenda to the public. I firmly believed that as the truth unfolded the citizens would not tolerate the misconduct that had been occurring within the sheriff's office, and steps would be taken to correct the problems.

After summary judgement was completed, the only thing left was to wait for the trial to begin in October. It still seemed like a long way off. The anticipation was overwhelming. Randy kept me busy at his office working on preparing our case for trial. There were more than forty thousand documents which he intended to present as evidence. It was an organizational nightmare, attempting to arrange everything in an orderly fashion. Randy was continually remarking that we had to keep the jury's interest up during the court proceeding, advising if the jury gets bored or disinterested, we could lose them. We spent the days, and sometimes into the nights organizing and preparing our case. Randy definitely kept me busy and it helped to pass the time. It began to feel like I had a job to go to, and I was doing something constructive. I needed that, it gave me time to adjust to being retired.

Capt. Hill called me one night in the middle of September. It was around 9:00 p.m. He told me he had received a telephone call from Deputy Baker. The call was to inform him that Sheriff Johnston had been in the sheriff's office every night for the last week. He advised Johnston would come into the office around midnight and then lock himself in his private office. Johnston took the paper shredder out of the record's office and put it in his office. He had been shredding papers all week. Baker remarked he did not know what Johnston was trying to hide, but he has been really busy destroying the documents.

Deputy Baker went on to relate to Capt. Hill that Sheriff Johnston has been letting everyone around the office know he was not happy with Judge Swanlund's ruling on summary judgement. Johnston kept remarking, "they will pay." Capt. Hill advised me to be careful stating that Baker said he had never seen Johnston so upset.

I remarked to Capt. Hill that I realized Sheriff Johnston was upset. Every time the sheriff is upset, I get hang up phone calls. They seem to come right after an incident involving the sheriff. An incident that makes him irate. I told Capt. Hill I had received more than three hundred and fifty hang up calls since my problems with Johnston started. They're the type of call where the person just stays on the line, but does not say anything. The hang up calls had become more frequent since summary judgement and I also had been receiving threatening calls. I told Captain Hill I got one call where a stern and rather harsh voice stated "I'm coming for you." I received repeats of that same call over a dozen times now, just since the Summary Judgement ruling.

Capt. Hill and I talked for over an hour. We talked about everything and nothing. It was comforting to both of us to have the other one there just to listen. I guess it was kind of a therapy for us, at any rate it always seems to help.

Two nights later, while my wife and I were sleeping, it all came very close to ending for us. I had been having trouble sleeping. In fact, over the last two years, since my problems at the sheriff's office began, my sleeping habits had been sporadic.

I was unable to get to sleep, or else I would sleep for about two hours and then awake and not be able to go back to sleep. Most nights, in fact almost every night, I would find myself up in the middle of the night watching television or working on paper work for the court case. The lack of regularity in my sleeping habits created a situation where when I did sleep, I was usually so exhausted that I would fall into a deep sleep. On this particular night, that was the case. I finally fell asleep around 2:30 a.m., and I fell into a deep sleep, the type of sleep it is very hard to arouse from, and if you are awakened, it seems abrupt. You find yourself in a state of drowsiness and disoriented.

Then suddenly, in the middle of the night, our dog, a female German Shepard named "Levi Jean," woke us. She jumped onto our bed and began barking at us. We were both startled. It was not normal behavior for "Levi." I was in a state of confusion, partly awake, and partly feeling the incident was a mere dream. I rolled over, pretending or maybe not really realizing what was happening.

Just then my wife, Sherry yelled.

"FIRE, FIRE, OH MY GOD, HONEY, HONEY WAKE UP, FIRE, OH MY GOD!"

I was still in a mystified daze. I was having difficulty comprehending my surroundings.

Sherry continued to yell, as "Levi" stood on the bed, barking endlessly.

Finally, I awoke to the point of realizing what was happening. Our home of nearly thirty years was being consumed by fire. The flames were everywhere and the heat, the heat was so intense. Smoke filled our lungs with a burning sensation. As we tried to breathe, we began to cough. Our eyes watered and our throats felt like they were on fire themselves. We jumped out of bed onto the floor and tried to find a path to crawl to safety.

We grabbed some blankets off the bed and threw them about us in an attempt to protect ourselves from the heat and smoke.

As we fought to survive, we became overwhelmed with the sinking feeling that our lives would end in this fiery tomb.

We were surrounded by the raging flames. I yelled to Sherry to lay still. I got back up onto our water bed. The mattress was exposed after we had torn the bedding off to cover us. I started biting at the mattress in an attempt to break it. "Levi Jean" observing what I was doing, began biting at the mattress too. We were able to tear it and the water poured out over the floor. There was just enough water that it slowed down the flames and created somewhat of a path for us to use to get to the door.

We fought with every bit of strength we could muster to get to the back door and to safety. We crawled on our bellies, our faces down to the ground with our noses rubbing the carpet in an effort to breathe. It felt like it took forever. "Levi Jean" stayed right beside us, every inch of the way. We finally made it to the back door. The flames were flaring and bounding about, destroying everything they touched. I reached up and opened the back door. At that very instant, as the door opened and the fresh air hit the wall of fire consuming our home, flames shot like a huge wave on the ocean over me toward the open door. The blankets we were wrapped in being soaking wet, is all that saved us. Once outside, they caught fire. We dropped the blankets away from us and rolled out onto the lawn. We just lay there on the ground coughing and gasping for air. "Levi Jean" stood over us. She had melted hair and burnt paws, but survived. She stood there over us, more concerned about us than anything else. Sherry and I looked up at her, after we caught our breath. Her tail was wagging. We hugged her. She had saved our lives. She was our hero.

We continued to just lay there on the ground in a state of bewilderment. You hear about fires all the time, but you never really understand the power of fire until you experience it. I never want to experience it again. Likewise, you cannot begin to realize or comprehend the trauma you face in a fire until it happens to you. The flames, the heat, and the smoke were consuming beyond belief. You have little choice but to flee in an attempt to survive. We thanked God that we had survived.

As we lay there on the ground, we had a sinking feeling of desperation. Had someone just tried to kill us? I knew, I just knew, the fire was no accident.

The fire department arrived a short time later. It was too late to save our home. It was totally destroyed. Along with our home, we lost all our possessions. A thirty-year accumulation, a life time of little things we held dear to us. We had raised our children in this home. I firmly believe the little things, the treasuries of memories lost, hurt the most. These were things that could never be replaced. They were taken from us, gone forever, except for in our hearts and minds.

The county fire marshal and the sheriff's office arson detective also responded to the scene of the fire, after the fire department notified them that they believed the fire to have been an arson fire. There were six points of origin to the fire. The fire itself was caused by a mixture of gasoline and diesel fuel being spread about. There were large areas surrounding the house that were soaked with diesel fuel. It appeared that the gasoline was used to ignite the diesel. There were no suspects. Well, at least, no real suspects, and there was very little evidence found at the scene.

Randy arrived at the scene approximately an hour after the fire department got there. One of the deputies on duty had heard the call on the police radio, called him, and told him about it. He followed us to the hospital. Sherry and I rode in the ambulance. "Levi Jean" rode with Randy. He took us to his residence after we were checked out and released from the hospital. He advised us that we could spend the night at his place and in the morning he would help us think about relocating. We agreed. We really did not have any choice. We had no where that we could go. We were exhausted and in need of rest. Randy had become more than just our lawyer. He had become a close friend. His wife, Patty, had also become a very close and good friend. She was constantly calling Sherry and checking on her and how things were going. The two of them seemed to hit it off from the start. We were pleased and grateful they were there for us and opened their home to us, the way that they did.

Sherry and I tried to get some sleep, but neither one of us could sleep. We rested for a couple of hours and then got up. We went downstairs. Randy and Patty were sitting in their livingroom drinking coffee. Patty got Sherry and me some coffee and we joined them in the livingroom. Randy looked at us with a concerned look on his face. He asked us how we were doing. We both remarked that we were not sure. We were still rather shaken up by the entire situation.

Randy remarked:

"You know, you guys are not safe. Someone is definitely trying to kill you. The fire was no accident."

Randy paused, and then continued:

"There is no proof, but my guess is Sheriff Johnston most likely is behind the arson fire and the attempt on your lives. I want to hide both of you out at this rental house I have, until after the trial. The house is furnished and currently vacant. You guys can stay there for free. It's a perfect place to hide you out. I own the house with my business partner, but the house is in his name, not mine. So there is no way anyone could even trace the house back to me, if they were attempting to find out where you might be staying."

"You guys need to hide out and basically disappear for the next two weeks until the trial starts and keep a low profile during the trial. This house would be a perfect place for that." We agreed and thanked Randy for all his concern and help.

He shook his head in reply and then stated:

"You know that the arson investigator of the county is "one of Johnston's boys." They will probably never develop any useable evidence or suspects in the arson."

I agreed with him.

Randy advised that he would contact Jason, and see if the FBI would get involved in the investigation. The reality that we were playing for keeps really hit home with us. There was no other logical explanation for anyone trying to kill us. It had to be related to the up coming trial, at least that was our firm belief.

Later that day, Randy took us to his rental unit and got us settled in. It was a small but nice two bedroom rambler located on a dead end "cul de sac." Patty arrived at the home shortly after Randy dropped us off. She had gone to the grocery store and picked up bag after bag of food items for us. She even got us tooth brushes and personal grooming items. They thought of everything. Randy came back later that evening with a televison and radio for us. He also just wanted to check on us and see how we were coping.

Over the next couple of days, the trauma of our physical loss of possessions and our home began to sink in. It hurt. We tried to focus on our survival and move on. We were ready for trial. We were more than ready to get the entire nightmare behind us and get on with our lives. Randy and Patty continued to go beyond the call of duty in taking care of us and seeing to our needs. They daily checked on our physical and mental well being. It was nice to have their concern, we needed it, and it gave us strength. Randy told us that when the trial began, he would pick us up and transport us to trial each and every day. He did not want us to be alone nor to give whoever was trying to kill us, an opportunity to catch us out and about by ourselves.

CHAPTER THIRTEEN

TRUTH A SIMPLE CONCEPT, YET DIFFICULT TO ACHIEVE, DISTORTED BY ONE's LACK OF COURAGE, OR JUST BY SELF- SERVING MOTIVATION.

There I sat, my eyes wandering around the court room. I had never been in Federal Court before, it was quite a sight. The large columns, the marble floors, and the ceilings that reached at least three stories high. My mind pondered the events of the last two years, the events that brought me to federal court and my trial against Sheriff Johnston. Randy began to speak to me, but I did not hear him. I did not hear the words nor even realize his presence. My mind was kind of in a daze. He reached over from where he was sitting and touched my shoulder. The touch brought me back to reality, back to the moment of time that I left.

Randy whispered to me "It's time, we have to stand while the judge enters the court room."

It was September 30, 1996, we were seated in the Federal Court room preparing to make the jury selection in my civil suit against Sheriff Johnston. The actual trial was scheduled to begin the next day.

We all stood while the Honorable J.D. Swanlund, the presiding judge, entered the room. He then had the bailiff bring in approximately sixty people who were the prospective jurors. They were made up of all kinds of people, from all walks of life. There were some prospective jurors that were barely out of school and then there were others that were old and retired. Each of the jurors had been given a number. They were referred to by their number.

After the prospective jurors were seated, the jury selection began. It started with Randy and Mr. Custington each asking a series of questions to each of the prospective jurors. It was, to say the least, an interesting process designed to determine if a person could and would be fair and impartial. I would say that it was, in fact, just a process which enabled the attorneys for both sides to make an educated guess based on the answers given to a minimal amount of questions.

Randy and I sat on the right-hand side of the court room. Mr. Custington, Mrs. Pitts, four attorneys from Mr. Custington's law firm, Sheriff Johnston, Undersheriff Deiter, and Chief Halsted all sat on the left side of the court room. It gave the appearance of the "little guy" going up against the "corporate giant."

I would have to say, with all honesty, that both Randy and I felt intimidated by Mr. Custington and his army of assistants and consultants. We did not have the resources nor the expertise that Sheriff Johnston had available in his defense. We did not even have the courtroom experience that his attorneys possessed. This was in fact, the biggest case of Randy's career as an attorney. It was also the first trial that Randy ever handled in federal court. Intimidated yes, scared yes, all we had in our corner was the truth and a dedicated determination to succeed. We knew in our hearts that the truth would prevail.

We tried to pick prospective jurors that appeared to be sincere, honest, and down to earth. The men and women that made up the prospective jury basically consisted of two types of people: those that wanted to be there and considered it an honor and duty to sit on a jury, and those that were there because they had no choice. One thing that I found interesting was the fact that the attorneys, especially Randy, really did not concern himself with whether the prospective juror wanted to be there or not. He was only concerned with the type of person he or she was and their ability to think independently in determining the truth. He was looking for individuals that were not afraid to make decisions based on the facts given, people that would keep an open mind. People who through their own life experience could see through any "smoke screen" that the defense might use to cloud or overshadow the truth.

The process of picking the jury lasted the entire day. Each side was allowed to refuse up to three prospective jurors "without cause." During the selection process, each candidate was asked if there was some reason that they felt they could not sit on the jury. Out of the sixty prospective jurors, about twelve of them asked to be excused for a variety of reasons. Nine of them were excused by Judge Swanlund. For most of those released, the reason stated was that sitting on this particular jury would create a conflict of interest. The judge felt their conflicts could prejudice them in one way or another in regards to the case before them. Seven other prospective jurors were excused due to medical reasons that would not allow them to be able to participate in three to four weeks of trial. There were forty-six candidates left from which to choose.

The process involved in picking the jury consisted of first eliminating all the candidates who were to be excused for "cause." The jurors are then taken in numerical order starting with the lowest number. We got to go first. We would strike a juror. Mr. Custington and his side would then strike a juror using one of their three rights of refusal to eliminate that person. The procedure continued in that manner until both sides used up their three "strikes," or options of refusal. After the refusals were exhausted, the remaining jurors were picked in numerical order starting with the lowest number left and ruled to be acceptable. The jury was finally empaneled.

Randy consulted with me on every selection that he made from the prospective jurors. We were pleased with nine out of the twelve jurors chosen. The other three jurors we had some reservations about, but really did not have any choice in the matter. We were stuck with them and could only hope that they would see that justice was served. We had used up our three "strikes" by eliminating those prospective jurors we were most concerned about.

In a civil constitutional law case held in federal court, all of the jurors have to agree on the decision reached in order for us to win our case. The decision has to be unanimous or else we lose the case. In that regard, the jury selection is an extremely important process, it had to be done right or it could cost us everything. We had some reservations, but, all in all, felt good about the empaneled jury.

Randy made the comment that the jury consisted of intelligent individuals that he felt would be able to determine the truth from the bullshit presented at trial. He thought that we had the best jury possible to hear the case. He had a positive attitude that things were going to work out.

The day ended with the new jury being given the preliminary jury instructions. Each juror was instructed that they were not to draw any conclusions nor make any decisions concerning the matter involved until both sides present their case and they are sent into the jury room for deliberation. They were further informed that they were not allowed to discuss the case or any of the court proceedings with anyone inside or outside of the court room prior to deliberation. They were told they were not even allowed to discuss the case or any testimony given among themselves until deliberation.

Finally they were instructed that the statements made by the attorneys in this case were not evidence or facts but their respective opinions and argument. They were to view what the attorneys stated as argument and not facts. The facts in the case would consist of testimony given by witnesses from both sides as well as any physical evidence that is submitted and accepted by the court as evidence. Judge Swanlund informed the jury that it was through the testimonies and physical evidence that they were to make their decision in the case. The jury was then adjourned until 09:00 a.m. the next morning.

Randy and I left the court room. It had been a long day. We were both exhausted.

Randy remarked: "Well, it's started. I firmly believe that we are off to a good start. We have a sharp jury. They'll see right through Sheriff Johnston and his smoke screens. I've seen a lot of juries and believe me we got a good one. Things are all going to work out, you'll see."

Randy smiled. I told him, I certainly hoped that he was right. He reassured me that things were going good. He told me to try and relax, remarking once again that everything was going to work out. The ride home was rather a quiet one. We were all deep in thought over the anticipation of the start of the trial in the morning. I knew I was not going to get much sleep that night.

I was right; that night was spent tossing and turning. Thoughts of the trial kept racing through my mind. My body was exhausted, but my brain just would not slow down. The trial was not just about bringing Sheriff Johnston and his administration down. It was, more importantly, concerning validating that I was, in fact, the victim, and I did not do anything improper or illegal. The jury, by convicting Sheriff Johnston, would enable me to bring about closure. It would allow me the satisfaction that I ended my law enforcement career on a successful note. It would enable me to be able to move on with my life.

I guess, for me, the trial itself was about me and not Johnston. Johnston and his administration might be the ones on trial, but in my mind, so was I. This final chapter would determine whether or not I wasted the last twenty three years of my life. It would decide for me if the system really worked, the justice system that I had devoted my entire life to protecting and enforcing. Thoughts continued to randomly bounce about my mind as my alarm clock suddenly rang. It was morning, October 1, 1996; the first day of the actual trial had arrived.

Randy picked Sherry and me up around 6:30 a.m., and we made the hour and half drive to the Federal District Court House. Traffic was heavy and moving rather slowly as we made the trip.

We spent the time in Randy's vehicle going over the witness list, discussing the witnesses that Randy intended to call for that day. Randy's wife, Patty, came with us. She came every day to court to lend moral support to Sherry and me. Her cheerful demeanor was an inspiration to us all. We enjoyed her company and welcomed her support.

The procedure followed in the trial was that we would present our case first. We anticipated that our case would take approximately two weeks, just to get all our witnesses to testify. Then Mr. Custington would put on Sheriff Johnston's defense, which we were told would take about another week of testimony. This would be followed by three to four days of rebuttal testimony and then final arguments by both the attorneys. The case would then go to the jury for deliberation and a verdict. We had a long drawn out process to face. It took two years to get here and now it had finally arrived. We drove to the court house in positive anticipation that we would succeed, but yet there was still the intimidation of the power house of attorneys representing Sheriff Johnston and the others.

The trial started promptly at 0:900 a.m., with opening statements. First Randy and then Mr. Custington gave the jury their opening statements. Randy began by outlining to the jury how my civil rights had been violated in regards to my freedom of speech. He told the jury how Sheriff Johnston first perceived that I was going to support his opponent, Atwater in the 1994 Sheriff's election. He explained how Sheriff Johnston took steps to intimidate me in an attempt to prevent me from supporting Atwater. He then went on, outlining how I felt like a victim of politics and finally, how I went public supporting Atwater.

Randy covered the steps of retaliation that Sheriff Johnston, Undersheriff Deiter, and Chief Halsted executed against me for supporting Atwater. Randy paused. He looked at each one of the jurors individually, his eyes making contact with each and every one of them, one at a time. He had their full undivided attention. He continued, stating that what they did to his client was wrong. It was, in fact, a clear-cut violation of my constitutional rights.

Randy then commented that there was even more. He told the jury the story of how a group of deputies, including myself, went to the FBI requesting a Grand Jury investigation into the activities of Sheriff Johnston. He advised them that my decision to go to the FBI was made only after information came to light that Sheriff Johnston was possibly involved in criminal activities. Randy went on, advising that I felt it was improper to become involved in investigating my own supervisors and the proper avenue was to request the FBI to investigate. He then informed the jury that one of the functions of the FBI was to investigate the police on matters involving law enforcement personnel who are suspected of violating the law. Randy remarked that it was the proper procedure for me to have taken. He then detailed the steps of retaliation taken by Sheriff Johnston, Undersheriff Deiter and Chief Halsted toward me for going to the FBI and requesting an investigation.

Randy stopped. He looked up at the jury with a concerned look upon his face. "Ladies and gentlemen of the jury, the facts that we will demonstrate in this case will show that my client," Randy pointed at me, "acted in a proper, responsible and a professional manner. Each and every action he took was within his constitutional rights as well as morally and ethically the correct thing to do. Sheriff Johnston and his administration however, acted improperly and clearly in violation the sergeant's rights. Then they intentionally took steps, direct and calculating steps to retaliate against my client. As you see the story unfold in this court of law, I know you will agree with me that the behavior of Sheriff Johnston, Undersheriff Deiter, and Chief Halsted was, and is, unacceptable and will not be tolerated." Randy then thanked the jury and returned to his seat.

Randy did a good job with his opening statement. I was happy with the way it went. I also was pleased to see how interested the jury appeared. They seemed to be listening to every word Randy had to say.

Mr. Custington got up and approached the jury. He began to deliver his opening statement. I listened intently, wondering exactly what he was going to say in their defense. Neither Randy nor I actually knew the strategy behind Custington's defense of Johnston.

He started out by advising the jury that his client, Sheriff Johnston, has been sheriff of Kingston County for more than seventeen years. He was elected sheriff four times, each time by a wide margin of votes. He is a dedicated police officer who has brought about many positive changes in the sheriff's office. He is not a criminal and does not violate individuals' rights.

Mr. Custington paused for a moment and then continued.

"What this trial is all about is perception, choices, and consequences."

"The sergeant here," he pointed at me, "The sergeant developed the misconception that Sheriff Johnston tried to intimidate him for supporting his opponent in the 1994 election. This is totally and absolutely false. Sheriff Johnston wanted to talk to the sergeant, yes, but not to intimidate him. Sheriff Johnston is a man that has always practiced hands-on supervision. He always goes out into the field to be with his men. This entire case is one where the sergeant overreacted, based on his own false perceptions. Then, as we will demonstrate in this court, the sergeant made the wrong choices and was unwilling to accept the consequences for his own actions. It was easier for the sergeant to blame the sheriff than admit that he, himself, was in the wrong."

Mr. Custington continued.

"The evidence presented will show that Sheriff Johnston and his administration acted properly. It will clearly demonstrate that they are the true victims in this case. You the jury will see that the sergeant's entire case is based on misconceptions which drove him to make the wrong choices and that he refused to accept the consequences of his actions."

Mr. Custington had large display posters that he set up in the court room. The posters listed me, misconceptions, unrealistic perceptions, choices, and consequences all in capital letters. On another poster, it listed each of the perceptions; choices that they claimed I had made. A third poster listed Sheriff Johnston's accomplishments over the course of his seventeen-year career. The poster idea was a smart maneuver on Mr. Custington's part. Seeing items in bold print tends to make people believes that it is true. Mr. Custington spared no expense in the material he designed to press the issues of their defense.

Mr. Custington hammered home to the jury misconception, choices, and consequences.

"No ones' rights were violated here and there was no retaliation taken against the plaintiff in the case." He continued. He then thanked the jury and returned to his seat.

Judge Swanlund advised Randy to call his first witness. Randy called Capt. Terry Hill to the stand. Capt. Hill walked into the court room. The judge swore him in and he sat down at the witness stand.

Randy began his examination of Capt. Hill by asking him to relate his career as a deputy sheriff working for Kingston County Sheriff's Office to the jury. The captain detailed his career. He advised that he was a twenty-five-year veteran of the sheriff's office. He had been a captain for the last fifteen years. His duties as captain were that of an administrator over- seeing patrol operations. He had worked for many years, ever since becoming captain, on the day shift with weekends off. He worked plain clothes as opposed to being in uniform. Captain Hill had received a variety of awards over the years for outstanding service. He never had any disciplinary action taken against him.

Randy asked Capt. Hill if his status with the sheriff's office changed and if so to describe when and how his status changed. The captain began to describe the changes that came about as a result of the 1994 sheriffs' election. He said in the summer of 1994, ex-deputy Atwater came to him and asked him if he would be his undersheriff, if Atwater won the election for sheriff. Captain Hill told Atwater he would accept the position of undersheriff. It became known publicly that he was supporting Atwater for the position of sheriff in the 1994 election.

Captain Hill went on to relate that shortly after it was announced that he had agreed to be Atwater's undersheriff, he was contacted by Chief Halsted. The chief informed him that he made a terrible mistake by agreeing to be Atwater's undersheriff. He should have told Atwater to "get fucked." Chief Halsted then warned Captain Hill that his career was over, if Atwater lost the election.

Captain Hill related that within a day or so of the announcement that he was going to be Atwater's undersheriff, he was contacted by Undersheriff Deiter. He was informed by Deiter that Sheriff Johnston was not pleased with his decision to support Atwater, nor to hear that he agreed to be Atwater's undersheriff. Undersheriff Deiter then remarked that Sheriff Johnston had a way of getting even with those that refused to remain loyal to him. He implied to Capt. Hill that he made a serious mistake in casting his support for Atwater and he had better fix it, before it became too late to save his career.

Capt. Hill continued, saying that a couple of days later, Sheriff Johnston came to see him at the precinct office. The sheriff told him he was upset with his decision to be Atwater's undersheriff. Sheriff Johnston informed him that he should remember that even if Atwater won the election, he would still have to work for him for another three months, until Atwater would take office at the first of the new year. Sheriff Johnson remarked that three months can be an awfully long time and a lot can happen to a person's career in that period of time. He then looked directly into Capt. Hill's eyes and remarked that those that support Atwater will pay and he will get even with each and every one of them. Sheriff Johnston smiled and told Captain Hill that he always liked him, so he was going to give him some good career advice. He told the captain,

"You better reconsider your decision to support Atwater."

Randy stood up from his chair and asked Captain Hill how he felt after his conversation with Sheriff Johnston.

Mr. Custington jumped up from the defendant's table yelling "I object. It calls for conjecture. I object."

Judge Swanlund sustained the objection.

Randy withdrew the question. He then continued with his

line of questioning of Capt. Hill. He could see the jury was engrossed in what Captain Hill had to say.

"Who won the election?" Randy asked.

"Sheriff Johnston did." Capt. Hill replied.

"What happened to you after the 1994 election?"

Captain Hill repeated the question, as he looked directly at the jury.

"Well," He replied, "The day after the election, I was contacted by Chief Halsted at the precinct office. He told me that I was being reassigned to swing shift. My days off were changed from weekends to week days. My duties as administrator overseeing patrol operations were removed. I was required to wear a uniform again, after fifteen years of working plain clothes. I was basically reduced to the position of patrol sergeant but allowed to retain the rank of captain."

He advised that Chief Halsted told him he was to help the sergeants out and fill in where they needed him. He no longer had any duties directly assigned to him. Capt. Hill then stated that later he had a conversation with Undersheriff Deiter who told him that he would remain on swing shift the rest of his career. The undersheriff then told him if he wanted to retire, the administration would not fight him on requesting retirement. Deiter further advised Capt. Hill that if Atwater had been successful in defeating Sheriff Johnston for the position of sheriff, then Johnston, Halsted and he would all have lost their jobs, since both Halsted and he held positions appointed by the sheriff.

Capt. Hill related to the jury how Undersheriff Deiter informed him, now that Sheriff Johnston won the election, those that supported Atwater should worry about their careers because they are in jeopardy.

Randy continued to ask a series of questions concerning Sheriff Johnston, Undersheriff Deiter and Chief Halsted.

Capt. Hill testified that Undersheriff Deiter informed him Sheriff Johnston was considering pulling my commission card. Capt. Hill pointed at me as he told the jury "the sergeant over there had been suspended the day after the election. Sheriff Johnston wanted to get rid of him and did not want the sergeant to be able to return to work. If he did, the sergeant would not be able to work as a police officer. The commission card is the authority that gives the police powers to an individual. Sheriff Johnston advised Deiter that since he is the one that signs and issues the cards, he should be able to take them away if he wants to." Undersheriff Deiter told Capt. Hill they were looking into the possibility of doing that to the sergeant. Capt. Hill told the jury how a couple of days after the 1994 election, "the sergeant over there," again pointing at me, "was suspended. It was announced at the "Brass Meeting" of sheriff supervisors, the sergeant was suspended for an undetermined amount of time, and he was the focus of internal affair's investigation stemming from him filing a claim for damages against the sheriff for violating his rights."

Sheriff Johnston, Undersheriff Deiter, and Chief Halsted, all three of them, sat there in the court room at the defendant's table glaring at Capt. Hill. It was obvious to everyone in the court room, including the jury, that Capt. Hill was under an extreme amount of pressure as he sat there on the witness stand. Capt. Hill maintained his composure, although he was feeling very shaky and nervous as he spoke. He came across AS honest and sincere in his answers. Equally important, he came across as a broken man whose career had been destroyed and it had an effect on the jury.

Randy asked Capt. Hill if I was eventually allowed to return to work at the sheriff's office.

Capt. Hill responded that I did return to work around January of 1995.

Randy then asked the captain if he observed how I was treated differently, after I returned to work in January of 1995. Capt. Hill advised the jury that after I returned to work, he noticed that Sheriff Johnston and Chief Halsted both appeared to micro-manage my every action and look for things that they could come down on me for. He stated that the sergeant continuously was made to justify his decisions, and was basically held to a higher degree of accountability than any of the other supervisors.

Capt. Hill told how I would ask him to witness reports that I was required to turn into Chief Halsted. He then stated that on at least two occasions I was accused of not turning in reports that he had witnessed me turning in. He stated that during the entire year of 1995, Sheriff Johnston, Undersheriff Deiter, and Chief Halsted continually attempted to invent reasons to have me investigated for misconduct or for not performing my duties.

Randy switched the topic away from me and asked Capt. Hill about the anonymous letters that he received.

Capt. Hill stated that starting around Christmas of 1994, his wife and he began receiving anonymous letters. He related that the letters started out accusing each of them of having affairs and cheating on the other. He then described the letters that followed as threatening in nature. He stated he tried to get the sheriff's office to investigate the letters, however, Undersheriff Deiter refuse to allow the letters to be investigated.

Randy asked Capt. Hill a series of questions concerning the FBI investigation.

Capt. Hill said that after the anonymous letter of October 19, 1994, came out, listing criminal activities involving Sheriff Johnston and his administration, information concerning Sheriff Johnston's involvement in criminal activities began to surface and was circulating among the deputies. He stated those deputies who were known to have supported Atwater in the election, began receiving documents concerning unlawful activities involving Sheriff Johnston and others. The documents were coming to those deputies anonymously. Capt. Hill remarked that he too began receiving documents, and information concerning Sheriff Johnston, Undersheriff Deiter and Chief Halsted being involved in illegal acts.

He advised that we turned all the material we received over to Randy. Capt. Hill remarked there were some serious allegations made against the sheriff and he felt obligated as a law enforcement officer to have the allegations investigated.

He remarked "In fact, many of us felt obligated to do something about the information that came to light. It was decided upon that the FBI was the proper authority to conduct an investigation into these matters."

Capt. Hill advised the jury that Randy set up the meeting with the FBI. He stated eleven deputies, accompanied by Randy went to the FBI's office and turned over all the documents and information that we possessed to the FBI.

Randy asked Capt. Hill:

"Of all the deputies that went to the FBI, how many of those deputies are still employed and working at the sheriff's office."

Capt. Hill replied. "Two."

Randy questioned "What happened to you and my client?" {he pointed to where I was sitting} "Well," Capt. Hill began to answer "The sergeant over there and myself were suspended for possession of illegal documents, reference the papers that were given to the FBI. We both were found guilty by an in-house investigation and would have been terminated if we both didn't retire, so we both retired. Neither of us wanted to retire. We were not ready to retire. We had no choice, we had to retire or get fired."

"And what happened to all the others?"

Randy questioned.

"Well, two of them were fired by Sheriff Johnston. Five others were all subjected to internal affairs investigations that would have resulted in their termination, but they either quit or retired prior to being fired."

Capt. Hill remarked that every one of the internal affairs investigations against those deputies were intiated by either Sheriff Johnston or Undersheriff Deiter.

Randy requested Capt. Hill to explain the procedure followed in an internal affair's investigation.

Capt. Hill explained "The sheriff, under his authority as chief administrator, would order an internal affairs investigation based on a complaint filed against the officer in question. The complaint could come from an individual inside the police department or a citizen in the community. Sheriff Johnston would then appoint an officer of his choosing to handle the investigation and gather all the facts and information related to the complaint. Our county is a small county and does not have an internal affair's division such as you find in the larger cities. The officer assigned to handle the investigation would turn all the information and evidence he had gathered over to the Sheriff. The sheriff and undersheriff would then get together and decide the guilt or innocence of the party involved."

Randy asked Capt. Hill:

"In regards to yourself and my client, who decided that you and the sergeant were guilty of the charges filed against the two of you by the sheriff and the undersheriff?"

"They did" Capt. Hill replied.

Randy question Capt. Hill in detail concerning his knowledge of the actions taken against me by Sheriff Johnston, Undersheriff Deiter, and Chief Halsted. Randy's questioning lasted the entire day.

When the first day of the actual trial ended, Randy was pleased with the way the testimony went. He was equally happy with the interest the jury appeared to be showing in the case. He advised that he kept glancing over at the jury. They were listening intently and at times appeared to be on the edge of their seats waiting to hear what was coming next. Randy remarked even Johnston, Deiter and Halsted helped our case today by glaring at the captain. He advised he noticed that some of the jurors picked up on the evil looks they were throwing out at Capt. Hill. It appeared to him the jury members were not pleased with them.

Randy decided he was going to rate every day of trial. He decided to rate each day on a scale of one to ten, with one being very bad for us and ten extremely good. He rated the first day as an eight, stating that the only thing that hurt us to some degree was Mr. Custington's opening statement which implied to the jury that I was the bad guy and made the wrong choices. He was pleased with Capt. Hill's demeanor on the stand and thought the captain's answers painted a clear picture to the jury of how things were going on at the sheriff's office around the time of the election of 1994 and afterwards.

As we rode home with Randy that night, we were exhausted but happy and excited about how the trial was going.

October 2, 1996, the second day of trial began with Mr. Custington starting his cross examination of Capt. Hill. It was rather obvious from Mr. Custington's line of questioning that he was making every effort he could to discredit Capt. Hill's testimony. Capt. Hill did an exceptional job of maintaining a professional demeanor while answering each and every question asked honestly and accurately.

Mr. Custington asked "Captain, you and the plaintiff broke into Sheriff Johnston's and Undersheriff Deiter's offices and stole documents, didn't you?"

Capt. Hill replied "No, absolutely not."

He looked directly at the jury when he gave his answer. The jurors could see the honesty in his response.

"You didn't steal some of the documents that were turned over to the FBI?" Mr. Custington demanded to know.

"Most certainly not." Capt. Hill responded.

"Isn't it true that you and the plaintiff conspired to destroy Sheriff Johnston's good name?"

"No, that is not true." Capt. Hill answered.

"Isn't it true, the only reason you went to the FBI was to embarrass the sheriff?" Mr. Custington asked.

"No, that is not true." Capt. Hill responded.

Mr. Custington kept shooting questions back at Capt. Hill as soon as Capt. Hill would answer.

"You knew that the sheriff did nothing wrong and was not involved in any criminal activity at all, didn't you?"

"No, that is not true; in fact, I personally had knowledge that Sheriff Johnston did break the law."

Capt. Hill had witnessed Sheriff Johnston a few years back when he was running for sheriff, break into a local convenience store. Sheriff Johnston bragged that he would break into a store and then call the owner. He would tell the owner that he chased the burglars away in an attempt to catch them, while he was out patrolling the area. Johnston would gain support from local merchants who thought he was actually out at night going the extra mile to protect them and their property. This particular time that Capt. Hill witnessed the incident, occurred one night after a meeting that he attended with Sheriff Johnston. The sheriff was driving, while Capt. Hill was a passenger in the sheriff's car.

Sheriff Johnston stopped his patrol unit by a small grocery store that was closed. He got out of the vehicle, advising Capt. Hill to watch this. He then walked up to the front glass door to the store and smashed the glass to the door with his flash light.

Capt. Hill was shocked and caught completely off guard by the actions of the sheriff. Sheriff Johnston then went into the store and helped himself to a candy bar and soda pop. He motioned to Capt. Hill to come inside. Capt. Hill reluctantly walked into the store. He observed Sheriff Johnston picking up the phone and calling Cen. Com. He advised the dispatcher that Capt. Hill and he just discovered a burglary in progress to the convenience store and chased the burglars off. He looked over at Capt. Hill while he spoke to the dispatcher. He winked at the captain and smiled. Capt. Hill just stood there with a puzzled look on his face. Sheriff Johnston requested Cen. Com. to notify the owner, and have him respond to the store.

The owner arrived at the store a short time later. Sheriff Johnston explained to the owner how they scared off the burglars that were breaking into the store. The owner was impressed. He thanked Sheriff Johnston for his dedication and observations in checking his business. Capt. Hill was in total disbelief. He was shocked at the actions of the sheriff. He could not believe that this was occurring. He was at a loss as to what he should do or say, so he decided to say and do nothing.

That entire night played before Capt. Hill's mind as he sat there on the witness stand. He was aware that Judge Swanlund had ruled in "Motions in Liminee," that he was not allowed to tell the jury about Sheriff Johnston and the burglary. With that in mind, he did not elaborate on his answer. He stopped with, "no, that is not true. I know the sheriff has in fact broken the law." Mr. Custington, I guess, was equally aware of the "Motion in Liminee" ruling. He did not pursue the question any further, but rather changed the subject.

The jury looked somewhat confused. They expected Mr. Custington to ask Capt. Hill what laws he was aware that Sheriff Johnston had broken. When the question was not asked, it gave the appearance that Mr. Custington was attempting to conceal the truth from them. Juries in general do not like it when one of the attorneys comes across trying to hide and conceal things from them. It turns them off to that individual and makes them feel that they cannot trust them. They were developing that kind of a feeling for Mr. Custington and that was good for us.

Mr. Custington spent half the court day in cross examination of Capt. Hill. He finished just as we reached the noon break.

The afternoon session started with Randy calling the second witness in our case. He called one of my medical doctors to testify as to the physical and emotional trauma that I experienced, brought on by the actions and incidents caused by Sheriff Johnston and his administrators. Randy's examination was brief, covering only the issues that he thought it was necessary for the jury to hear and understand.

Mr. Custington proceeded to cross-examine the doctor. He attempted to get the doctor to state that I was paranoid. She advised him that I was not. The doctor stated that paranoia is based on illusion. It is unjustified fear cause by one's imagination bringing about unrealistic concerns and worries. She stated the fears and concerns which I had experienced were based on actual facts and events in my life. They were caused, directly and indirectly, by Sheriff Johnston, Undersheriff Deiter, and Chief Halsted.

Mr. Custington was outraged by her response. Everyone in the court room could not help but to observe that he was upset and taken back by her statement. Apparently, he had thought, for some strange reason, she was going to say I was paranoid. He should have realized, however, she would have answered the "paranoid question" in that way. In my deposition, he had asked me if I was paranoid and I had told him my doctor's response, which was the same response she stated here. I, myself, was concerned if I might just be paranoid, and I had asked my doctor that same question. I think the word "paranoid" is one of those words that we all use incorrectly more often than not.

Mr. Custington fired back another question at the doctor.

"You do not know that Sheriff Johnston, Undersheriff Deiter, and Chief Halsted caused the events that gave concern to the plaintiff, do you?"

"Yes, I believe I do" She responded.

"No, your assuming they are responsible because of things that the plaintiff told you, isn't that correct?" Mr. Custington asked.

"Well, I guess you're right to some degree. My belief is based on information I received from talking to the plaintiff." The doctor replied.

Mr. Custington responded.

"So if the plaintiff didn't tell you everything or didn't tell you the truth; then your belief could or would be wrong, isn't that correct?"

The doctor became defensive as she answered Mr. Custington's question.

"No, my diagnosis is not wrong. The plaintiff is not paranoid."

She continued, explaining that part of the process of making some diagnoses is based on the patient's perception of what is actually occurring.

She said: "The actual occurrence of events are not that important. It is the perception of the individual that determines if a paranoid condition exists, and to what degree."

The doctor then continued, advising further, "From what was happening in the sergeant's life, I, as a doctor would have been alarmed and concerned about his mental and physical health if he did not have concerns and worries over his current situation at the sheriff's office. It was normal for the sergeant to be fearful and cautious. I, myself, was well aware of Sheriff Johnston's power and control over my patient. I was equally aware of the incidents of behavior which questioned the sheriff's conduct and demeanor. The entire situation created a hostile atmosphere for my patient and others employed there. I further believe an actual threat of physical danger existed for my patient, and that threat was a constant in his life."

Mr. Custington shook his head. He decided to drop the issue, realizing the more he allowed the doctor to talk, the more damage he was doing to his own case.

"No further questions." Mr. Custington advised. He turned and walked back to his seat at the defense table.

The next witness that Randy called on my behalf by way of deposition was a newspaper editor who had passed away a couple of months prior to trial. I remember, oh, so well, how I learned of his death. Randy and I walked into the conference room where depositions were being held. Sheriff Johnston and Mr. Custington were already in the room. As we walked into the room, we overheard them laughing about the editor's death, remarking that we would not be able to use him against them now that he was dead. I found it very distasteful and irritating that life could mean so little to them. This man, the editor, had a family and loved ones who would miss him dearly. There was no reason or justification in finding pleasure in his death, just because it served their best interest.

We had taken the editor's deposition prior to his death. Since the subject is now deceased, a reading of his deposition takes the place of his testimony.

Randy read the deposition to the jury. In his deposition, the editor advised; back in 1994, Sheriff Johnston telephoned him prior to the time he had spoken to me. Sheriff Johnston warned him on the phone that I might be calling him. He stated, the sheriff told him that I was a disgruntled employee who had been passed over for promotion. The sheriff further informed him that he {Sheriff Johnston} had received information that I was involved in illegal narcotic activities in regards to an undercover operation.

The deposition went on, stating I informed him of the meeting I had with Sheriff Johnston on October 10, 1994, and of the interview by Chief Halsted on October 25, 1994, when I was accused of writing the anonymous letter.

Randy continued to read the deposition. It stated that I told the editor I felt I was intimidated by Sheriff Johnston and was a victim of politics. It cited the reasons why I called the editor. I wanted to make a public announcement that I was supporting Atwater for sheriff in the 1994 election.

The nice part of the reading of the deposition into the record was the fact that Mr. Custington was not given the opportunity to try to discredit the witness or to down play the testimony to the jury. The editor's deposition was admitted as read into evidence.

The procedure, concerning physical evidence, followed in trial was after a witness identifies the evidence to the jury, the attorney can move to have that piece of evidence admitted. The judge then makes a ruling, either admitting or denying that particular item. All of the evidence that the judge admits goes to the jury to be used in deliberating the case at the end of trial.

After Randy completed the reading of the newspaper editor's deposition and got it admitted, the jury was excused for the day. After the jury departed the court room, Randy requested to approach the bench. Judge Swanlund told him to come forward. Randy then asked the judge to reconsider one of the "Motions in Liminee." He asked Judge Swanlund to allow Mr. Falkner, the county coroner, to be allowed to testify as to a certain conversation he had with Sheriff Johnston. This was a conversation in which Johnston told Mr. Falkner he was going to get every one of the deputies who had gone to the FBI. He would make them sorry, and they were going to pay. Randy argued that talking to the FBI was in fact protected speech under the first amendment rights of the U.S. constitution and, therefore, Mr. Falkner's testimony was imperative in demonstrating violations of my constitutional rights by Sheriff Johnston.

Judge Swanlund ruled that Mr. Falkner would be allowed to testify, but only to that part of his knowledge involving the conversation he had with Sheriff Johnston, dealing with the deputies who went to the FBI. There were other conversations where Sheriff Johnston made threats to Falkner. Those conversations were still held by the judge to be in "Liminee" and not admissible to be mentioned in front of the jury. Randy was pleased; he was able to convince the judge to allow Mr. Falkner's testimony involving threats against the deputies that went to the FBI.

Two days of the actual trial was over with. Randy felt everything was going well. He rated the day as another eight. I personally just felt nervous. We still had a long drawn out process ahead of us.

On the third day of trial, Randy called Sheriff Johnston to the stand. Right from the start, Sheriff Johnston displayed his political charisma. This type of charm enabled him to get reelected to the sheriff position four times. His demeanor appeared very attentive, concerned, and a little nervous, but full of confidence in himself. When he answered questions, he would turn directly toward the jury and in a strong and positive voice relay his answer directly to them. My heart sank when Sheriff Johnston began to speak. He came across so smooth, as the sentences poured from his lips. I was afraid the jury would buy his bullshit. He, after all, was a professional speaker. His answers were articulate and convincing. He had an answer, or I should say, a rational excuse for everything asked of him. I looked over to the jury to observe each one of them. They were all giving Sheriff Johnston their undivided attention.

Randy's first series of questions to Sheriff Johnston were merely basic background questions. The sheriff took advantage of that line of questioning to expound on his career and accomplishments. Randy proceeded to question him concerning his contact with me on October 10, 1994. I sat on the edge of my chair, listening in disbelief as the sheriff recalled the events of the meeting he had with me that night.

Sheriff Johnston advised the jury he did contact me that evening because of concerns that he had over a conversation with a local newspaper editor. He related the editor had told him that he received information that I was involved in illegal narcotic activities regarding an undercover sting operation I supervised and worked, in 1989. He went on to state that I had always been a good cop and he wanted to confront me with this information. He did not believe it was true and he wanted to hear my side of the story first hand.

Sheriff Johnston paused, his eyes wandered across the panel of jurors. He then continued, stating that I became angry at him over being accused of being involved in illegal activities.

"I tried to calm the sergeant down" the sheriff stated and he then continued.

"It was impossible to do. The sergeant's demeanor was out of control and full of hostility. He raised his voice and began yelling at me."

Johnston shook his head at the jury, as if to say, he did not know how to handle the sergeant.

He stated:

"The sergeant told me that he was not going to tolerate my behavior and the things I was saying to him. He said that we had a long history and that I knew he was a good cop. He just seemed to be yelling and carrying on, not really making a lot of sense. Then out of the blue, the sergeant tells me he was going to be Atwater's chief of detectives after Atwater wins the election."

Sheriff Johnston stopped talking and reached over and took a drink of water. I was taken back, I could not believe the lies the man was telling under oath. I was astonished by his elaborate story. He was a mockery to truth and justice. It made me sick. I was also scared with the fact he told the lies so convincingly.

Randy continued to question the sheriff concerning the events and incidents that occurred during the 1994 and 1995-period. I began to realize a distinctive pattern of behavior by the sheriff on the stand. He was constantly clearing his throat prior to answering the question asked of him and he was drinking a lot of water. In fact he went through an entire pitcher of water while he was on the stand and even requested a second pitcher while he sat there answering questions. I hoped the jury was picking up on these two behavioral functions of the sheriff. I hoped they might hold significance in determining how truthful Sheriff Johnston was being in his testimony. I had come to realize, after years of interviewing people, that the subconscious traits demonstrated by an individual are often an obvious sign of deception. The most nerve racking part of a trial is that you just never know what the jury is thinking.

Randy asked Sheriff Johnston:

"Who ordered Chief Halsted to investigate the sergeant on October 25, 1994, in reference to the anonymous letter that had circulated claiming issues of wrong doing by you and your administration?"

Sheriff Johnston turned his attention back to the jury and began to speak once again. His voice was calm with a touch of concern in his delivery as he spoke.

"I ordered the chief to talk to the sergeant. We received information that the sergeant was involved in the anonymous letter. I wanted the matter cleared up. I never really thought the sergeant was involved. When the chief talked to the sergeant, he told him that he was not involved and as far as I was concerned that was the end of it. There was really no actual investigation that took place over the possibility the sergeant was involved in the anonymous letter."

Randy asked the sheriff if any other deputy was ever interviewed by him or at his direction concerning the anonymous letter.

"No."

Randy continued with a series of questions until all the events involving his actions toward me were covered. It took the rest of the court day. When we left the court room that evening, we were all exhausted. It had been a long and intense day. Randy remarked that it was a hard day to call in regards to his rating system. He advised that it all hinged on how the jury took Sheriff Johnston. He related that he was impressed with how well the sheriff carried himself, and that he came across as a dedicated professional. Randy commented he might have hurt us today. He rated the day as a six, on the scale of one to ten. Stating that even if Johnston hurt us, it wasn't that bad. Needless to say, Randy did not do anything to build my confidence with his comments and rating. There again, one of the things I like most about Randy was his honesty in calling it like he saw it. I was not always happy with his comments, but I appreciated him making them; it helped me keep a proper perspective on the issues at hand.

The fourth day of trial began with Mr. Custington cross-examining Sheriff Johnston. He filled the court room with giant charts. The drawings designed for "illustration purposes only," at least that was how they were referred to. The charts were professionally prepared. They looked very impressive. There was one chart that chronologically covered the history of Sheriff Johnston's career. It made the sheriff look like an outstanding administrator, with a multitude of accomplishments. The second chart was titled "The Sergeant's Choices." It listed the events that occurred in 1994 thru 1995 in one column, and a second column read "Wrong Choices Taken By The Sergeant." There was yet a third chart titled "Proper Administration Actions." It listed all of the actions they alleged to be positive acts. They wanted the jury to believe these were positive and justified actions of Sheriff Johnston and his administration. The fourth chart was titled, "Violations Committed By The Sergeant." There were even more charts covering just about everything, each containing justification for their demeanor and actions. They were an illusion of rationalization, in more accurate terms.

Randy looked at me. We were both in disbelief. The jury seemed to be disappearing from our view as Mr. Custington's staff kept setting these charts up in front of us. Each chart was three to four feet wide and approximately five feet in length.

People in general tend to believe what they see in print is true. If that was the case, these charts could hurt us badly.

Randy objected to the use of the charts. Judge Swanlund ruled that the charts were admissible for "illustration purposes only."

Randy then requested that the charts be moved away from in front of the Plaintiff's table, advising that they were obscuring our view of the jury. Judge Swanlund advised Mr. Custington to move the charts so they would not block the plaintiff's table.

Mr. Custington began his interview of Sheriff Johnston, by having the sheriff detail the high points of his career.

Sheriff Johnston responded by advising that his position was similar to being the C.E.O. of a twelve million-dollar business. He then went on and on; it sounded like a campaign speech. Sheriff Johnston was the youngest person in the state's history to become sheriff. He also was involved in many positive changes in the evolving field of law enforcement over the years. These items where not the issues that were on trial: they were however used by Mr. Custington and the sheriff to cloud the real issues of this case.

Randy followed up with redirect of Sheriff Johnston after Mr. Custington completed his cross examination. Pieces of evidence kept getting admitted by both sides, after each piece was identified by testimony.

The afternoon session consisted of testimony from Deputy Lori Plankin, Deputy Michael Baker, and Sergeant Wayne Newton. It was obvious by each one's demeanor that they felt intimidated and nervous on the stand giving testimony against Sheriff Johnston. In fact, the jury witnessed just how scared they actually were. It was enlightening to the jury, regarding the problems that existed within the sheriff's office.

Lori Plankin testified to Sheriff Johnston making statements at a Dare Officer's meeting that he would get the thirty deputies that voted against him in the guild vote for endorsement and how those officers would pay.

Mike Baker gave testimony regarding conversations he had with Sheriff Johnston: the conversation, whereby Sheriff Johnston made comments of getting the deputies that supported Atwater and the conversation concerning the deputies who went to the FBI. Deputy Baker's voice trembled as he spoke, answering the questions Randy asked of him. There was no hesitation in his speech. He came across as honest and very sincere. It was obvious that he was scared. The tone of his voice and his demeanor had an impact on everyone in the court room.

I felt sorry for both Lori and Mike. Sorry they had to be put through this process of testifying. I also had a lot of respect for their moral conviction and courage in taking the stand and telling the truth especially when they both realized the effect it would have on their careers.

The last one to take the stand for the day was Sergeant Newton. He had avoided the truth in giving his deposition a few months back. He advised Randy prior to testifying that he was going to tell the truth on the stand and he would not tell any more lies. He was done being intimidated by the sheriff and his attorney.

Randy had told me that Sergeant Newton's testimony could help us or hurt us. It would depend on whether he would be honest or not. Randy advised he could get up on the stand seeing the sheriff and go back to lying. He just did not know. He hoped for the best. He hoped that Sgt. Newton would hold up and be honest.

Randy began questioning Sgt. Newton. "Isn't it true that when I took your deposition in this case that you were less that honest and not completely truthful in your answers?"

"Yes, that is correct" Sgt. Newton replied.

"Why were you not truthful?" Randy asked.

Sgt. Newton began to answer. "I was intimidated by the process. I had been contacted by Mr. Custington prior to giving my deposition. Mr. Custington had advised me how he wanted me to answer certain questions that he anticipated you would be asking. He . . . "

Mr. Custington jumped up from his chair, cutting Sgt. Newton off in the middle of his sentence. He began to object to Randy's line of questioning. Judge Swanlund kept overruling Mr. Custington's objections and allowing Randy to continue. Sgt. Newton went on;

"Mr. Custington told me in the interview we had prior to my deposition that I was to answer every single question with either "no" or "I do not recall at this time.""

Randy asked Sgt. Newton. "Are you prepared to tell the whole truth here today?"

"Yes, yes I am."

Sgt. Newton replied.

"Did anyone prepare you as to what or how to answer any anticipated questions that could be asked of you here today?"

Randy inquired.

Sgt. Newton answered "I was ordered by Sheriff Johnston to meet with Mr. Custington at the county's personnel office. In fact, all the deputies testifying in this case were ordered to meet with Mr. Custington prior to testifying."

"I . . . "

"Objection, I object." Mr. Custington yelled drowning out Sgt. Newton's voice.

"Overruled,"

Judge Swanlund snapped back. It appeared that the honorable judge was very interested in Sgt. Newton's testimony.

Sgt. Newton continued "I went into the interview room to talk to Mr. Custington. He began to go over the testimony I was going to give in this trial. He started to direct me as to how I was to answer certain questions, if they were asked of me. I became upset and informed him that what he was doing was not right. I think it was at that very moment that I realized exactly what was happening to me through the deposition process and everything. I was being compromised. I had been less than honest because I feared for my career and also out of sense of misplaced loyalty to Sheriff Johnston and the sheriff's office."

Sgt. Newton paused.

Mr. Custington objected once again to the line of questioning.

Judge Swanlund commented that he was sure Mr. Custington objected, but the objection was overruled.

Sgt. Newton began to speak again. "I got up, and told Mr. Custington that I was going to tell the truth when I was called upon to testify in court. I informed him that no one, absolutely no one, was going to influence my testimony or tell me what to say. When I stood up, Mr. Custington got up and got right into my face. He warned me that if I valued my career, I had better sit down and listen to him. I turned and walked out."

Randy began to ask Sgt. Newton a series of questions concerning Sheriff Johnston. Sgt. Newton kept his word. He answered each question truthfully. Each answer he gave damaged Sheriff Johnston's defense and helped to strengthen my case against the sheriff. I gained back a lot of respect for Sgt. Newton, respect that I had lost when he was less than honest in his deposition.

Sgt. Newton testified that Sheriff Johnston was obsessed with power. He advised that he "experienced concern over Sheriff Johnston's demeanor and that he warned his deputies to be extremely cautious around the sheriff." He went on to state that

"Sheriff Johnston was a very vindictive person. On more than one occasion, Johnston made comments that he would get those deputies that supported Atwater and who went to the FBI." He said, "they would pay and their careers were over."

Randy asked Sgt. Newton one last question.

"Why did you lie in your deposition?"

Sgt. Newton replied.

"I, I," he repeated himself, "did it out of a sense of loyalty to the sheriff's office and to Sheriff Johnston. I have more than twenty years of service to the department. I felt pressured, scared, and I was told by Mr. Custington it was the right thing to do. I don't know—I knew it was wrong."

Mr. Custington once again stood up; "Your Honor, I object."

Judge Swanlund replied, "I bet you do. Sit down. Your objection is over ruled."

Randy ended his examination there.

Mr. Custington began his cross examination of Sgt. Newton. He started by picking up Sgt. Newton's deposition. He walked over to the witness stand and handed Sgt. Newton a copy of his deposition. He then advised Sgt. Newton to turn to a certain page in the deposition and to read that section to the jury. Sgt. Newton turned to the jury and read the section requested.

"Sgt. Newton," Mr. Custington asked, "Is that the answer you gave in your deposition?"

"Yes, that is the answer I gave."

"And now your stating here in the court room today, that statement that you gave is not true?" Mr. Custington questioned.

"Yes, that is correct. It is not true." Sgt. Newton answered.

He looked at the jury as he gave the answer. Everyone in the court room could see the pain on Sgt. Newton's face. We could feel the emotion being reflected in his voice. Yet, he sat straight and tall as he answered each question without hesitation. Here sat a man admitting he lied, admitting his mistakes, regaining his pride and integrity with each word that he spoke. On the stand that day during the cross examination process by Mr. Custington, Sergeant Newton made peace with himself and was ready to accept the consequences of his actions.

One after one, Mr. Custington pointed out the lies' Sgt. Newton had told in his deposition.

Sgt. Newton continued to respond. "Yes, that is correct. That is what I said then and this is what I am saying now."

Mr. Custington concluded his cross examination by asking Sgt. Newton: "Do you believe Sheriff Johnston acted improperly and vindictively in his actions against the sergeant, the plaintiff in this case?"

Mr. Custington pointed over at me as he spoke.

"Yes, I do," Sgt. Newton replied.

"Isn't it true, Sgt. Newton, that you just admitted to everyone in this court room, including the jury, that you are a liar and you lied on your deposition?" Mr. Custington asked in a demanding fashion.

The courtroom silence was overwhelming as Sgt. Newton answered the question.

"Yes, sir."

"So why should anyone believe what you're saying now?" Mr. Custington demanded.

He put his hands up in the air in disgust advising that he withdrew the question and had nothing further to ask the witness. Sgt. Newton was excused from the witness stand and exited the courtroom.

Randy and I discussed the events of the day as we drove home that evening. Randy felt the jury could go either way with Sgt. Newton's testimony. It could help or hurt us. It all depended on what the jury perceived to be true from Sgt. Newton's testimony. Randy rated the day as a six on the scale of one to ten. Advising, it all depended on how the jury viewed Sheriff Johnston's testimony as well as Sgt. Newton's testimony. He just did not know. He felt that even if they didn't believe Sgt. Newton and it did hurt our case, it was minimal and everything was still going well.

I felt that I really had lost all objectivity involved in determining how the trial was going. I was just too closely involved to really be able to evaluate the day's proceedings with any accuracy. I just kept telling myself that with each court day that passed, I was one day closer to finding closure and getting the entire ordeal behind me. I looked forward to closing this chapter of my life once and for all.

October 4, 1996, the fifth day of trial, Undersheriff Deiter took the stand. He spent the entire day giving testimony. The undersheriff was a smooth talker who came across well. He was professional in appearance and articulate in his answers. Even when Randy would catch him giving testimony that was contradictory in nature, as to statements made by Sheriff Johnston, he always had an answer. He would rationalize the inconsistencies in their testimonies without missing a heart beat. His rationalization would even make sense and would be given with convincing delivery. I concluded that he was an accomplished liar and excelled in the field of deception. I could only hope and pray that the jury would see through his polished outward manner and reach the same conclusion.

The court day was long and drawn out. We were tired when we finally arrived back at Randy's residence that evening. Sherry and I went back to Randy's to work on assisting Randy prepare additional items that we wanted to cover in the trial. It was also a chance for all of us to do some brainstorming on how the trial was going, as well as any strategy thoughts we could come up with to improve our case.

Capt. Hill came by Randy's residence that evening, arriving just as we were getting out of Randy's vehicle to go into the house. He parked his car and walked over to the four of us who were standing in the driveway. He had somewhat of a smile on his face. He was carrying a large basket wrapped in colored cellophane. It was one of those types of baskets that people get at Christmas time, the type containing summer sausage, snacks, candies, wine and crackers. He handed the basket to me, stating "a bunch of the deputies all contributed to getting this for you and Sherry. It just a little something to let you guys know we care and are supporting you."

I read the enclosed card. "Men of integrity are the hands that hold the world together." It was signed by many of the deputies and their wives, wishing us luck and giving us their support and prayers that the truth will prevail in our court case. Sherry and I were both taken aback by the support and friendship we continued to receive at our time of need throughout the entire ordeal.

The sixth and seventh day of trial were filled with testimony by the deputies. One after another, Randy called in the deputies who gave testimony concerning Sheriff Johnston and the administrations demeanor and behavior. They testified, citing incidents of retaliation as well as vindictive actions undertaken by Sheriff Johnston, Undersheriff Deiter and Chief Halsted toward myself and others in the department who had either supported Atwater or went to the FBI, or did both.

Everyone that Randy called as witnesses to our case portrayed a demeanor that was obvious to the jury and those in the court room; they were scared and uncomfortable being on the stand. Each of them realized that their own careers were in jeopardy just by testifying. Each one of them came across as honest and sincere in answering the questions asked of them. Deputy Frank Tooney, Deputy John Farrell, Deputy Steve Farrell, Deputy Teri Willis, and Deputy Ed Talgon were among the deputies who testified.

Following the testimony given by the deputies, Randy called June Milton, a retired city mayor to the stand. She told the jury how Sheriff Johnston pressured her into firing two of the police officers that were employed by the city in which she was the mayor. She advised that at the time that she fired the officers, the sheriff had informed her that the two officers were involved in drugs and that he had personal knowledge of their drug related activities. The two officers were probationary officers at the time of their firing. June stated that because of their probationary status, they could be terminated without stating any just cause for the termination. She advised that she fired them under the direction of Sheriff Johnston and his statements concerning their drug involvement. She later learned from Sheriff Johnston, himself, that the main reason he wanted them terminated was because they were supporting Johnston's opponent back in the 1990 Sheriff's election.

Retired Mayor June Milton continued to testify, advising the jury of how Sheriff Johnston would rave and carry on about certain individuals who refused to go along with his plans. She related that to Sheriff Johnston, you were either a supporter or the enemy. There was no such thing as middle ground. She advised how the sheriff would label anyone who did not go along with him as a "Judas" or "traitor." She basically gave testimony concerning her experience and observations in dealing with Sheriff Johnston's vindictive behavior over the period of time that she was mayor.

June Milton's testimony was followed by Randy calling Ted Falkner, the chief coroner for the county, to the stand. Judge Swanlund had reconsidered Randy's request concerning allowing Ted Falkner to testify. He did, however, limit Mr. Falkner's testimony. He was only allowed to testify what Sheriff Johnston told him concerning the deputies that went to the FBI.

Chief Coroner Ted Falkner was sworn in.

Randy approached him and asked: "Would you please tell the jury about the conversation that took place between Sheriff Johnston and you concerning the deputies that went to the FBI."

Chief Coroner Ted Falkner responded,

"Well, I believe it was shortly after Sheriff Johnston learned that a group of deputies had contact with the FBI concerning his conduct and behavior that he contacted me. Sheriff Johnston came storming into my office and began yelling. He told me that ten or eleven deputies went to the FBI requesting that a Grand Jury investigation be initiated against him. He then informed me that one of my Deputy Coroners went with the Deputy Sheriffs to the FBI."

Ted Falkner continued:

"Sheriff Johnston was furious. He was screaming and cussing. He told me, he would get every one of those fuckin deputies and they would pay. He would see that their careers are over and make them wish that they never tried to mess with him."

"The sheriff just kept repeating himself. Stating, they'll pay. They'll pay."

"Sheriff Johnston demanded that I fire the deputy coroner that went to the FBI with the deputy sheriffs."

Randy asked, "So what did you tell Sheriff Johnston when he demanded that you fire one of your employees?"

Ted Falkner responded: "I kicked Sheriff Johnston out of my office. I told him his behavior was unacceptable."

Randy advised Judge Swanlund that he had nothing further and he was done with his examination of the witness. Mr. Custington then did cross examination of Mr. Falkner, as he had done with every one of the witnesses Randy had called to the stand.

Mr. Custington's cross examination of Mr. Falkner did little to impact or discredit his testimony.

Randy and I were both pleased with the manner in which all our witnesses testified, as well as to their demeanor of professionalism and honesty that they displayed to the jury. They came across well and the jury seemed receptive to the facts they outlined. Our confidence was building. We felt the trial was going well. We also, however, realized that Mr. Custington still had his "Case in chief," to present to the jury. The trial was far from over and we had not won yet.

The local newspapers were a great disappointment to us and to all of the deputies that wanted the public to be aware of the true facts concerning Sheriff Johnston and the sheriff's office. The newspapers, especially the daily paper seemed to be rather biased in their reporting of the trial. Each day the headlines supported Sheriff Johnston and portrayed him as wining the law suit. The articles were one sided, for example, one article advised that a "group of disgruntled deputies," was attempting to smear Sheriff Johnston. Another example was the paper stated that Sheriff Johnston was a victim of political assassination by his opponents.

After Retired Mayor June Milton and Chief Coroner Ted Falkner testified, my wife, Sherry, over heard Sheriff Johnston telling one of the reporters covering the trial not to print either one of their testimonies in the paper. The paper never made mention that either one of them even testified. It was our opinion and belief that the local daily paper was in Sheriff Johnston's pocket. We also firmly believe that the actions of the local paper by not reporting the truth and doing so objectively did a deliberate disservice to the public and the community who had a right to know exactly what was occurring within their local sheriff's department.

CHAPTER FOURTEEN

ENHANCING ONE'S CREDITABLITY HINGES ON UNDERSTANDING THAT ONE DOES NOT HAVE A HIDDEN AGENDA, AND ESTABLISHING FIRM BELIEF, ONE'S STATEMENTS ARE TRUE AND ACCURATE.

On the eighth day of trial, Randy called Chief Halsted to the stand. Randy's strategy in trying our case was to call Sheriff Johnston, Undersheriff Deiter, and Chief Halsted, all as our witnesses. Randy felt there were certain questions that he wanted to ask them that he might not get a chance to ask in redirect. In redirect you are only allowed to ask questions that relate to the questions the other side asked in direct, which limits your ability in getting in certain facts that you want the jury to hear. His strategy was working well. We were getting the questions we wanted asked, and getting the answers we wanted on a lot of the issues. Issues that would all be tied together before the trial concluded. A bonus to calling Sheriff Johnston, Undersheriff Deiter, and Chief Halsted, that we did not plan on, was the fact that the three of them kept contradicting each other. Some of the contradictions were so obvious we were certain that the jury caught them.

There were others that were not as recognizable. Randy would attempt to discreetly point them out to the jury.

Chief Halsted came across to the jury as a man of minimal intelligence with a rough and rather crude demeanor. There was no doubt in the juror's minds that he would do whatever Sheriff Johnston asked of him. In fact, he testified to that on the stand. Randy questioned him in detail concerning the events that occurred during the years of 1994 to 1995, starting with Deputy Atwater's announcement that he was running for sheriff and continuing until the time of my suspension in December. He covered Chief Halsted's actions toward myself and other deputies. He also covered the actions of Sheriff Johnston and Undersheriff Deiter. Randy concluded his direct and Mr. Custington completed his cross examination all by the noon break.

The afternoon session began with my wife, Sherry, taking the stand. Randy questioned her, concerning the effects the actions of Sheriff Johnston, Undersheriff Deiter, and Chief Halsted had on me and on our family life. She answered each question clearly and without hesitation. Her answers were sincere and straight forward. They came with such emotional impact that by the time she was done you could have heard a pin drop; she had the undivided attention of everyone in the court room. It was the first and only time she had ever testified in court and she did exceptionally well. I looked around the court room and over at the jury. There was no doubt that they felt her pain and realized the trauma we had gone through.

Randy turned to me, as she walked back to the plaintiff's table and remarked:

"If Mr. Custington is smart; he won't even conduct a cross examination of her."

Sherry's demeanor on the stand was straight forward and professional, but dramatic. It was obvious, she was holding back the tears. It was equally apparent that the entire ordeal which we had experienced through the actions of Sheriff Johnston and his administration would have long-term effects on our lives. Mr. Custington got up from his seat at the defense table and informed Judge Swanlund that he had no questions to ask Sherry and would not be cross examining her. Judge Swanlund called the afternoon recess.

Sheriff Johnston, upon the start of the recess, immediately got up from his seat and walked over to the local reporter from the daily paper. She was seated in the rear of the court room.

Once again, he was overheard advising her as to what he wanted her to do. He informed her that he did not want her to even mention that Sherry testified, and by no means print anything that she said on the stand. The reporter assured the sheriff that nothing would be mentioned in the paper. Hearing the comments Sheriff Johnston had made to the reporter just enhanced our belief that he controlled the newspaper.

The court day ended with me taking the stand and beginning my testimony. Randy had it planned that I would be the last witness called for our side before we rested our case. It was just the start of my testimony, testimony that would keep me on the stand for the next four long and tedious days.

Randy began by having me detail my background to the jury, explaining the training and work experience I had received over the twenty-three years I served as a commissioned police officer employed by the sheriff's department. He apologized to the jury for the time spent going over my background. He told them he realized in covering such things as training and background that they were, at best, boring but necessary in order for them to understand the type of individual and police officer I was. Randy had only started with my testimony when the court ended for the day.

We exited the court room, taking pleasure in the fact that another long day was over and behind us. We were pleased with the way it was progressing. It was going well. Randy rated the day as a nine on the scale of one to ten.

October 10, 1996, started early that morning. It was a beautiful day; the sun was just beginning to rise and there was a light breeze in the air when Randy arrived to pick us up for the ride over to the federal court house. This particular morning Randy's wife

Patty had decided to stay home. She had to run some errands for her mother. Since there were only three of us making the commute, Randy drove his oversize four by four pick-up truck. It was a large Ford, with big tires, so the cab of the truck sat high off the ground.

The day started out, basically, the same as the other mornings before court. The hour or so ride to the Federal Court house was spent talking about the trial. I would take notes during the trip. Writing down notes when topics were being discussed, brought up issues of importance that we needed to remember. In fact, it got so I kept a tablet on my lap, and a pen in my hand during the entire travel time. The first couple of days going over it became somewhat of a joke. I would no sooner put the notebook paper back into the brief case and put my pen away than Randy would say,

"Oh, and write this down; it's important to remember."

So I got in the habit of just holding on to the pen and paper during the entire trip. I guess you could say that the commute time was well-spent, working on our strategy for that coming day's trial.

I really was not looking forward to being on the witness stand the entire day, but I realized that I did not have any choice in the matter. I also knew that I would be extremely happy when my testifying was said and done.

We were about three blocks away from the Federal Court house when suddenly, out of nowhere, it happened. A white sedan veered in front of Randy's truck. Randy had to slam on his brakes to avoid impact. We observed a subject in the passenger side of the vehicle pointing a dark object at us. It all happened so fast that we did not even realize that it was a gun until the sound of gunfire rang out, filling our hearts with sheer terror! It was so loud that the first couple of shots sounded like individual explosions. I reached out to Sherry and pushed her down toward the floor boards of the truck's cab. Time instantly slowed down beyond belief. It slowed to a point of acute awareness. Anxiety and panic overwhelmed us as shattering glass seemed to flutter about the cab of the truck, like feathers floating down from the sky.

Randy punched the accelerator pedal to the floor as he tried to duck down into the seat. The truck lunged forward, impacting the rear quarter panel of the shooter's vehicle. Randy's foot hitting the gas pedal was just a reaction and not an intentional maneuver on his part. It did possibly, however, save our lives. Randy's truck accelerated with tremendous force knocking the shooter's vehicle into a tail spin, causing the driver to momentarily lose control as the car crashed through a picket fence and across the green grass of someone's yard. Randy's truck was out of control as well. It went up over the sidewalk and came to rest just inches away from crashing into the wall of a small business. The entire incident lasted but a brief couple of seconds; it was basically over almost before it started. It did, however, seem like an eternity of time to us as we experienced the sequences of events unfolding. The shooter's vehicle was not immobilized and they were able to flee the scene. My heart was pounding in my ears like a bass drum at a rock concert, when I heard some sort of voice calling out.

"Are—you—guys—all—right?—"

It was Randy yelling. His voice could hardly be heard over the pounding in my ears and chest. The words slowly came out. It was difficult to understand exactly what he was saying. Randy repeated himself, this time saying;

"Are you guys okay?"

Sherry and I both acknowledged, "Yes, we think so."

We just sat there in the cab of Randy's truck, covered with glass from the broken windshield. The three of us were all stunned and a bit bewildered. We were just victims of a drive by shooting. Some individuals unknown to us had just attempted to take our lives. It created a range of emotions within us dominated by anger. We exited the vehicle while scanning the street for the white sedan. We were not certain that the vehicle would not be returning and making a second pass at us. The white sedan was, however, gone and did not return. We could hear the sound of sirens as the police responded to the scene of the incident. We just stood there looking down the hill at the Federal Court house wondering if this attempt on our lives was directly related to the trial, or just an uncanny coincidence. Logic told us that it was, in fact, related to the trial, it was the only thing that made sense. There was, however, no proof.

The entire incident happened so fast, not one of us got the license number nor a description of the driver or passenger in the suspect's vehicle. The only thing the three of us could say with certainty was that both the suspects were white males, possibly over thirty years of age.

The police arrived and took charge of the scene. They wrote the incident off as a "random drive by shooting." The suspects were never located. The interesting part of the situation was that the white sedan was never located, either. Normally, in drive by shootings the vehicle involved is usually stolen and will be found abandoned—that, however, was not the case in this incident. We all knew in our minds that it was more than just a random act.

We arrived at the Federal Court house just as trial was about to begin. Sheriff Johnston looked surprised to see us, at least, that was the impression that I got from the look on his face. Later that day, when I spoke with Sherry and Randy, they both acknowledged that they had the same reaction when they observed Sheriff Johnston's appearance as we walked into the court room. I guess you could say that the only thing we did know and believed with all certainty was that our lives were in danger and the sooner that we got this trial over with, the better it would be for our safety and survival.

Randy informed Judge Swanlund of the ordeal we had just experienced with the attempt on our lives. The judge asked if we wanted to have a recess from the court proceeding today, due to the trauma we suffered. Randy checked with Sherry and me. We all decided to continue. We wanted to get the trial behind us without delays. Randy then informed Judge Swanlund that we declined the recess and wished to move on with the trial.

The day's trial proceedings began with me returning to the witness stand and Randy continuing with his lines of questioning that he had started the day before.

I took a deep breath, I needed to calm down and concentrate on the questions being asked of me. Relax, relax, relax, I told myself. I took another deep breath and repeated the words in my mind. Relax, relax, relax. I could feel my mind kicking in and gaining control as I began to slow down and relax. I repeated the words' three or more times, each time taking in deep breaths and releasing them slowly. It was working, I was about as ready as I could be considering the ordeal we had experienced. I was ready to testify and get this thing over with.

Randy kept me on the witness stand for the next two days. First covering my education and background, and then relating to the jury my experiences and accomplishments over the twenty-three years I spent as a police officer. Randy attempted to give the jury an overview of my career. He covered everything, from my receiving the police officer of the year award in 1982, to my two tours working deep undercover in narcotic operations.

He went into the problems that I experienced in the sheriff's office starting with Sheriff Johnston's conversation with me on October 10, 1994, followed by the treatment I received from Undersheriff Deiter and Chief Halsted throughout 1995.

The technique that Randy used in his line of questioning was designed to be complete without overstating the facts involved in the case. We wanted to hold the jury's interest and prevent them from becoming bored or confused. Randy had explained to me that the demeanor of the jurors was fragile at best. A good juror wants to be educated on the facts of the case but can get turned off quickly if they come to the conclusion that you are wasting their time. We did not want to turn the jury off. We made every attempt to hold their interest. We stated only the facts that we considered directly related to the case.

The jury appeared to be very interested in what I had to say. I felt a bond growing between myself and the members of the jury.

It was a rather unique experience at best. The only real contact I had with the jury members in this case was an occasional eye contact while giving my testimony, yet I sensed understanding, compassion, and respect in their eyes. I really did not know if it was just my imagination or for real. I felt and firmly believed it was real. I needed to believe it was real and sincere to give me the strength to proceed.

October 15, 1996, began with Mr. Custington's cross examination of me. It would prove to be the most difficult part of my testimony. He had a reputation of tearing witnesses apart on the stand. Randy had warned me that Mr. Custington would do everything in his power to undermine my statements and destroy my creditablity. Randy went on to explain to me that once a question is asked of me, I had the floor to answer the question and could not be interrupted or stopped by Mr. Custington as long as my answer stayed within the perimeters of the question. He advised that if I strayed outside the perimeters of the question then Mr. Custington could step in and stop me from answering and also have my answer stricken from the record.

Randy told me to take my time in answering, making certain to stay within the topic. He then explained to me, if any questions "opens a door" take advantage of it and get the testimony in. He explained to me the only way we are allowed to get testimony involving items restricted in "Motions in Liminee" into the case, is if the other side, Mr. Custington, brings up an item and "opens the door."

Randy began to lecture me. He advised me not to allow Mr. Custington to "get to me." I needed to maintain a professional image and appearance on the stand in order to demonstrate to the jury that I was giving my full and undivided attention to the issues and questions at hand.

I told myself that I needed to take my time. I needed to repeat each question asked, analyzing each and every word involved in the question prior to giving an answer. I had to insure that I understood the meaning of each word so that my answer could not be twisted and used against me. I was determined not to become a victim for one of Mr. Custington's traps.

Mr. Custington began his cross examination with hard-hitting questions right from the start. He, too, was determined. He was determined to tear me down and destroy my creditablity in the eyes of the jury.

"Sergeant, you worked undercover in two highly successful undercover operations, isn't that true?" Mr. Custington asked.

"Yes, that is correct." I answered.

"In order to be successful as an undercover officer, you have to be a very good actor, don't you?" Mr. Custington enquired.

"No, I don't believe that is an accurate statement." I responded.

"Well sergeant, explain to the jury why this is not an accurate statement" Mr. Custington demanded.

"An actor reads from a script and portrays something that he is not." I stated,

"Isn't that exactly what you did when you worked undercover? Didn't you portray something that you were not?" He quizzed.

"No, not exactly," I answered.

"Please explain what you mean to the jury," Mr. Custington directed.

I turned to the jury. It appeared that all of the jurors were sitting on the edge of their seats waiting to hear my response. I began to respond. "The characters that I portrayed when I worked undercover were based on experiences from my life. An example; when I infiltrated organized crime, my character was that of an outlaw motorcycle rider who was a wood carver by profession. I have been riding motorcycles since my teenage years. I also have been making wood carvings for more than thirty years and even had a booth at the local fair where I sold the carvings and put on demonstrations of them being made." I repeated, "the character I represented myself as, was based on truth. The truth was drawn from my actual experience."

"In order to be successful as an undercover officer, you have to be believable. People in general are not stupid. If the character which you portrayed, is based on a lie, they will see right through it. Truth is the key to successfully building an undercover identity."

Mr. Custington was not happy with my answer. You could see it in his face. The jury could see it.

"Well, sergeant, what about the "Wild Willie" operation; was that based on truth as well?"

He asked.

"Yes it was. In the "Wild Willie" operation, my character was that of a burnt out Vietnam veteran who relocated to the area from California. I am a veteran of the Vietnam era and I did originally relocate here from California some thirty years ago." I responded.

"In the "Wild Willie" operation, you portrayed Wild Willie, isn't that correct?" Mr. Custington asked

"Yes."

"It was a very successful operation, resulting in more than 336 arrests of suspected drug dealers, isn't that correct?" He asked.

"Yes, in fact it still holds the record of being the most successful undercover operation in the state's history." I stated.

"You testified in court on many different occasions didn't you?" Mr. Custington kept firing questions at me.

"No, not really." I replied.

"Well, sergeant, if "Wild Willie" resulted in more than 360 suspected drug dealers being arrested, then you must have testified hundreds of times, haven't you? In fact, I would have to say that you are an expert in testifying in court, aren't you?"

He smiled at me when he asked the questions. You could see his mind working. He was attempting to discredit me with the jurors by making them believe that I was this great actor, who had testified hundreds of times and I was just putting on a show for them here on the stand. I looked over at the jury, turning my attention away from Mr. Custington and began to answer.

"No, I do not believe I am an expert witness. I have not testified in a court case for probably more than ten years, with the exception of this case here. In regards to the "Wild Willie" operation, everyone that I arrested pleaded guilty, I never went to court on a single case."

Mr. Custington shook his head. He went back over to the defendant's table and started flipping through pages of his notes. He then returned to the podium, and began asking me a series of questions concerning the events that occurred over the 1994 and 1995 years. The questions were basic and related to the line of questioning that Randy had already covered in direct examination. Still I had to be very careful in my answers. Mr. Custington had a habit of altering the question just enough to give it a slightly different meaning.

He then changed the line of questioning and began to ask me questions from the depositions he had taken from me over the last two years. Randy could have objected to Mr. Custington's line of questioning because it went outside the scope of questions that he had asked in direct examination. He decided to allow Mr. Custington to continue; he felt that I was doing well in answering the questions asked, and he thought just maybe if he gave Mr. Custington enough rope, he would hang himself.

Randy had developed enough faith in my ability to answer the questions properly that he wanted to allow Mr. Custington all the leaway he could, hoping that his line of questioning would blow up in his face and turn the jury off. He was taking a calculated risk, but felt it was in our best interest.

Mr. Custington continued with his questioning.

"Isn't it true that in your deposition under oath, you were asked if you were aware of Sheriff Johnston ever being involved in any criminal activity and you answered no?"

I took a breath. I kept telling myself mentally to relax. I looked directly at Mr. Custington and began to answer.

"Mr. Custington, you are constantly taking statements out of context that I made and then asking me a question that is inaccurate. This creates a problem with me being able to give you a direct answer."

My response forced Mr. Custington to pull out my deposition and read the original question and answer to the jury. He was reluctant to do so. Randy asked the judge for a reading of the transcript of my deposition to the jury.

The question asked during the deposition was:

"Prior to October 10, 1994, were you aware of Sheriff Johnston being involved in any criminal activities."

My answer was:

"No."

It demonstrated to the jury the deception used by Mr. Custington in the line of questioning he was using when asking me certain questions. The fact he omitted the date made the answer I would have given at the time of my deposition incorrect, based on my present knowledge. The jury was able to gain insight into Mr. Custington's defense and his deceitful nature. Mr. Custington continued to drill me with questions. The timing of the next series of questions could not have been better.

Mr. Custington asked: "You took notes on everything that occurred at the sheriff's office starting on October 10, 1994 and continuing until the last day that you worked there in December of 1995, isn't that correct?"

I responded with: "No! That is not correct. I did not take notes on everything that occurred. I only took notes on incidents and information that I felt were important to protect myself and my career."

Mr. Custington continued: "Turning to the section in your notebook which covers the middle of March of 1995, could you read that section out loud to the jury."

I paused for a moment while I attempted to find the section that he wanted me to read.

Randy objected. Judge Swanlund called for the morning recess, advising that he would take the issue of the objection up out of the presence of the jury. The jury was excused and sent on break. Randy advised the Judge that the "Motions in Liminee," stated that we are not allowed to submit any of my notebooks, as evidence in this case. If Mr. Custington is permitted to present a small insert from my notebooks to the jury, it "opens the door" and he would demand the court to allow all of my notebooks admitted as evidence. Randy went on to advise that if the court does not allow the notebooks to be entered as evidence, he would be forced to have me read everything in the notebooks to the jury if Mr. Custington is allowed to continue.

Judge Swanlund denied Randy's request, then turned to Mr. Custington.

"Mr. Custington, I'm leaving it up to you whether you withdraw your last question or continue. However if you continue, Mr. Town may at that time request all the sergeant's notebooks be entered as evidence and I will entertain that motion at that time. It's up to you as to what you wish to do."

Judge Swanlund stopped and looked directly at Mr. Custington.

Mr. Custington appeared upset. He hesitated, and then told the judge that he would withdraw the question.

After the morning break, the questioning continued. I thought to myself, the jury had to be wondering what happened to the last question before the break and what exactly was in my notebook that was skipped over. I hoped the jury didn't think I was trying to hide anything from them. I wanted the jury to know that I had nothing to hide. Mr. Custington kept firing one question after another at me. I articulated the question in my mind and then tried to answer as briefly and accurately as possible.

Every question Mr. Custington would ask contained words which had double meaning. Words that made it difficult to answer the question asked. I was constantly requesting clarification of the meaning of certain words or phases. The process was wearing both of us down. Toward the end of the day, we were both exhausted from the mental tension.

Mr. Custington asked me another question. It would be his last question asked of me. I once again asked him for clarification of certain double meaning words he used in the sentence. My persistence got the best of him and he lost it.

"Oh, I forgot you have difficulty understanding the simplest things, and I have to drawn you a damn picture. Let me state it plainly so any stupid person can understand it" he shouted.

His words echoed through the court room. The jury was taken aback and looked shocked by the outburst. Judge Swanlund who was sitting back rather comfortably in his chair, rose quickly and sat erect.

Mr. Custington realized that he had lost it. He looked perplexed. He withdrew the question, stating that he had no further questions of me.

Randy stood up and advised the judge and the jury that the plaintiffs case in chief was completed and that we rested.

We were done with our case. Now, it was Mr. Custington's turn to present Sheriff Johnston's defense to the jury. Judge Swanlund advised that court would be in recess until tomorrow morning when the defense could begin their case.

We felt good that we were done. There was some relief knowing that part of the case was over. Randy rated the day as an eight on the scale of one to ten. The lowest he had rated anyone one day was that of a six. He felt that everything was going better that he even anticipated.

He remarked:

"You just never really know what the jury is thinking."

CHAPTER FIFTEEN

A "LIE" EXPOSED CARRIED MORE IMPACT THAN THE TRUTH TOLD, AND SERVES TO ENHANCE THE TRUE NATURE OF THE "BEAST."

On October 16, 1996, Mr. Custington began his defense of Sheriff Johnston, Undersheriff Deiter, and Chief Halsted. It was, also, Sherry's birthday. It hurt me that we would have to spend the entire day in court. It was not really the way that anyone, especially someone special to you, should have to celebrate their birthday. Birthdays have always been important to us. They were a celebration of life and survival. We looked upon them with recognition and importance, that landmark, our trip down the path of life.

Mr. Custington began his defense by calling his first witness. He called the sheriff from another county within the state. He advised the jury that this sheriff was considered an expert witness in the field of handling police administrations, including policies and procedures. The sheriff began his testimony by advising the jury that he had degrees in law enforcement from a variety of colleges and that he, also, had a Master's degree in business administration. He advised he had been involved in running police departments for more than twenty years.

He told the jury that Sheriff Johnston gave him a copy of the internal affair's investigation that they had conducted against me and that he reviewed the investigation. He advised that from the information supplied to him, he concluded that Sheriff Johnston and Undersheriff Deiter were justified in ordering an internal affair's investigation against myself and Captain Hill. He continued to report that it was his expert opinion from the information gathered in the investigation they were justified in finding Capt. Hill and me, guilty of the charges brought against us.

Now, an expert witness is basically supposed to be an individual who through his training, education, and years of experience, has developed an expertise in a particular field. An expert witness is also supposed to be an impartial witness that is there to testify only to the opinions and conclusions he or she has reached from studying the facts and evidence in the case. Randy began his cross examination of Mr. Custington's so-called expert witness, after Mr. Custington concluded his direct examination. Randy was able to get the sheriff to admit that he and Sheriff Johnston were longtime friends whose friendship had evolved over a twenty-year period. He pointed out to the sheriff, when he reviewed the internal affair's investigations, there were certain facts and pieces of evidence, which were denied to him. Randy was attempting to get the witness to change his testimony in regards to his conclusion that Sheriff Johnston and Undersheriff Deiter were justified in finding me guilty. The sheriff stood fast in the statements he had previously made during direct testimony. He kept insisting that Sheriff Johnston and Undersheriff Deiter were justified in every action that they took during the entire internal affairs process.

Randy failed in getting this man to change his testimony; however, the last question that Randy asked of him did put reasonable doubt to everything he had told the jury. Randy asked him if he was ever sued by any of the deputies that worked for him, for violating their civil rights. He paused for some time. Randy repeated the question. He began to speak, advising that the cases were thrown out in summary judgement. Randy once again asked him if he had been sued by any of the deputies that worked for him for violating their constitutional rights.

Randy told him:

"Just answer the question, yes or no."

The sheriff paused again and looked over toward Sheriff Johnston, he then turned back toward Randy. The demeanor and expressions he displayed had to impact the jury to his true nature.

"Yes." He answered.

Randy repeated his answer. "You are telling me and the jury that you have been sued for violating your own deputy's constitutional rights, is that correct?"

"Yes." He acknowledged once again in the affirmative.

Randy then asked him how many times he had been sued for violating his own deputy's civil rights. He acknowledged that he had been sued three times. Randy turned to the jury and kind of rolled his eyes in disgust.

He advised: "No further questions of this witness" Randy returned to his chair at the plaintiff's table.

Mr. Custington then called his second witness. Another expert witness. This time it was a police administrator, an assistant chief, of one of the larger cities within the state.

His credentials were more impressive than the sheriff that testified previously. He possessed a variety of master's degrees in business and police administration fields. He had, also, been involved in organizing and structuring of different police agencies around the country. During the course of his career, he supervised the internal affair's division of a major metropolitan police department.

Mr. Custington began to question him in a similar fashion to that he used in questioning the sheriff. He answered all the questions asked of him in a matter of fact manner, coming across as a dedicated professional. He advised the jury he was supplied the reports and information available in regards to the internal affair's investigations involving Capt. Hill and me. He stated he had studied the information provided and concluded that Sheriff Johnston and Undersheriff Deiter were justified in the actions that they had taken. He further informed the jury that Sheriff Johnston and Undersheriff Deiter had a responsibility to conduct the internal affair's investigation and failing to do so would have been wrong.

His testimony was damaging to our case. Randy finally got his turn for cross examination of the man. Randy began questioning him in detail as to the information the Sheriff and Undersheriff had supplied to him within regards to the facts and evidence involved in the internal affair's investigations. It was determined once again that Sheriff Johnston and Undersheriff Deiter only supplied him with the facts that they wanted him to know. He was unaware that the so called illegal tape recording was recorded by my answering machine without my knowledge. He equally was not aware that the possession of unauthorized documents involved papers that went to the FBI involving investigating Sheriff Johnston and his administration of committing illegal acts.

Randy informed him that I was never in possession of the documents that I was accused of possessing and that there were no facts in the internal affair's investigation proving that I was ever in possession of these documents. Randy asked him if he was aware from the information supplied to him that Capt. Hill and Chief Halsted were both made aware of the sexual Harassment complaint involving Deputy Willis. He advised that he was not.

After Randy detailed the information that Sheriff Johnston and Undersheriff Deiter failed to provide him in his evaluation of the merits of the internal affair's investigation, he asked:

"With this new knowledge, would you change your conclusions and opinions concerning the merits of the internal affair's investigation?"

The Police Administrator advised the jury:

"If the information being relayed to me today in this court room is accurate, it would change my opinion."

He continued to state: "Based on the information received here today, the act of even conducting an internal affair's investigation against the plaintiff would have been retaliatory in nature and wrong."

He then advised: "The results of the internal affair's investigation should have cleared the sergeant of the charges against him."

This second expert came across as an honest dedicated individual who was impartial and did not possess any hidden agenda. Randy's being able to turn him around and testify in our behalf served to weaken Mr. Custington's defense.

Randy was, to say the least, quite pleased with himself, when he completed his cross examination. I felt good about the job Randy did as well. He was able, once again, to demonstrate to the jury that Mr. Custington was still attempting to deceive them. What is more important, he was able to change one of Sheriff Johnston's expert witnesses into an expert witness on our behalf and get the man to conclude that Sheriff Johnston and his administration acted improperly in their actions toward me. This factor alone would prove to be a significant impact to the case when the trial finally would go to the jury.

The rest of the day in court was spent with Mr. Custington parading all of Sheriff Johnston's top administrators on the stand. Each one of them was an individual who held the position and rank that they possessed due to an appointment by the sheriff. After the administrators all testified, Mr. Custington had some of the mid-level supervisors testify on Sheriff Johnston's behalf. I anticipated that Mr. Custington's strategy was going to be to attempt to assassinate my character and reputation through the witnesses he called to the stand. To my surprise and delight, I was wrong. Instead, he asked each and every one of his witnesses the exact same questions, and they all gave the same basic answer.

Mr. Custington asked:

"Did you ever observe Sheriff Johnston, Undersheriff Deiter, or Chief Halsted act inappropriately toward the plaintiff in this case?"

The answer Sheriff Johnston's witnesses all gave was: "No."

Mr. Custington would then ask: "Are you aware of any incident were by Sheriff Johnston or anyone from his administration violated the sergeant's constitutional rights or retaliated against the sergeant for his support of Sheriff Johnston's opponent in the 1994 election?"

Again the answer given by all of Sheriff Johnston's witnesses was:

"No."

Mr. Custington asked other questions of the witnesses: he asked basic questions concerning their length of career with the sheriff's office and different procedures that were followed within the department. It became rather apparent that Mr. Custington's defense was to create doubt by demonstrating a preponderance of testimonial evidence to the jury that Sheriff Johnston and his administration acted appropriately.

He wanted to convince the jury that all of his witnesses believe Sheriff Johnston, Undersheriff Deiter, and Chief Halsted were excellent administrators who would not engage in violating anyone's rights. He, actually, did an excellent job in getting his point across to the jury. I looked over at the jury more than once during the testimony being given. Each of the jurors appeared to be listening intently to the testimony being given.

Randy cross examined each witness after Mr. Custington completed his direct examine. Randy asked each of the witnesses basically the same questions and once again each of the witnesses gave the same answers to the questions asked.

Randy asked:

"Are you in a position or do you hold a rank, that was appointed to you by Sheriff Johnston, or are you currently on probation status with the position that you hold at the sheriffs' office?"

Each and everyone of Sheriff Johnston's witnesses answer:

"Yes."

Randy asked them:

"Being appointed or on probation status, isn't it true that Sheriff Johnston has the authority to remove you from the position you hold without cause or without having any special reason, if he so desires?"

Once again the answer given by all the witnesses was:

"Yes."

Randy questioned the witnesses: "Were you involved in the internal affair's investigation against the sergeant or Capt. Hill?"

They all answered: "No."

Randy continued: "Did you even work with my client, at any time over the last two years?"

Randy pointed over to me, as he asked the question.

"No," was the answer given, by everyone that he quizzed.

Every one of the witnesses had a hidden agenda, so to speak. Each of them stood to lose their status in the department if they did not testify for Sheriff Johnston. Randy was able to demonstrate this to the jury. By the end of the day, when we departed the court house, we were extremely pleased with the events of the trial. Randy rated the day at a ten, on the scale of one to ten. Mr. Custington's defense of Sheriff Johnston, had only helped to fortify our case against him.

We were totally dismayed when we read the headlines in the local newspaper the next morning. It read.

"Sheriff Johnston's administrators and top officials all testified that the sheriff acted appropriately. Expert witnesses gave testimony justifying Sheriff Johnston's actions."

Our commute to the federal court house that day was spent discussing the miscarriage of justice created by the local newspaper for refusing to publish the truth. The citizens of the community had a right to know the facts, but still they were being kept in the dark by the local media. It was wrong, but there was nothing that we could do about it.

The court day started with Undersheriff Deiter taking the stand. Mr. Custington began questioning him in direct. The undersheriff answered a series of questions justifying the actions taken by Sheriff Johnston, Chief Halsted, and himself in regards to the treatment they took against Capt. Hill and me. Undersheriff Deiter did an excellent job portraying himself as a fair and impartial administrator. I was even impressed with his demeanor and answers given on the stand. I was, also, concerned that the jury would believe his bull shit. He came across as very convincing and even sincere. He was to say the least, "smooth."

It was going to be up to Randy in his cross examination to bring out the truth. It would be a tremendous challenge for Randy, considering what an accomplished liar Deiter was. Mr. Custington finally finished with his direct and Randy began his cross examination.

Randy began to ask Undersheriff Deiter a series of questions.

"In the internal affair's investigation against my client, you found him guilty of possessing documents that he was not authorized to possess, is that correct?"

Deiter answered: "Yes, that is correct."

Randy then asked him: "What documents, exactly, did he have which were not authorized for him to have in his possession?"

Undersheriff Deiter got a rather puzzled look on his face and hesitated briefly. He then stated, "I don't know."

Randy looked at the undersheriff and then glanced over to the jury. He then continued.

"You found my client guilty of possessing unauthorized documents, but you cannot tell the jury what documents you found him guilty of possessing?"

"Well, Well, the documents that went to the FBI."

Undersheriff Deiter said.

"Undersheriff, you heard testimony here in this court room that I took the documents to the FBI and not my client, isn't that correct?" Randy asked.

"Yes, that is correct." The undersheriff answered.

Randy asked again.

"So, tell me, which documents my client was found guilty of possessing."

The undersheriff was beginning to become flustered. He paused and glanced over at Mr. Custington, as if to ask Mr. Custington to help him. He then stated, "I, I, ah don't really know."

Randy had him exactly where he wanted him. He continued relentlessly with his questioning. "So you found my client guilty of possessing documents but you do not know what documents, if any, he actually possessed that were in fact, unauthorized for him to possess, is that correct?"

Mr. Custington jumped up from his seat at the defense table. He objected. He advised the judge that the question had previously been asked and answered.

Judge Swanlund looked over to Randy for a response. Randy informed the judge that the specific documents in question have not been identified and it was an important issue for the jury to have knowledge, of deciding the merits of the internal affair's investigation.

Judge Swanlund overruled Mr. Custington's objection.

Randy repeated the question to Undersheriff Deiter.

"Well, ah, well, ah, yes," Deiter replied.

"You do not know what documents. Is that, what I am hearing you say?" Randy demanded.

"Yes that is correct," Undersheriff Deiter acknowledged.

Randy changed the topic and asked: "Isn't it true that the prosecutor refused to charge my client with illegal recording, in reference to the answering machine tape, of the conversation that occurred between you and him?"

"Yes, that is true." Deiter replied

Randy continued:

"In the internal affair's investigation you found my client guilty of that recording, citing it was an illegal tape recording and a violation of the law, isn't that correct?"

"No, I didn't. The sheriff did. It wasn't I." Deiter stated, in rather a defensive voice.

Randy then asked:

"But my client was found guilty of making an illegal tape recording as a result of the internal affair's investigation correct?"

"Yes." Deiter replied.

Randy got what he wanted from Undersheriff Deiter concerning those issues, so he once again changed the subject. He asked:

"Did you tell Capt. Hill that my client was going to be Atwater's Chief of Detectives?"

"Well, yes, but I, I said it as kind of a joke." Deiter replied, hesitating as he spoke.

"So you actually started that rumor about my client being chief of detectives for Atwater, didn't you?" Randy asked in a demanding voice.

"Well, I guess, I mean, I really don't know. I am, well, I am not really in the habit of starting rumors. You know, I, well I . . . "

Deiter responded.

Randy advised that he had no further questions. He kept the line of questioning simple, and he did it. He exposed Undersheriff Deiter's true demeanor to the jury. They now had an insight as to Deiter's actual character. Undersheriff Deiter stepped down from the witness stand and walked back to the defense table. Sheriff Johnston was sitting at the defense table just glaring at the undersheriff. Everyone in the court room who happened to glance over at the sheriff, could see the anger and disappointment on his face as he stared unmercifully at Deiter.

Deiter himself no longer appeared to be a man in control. He returned to his seat stripped of the confidence he had taken to the stand.

Mr. Custington called Chief Halsted to the witness stand. His testimony was similar to Undersheriff Deiter's. Mr. Custington asked him a series of questions, whereby his answers justified the actions taken by Sheriff Johnston, Undersheriff Deiter, and himself against me.

Randy cross-examined Chief Halsted, once Mr. Custington completed his direct. His cross examination was less dramatic than that of undersheriff's. He kept it brief, catching Chief Halsted in one contradiction after another of the testimony previously given by Sheriff Johnston and Undersheriff Deiter.

Each time Randy would point out a discrepancy, Chief Halsted would reveal his callus, uncaring nature. Randy felt Halsted's own demeanor was more than enough to turn the jury off and destroy his own creditablity with them. He ended the cross examination before the jury lost interest.

Sheriff Johnston maintained a disgusted and upset look on his face the entire time that Chief Halsted was on the stand being cross examined by Randy. When Chief Halsted departed from the stand, Sheriff Johnston just shook his head in disapproval.

Mr. Custington called Sheriff Johnston to the stand. He had to call him twice. The sheriff was preoccupied with the prior testimony, and did not even hear his name being called. The second time Mr. Custington called the sheriff, it brought him back to reality. He looked embarrassed as he walked up and sat down at the witness stand.

Sheriff Johnston immediately grabbed the pitcher of water sitting by the witness stand and poured himself a glass of water. He drank it down rather rapidly and refilled his glass. Each and every time he took the stand, he would drink glass after glass of water and even request a new pitcher while he testified. Randy and I would joke that lying must make a person thirsty. Sheriff Johnston seemed to gain his composure rather quickly. It was obvious once again he was responding like a politician, campaigning the jury.

The court day ended shortly after Sheriff Johnston took the stand in his own defense. Randy and I were once again happy with the proceeding of the day and the realization that it soon would all be over and behind us. It could not end too soon as far as I was concerned.

October 18, 1996, the trial day began with the continuation of Sheriff Johnston's testimony. Mr. Custington asked question after question of his client. The questions were designed to portray Sheriff Johnston as an honest, dedicated individual who performed his duties and responsibilities with proper motivation. They were also designed to portray me as a misguided, disgruntled employee.

I sat there in the court room listening to every word. Sheriff Johnston always came across well in a controlled setting. If the jury was buying the story that he was telling, we would be in trouble. Mr. Custington finally finished with his direct examination and Randy then got his last chance to question Sheriff Johnston in cross examination.

Randy went immediately into asking articulate questions concerning the course of events which started back in 1994. Randy had told me time and time again that a jury, any jury, does not like to sit there having their time wasted with games. A jury wants the truth, the plain and simple truth. If you cut to the chase and take your chances with the truth, the jury will hold their interest high and reach the proper decision.

Randy asked Sheriff Johnston:

"Do you actually believe my client wrote the anonymous letter that circulated back on October 19, 1994?"

Sheriff Johnston responded: "In the beginning, when I first received the letter, I wasn't sure if he was involved in it or not. Now, I believe he did write the letter."

"Why?" Randy asked.

"Because the sergeant admitted that he wrote the sixty-six allegations that went to the FBI, requesting that they investigate me. The anonymous letter, and the letter that went to the FBI are very similar in nature, as well as design. I now know he did it."

Sheriff Johnston replied.

Randy could not believe the words that just came from Sheriff Johnston's mouth. He had been attempting to get the sixty-six allegations that went to the FBI admitted as evidence in this case since the beginning of trial, but had not had any success. Sheriff Johnston just put out the welcome mat and opened the door for Randy to be able to get the sixty-six allegations admitted.

"Your Honor, I move to admit the sixty-six allegations that went to the FBI as evidence, at this time." Randy requested to Judge Swanlund.

Mr. Custington stood up by the defense table where he had been sitting and yelled out.

"I object."

Randy responded.

"Your Honor, Sheriff Johnston just alluded that there were

similarities between the anonymous letter of October 14, 1994, and the sixty-six allegations that went to the FBI. There are not. In order for my client to defend himself against Sheriff Johnston's testimony here today, the jury needs to see both documents for themselves. The jury then can decide on their own the merits of Sheriff Johnston's testimony."

"Motion granted, the sixty-six allegations will so be admitted as evidence," Judge Swanlund directed.

Sheriff Johnston looked extremely upset; he realized that he just committed a major error in his own defense. He did not want the jury to see the list of sixty-six allegations of wrong doing involving himself and others close to him. He knew that once the jury saw the list of criminal activities which related back to his involvement, it could destroy any creditablity he had with them.

During the entire trial, Mr. Custington had been successful in preventing the list of allegations from getting into evidence.

Now it was going to the jury. Sheriff Johnston began to sweat as he sat restlessly in the witness box. He began again to drink glass after glass of water from the pitcher sitting by the witness stand. He face became red and flustered. It was obvious to everyone in the court room that he was upset with what had just occurred.

Randy continued with his questioning.

"After Charles Atwater submitted his public disclosure form stating his intentions to run for sheriff in the 1994 election, did you have a conversation with your sister? Did it result in your ordering an internal affair's investigation to be conducted against Atwater for inappropriate behavior?"

"No! Absolutely not," Sheriff Johnston responded.

Randy continued his questioning:

"Well, Sheriff Johnston, was there in fact an internal affair's investigation conducted against Atwater for inappropriate behavior?"

"Yes, there was," Sheriff Johnston stated.

"Did you order the internal affair's investigation to be conducted against Atwater?" Randy questioned.

"Yes." Sheriff Johnston answered.

"Was Charles Atwater found guilty of inappropriate behavior as a result of the internal affair's investigation against him?" Randy asked.

Sheriff Johnston responded: "Yes."

"Did your sister initiate the complaint against Charles Atwater at your request?" Randy asked.

"No, absolutely not."

Sheriff Johnson stated in a defensive tone.

"Did you have a conversation with your sister concerning Charles Atwater prior to making the decision to initiate an internal affair's investigation against him?" Randy questioned.

"No, I did not." Sheriff Johnston responded.

"Sheriff Johnston, did you talk to your sister prior to initiating the internal affair's investigation against Atwater?" Randy asked again.

"No, I did not."

Sheriff Johnston was looking extremely uncomfortable as Randy continued to drill him regarding his sister.

"You are telling me that you did not have any conversation whatsoever with your sister prior to ordering the internal affairs investigation against Charles Atwater; is that correct?" Randy restated and asked again.

"No, I did not talk to my sister. Sheriff Johnston stated, this time in a stern and commanding voice.

Randy then asked the sheriff one final time. "Are you certain that you did not talk to your sister?"

Sheriff Johnston was attempting to maintain his composure. He took another drink of water and turned to the jury. He looked at the jurors, his eyes wandering across the jury booth. He then responded.

"No, I did not talk to my sister concerning Charles Atwater, before or after the internal affair's investigation. And, if I may say so, Charles Atwater was investigated for inappropriate behavior after we received a citizen complaint against him. It was standard procedure to do so, no matter who the deputy is that has a complaint filed against him. The fact that he announced he was running for sheriff had nothing to do with the internal affair's investigation. We did what was right and appropriate, and I stand behind the decisions I have made, and take full responsibility."

Sheriff Johnston had regained his composure and was back to campaigning the jury. He came across very convincingly. It made Randy appear to be unjustly badgering him.

Randy did not say a word, instead he turned away from Sheriff Johnston and walked over to the plaintiff's table. He reached down onto the table and picked up Sheriff Johnston's deposition. It was a transcript of the deposition that Sheriff Johnston gave some six months earlier.

Sheriff Johnston saw the deposition in Randy's hands and realized what it was and what it contained. He turned white as a ghost and began to panic.

Sheriff Johnston blurted out:

"Well, Mr. Town, if you are going to get my deposition, then yes, yes, I did talk to my sister."

Sheriff Johnston's face turned instantly red and flustered as he realized what he had said. He turned quickly, glancing at the reaction of the jury, and then looked about the court room. He looked bewildered, devastated, as he grabbed the glass of water sitting in front of him and began to drink. It was obvious to everyone in the court room that he just got himself caught in a lie, a lie which Randy gave him every opportunity to avoid. It was also a lie that he compounded over and over again.

No one in the court room could believe what had just transpired. Sheriff Johnston had demonstrated his true nature to everyone there. We all just kind of sat there in a state of shock and dismay over the sequence of events that unfolded before our eyes.

Mr. Custington dropped the pen that he was holding in his

hands and placed his hands to his head. He lowered his face downward toward the table, holding his head.

Dead silence filled the courtroom. The silence was overwhelming. It was as if time had become suspended. It only lasted a brief second, but it seemed like forever.

Randy had a lot more questions that he had intended to ask of Sheriff Johnston. He decided, however, to stop. He felt the impact of Sheriff Johnston being caught in a lie was dramatic conclusion that would stay with the jury during the deliberation process. He did not want to lose that advantage that Sheriff Johnston had just given.

"No further questions."

Randy stated.

Mr. Custington looked up. He then stood up; he took maybe two steps and then stopped. His face was full of hesitation. He paused in front of everyone and then advised:

"Your Honor, the defense rests their case."

Mr. Custington then returned to his seat. He had the appearance of a defeated man upon his face as he just sat there with a blank stare.

The court was recessed until Monday, October 21, 1996, when both sides would submit their closing arguments to the jury prior to the jury going into deliberation on the evidence in the case.

As we departed the court house that afternoon, I noticed a distinctive change in the behavior of Sheriff Johnston, Undersheriff Deiter, and Chief Halsted. Every day, since the trial began, you could observe the three of them walking almost hand in hand, joking and appearing to not have a care in the world. They always appeared to be having a good time socializing and carrying on conversations as they walked back to their vehicles. They appeared to be inseparable comrades. Today, however, they appeared to be strangers, each of them walking quietly, separately, back to their cars. There was a good ten feet of distance between them, as they each walked alone, down the city sidewalk.

An interesting aspect, the following morning, was the fact that not one of the local news papers mentioned that Sheriff Johnston was caught in a lie on the witness stand. The reporters were in the court room when he lied. They all saw it. They were still protecting this man, and denying the truth to the citizens of the community. This disturbed and concerned us.

CHAPTER SIXTEEN

JUSTICE IS ACHIEVED ONLY WHEN TRUTH TRIUMPHS OVER DECEIT, AND MEASURES ARE TAKEN TO PREVENT ITS RECURRENCE.

The last day of the trial finally arrived after a long weekend. The weekend seemed to pass by in slow motion, with the anticipation of the case going to the jury. Randy spent the time working on his closing argument that he had to present to the jury. I assisted him. Each side had one hour to give their closing statements. It was barely enough time to cover the high points of the three-week long trial. We kept condensing the material, while carefully attempting to articulate the wording in order to ensure that everything of importance that was needed to be said was told to the jury. Randy actually didn't get his closing argument finished until around three a.m. that morning.

The ride to the court house was spent with Randy going over his closing statement. He handed me a typewritten copy of it and then recited it from memory. We finished going over it just as we arrived at the federal court house.

"What do you think of it?" Randy asked.

"It's great, I think you'll get the facts across and will be able to hold on to the jury's interest, every step of the way."

I stated.

Randy nodded his head in agreement.

"Good, well, let's get up to the courtroom." He said, just as we pulled into the parking lot of the federal building.

The trial began at nine, a.m., with Judge Swanlund presiding. The procedure followed for closing arguments was that Randy would go first. He was given forty-five minutes to speak to the jury. Mr. Custington would then be given one hour to speak to the jury followed by Randy having fifteen minutes to rebut Mr. Custington's closing remarks. The system was designed to allow the plaintiff's side the opportunity to have the first and last words on the case being tried.

Randy began his closing argument, he spoke softly but firmly, his voice filled with compassion and understanding.

"This case is not just about my client. Rather, it is a case concerning you, me, and our children. This case involves each and every one of us. It is about protecting our constitutional rights."

"Ladies and Gentlemen, the decision you reach in this case is extremely important and involves protecting all of us from corruption and violation of the very core of our democratic society. If we allow any elected official, anyone that we have given a position of authority, to violate our public trust, we are, in fact, condoning the undermining of our very own constitution. You have the power. The power to defend our constitution and at the same time, send out a message. A message that this type of conduct, of violating our trust, will not be tolerated. It will not be tolerated by whom? By us, we the people, will not tolerate it."

Randy was doing well. He was not just giving a speech or a lecture, you could tell by the emotion he was expressing that he was actually into it. I mean that he got into it with his entire body and soul. Even more so than that, he had his heart into his speech. His delivery was so intense that even if the world was to come to an end, I'm not sure that anyone would have even noticed. Everyone in the court room, including the jury, was giving him their undivided attention. Randy continued giving a brief summary of the items that were covered in the trial.

"My client described Sheriff Johnston as a reactionary, a figure head, who ruled by intimidation and fear. He described Undersheriff Deiter as a fixer, planner, and an enforcer. He described Chief Halsted as a dictator and a "yes" man for the administration."

"You heard the testimony of the various deputies who testified. They each substantiated my client's description of the administration. You heard them testify not only to the treatment they witnessed my client received, but also to the unfair and biased treatment many of them received, as well. And, why were they treated this way? Why? Why? I will tell you why. All because they chose to support Sheriff Johnston's opponent in the 1994 election."

"Why? Why? Because after they learned of criminal activities possibly involving Sheriff Johnston and his administration, they decided to go to the FBI and request a Grand Jury investigation."

"Realize, Ladies and Gentlemen: just think about it. Testimony in this trial, over and over again, cited Sheriff Johnston as making statements, saying that he would "get" those who supported his opponent. Likewise, Sheriff Johnston stated again and again, he was going to "get" those that went to the FBI."

"And he did. He did. All but one of the deputies who went to the FBI have been either fired, or forced to retire or resign depending on their particular situation. All but one, and that one has received two written reprimands since the 1994 election. And Sheriff Johnston is still there. And he is still doing the same thing. Can you believe that?"

"My client was singled out and treated differently because he supported Sheriff Johnston's opponent, and because he reported allegations of possible criminal activities and inappropriate behavior to the FBI. Ask yourself, what did my client do that was wrong? What did my client do to deserve the treatment that he received?"

"Think about the testimony you heard in the court room. The sergeant's story, my client's story, never changed. The stories told by his witnesses maintained consistency. Now think about Sheriff Johnston, Undersheriff Deiter, and Chief Halsted's stories. The three of them could not even keep their so-called facts straight between themselves. They lied. They lied. Their defense is full of inconsistencies and lies designed to keep you, the jury, from realizing and understanding the truth involved in this case."

"Remember, when I asked Sheriff Johnston about the issue of his sister being involved in the Atwater internal affairs investigation. He said, 'no, no, no, absolutely not.' Then, I turned and picked up his deposition and he remarked; 'Well if you are going to get my deposition, Mr. Town, yes I did talk to my sister.' Yes, she did call me.'"

"This incident only goes to show the deceit and lies used by the defendants in this case. They do not want you, the jury, to know the truth. Why? Because they know they are in the wrong. They know they violated my client's civil rights."

"My client, on the other hand, tried to tell you everything. He has nothing to hide. The decision is yours, Ladies and Gentlemen. Your decision is important and will affect each and every one of us. It will affect the future and strength of our constitutional rights. I have every faith in you, the jury, that you will reach the right decision in this case. Thank you for your time."

Randy walked over to his seat at the plaintiff's table and sat down. His closing argument was not just the words that he recited to me during our ride to the court house that morning. Words are merely words. His speech came from the heart. It was touching. It had impact. It inspired, in the jury, a sense of power and obligation that encompassed our future. This trial was no longer an individual rights violation case. Randy had elevated it to a much higher plane.

Randy looked over to me, he could tell by my eyes that I was pleased with his closing statement. I sat there, proud. I could not have said it better myself. I was satisfied, win or lose, we had done the very best that we could. I would have no regrets, no matter what the final outcome would be. Randy and I had become an interactive team. A relationship had developed between us built on mutual respect and admiration. We had become the best of friends, a friendship that I firmly believe will last a life time.

Mr. Custington took the floor and began his closing argument. He filled the court room with large charts. They appeared to be professionally constructed. The charts were used for illustration purposes only. I believe the only reason he used the charts were to enhance his defense. People sometimes believe what they see in written word has to be the truth. Mr. Custington was hoping to influence the jury in that manner. Some of the charts were the same ones that he used in opening statements. Others were ones that none of us had seen before. Randy and I objected to the use of the charts, but there was nothing that we could do about them. It was perfectly legal, so no formal objection was made by Randy.

After setting up all the charts, Mr. Custington addressed the jury:
"This case is about personal choices, logical consequences, and misplaced blame. It is not about politics, violations of constitutional rights, nor retaliation."

"You heard a majority of the supervisors from the sheriff's office all testify that they never, and I repeat never, witnessed my clients violate the sergeant's constitutional rights. They all testified that they never even once observed Sheriff Johnston, Undersheriff Deiter, or Chief Halsted retaliate against the sergeant, or anyone else in the department, for that matter."

"The sergeant made the personal choice to support Charles Atwater in the 1994 election. That was his right to do so. Sheriff Johnston respected the sergeant's rights. It was the sergeant's misconception of the sheriff that caused his belief that he had been violated. The plaintiff was more concerned about politics than he was about doing his job as a patrol sergeant. The sheriff's administration reaction to the sergeant's behavior was the same reaction that they would have had toward anyone in the department that was slacking off and not doing their job."

"The plaintiff refused to accept the consequences caused by his own actions. This resulted in misplaced blame and unjustified behavior toward Sheriff Johnston, Undersheriff Deiter, and Chief Halsted."

"You heard the two expert witnesses testify that the sheriff was justified in ordering an internal affair's investigation against the sergeant. You heard them state the internal affairs investigation was conducted properly. They each advised they had reviewed the internal affair's investigation including the process and procedures followed, and concluded that the sergeant was guilty of the violations cited."

Mr. Custington was smooth in his delivery. I glanced over at the jury members who appeared to be listening intensely to his every word. He continued.

"There were absolutely no violations of constitutional rights, no retaliation taken toward the sergeant. What there was, was accountability. The sergeant was held accountable for making the wrong choices. He was held accountable for his actions. The sergeant over reacted and blamed his problems on the sheriff and his administration. He looked for someone else to blame rather than himself. The plaintiff failed to accept responsibility for his own actions and that is the real reason that we are all gathered here in this court room."

"Now let us step back and examine the evidence that was presented against my clients in this case. The "Big picture," I present to you in all honesty, is that there is no real evidence which was presented in this case. No hard, fast evidence was ever presented against my clients. If you look at all the testimony, what you have is a small group of "disgruntled" employees and their perception of misconduct by the sheriff's administration. There was no actual misconduct and there are no facts or evidence that clearly demonstrate that there ever was."

"I wanted to take a few minutes to go over the special verdict form that will be supplied to each of you on the jury. I realize that Judge Swanlund will be explaining this form to you. I also realize, having been involved in many of these types of cases over the course of my career, that these forms can be quite confusing and you might have difficulty understanding what the Honorable Judge is attempting to explain to you. Therefore, I took the liberty of having illustrated posters of the special verdict form made up so that we can go over them."

Mr. Custington then set up the large illustrations of the special verdict form. I was personally alarmed by what I saw. Not only did Mr. Custington have the questions of the special verdict form listed on the posters, he also had the answers marked. The answers were all marked in his client's favor. I thought it an outrage that he was actually telling the jury how to vote, but it was a perfectly legal maneuver on his part and one that was tolerated. I just sat there attempting not to show any emotion, as I listened to Mr. Custington addressing the jury. "Now, Ladies and Gentlemen of the jury, let me read these questions to you." Mr. Custington picked up a long stick type pointer and pointed to question one as he began to read it aloud.

"Question #1. Have the plaintiffs established by preponderance of the evidence that Patrick Johnston, Charles Deiter, or Ray Halsted intentionally engaged in acts of retaliation against the plaintiff for having exercised his federal civil rights secured by the U.S. Constitution?"

Answer: _____yes _____XXX___no

Mr. Custington looked directly at the jury advising them that they had to mark "no" as the answer to this question. He stated that they really had no choice in the matter. The evidence just was not presented to allow them to reach any other decision but to mark "no."

He then continued, going on to the next question.

"Question #2. Have the plaintiffs established by preponderance of the evidence that retaliation against the plaintiffs was a substantial or motivating factor in the acts of Patrick Johnston, Charles Deiter, or Ray Halsted?"

Answer: _____yes _____XXX____no

Here again you have no choice but to mark "no." There isn't any evidence that was presented in this case which established retaliation ever took place against the sergeant. The plaintiffs had an obligation to provide you, the jury, with the power of proof, to convince you that my clients violated the sergeant's rights and retaliated against him. The proof has to be overwhelming and it simply is not there. Why, because my clients are innocent. There is no proof because they did nothing wrong."

I glanced over at the jury. I tried not to stare. I was appalled. Mr. Custington, representing himself as an officer of the court with years of experience, was allowed to stand there in front of the jury advising them exactly how to vote. It concerned me that all he needed to do was convince one of the jury members. Convince them that they had no choice in how they voted and I would lose the case. I did not believe it was right. Still, I tried to maintain my composure and not show any visible signs of my emotions. Mr. Custington went on.

"I could go over the other questions on the special verdict form, but I do not want to waste your time," Mr. Custington stated, then he paused before continuing. If you answer 'no' to the first two questions, you will not have to proceed in answering any of the other questions. You will have fulfilled your obligation as a juror and you will be finished with this case. I see no sense in going over the other questions since those two questions are all that you really have to answer."

"After you complete question one and two with a 'no' answer you are done."

"In closing, I wish to point out to you, the members of the jury, that my clients had nothing to gain by retaliating against the plaintiff. Further, you must realize that in order for my clients to have retaliated against the plaintiff, by definition, their actions had to be solely and substantially motivated by revenge. This was not the case. As long as there are not any other reasons involved, their actions were proper."

"So Ladies and Gentlemen of the jury, remember Sheriff Johnston, Undersheriff Deiter and Chief Halsted are all innocent.

The answer to question number one and two is "no"."

"Thank you for your time."

Mr. Custington returned to his seat and sat down. Randy got up and walked over to the jury. It was time for his final rebuttal statement, the last step in closing arguments.

Randy stood in front of the jury and just looked at them. He did not say anything. He made eye contact with each and every one of them, one at a time. The court room filled with dead silence. Randy looked away and glanced around the court room. He then directed his attention back to the jury and began to speak. He spoke softly with sincerity and confidence in his voice.

"Ladies and Gentlemen of the jury, as I stand here before you today, I am not going to insult your intelligence by attempting to tell you how to vote. That decision is up to you and only you to make. You have all the facts and evidence that we were allowed to present. You make the decision."

"Now, if you find Sheriff Johnston, Undersheriff Deiter, and Chief Halsted guilty, then you have to decide the proper punishment to impose. This is a civil case. The way that you punish them is monetary. I'm not going to tell you how much to impose. I do want you, however, to realize, the larger the judgement you make, the more the guarantee this type of behavior will not occur again. You need to send a message to all those in positions of authority that violations of our constitutional rights will not be tolerated. Those who violate our rights and retaliate against us will be held accountable and have to pay the price."

"There is not a dollar value or amount that will make up for the pain and suffering my client's experienced over the past two years. The ordeal the sergeant and his wife went through will haunt them for the rest of their lives. The sergeant's career is over, but his life must go on. Your decision in this case will affect him forever."

"Thank you for your attentiveness in this case and for the sacrifices you have made in your own personal lives by sitting here on this jury."

Randy returned to his seat at the plaintiff's table. The court case was over. Judge Swanlund ordered the jury into the deliberation room to decide the case. It was 11:30 a.m., on October 21, 1996. Two years and eleven days since the entire incident began. All that was left was the wait. The wait while the jury decides the case and returns with a verdict. The anticipation was overwhelming.

Randy, Sherry, and I stayed at the court house the entire afternoon waiting for word from the jury. At 4:30 p.m.,

We were advised that the jury was excused for the night and would resume deliberation at 09:00 a.m., in the morning. As we drove home that evening, Randy remarked.

"The jury has now been out for more than five hours. That is a good sign for us. If they were going to find them not guilty, it wouldn't take this long. I got a good feeling that we've won. It will take time for the jury to determine the extent of damages."

During the drive home, Randy was happy. Sherry and I were just nervous.

That night, Sherry and I did not get much sleep. In fact, I am not sure either one of us really got any sleep whatsoever.

We spent hours talking about everything and about nothing. We prayed to the Lord that the truth would be seen by the members of the jury, and the truth would triumph. We also came to a peace with ourselves that no matter what the verdict was, we would get on with our lives, with the realization and satisfaction that we did what we had to do. We were proud that we stood up.

The next morning, October 22, 1996, we were back at the Federal Court house waiting for the verdict. Capt. Hill and his wife Eileen, met us at the court house. They decided they would wait with us for the verdict to come in. The anticipation was indescribable, and the minutes seemed to pass extremely slowly. Sherry tried to read a magazine. Randy sat reading a book. He would occasionally look up and smile. I couldn't focus enough to sit down and read anything. All I could do was pace. I walked about the Federal building, my mind racing with my thoughts. They were thoughts of everything, and of nothing. It was an emotional time for us all. The reality was that you never really know how much the jury comprehended, or for that matter, what the jury was actually thinking. Until the verdict comes in you can only speculate, but you never really know. I guess that is the part that drives you crazy and puts your nerves on end.

Finally, at 04:00 p.m., the court clerk advised Randy that the jury had reached a verdict. Court would reconvene in one hour with the verdict. Randy turned to the rest of us who were standing by the benches in the lobby.

"Well, the verdict is in. We will know the outcome in an hour" He said. His voice was full of excitement.

Another hour, I thought. I prayed the jury saw the truth and reached the proper verdict. An hour passes very slowly when you are full of anticipation, but at least it passes just the same. Finally, the time had come. We walked into the court room and sat down. It had become a familiar place to us after three—almost four weeks.

Mr. Custington, Ms. Pitts, and Sheriff Johnston were sitting at the defense table. Undersheriff Deiter, and Chief Halsted were not in the court room.

We all rose from our seats as the jury entered the court room, followed by Judge Swanlund. As we sat down, it was announced that the court was back in session. Judge Swanlund called for the jury foreman to rise. A man in his later thirties stood up.

"Has the jury reached a verdict?" Judge Swanlund asked.

The foreman replied: "Yes, your Honor, we have reached a verdict."

The judge motioned to his court clerk to get the papers containing the verdict from the foreman. The foreman then handed the verdict to the court clerk, who in turn took it over to Judge Swanlund. The judge then read the verdict to himself.

Time seemed to pass even slower than before. I looked over toward my wife, we made eye contact as I reached out and grabbed her hand. We stared at each other, not saying a word. The anxiety was intense.

Finally, the judge handed the verdict form back to the court clerk, who returned it to the jury foreman.

"Would you please read the verdict to the court." Judge Swanlund requested.

The foreman began to read from the special verdict form.

"Question #1. Have plaintiffs established by a preponderance of the evidence that Patrick Johnston, Charles Deiter, or Ray Halsted intentionally engaged in acts of retaliation against the plaintiff for having exercised his Federal Civil rights secured by the U.S. Constitution?"

Answer: "yes"

The foreman pause briefly and then continued:

"Question #2. Have Plaintiffs established by a preponderance of the evidence that the acts of retaliation by Patrick Johnston, Charles Deiter, or Ray Halsted, were done maliciously or with reckless disregard of Plaintiff's rights?"

Answer: "yes"

My wife, Sherry, squeezed my hand. I looked over at her, just a glance. Her eyes were tearing up. She was full of emotion, as was I. She was happy and proud. Our love and faith saw us through this ordeal. We had won, for this we were grateful and thank God.

The foreman continued:

"Question #3. Which of the individual defendants intentionally engaged in acts of retaliation that deprived the Plaintiff from exercising his Federal Civil Rights secured by the U.S. Constitution?"

Answer: "Patrick Johnston and Charles Deiter"

"Question #4. Have the Plaintiffs established by a preponderance of the evidence that the acts of retaliation by Patrick Johnston, Charles Deiter, or Ray Halsted, were a proximate cause of damages to Plaintiffs?"

Answer: "yes"

"Question #5. Amount of Plaintiff's compensatory damages?"
Answer: "$10,000,000.00"

"Question #6. Amount of Plaintiff's punitive damages?"
Answer: $12,000,000.00"

Judge Swanlund asked the foreman if the decision reached by the jury was a unanimous decision.

"Yes, it is your Honor." The foreman replied.

I looked over at Sheriff Johnston. He sat there, just staring at the jury with a fiery piercing stare in his eyes. He looked stone cold, full of hatred and anger. His demeanor could be characterized as scarey at best.

Judge Swanlund, polled the jury members. This is a process where by he asked each one of the jurors in open court if the decision reached in this case was their decision and their decision alone. Each and every juror, one by one, responded verbally, acknowledging that the verdict reached was their decision.

The judge being satisfied with the verdict, thanked the jury for their dedication and then excused them. Judge Swanlund then announced that the trial was over and exited the court room.

Sherry and I hugged each other. We both then hugged Randy. It was unbelievable. We had won. Someone finally had beaten Sheriff Johnston. What is more important, the truth had won. The system did work, the very same system that I had doubted while the course of events leading up to the trial unfolded, the system that I had dedicated my life to upholding as a law enforcement officer. The system that Sheriff Johnston had abused and used to destroy my career. In the end, justice came through.

Words could not begin to capture the emotions that I was feeling. Capt. Hill and his wife walked up to us. They both had tears in their eyes as they hugged us. I will never forget the powerful emotions experienced by all of us at that very moment.

Sherry and I would have been happy to have just won even if we only won a dollar. To us this case was not about money, it was about right and wrong, truth and justices. I don't think the fact that we were just awarded $22 million even began to set in or played a part in our feeling of victory. It was for a triumph of truth. It gave the trauma that we had experienced over the last two years some sort of relief and satisfaction.

As we turned to walk toward the door to exit the court room, we were passed by two men in dark colored suits. They entered the court room and walked directly over to the defense table where Sheriff Johnston was standing.

"We are from the FBI." One of the gentlemen stated. He then

continued to address Sheriff Johnston.

"You will have to come with us, Sheriff. You are being taken into custody on a variety of charges involving political corruption and conspiracy."

I did not even turn around. I did not need to hear anymore. None of us did. We knew what it was all about. We walked tall, as we left the court room that day. The tallest and proudest we probably have ever been. or will be again, in our lives.

A barrage of reporters and cameras flashing hit us as we walked out into the lobby of the Federal Building.

"No comment, no comment,"

It was our only response. After all, it had all been said, it was over.

During the course of this story, you might have noticed that I never once mentioned my name. I was always the sergeant, or plaintiff. I did not see any sense in mentioning my name since after this ordeal ended, my name had to be changed. My wife, Sherry and I just disappeared into society.

We never have to work again, but it's not in our nature not to work. Life has always been full of adventure and excitement for us, and we would not have it any other way. We decided to dedicate our lives to fighting political corruption and the abuse of power on a small scale, one community at a time. After all, power without accountability hurts us all. We cannot tolerate it. We will not.

Thank you, and remember to enjoy your life.